SHATTERED STARS

HANNAH HAZE

Copyright © 2024 by Hannah Haze

All rights reserved.

No part of this book may be reproduced in any form or by any electronic or mechanical means, including information storage and retrieval systems, without written permission from the author, except for the use of brief quotations in a book review.

Front cover designed by Covers by Christian

Edited by Buckley's Books

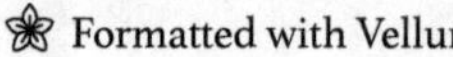 Formatted with Vellum

FOREWORD

This book is a 'why choose' bully paranormal romance with one female main character and more than one potential love interest. These love interests are ruthless and at times brutally unkind. There are scenes that some readers may find uncomfortable including violence and gore. For more detailed content warnings, please visit my website.

If you spot any typos in this book, please drop me a line so I can make it right: hannahhazewrites@gmail.com (Or just drop me an email anyway. I love to chat!).

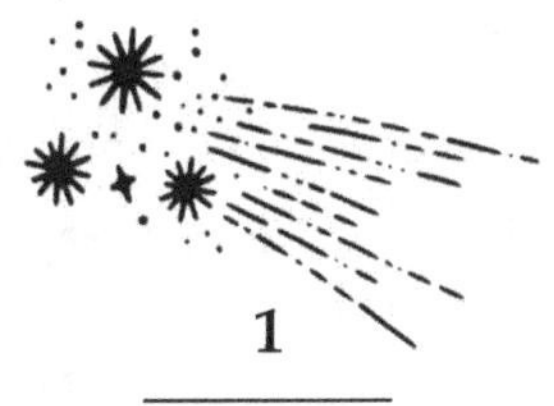

1

——————

T ristan

I'M high as a fucking kite; all the adrenaline and adulation from that match still thumping though my veins, desperate to go somewhere, fizzing so strongly I can feel the ends of my fingertips practically singing with magic.

Usually I'd pump all this fucking energy right between some girl's thighs. Hell, on a night like this, I'd fuck girl after girl, not giving a shit whether that breaks their hearts and hurts their feeble goddamn feelings.

But things are different now.

So different, I hardly recognize myself.

I'm not interested in just any girl.

There's only one I want to unleash all this energy on, and I'm staying as far away from her as I fucking can.

That leaves me with only one alternative. An alternative that has the blood leaping in my veins with excitement.

I kick the half-dressed girl perched on my knee off my lap and rock up onto my heels, scanning the party.

Spencer's not here, but there's enough noise from outside to know the party's spilled out into the gardens.

I crash through the dancers, ignoring the people that call my name and brushing away hands that try to grab me.

I find him leaning against a tree, staring into space, far away from all the other revelers who are dancing and singing and fucking.

He's no longer clutching the trophy and he doesn't look like a man who just won his team – damn his school and his country – the most important match of all our careers. He looks defeated.

"Hey," I say, jerking my chin at him and catching his attention. "You want to get out of here?"

He swings his gaze around slowly.

"Where?" he asks.

"The warehouse."

Something in his eyes gleams immediately and he nods his head.

"Just us?" he adds.

I glance at all the drunk fools in the garden and falling out of the common room. It's mostly losers and hangers-on. Most of the other jocks and cheerleaders have disappeared, probably off fucking each other somewhere.

"Yeah, just us," I say, smacking him on the shoulder.

We take my car, parked in the underground parking lot, even though Spencer hisses about the fact it's not built for a giant like him.

"It's faster than your truck, man," I say, revving the engine and making the machine roar. "And I want to get there quickly, you know."

He does. His body's jerking and twitching with untapped energy just like mine.

We dissect the match as I speed us along the dark country lanes towards the glowing city in the distance, debating how we could have played things better, congratulating ourselves on the plays we nailed, discussing how we'll do things differently in the future. Although it's mostly me doing the talking, he sits there grunting his agreement or shaking his head.

"They never stood a fucking chance," I say with a grin. "We had those fuckers from the start."

Spencer nods again but doesn't smile. He seems lost in his thoughts.

"What's with you?" I ask. Usually, I wouldn't be able to get him to shut up about this stuff. He'd be gloating his fucking head off. Instead, he stares straight ahead, out of the window. "You got knocked on the head or something?"

"Summer went for the Pig Girl this evening."

"When?" I say, sitting up straighter in my seat, glancing at his face.

"Fuck, I don't know. An hour or two ago."

"What happened?"

"Summer started on her – wanted her to kiss my feet or some such shit. And Pig Girl retaliated – head butted her. Broke Summer's fucking nose."

I can't help a chuckle, shaking my head in disbelief. She head butted her? Broke her nose? That pathetic scrap of a girl never ceases to amaze me. That's half the fucking problem. I can't predict what she'll do next and it excites me like nothing else does; keeps me waiting, watching.

"She did that? Fuck! I wish I'd seen it!"

"Yeah, she did." The corner of his mouth tugs up into a

smirk. "It was kind of awesome to see Summer put in her place for once."

I chuckle some more. Yeah, I bet that was something to behold. Then the amusement dies on my lips.

"Summer won't let it stand," I say, tugging on the gear stick and speeding us into the city streets.

"We'll see," he says, the half-smile vanishing.

We're quiet for the remainder of the journey, both lost in our thoughts. I'm not as confident as he is about the girl being able to handle Summer Clutton-Brock. You don't end up head of the cheerleading squad – most popular girl in the school – without perfecting your skills as a mega bitch. Summer's had years of training and practice. She knows how to manipulate people. She knows how to tear them apart. How to make them suffer.

An unease brews in my stomach. I don't want Summer messing with her. I want Summer as far away from her as possible. I shouldn't care. I shouldn't give two shits about what happens to her. And yet I do. I'm far too interested, far too vested. I huff out air through my teeth. It's clear I need to get a handle on myself and I'm even more impatient to arrive at the Warehouse.

The parking lot out in the far stretches of the docks, crouching in the shadows of the mountain-like tankers, is full to the brim. A mixture of priceless vehicles like mine, motorcycles and beat-up trucks. This place attracts all kinds. The very richest and the very poorest. All wanting to feel their knuckles split and taste blood in their mouth.

I lock up the car and add a spell or two in case some punk thinks he's going to steal my ride. When I'm content, we wave our hands in front of our faces, dark masks forming over our cheeks and across our brows. The magic will prevent anyone from spotting who we really are. Then I follow Spencer through the maze of vehicles to the warehouse standing on the far side of the lot. There isn't just one man guarding the door, there's a whole group, each wearing a weapon strapped across his body, eyes shaded by dark glasses even though it's the frigging middle of the night.

They nod when they see us both, parting to let us through without a word. They may not know our true identities, but they recognize us, nonetheless. They know we are here to fight, not to cause trouble.

We walk down an empty corridor and through into the towering space of this deserted warehouse, the noise hitting us immediately.

It's not like the roar of the crowd at the match. It's hungrier, more desperate, more fucking dangerous. It has the adrenaline leaping in my veins and my feet moving that much faster.

We can't see the match taking place in the center of the space – the crowd is at least six people deep – but Spencer barges his way through, receiving no complaint and soon we're standing at the front watching the battle.

Six men, all shirtless, blood on their hands and running down their faces, are dueling. Only it's not like back at the academy. No safety vests here. No rules, no restrictions. You fight until your opponent concedes. Bones are broken, flesh ripped, muscles torn. It all gets fixed in the end. There is the occasion, of course, when things have gone too far, but that's the risk you take. That's why it makes the adrenaline buzz in my body. That's why I'm bouncing on my toes, my magic sparking on my fingertips. It's low after the match. But I don't give a shit. I want to tear everything apart. Besides, I'm sure my magic, even depleted, is a hell of a lot stronger than most of the fuckers' in this place.

We watch, side by side, as the three men dressed in dirty

jeans grasp the upper hand, plowing their magic and their fists into the bodies of the other three men; this team dressed in sweatpants.

Magic swoops and spins in the air, the crowd ducking to avoid stray shots, pushing a man back into the ring's center when he stumbles with the force of a fist.

One man ends up on his knees, his face punched again and again, until his whole body sways and his eyes lose focus. His friend catches him by the shoulder before he face plants onto the bare concrete floor, and lifts his free hand into the air.

"Concede," he calls out. The crowd groans, disappointed the fight has ended, but the three men in jeans roar, hugging each other, and pumping fists into the beam of lights erected overhead.

The adjudicator comes to shake their hands as the unconscious man is hauled out of the ring by his two friends, and a wad of notes is thrust between the three winners. Then the adjudicator is spinning round to face the crowd.

"One-on-ones," he yells. "Any takers?"

I look at Spencer and he nods, both of us thrusting our fists into the air. Around the ring, several other men do too. The adjudicator strolls around the ring, examining each of us in turn. In front of me, he stops, peering through the holes of my mask and into my eyes. The magical disguise is powerful, but I'm sure many here tonight could take a good guess at my identity.

"Golden Boy," he says, "we haven't seen you in some time."

I crack the knuckles of my right hand in my left, swinging up and down on my toes. I nod.

"Hmmm," the adjudicator says, "who wants to see the Golden Boy fight?"

A roar erupts around the ring. They know I'm good.

The adjudicator chuckles. "The crowd has spoken."

I walk into the middle of the ring, under the hot lamps, rolling my shoulders, and tipping my head from side to side.

The adjudicator peers up at Spencer but continues to walk around the ring. He knows from experience we won't fight each other. He stops before a tall man instead – a man who looks more like a tank than a fighter, his body straining to break free of the black vest he's wearing.

He's new. I've not seen him before and I'm guessing the adjudicator hasn't either.

"What's your name, fighter?" he asks.

"Crusher," the man says with a grin that shows he's missing teeth. I smile to myself. It means the man is either too dumb to fix his own teeth or so dumb he's chosen not to. Either way, I could defeat him blindfolded with my right arm tied behind my back. Maybe this isn't going to give me the relief I'm after. Then again, the man speaks with an accent similar to that Andrew kid. The one I know betrayed the pig girl to Barone. Maybe I'll enjoy making him suffer.

"Haven't you got someone a little bigger? More of a man to fight," the dude says.

I smile at him. The adjudicator smiles at him. Half the fucking crowd smiles at him.

He really is dumb.

But he's also strong. Fucking strong. And faster than a man that beefed up should be.

Doesn't matter though, half the fun is letting them think they're winning, defeating me. Letting their knuckles slam into my cheek, and feel all that pain crackle through my body. Let them crush a solid shoulder into my rib cage and hear the crack. Let them pound me. Let me taste blood in my mouth. Let me feel hungry for it.

It's nothing I haven't felt a million times. A million beatings. Everyone making me more powerful. Stronger.

I spit bright red saliva onto the dirty floor and peer up at the man, hunching over like he's ready to sprint at me, his shoulders heaving like a bull about to charge.

I wait for him to move, lifting my fist and striking him right in the center of his fucking head, pummeling all my magic behind the strike. It stops the fucker dead in his tracks and there's an impressed gasp that spins around the circle watching us. I flick my fingertips and the man lifts through the air, high above our heads. I twizzle my fingers next and he spins so fast I'm surprised he doesn't vomit. Then I drop my hand and the man drops too, falling through the air and landing with a thump and a groan.

He's crumpled on the ground now, moaning. This was far too easy and I'm not nearly satisfied enough.

This isn't the thrill it used to be. Neither is grabbing the scruff of his vest and smacking my fist into his dumb face over and over again, until he's begging for mercy; the teeth he has a bloody mess, his nose the same.

Nothing's a thrill any more. Nothing.

And I'm not sure how much more of it I can take.

Because I'm beginning to realize that all I want is the thrill of her. The touch of her. And the taste. Fuck, even the scent of her. The only thing that makes my blood shimmer.

I want her. And I don't think I can fight this any longer.

2

R hi

I LIE in Stone's arms in his bed, the darkness of night withering away around us and the first fingers of dawn creeping in through the gaps in the curtains.

I don't want day to chase away this night. I want to lie in this moment, in our own little world forever. Because as the room turns a deep shade of gray, I know we have to face whatever's coming next. And experience has taught me that whatever that is, I am unlikely to like it.

"You're too much of a pessimist for someone so young," Stone whispers, stroking back strands of hair from my face.

I nuzzle closer into his embrace, loving the feel of his warm skin against mine.

I never knew being with someone could feel like this, that the press of their body against mine would feel so intoxicating. I thought the sex would be the exciting part –

and yes that is damn, damn good – but this, these moments ... is it strange to like them more?

"No," he whispers into my ear.

"So you're going to let me stay?" I ask, with mischief in my eyes.

"You know I don't want you to go."

"But you're going to kick me out of your bed anyway."

"Not kick," he says, "gently nudge." I scowl at him and he sighs. "You know I don't want you to go, Rhianna. You know I'd rather spend the next few hours fucking you into this mattress until you're actually begging me to stop."

"I don't think I'd ever beg you to stop," I admit, combing my fingers through his beard in a way I've been dying to do since I met him. He catches that hand in his and kisses my palm softly.

"You're making this very hard for me." I go to argue some more, but he beats me to it. "We can't risk someone seeing you leave this cabin, Rhianna. We can't risk someone catching us together. You have to go before morning rises."

"Why does it matter? You're my fated mate. I'm yours. Surely the rules won't apply to us."

He closes his eyes, real pain flashing across his face. "It will matter. It will probably matter more. Besides, if they learn about us, how long before they learn of you and Azlan too? And then there will be questions for all of us."

"Why does it matter to them who we're sleeping with?"

He twerks an eyebrow at me. "Rhianna, you are not as stupid as you look." I pinch his toned abs for that dig. "You understand enough of this world to know how things work now. Fated mates are believed to be strong and powerful. A woman with two fated mates – and not just any mate–"

"Phoenix Stone!" I tease.

He lifts his eyebrow again. "No one's going to give a shit

about me. I'm talking about Azlan. The man in black. The authorities' enforcer. Heir of the Kennedy family."

"I give a shit about you," I say.

"You do?" he says, rolling on top of me. "How much of a shit?"

I pinch my finger and thumb together. "Just a little one. A teeny tiny one."

"Humph," he says, "then I take it back. No nudging. I'm definitely kicking you out."

I wrap my arms around his neck and smile up at him. His eyes are so beautiful – blue like the sky at early morning – I could stare into them for an eternity.

"I don't think it's just my eyes you like, sweetheart," he says, grinding one very large, very hard cock against me.

"That's true. I like your bike too."

"That's it!" he says, unclasping my hands, rolling off me and flinging back the covers. "Out!"

I pout at him and refuse to move. "I don't want to go," I say.

The tease in his features dies away and something more tender replaces it in his expression, something I'd never seen until last night.

"Rhi," he pleads.

"It's going to hurt," I whisper, my hands falling to rest on my belly. I've been here before. I know just what it's like. And this time I fear it might be even worse. The two bonds in my core, locked together in place, seem stronger than ever, more powerful, more unbreakable.

"We'll see each other soon enough," he says, kissing my hands, kissing my stomach, kissing my shoulder.

"That's not what I'm saying. Separating will be agony. The bond ..."

His eyes drop to my stomach and then to his. "Ahhh," he says.

"It took days to be able to bear being even a few paces from Azlan's side."

A smug grin lands on his face. "Erm, sweetheart, I'm guessing you and Azlan didn't ..." he pauses, "consummate the bond straight away."

I shake my head. "Not until after I left the hospital."

"That was causing the pain."

"I know that. But it took a lot of–"

"Fucking," he growls, diving back towards me. "Well, I think we did a lot of our own fucking last night."

"Maybe not enough," I say innocently into his face.

"You think we should do some more?" he asks with a look of feigned concern.

"Just to be on the safe side," I say, trailing my fingertips down the inks on his chest.

He chuckles. "You are such a fucking brat. And I am so doomed."

"Are you complaining?" I say, wrapping my legs around his waist and encouraging his hard cock inside me.

His eyes flutter shut and he groans. "Fuck, no."

He rocks and grinds into me and I watch as the light gradually brightens across his face, those eyes of his never leaving mine.

We come together, quietly, both exhausted by everything that's gone before, our bonds thrumming with energy, our bodies damp with sweat.

He kisses my cheeks and my eyelids, my jaw and my lips, and then he hauls me out of bed, and leads me to the bathroom.

I've dried come and arousal on my thighs, and he runs the sponge under the warm tap and settles down on his knees, ready to wash it all away. He's lifting the sponge to my leg when he halts.

"What?" I ask, glancing down at him.

He growls and slides his fingers up towards my pussy, capturing a dribble of fresh come that's escaped my hole. "Don't waste it," he growls. Pushing it back up inside me with his fingers.

I stare down at him. My body trembles. That was hot and yet also ...

"You don't think trying to knock me up would add to our problems?"

"I did the birth control spell, remember?" he says, cleaning me with the sponge. "I'm not trying to knock you up."

"Then, why–"

"It's just where I want it, okay?" he says gruffly, stumbling to his feet and handing me my dress. It's still ripped and stained with mud and blood. When I drag it on, I look like I just stumbled out of a fight. One sweep of his hand, though, and the dress is good as new.

He takes my hand and leads me to the door of his cabin. "Take the back paths, not the main ones. And if anyone asks where you've been–"

"I'll tell them I was going for an early morning walk."

"Rhianna," he says, twisting me around to look at him and resting his hands on my shoulders. "That is lame."

"Can you come up with a better explanation for me wandering around campus early in the morning in yesterday's dress?"

He thinks about this for a moment.

"Shit," he mumbles. "Then for fuck's sake, don't let anyone see you."

I lift his palms from my shoulders and hold his hands in mine.

"When will we be able to see each other again, like this?"

He hesitates. "I'll find us a way." He squeezes my hands. "Keep the bond open."

"And Azlan?"

He frowns. "What about Azlan?"

"We need to tell him about this."

"I'm pretty sure he will have felt it happen."

"You think?"

He shrugs. "He's not going to be angry about this, Rhi. It's what he wanted."

"We still need to tell him."

"You're right. I'll talk to him."

"No, I think I should do it." He nods. "And Stone ..." I hesitate, but he reads the thoughts in my mind anyway.

"I know, Rhi. I know I have a lot more to do to make things up to you. I know I treated you like shit when I should have been treating you like the most precious thing on Earth. I know I fucked things up and I promise I'll make it up to you."

"You'd better," I say with a stern frown. He bends his gaze to mine, giving me his best remorseful puppy-dog eyes, and I can't help but laugh.

Then he kisses me, a long lingering kiss that tells me just how reluctant he is to let me go. A feeling I experience as strongly all through my body. But soon, I'm stepping out into the gray morning and, with my tracking senses alert, tiptoe along the less well-trodden paths towards my dorm.

I needn't have bothered being so cautious, though. Campus is as dead this morning as it was the day after Founders' Night. In fact, I make it all the way back to my dorm without meeting one single person.

When I reach our room, I wave away Winnie's locking spell and creep inside the room. Winnie stirs from her sleep as I tiptoe inside, stopping to bend down and stroke my palm over a sleeping Pip's form.

Winnie rolls over and rubs her eyes. "Rhi, is that you? What time is it?"

"5.25 am Winnie. Go back to sleep."

She doesn't though, instead she bends her elbow and rests her cheek on her palm.

"Were you with Stone this whole time?"

After a string of increasingly anxious messages demanding to know where I was, I'd confessed to Winnie I was with Stone. I neglected to include any details in my messages though.

"Uh huh," I say, stepping out of my dress and into my pajamas.

"Oh no you don't, Missie. I was up half the night worrying about you. You just ... disappeared. I was about to call the man in black and have him search for you."

I flop down onto the floor beside Winnie's bed and she peers into my face and gasps.

"What?" I say.

She sits upright.

"You sealed the bond. With Stone. Didn't you?"

"H-h-how the hell–"

"It's your eyes. It's something about your eyes. I remember they looked a little different after you bonded with the man in black. Brighter somehow. I don't know. I can't describe it. But now they're even clearer."

"Really," I say, standing and walking to the mirror and staring at my reflection. All I see is a girl with very flushed cheeks. A girl who's just had more orgasms in one night than she's probably had in her entire life.

"Do you think I'm crazy? For doing this?" I ask, meeting her gaze in the reflection of the mirror.

"No, I don't," she says earnestly. "I think it's the opposite of crazy. Resisting your mate, going against the forces of fate, that would be crazy. In fact, I think that could drive you to the edge of insanity. That's what they say, anyway."

I think of Stone's mom and nod.

Then I think of the others. The way it isn't only Azlan and Stone I feel drawn towards.

I return to my spot on the carpet beside Winnie.

She yawns and lowers her head back to her pillow.

"I hope he was sorry," she says. "I hope he begged for your forgiveness for all the shit he's put you through this term."

"He had his reasons."

Winnie tsks. "They always do. Don't forgive him too easily, Rhi. No matter how good he may be in bed." She grins. "And he's good, right? Please don't shatter all my illusions about that man and tell me he is a dud. Although, I guess room for improvement is not a bad thing. Teaching Trent some things has actually been a lot of fun–"

I whack my friend on the shoulder. "Winnie, last night was amazing. I don't think there's anything to teach the man."

"Yeah, I bet," she says, giggling. "I bet half those books on his shelves are sex manuals. I bet he knows tantric sex moves and how to make orgasms cosmic and–"

"Winnie!"

"Yes, Rhi," she says, grinning at me.

I take a deep inhale. "What if Stone and Azlan aren't the only ones? What if ... what if I do have other mates?"

She giggles again, but the sound dies on her lips when she sees how serious I am.

"Who?"

I give her two names. Not the third, because ... because ... that just can't be right!

The incredulous noise she makes when I tell her has Pip jerking awake in his bed and scuttling towards us both.

My best friend gapes at me as Pip settles himself in my lap, then shakes her head in disbelief before snorting loudly.

"You can't be serious?"

"I don't know," I say, hiding my face in Pip's upturned tummy.

"But ... but they've been treating you like shit."

"Well, the man in black and Stone didn't exactly welcome me with open arms, did they?"

"Yes, but they never set out to torture you, to make your life miserable, to actively belittle you."

"Hmmm," I say. Because Stone did chain me to a bed, throw ham sandwiches at my head and try to infiltrate my mind by force.

Yeah, none of my fated mates are exactly earning themselves gold stars here.

"Then again ..." she says, rolling over onto her stomach and reaching down to tickle Pip's exposed chin. "They do seem to have a rather unusual infatuation with you. Tristan especially. I've never seen him pay any girl any particular attention. Not even Summer. But you ... I mean, it's negative attention, but still attention."

"I'm probably imagining it. It's probably just my bond, all unsettled from the recent sealing of the bonds with Azlan and Stone," I say, not one bit convinced by this explanation. "More than two fated mates? That can't be possible."

"I mean it can be."

"Really? In fairy tales and–"

"Wait," Winnie says, "that reminds me of something."

"It does?"

"Uh huh." She reaches down to the floor, scrabbling for her phone and then typing away. "I might be misremembering ... it was a long time ago ..."

"What was?"

She looks up from her phone. "Huh?"

"What was a long time ago?"

"The story."

My brow crinkles, but Winnie's already jumping back to the two jerks that may or may not be my fated mates. "I just ... if they are ..."

"If they are, where does that leave me?" Heading for the mental hospital like Stone's mom?

Winnie rests her hand on my shoulder. "I'm sure you're right. That it's just a confusing time. You moved here from the backend of nowhere. You were thrust into a new world and way of life you didn't understand. You've been treated like crap by far too many people in this academy – that's got to be massively confusing. You're doing amazing, Rhi. If it were me, I'd probably have struggled to get out of bed most days."

"There are a lot of days that I do."

"What I'm saying is, with all your emotions tangled and confused like that, it's not surprising you might mistake some emotions for others. They do say there is a very fine line between love and hate," she says, looking unsure. "Because I simply can't believe two people could treat their fated mate the way Tristan and Spencer have treated you."

I kiss Pip's head. I hope she's right. I want her to be right. I don't want to be forced to make a decision like that: tie myself to two men who treat me badly or endure a life of madness and pain. Neither of those options sound even vaguely appealing.

"Anyway," Winnie says, leaning over her bunk to kiss my head in the way I just kissed Pip's. "Did you hear the announcement yesterday after the match or were you too busy banging the hot professor?"

"I didn't hear any announcement."

Winnie swings her legs out of the bed and her feet hit the floor, her face erupting into uncontainable excitement.

"There's going to be a ball in honor of the dueling team's victory in the cup."

"Tonight?" I say. I have nothing to wear to a ball and, though Winnie often acts as my fairy godmother, I don't think even she could magic a ball gown out of nowhere.

"No, not tonight," Winnie says, whacking my shoulder and shaking her head. "You remember how much work went into the Founders' Night party? A ball requires ten times as much work as that. It won't be for weeks."

"And a ball is a good thing?" I venture.

"Are you kidding me?" Winnie squeals. "There hasn't been one the entire time I've been at the academy. This is the first one."

"And you're pleased about that?"

"Rhi, Arrow Hart balls are legendary. In fact, my mom claims the night of the Arrow Hart ball was the night she fell in love with my dad." Winnie frowns. "I'm pretty certain it was the night I was conceived too."

"Balls sound dangerous."

Winnie gives me a hard look. "Rhianna Blackwaters, please tell me you are using contraception. I know we haven't had this little chat, but I assumed–"

"I'm using contraception," I say. "But," I add, lowering

my voice to tell her about what happened with Stone in the bathroom this morning.

"Woah," Winnie says, her eyes widening. "That is incredibly hot and–"

"Exactly," I say. "I don't understand men." Azlan, Stone, Tristan, Spencer: they all confuse the hell out of me.

"I think you understand them far better than you realize," Winnie says, grinning at me.

I wish she was right.

3

R^{hi}

Winnie wants to grill me some more after that but I'm yawning so much that she soon takes pity on me and lets me crawl into bed with Pip.

I don't wake again until past lunchtime and my first thought is Azlan. I said I would talk to him and I've already left it longer than I should. I hunt for my phone and send him a message. It's clear from his reply that he is reluctant to be seen at the academy again so soon after yesterday. We agree instead that I'll travel into the city by the campus bus and he'll meet me at the stop. It's Sunday after all and in honor of the match yesterday, I've been let off from gardening duties.

There is only one problem with this master plan. I need permission to go into the city from my head of house. From Tristan Kennedy.

I consider skipping away without it but there's a chance the campus bus driver will want to see my permission slip and besides I've been in enough trouble these last few weeks. I want to avoid any more for a while if I can. A long, long while.

All this means I'm going to have to swallow my pride and go beg Tristan Kennedy. Which I hate. Which I really, really hate. The idea makes me sick.

After I've showered, thrown on my usual attire of jeans and a t-shirt and braided my hair, I give myself a stern talking to in the mirror. Winnie's already gone off to spend her day with Trent, taking Pip with her, so there's no one to hear my little pep talk.

"I am not going to take any of his crap. I will remain calm. I will not let him get to me." My reflection catches my attention. My cheeks are still rosy, my eyes still shining. I realize I look so much healthier than I did when I arrived. With a self-reassuring nod at my reflection, I head to the Venus common room, assuming Tristan will be in his usual lair. To my surprise, when I step among the half-comatose and groaning bodies, passed out over the double bed, the sofas and even the floor, I find Tristan Kennedy isn't among them.

Strange.

It seemed like last night's celebration morphed into one giant orgy – one I'd assume Tristan would be right in the middle of.

I step over a half-dressed boy snoring by the door and back out into the gardens, pulling out my phone as I do.

If going to see him was bad, sending him a text message somehow feels worse. God, I despise this power he has over me and the way he likes to abuse it. But I want to see Azlan –

I need to see him – so once again I'm prepared to swallow my pride.

I type him a brief, perfunctory text message requesting permission. If I'm lucky, I'll get a simple 'yes' by reply which might be enough to satisfy any bus driver and will be proof enough I have permission.

Of course, this is Tristan Kennedy. Possibly the biggest jerk on the planet. He tells me if I want a permission slip, I'm going to have to come get it. From his room.

I growl reading that text.

AND WHERE IS *his highness's room?*

I TYPE OUT, then remember my promise to myself about keeping calm. I scrub that message out, sending a text that reads '*Directions, please*' instead.

As if it was in any doubt, Tristan's room turns out to be in the most expensive and luxurious of dorm buildings and his room is the penthouse itself. I huff and roll my eyes as I plod up the staircase. No wonder he tops the class at everything. It's not exactly hard when you're dripping in wealth and luxury.

I hover outside his door, noting all the handwritten notes pinned there, and debate whether there is a simpler, less dangerous way to get to Los Magicos. Like walking. Or flying on a broomstick.

Before I can change my mind though and walk away, the door swings open and Tristan is there in the doorway, wearing only a pair of gray sweatpants. Seriously?! Does this dude ever wear clothes?

Immediately, my stomach somersaults and my bond

pulls towards him, a vicious tug that's hard to deny. He's so good looking that sometimes it's hard to look at him. Like the sun, he's blinding. I can't be confused about this, surely? But I must be.

His lack of clothes is clearly a ploy to intimidate me or make me feel uncomfortable or basically torture me. I won't fall for it.

"Come in," he says, turning his back on me and sloping off into his vast room. As he does, my eyes run over his form of their own accord. His skin is golden and packed with solid muscle, his shoulders broad, his pants slung low, his feet bare. An ink trails over his shoulder – a tiger leaping, its eyes emerald-green like Tristan's. It stares back at me, baring its teeth.

I can't drag my eyes off it – or him. But then I see the dark outline of a bruise tracing the edge of his shoulder blade. It's the size of my palm and painted a mixture of blacks and purples. It makes me wince. Is that from the dueling match? And if so, why hasn't it been healed? There are no other marks on him.

I don't move from the doorway. His scent hangs heavy in the air. Stepping inside his room would be like stepping into a tiger's lair.

"I'm fine where I am, thanks." I glance towards the bed. Somewhere he must seduce all those countless girls. My stomach twists and that memory of him with that girl in the common room flashes through my mind. "Can I just have my slip, please?"

He halts, then spins on his toes, grabs my wrist and hauls me into his room, slamming the door behind him.

I let out an angry huff, already failing to keep my promise to myself.

Being in his room feels intimate and dangerous. His territory. There isn't even anyone else on this floor and his unmade bed is just there by the giant window, unmade and rumpled.

I expect him to adopt his usual bored posture, laying out on the bed, or slumping low on a chair. Instead, he stands to face me in the middle of the room, squaring up to me. I don't know how to feel.

The room, I note, is so bare it's hard to believe it's actually occupied. There's not even a picture of his family resting on his desk or a trophy balancing on a shelf. In fact, the only hint that the room is occupied at all is that messy bed and his dueling jersey slung over a chair.

I thought his room would be an ostentatious display of who he is. Overrun with all those awards, dripping with expensive belongings. I half expected the walls to be lined with gold and decorated with pictures of his beautiful face.

"You head butted Summer Clutton-Brock, busted her nose." Is it my imagination or does he say that with just the faintest hint of admiration?

I shrug.

"You're going to need to watch your back, little piggie. She's going to come at you with everything she has now."

"I'm not scared of a bully like her." Not when I have far more menacing enemies out to get me and far more dangerous complications plaguing my life.

"Maybe you'd be wise not to make so many enemies," he says, clearly thinking the same thing I am.

"It seems to come naturally to me," I say, smiling flatly and holding his gaze. He's shed his usual bored persona. His eyes are just like that tiger's today. Intelligent, predatory, challenging.

"Why do you want to go into Los Magicos?" he asks, with a jerk of his chin, his hands deep inside the pockets of his sweatpants.

"I don't actually think that is any of your business, Tristan."

He begins to pace across the room in obvious agitation, my bond tugging after him as he moves. It's so clear. I can't be wrong about it. I can't be wrong about the way he makes me feel. Against my will. I don't want to feel that way about him. I want to hate him.

"You want the slip, then you tell me the reason."

I know there is no point arguing. The more I fight, the longer this will take. If I play along, the quicker I get out of here. And I want to get out of here. The sensations in my gut are unbearable and I don't want to believe that this is real. I want to stay as far away from him as I can and convince myself it's not.

"I'm going to see Azlan," I tell him.

He hesitates for one second before turning to frown at me, the intensity when our gazes lock making me step away from him.

"Why can't he come and see you here?"

"It would look strange if the enforcer was seen here at the academy again so soon after the match."

"Azlan doesn't care about that shit."

"He cares about me," I say.

Tristan's eyes flit all around my face. "He's coming to collect you?"

"I'm going to take the bus."

He scoffs. "The bus? It's not safe."

"It's perfectly fine." I scowl at him. "I've told you where I'm going and why. Can I have my slip now?"

"He should be coming to collect you," he growls.

"He's going to meet me right off the bus."

"You have Renzo fucking Barone–"

"I'm aware."

"I don't think it's a good idea. It isn't safe. I'm inclined to deny your request."

"Azlan–"

"Azlan is a fool," he snaps, twisting away from me so I'm given another view of his broad back and the bruise resting across his shoulder. "Funny, he never used to be. It must be your influence."

"Nothing to do with me. It must be a familial trait," I snap back.

We're both quiet for a moment and my eyes stray right back to that bruise, so dark against his golden skin.

"Matron missed a bruise," I can't help blurting out, "on your back." It looks so painful, so brutal. The only flaw on his otherwise perfect body.

"What?" he says, shaking his head as if he's attempting to shake away the thoughts in his mind.

"There's a pretty bad bruise on your back. One I'm guessing the matron missed after the match."

He strolls to a full-length mirror hanging on a wardrobe door on the far side of his room and peers over his shoulder. The tendons on his neck tighten and the muscles on his shoulder ripple. I bite my lip.

"Matron didn't miss it," he says. "It's not from the match."

I frown, remembering the last time Tristan Kennedy looked beat up.

He attempts to hook his arm over his shoulder and touch the bruise but he can't reach it.

"Damn," he says.

I hesitate, calculating my options. "If ... if I heal it for you, will you give me the stupid permission slip?"

His eyes flick up to mine, all that electricity dancing in his pupils again. He licks his bottom lip.

"Do you actually know the spell, little piggie?"

I hold his gaze. "I saved my friend's life a few days ago," I whisper.

Interest sparks in his eyes.

"The Wence girl?"

I nod.

"What happened to her?"

I don't know why I tell him, but I do. Something tells me if I'm honest with him, if I share my secrets, he'll be more willing to give me what I want.

"We were attacked. By a group of soldiers."

He frowns. "That doesn't make any sense, little piggie. Are you making up stories?"

"It was back home. They were soldiers from the West."

He frowns. "Soldiers from the West in our territory. It doesn't make any sense. How would they get through our defenses?"

"Azlan says there've been several infiltrations."

His eyes flicker across my face as he takes in this information.

"Your friend – she was injured?"

"Yes, when we tried to get away. I saved her." A sense of pride blooms through my body and for once Tristan Kennedy doesn't say something snarky in return. Instead he holds my gaze and nods.

"Okay," he says finally. "Heal the bruise and I'll give you the slip." He stalks towards me grabbing my wrist again.

"But I warn you, Piggie, tell anyone about this and I'll make you regret it."

I examine his face, filled with curiosity. Why would it matter? Where the hell did he get this bruise? Why hasn't it been healed? And why is it some big secret?

"Turn around," I tell him. He gives me a hard look, then does as I say.

I reach up to his shoulder, but I have to stand on my tiptoes to reach properly and balancing while weaving complicated magic is going to be too hard.

"I need you to sit."

He drags the nearest chair towards him, the one with his prized jersey, and flops down. Firmly, I rest my hand on his shoulder, meaning to push him forward but as my palm connects with his flesh, electricity erupts in a hiss of sparks.

He leaps off his chair and I stare at him in disbelief.

"Did you fucking zap me, Pig Girl?"

"No," I say, shaking my hand, electricity racing from my fingertips up my arm. "I'm sorry," I add, "please, let me try again."

He glares at me but flops back down, this time hunching over his knees so I can reach his shoulder blade.

Closer to him now, I can smell his scent even more clearly and feel the heat radiating from his skin, his magic swirling in the air. I hover my palm over his skin this time, trying not to be distracted by the contoured lines of muscle that ripple there, or the tiger glaring up at me.

I close my eyes instead and whisper the words under my breath, feeling for the congealed blood under the surface, encouraging it to disperse, encouraging the injured tissue to heal.

As I do, I sense the traces of ancient bruises, of long-healed bones, of ripped and repaired flesh. Old dueling injuries? Fist fights from school? No, they are much older. Much, much older. I think of my own body, littered with the remnants of long-ago scars. Of how they formed.

I open my eyes and stare at the golden head of the boy before me, wondering if his life is not quite as golden as I always believed.

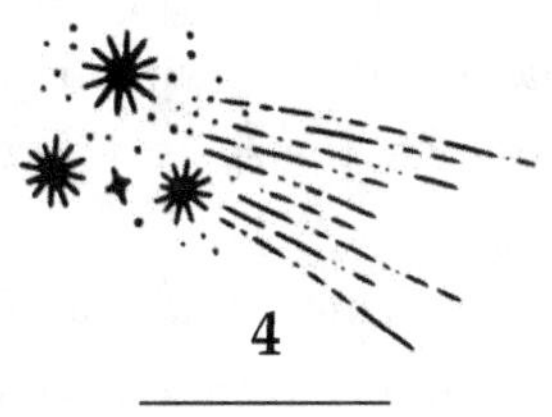

4

A zlan

I SCAN the afternoon's city traffic, searching for the first signs of the campus bus, growing ever more impatient with every car, truck and bike that passes.

This was a stupid idea. What if the bus was intercepted? What if it was forced off the road? What if the decrepit thing broke down out there on those lonely country roads?

But I'm being stupid. I'd know if she was hurt. I'd know if she was in danger. I'd feel it. The bond is strangely more powerful in my gut than it was the day before. Something has happened and I'm guessing that something is what she's so desperate to talk to me about.

I feel through the bond for her now and, as if my bond is dragging her closer, the bus bundles into view at that moment.

My body sags with relief, and impatiently, I slide off my

bike, pulling the hood of my cloak over my head and walk out to the sidewalk. The bus takes an age to chug the length of the street, caught by every frigging red light, but finally, it pulls alongside me, the doors swinging back and Rhianna standing in the doorway, the sight of her making my heart ache vividly in my chest.

She spies me and jumps down onto the sidewalk. We wait for the bus to go and then I offer her my hand. She takes it, her palm warm and inviting as I pull her into an alleyway and into my arms, kissing her as all the traffic streams past on the street and the sidewalks bustle with people.

"We'll go back to my place," I tell her when I'm finally happy to release her mouth from mine. "There's someone I'd like you to meet."

She looks at me quizzically and follows me to my bike. Then we're weaving our way through the city, her arms tight around my body, just like I want them. It's these moments I wish would last forever. Just her. Just me. The bike and the road.

When we reach my house, curiosity still shines in her eyes.

"Am I going to be happy to meet this person?" she asks, with a hint of suspicion.

"I hope so," I say, taking her hand in mine. "I'm hoping you're going to be friends."

"Well, as long as it's not Lucinda or one of your other ex-girlfriends," she mumbles.

"It's not," I say firmly, then add with a mumble, "and you're making it sound like I have a lot of ex-girlfriends."

She eyes me with more suspicion and I open the door, finding my sister waiting for us right there in the hallway, eagerness permeating out of every single one of her pores.

She's a lot like me: her hair dark and loose about her shoulders; her eyes dark too, and bright with excitement. She's tall like me as well, nearing half a foot taller than Rhi easily, though much slighter. Too slender if you ask me. A consequence of the stress of living under my uncle's control.

Today she's wearing a colorful bright scarf tied around her head; a chain of beads hang from her ears and around her neck and her dress is as bright and colorful as her scarf. It isn't an outfit she'd dare to wear in front of my uncle.

"Rhianna," she beams, rushing forward to clasp my mate's hands in her own. "I'm so pleased to meet you."

"Rhianna, this is Eleanor – Ellie, my sister."

"Yes, I know." Rhi smiles back at my sister. "I saw you in the Kennedy box at the match yesterday. It's nice to meet you."

My sister nods eagerly, her smile stretched wide. "It was a good match. Tristan played so well. You should have stayed to watch, Az."

Rhi's eyebrow twitches and she peers up at me in amusement. I guess she's never heard me called that before.

I snort. "Tristan had enough sycophantic fans there to cheer him on. Besides, I'm not exactly welcome in the family box right now."

The smile on Ellie's face fades to something sadder, an expression I see far too often these days. I've asked her a million times to come and live with me, away from the family – fuck, I've begged her. But she won't do it. She has an unerring ability to see the good in people – even when there's practically none there to see – and she is clinging desperately to the need to keep our family together, to have some kind of positive influence on their actions.

"If you talked to our uncle, if you took Rhianna to meet him–"

"I'm not taking Rhianna anywhere near him," I say firmly. "Come on, the two of you can get to know each other. I'll make us all a coffee."

"Herbal tea for me," Ellie reminds me.

"Yes, ma'am."

"And a cookie," she adds. I roll my eyes at her. "Oh, yes, I'm sorry, I forgot Mr. Muscle-man only eats raw eggs, grilled chicken and steamed vegetables."

Rhi giggles, obviously enjoying the way Ellie teases me.

"I'm very happy to serve you both cakes and cookies. You could both do with fattening up."

That shuts the two of them up and they follow me through to the lounge. I leave them perching on opposite sofas, grinning at each other a little nervously and go search the cupboards for something vaguely sweet, finding a slab of chocolate I think Rhi left here after her stay at the hospital. It's not cookies but I hope it will do.

When I return to them, I find Ellie's slipped off her sandals and tucked her feet underneath her as she recounts tales of our childhood, much to Rhi's obvious delight. My sister is much younger than me, closer really in age to Tristan than me, but we've always been close. Losing your mother at such a young age will do that to you. It's the other reason she won't wrench herself from our family. She lost one parent, she can't bear to lose another. It would break her heart. Doesn't seem to matter that he torments that heart on a daily fucking basis.

"Don't believe a word she says," I tell Rhi, smiling at my little sister fondly as I pass her a cup of some floral-smelling tea. "She has a very vivid imagination and a lousy memory."

"Lies." She laughs, swatting at my shoulder as I sink onto the sofa beside her.

Rhi takes her own cup from my outstretched hand and

sips at the rim. "Well, that's a shame. My opinion of you was taking a serious upward tick. Eleanor was just telling me what a devoted, protective older brother you were. But if it's all lies ..."

"It's not," Ellie says, resting her head on my shoulder. "I couldn't ask for a better brother. You're fortunate to have him as a fated mate."

"Not as fortunate as I am to have Rhianna," I say, meeting Rhi's gaze. She flushes with pleasure, the emotion clear in her bond. I make a note of it. The girl likes compliments and I intend to flood her with them. I haven't spoiled her nearly enough.

Tears form in the corners of Ellie's eyes. "I'm so happy for you both," she says, wiping at her face. "I've been so worried about him all alone. He's not meant for that. He deserves love, family, companionship."

"I think we all do," Rhi says quietly.

"Yes, I think we do." Ellie sniffs, another wet smile forming on her lips. "How did you meet?"

I open my mouth. Close it. Open it again.

Ellie swings her gaze from me to Rhianna.

"He was sent to capture me. I was an unregistered on the run," Rhianna says, plain and simple. She's not ashamed of who she is. She never has been and it's one of the things I love about the girl – her fiery, unwavering doggedness and resilience.

"Oh, I know that bit," Ellie says, blushing slightly and tucking her feet further underneath her. "But I wanted, you know, all the gory details. He never tells me anything," she adds in a whisper.

"I did tell you everything," I insist.

Ellie tsks. "Yes, all the facts. The date, the weather, the GPS location, blah, blah, blah. Rhianna, tell me what actually happened? Was it love at first sight? Was there an instant connection?" She claps her palms together and brings them to her chest.

I expect Rhi to pull a face and tell my sister about how I fired magical bolts at her.

Instead, she glances towards the window, the light catching on the bright green plants growing the other side of the glass.

"It will probably sound stupid, but ... it wasn't love at first sight ... but the moment I laid eyes on him, that very first time, I felt like I already knew him, that I'd seen the scene that unfolded already in another time and another place. He was familiar to me, like *déjà vu*."

"You probably saw my face. On posters and—"

"No," she insists. "It wasn't like that."

"Maybe you *had* seen him before," my sister says.

"We'd never met before," I insist.

"Not in this lifetime," she counters, "but maybe in another."

I scoff, shaking my head and directing my next words towards Rhianna. "My sister believes in all sorts of woo woo shit."

"You don't think fated mates is some serious woo woo shit?" Ellie says.

I open my mouth like I did before but I don't have any argument for that.

"What do you mean 'in a previous life'?" Rhi asks.

"It's what some people believe—"

"Hippies and—"

"Plenty of scholars," Ellie insists. "They believe that fated mates are destined for one another over and over again, through many lifetimes, in many different times and places. You are fated mates. Perhaps you have always been."

Rhi stares at her, the cogs clearly moving in her mind. "You don't believe in that?" she asks me.

"I don't know," I say simply.

"What did you feel when you first saw me?"

I close my eyes, remembering that moment out there in the dark clearing, the air alive with fragrance, the sky full with starlight. "I thought you were the most beautiful creature I'd ever seen."

This time she scoffs but I also feel that pleasure again through the bond and I hope she feels my honesty and emotion in return. I hope she knows just how much I mean it.

Eleanor's eyes flick from my face to Rhianna's.

"Tell me more about yourself, Rhianna," she says. "I want to know everything."

Rhi laughs. "There isn't much to know. I'm studying at Arrow Hart." She shrugs.

"She has a pet pig," I tell Ellie.

Ellie gapes at Rhi like she can't decide if I'm teasing her or not. "A pig?"

"Yes, Pip. He's my baby and my oldest friend." Rhi laughs again. "Now I probably have you worrying that your brother is bonded to a mad woman." Ellie shakes her head emphatically. "Oh but your brother thinks I'm crazy for owning a pig. He hates Pip."

"I don't hate him," I mutter.

"We had a pet rabbit when we were kids. It was meant to be the family's. But really it belonged to Az. They were inseparable. He used to take that creature to bed with him. The only time I've ever seen him cry was the day Bibkins died. Then and ..." She peers down at her hands and I swallow.

This time it's Rhi's turn to flick her gaze across our faces, but she doesn't push Ellie to continue. Maybe she senses how painful that topic is. For my sister and for me.

Ellie takes a sip of her tea and manages another smile, finding her composure again.

"I like your necklace," she says, pointing to a locket resting against Rhi's clavicle. One I've not seen before. "Was it a gift from Az?"

"Errr ... no." Rhi fiddles with the silver charm.

Ellie narrows her eyes. "Has my brother given you any presents, gifts? Flowers, perfume, chocolates?"

"Erm, no," Rhi repeats, twisting the chain around her fingers and refusing to look at me.

A wave of guilt crashes through my body followed by a violent smack on my arm.

"Azlan Kennedy!" Ellie says in outrage. "Rhianna's your fated mate and you've never bought her a gift?"

"Oh no, he bought me some bumper meals when we were traveling to Los Magicos–"

"Not good enough." Ellie smacks me again. "Rhi, I don't mean to be rude – please don't take this the wrong way – but do you have much money? I mean, most students don't. It's not like you're paid to attend the academy."

"The authorities are giving me an allowance," Rhi says.

"How much?" I ask, anger at myself now adding to the shame. She hesitates but my hard look has her spilling the information.

"That's all!" Ellie says in even more outrage before whacking me even harder. "That isn't enough to buy all the girlie things a woman needs."

"Like what?" I blurt out.

"Plenty of things." Ellie wags her finger at me. "Clothes, toiletries, makeup–"

"Rhianna doesn't need makeup. She's beautiful as she–"

"She doesn't need it. But maybe she wants it."

Rhi smiles, seeming to enjoy the berating my sister's giving me even more than the teasing.

"You need to take her shopping. I'd do it but ..."

"But?" Rhi asks.

"Ellie's already taken a big risk coming here today."

"It wasn't easy," Ellie says, that unease creeping back into my body as she winds her beaded necklace though her fingers. "Our uncle has spies everywhere, reporting on our every movement. I had to come up with some elaborate story, take a roundabout route." Her tea cup begins to shake in her hands and I rest my palm on her shoulder.

"Don't go back, Ellie. Stay here with me."

Ellie shakes her head, worrying at her bottom lip.

"Why not?" Rhi says. "You'll be safe here. Azlan will keep you safe." A warmth spreads through my chest. Pride. Does she believe that? Does she see how hard I'd work to keep Ellie safe? How hard I'm working to keep her safe?

Ellie shakes her head a second time. "I love my family. I can't help it. My uncle may be a cruel, ruthless man – sometimes father can be that way too – but they have our best interests at heart. I can't be separated from them."

"You'd really miss our uncle?"

The corner of Ellie's mouth twitches. "Maybe not," she confesses. "But I'd miss our aunt. I'd miss Tristan."

I snort and Rhi catches my eye. "Everybody talks about your uncle – Tristan's father?" I nod, "like he's the devil himself."

"Because he is."

Rhi's brow furrows. "What's so awful about him?"

I look at Ellie who peers down at her hands.

"He's manipulative, cruel, calculating."

"A lot of the people I've met in Los Magicos are," Rhi mutters.

Now my brow furrows. "Who?" I say darkly.

"It doesn't matter."

It does. I intend to question her about it once Ellie's gone.

"Trust me," Ellie mutters. "None of them are like our uncle."

"Not even the chancellor?"

I shake my head. "My uncle believes himself to be the most powerful magical on Earth."

"Is he?"

I hold her gaze. "I don't know," I say. For a while now, I've suspected I am stronger. Suspected Tristan may be too. But we've never challenged him, never pitted ourselves against him. I might be wrong. Maybe my uncle is hiding as many secrets from us as we are him. No, there's no doubt that he is. "My uncle thinks his power entitles him to the right to rule this country – for it to be his – like the old kings back in ancient times. If he were ever to be made chancellor, he would make it happen. He would make this country his. The current chancellor is the only man standing in his way. He isn't perfect, but he's better than my uncle."

"If your uncle is more powerful than the chancellor, how is the chancellor stopping him from taking over?"

"My uncle may be powerful but he is only one man and the people support the chancellor."

"You mean the council supports the chancellor," she mutters. "Ordinary people like me don't get a say."

"It's safer this way."

"Let's hope so," Ellie mutters, shuffling in her seat.

My gaze snaps to her face. "What do you mean by that, Ellie?"

"Oh," she says, fidgeting some more. "Just a bad feeling I have. Woo woo shit." She smiles half-heartedly.

"Ellie," I press.

She adjusts the scarf tied round her head. "It's probably nothing …"

"What is?"

"Our uncle, our father."

"What are they up to?" I say, my spine stiffening, a desire to pull my mate close almost overwhelming.

"I don't know for sure. But there's been meetings, messengers."

"There always has been." Something my uncle and father have worked hard to disguise but something unmissable when you live with them.

"Yes, only, I don't know, there seems to be more."

We're silent for a moment, all thinking. I doubt Ellie is wrong about this. Usually it would be something I'd question Tristan about but we aren't talking right now. I'll have to keep a watchful eye on the family, stay in close contact with my sister.

Rhianna gives me a hard stare, then she glances at her necklace.

"It's a cloaker," she tells Ellie, tracing her fingers over the design and changing the subject. "It was my mom's."

"A cloaker is a powerful charm," I say. "One that would help keep you safe, Rhi."

"Yep, but I don't know how to use it."

"You need to learn."

"I'm at Arrow Hart – which you keep telling me is the safest place I can be. I have you looking out for me – plus Stone. And, if you hadn't noticed, I'm pretty good at looking out for myself."

"May I?" Ellie asks, stretching out her hand.

Rhi hooks the necklace from her neck and holds it in her palm. Ellie takes the necklace from Rhi's hand, examining the intricate design. "It's very pretty." She closes her fingers around it and shuts her eyes. "I can feel it's magic."

"Do you know how to make it work?" Rhi asks.

"No, but I'll find out," Ellie says.

"Ellie's a complete bookworm and a nerd."

Ellie wags her finger at me. "Just because I actually bothered to work hard and got more credits than you at the academy."

"Bullshit," I say. "We all know how clever you are. She's a very skilled alchemist. If anyone can discover how to make your cloaker work, it's Ellie."

My sister beams, then turns to Rhi. "Leave it to me."

5

R^{hi}

"THANK YOU," the man in black says, when he returns from seeing his sister to her car. "For allowing me to introduce you to my sister."

I shake my head, smiling. "Are you kidding? I wanted to meet her."

"Yes," he says. "But I know you wanted to talk to me and I apologize that you had to wait."

"It's fine," I say, suddenly nervous, the smile faltering on my lips.

What if he's not happy about this? What if he's anything but? What if it hurts him? I don't want to hurt him.

"Rhi, what is it?" he asks, his brow furrowed. He can feel all my swirling emotions through the bond.

I take his large hand in mine and thread our fingers together.

"Stone," I say, pausing to steady my nerves. I'm not brave enough to hold his gaze, instead focusing on our combined hands. "Last night, Stone and I slept together. Last night, we sealed the bond between us."

He squeezes my hand, rubbing the coarse pad of his thumb over my knuckles. I'm too afraid to look at his face.

"What's wrong?" he asks.

"Wrong?" My gaze finally leaps to his concerned one.

"You seem unhappy. Are you regretting your actions? Did he–"

"No, no, none of that. I'm happy with this decision, Azlan. Really happy. Maybe I'm incredibly naïve and dumb and–"

"You're none of those things, Rhi."

I nod. "Maybe this is a crazy situation, one that's going to land us all in trouble. But the two of you – it just feels right. Maybe it would feel right even if the bond between us did not exist."

"So why the unease?"

"You," I say.

"Me?" His shoulders tense.

"I want you to be happy too, Azlan. I don't want to hurt you."

His face breaks out into a huge, broad grin, that seems to lift all the shadows from his face. "Rhi, I am happy about this."

"Really?" I say, unsure despite the contentment I feel through the bond. "Because the thought of you with another woman, tears me apart."

"But this wasn't some other man, Rhi. This was Phoenix. This was your fated mate."

"And that makes a difference?"

"Yes," he says adamantly. "Fate wants this for us."

"And so if there was another fated mate ..." He chuckles. "I'm serious, Azlan. I need to understand how this works. Is it just Stone or ..."

He shakes his head with indulgence. "I don't know for sure, Rhi, until I'm in that situation. But if fate were to give you another mate, I believe I'd be accepting of that."

"Even if he were an asshole?"

"Like Phoenix, you mean?"

"Worse than Phoenix?"

"Then I'd whip him into shape for you. Fate has given me you, Rhi, and I'm destined to follow you to the edge of the world and back again now, facing whatever else fate throws our way."

"That sounds like woo woo, Mr. Enforcer."

"Maybe I believe in more of the woo woo stuff than I would ever be prepared to admit to Ellie. Maybe having experienced the power of all this woo woo crap, I'm more of a believer in it. Just don't tell my sister."

"I liked seeing the two of you together. It gave me a glimpse of your softer side."

"Haven't you seen plenty of my softer side?" he asks, tugging me against his solid frame.

"A little, now and then."

He sighs. "You're right. Ellie's right. I haven't been the mate I should have been. I've looked out for you but I haven't cared for you like I should have. I'm going to make it up to you. I intend to spoil you from now on, little mate. Anything you want, I'll give it to you. Anything you desire, I'll buy it for you."

"Really?" I say with a tease. "That sounds expensive."

"Rhi, I've been a single man for a long time, working my ass off. I have an awful lot of money saved in my vault." He examines my face. "What did you have in mind?"

"A new bike." I grin at him cheekily.

"No," he says firmly.

"And why not?" I don't really want one. Well, that's a lie. I'd love a new bike. I miss the freedom my old one gave me. I miss riding it. But bikes are pricey and I could never truly accept a gift like that.

"I like you riding on mine with me."

"Yeah," I confess with a sigh of my own, "I like that too."

"I'll buy you your own bike to look at but not to ride. I want you on my bike with me," he says with such forceful possession my knees almost buckle. "But I'm going to buy you other things too, Rhi."

"You are?"

"I am. Starting with some new clothes. I'd get you the best room in the whole academy if it wouldn't look damn suspicious – you going from the shittiest room to the best."

"They'd all be asking questions about my new sugar daddy." I grin. "You know it's going to look really suspicious if I start walking around in a load of designer clothes. Besides, it's not really my thing."

"Well one thing I am definitely buying you is a new pair of fucking jeans!" He hooks his finger through the loop of my pants and tugs me closer still. "These have gotten ridiculously tight."

"You don't like them that way?"

"I like them far too much this way. All I want to do is squeeze this ass of yours." He slides his palm around to my cheek and does just that. Then he's grabbing the other cheek too, hoisting me up and carrying me through to his bedroom.

On the bed, we scrabble at each other's clothes like wild desperate people and when he has me down to my underwear, he pauses to tell me, "I'm also buying you new panties.

Lots of ridiculous tiny expensive pairs of panties. No one but me will see them so it won't matter."

"And Stone," I remind him.

He growls against my throat.

"Also panties like that don't sound very comfortable," I tease.

"Doesn't matter," he says, sliding my plain cotton briefs down my thighs. "You won't be wearing them for long."

When I'm bare for him, he spreads my thighs open, settling between them and inhaling deeply. "I can smell him inside you," he whispers. "Are you all sticky with him too?" He drags his fingers through my wet folds.

I moan, wriggling against his touch. Then he slides a thick finger inside me.

"Fuck, you are," he says. "All sticky ... full of him." He growls. "I'm going to fuck you now too, pump you full of my seed."

I remember how obsessed Stone was about this earlier today. Is it part of the fated mate thing? This obsession with wanting to pump me full of their come. And why is that so damn hot?

I grind against his fingers as he massages the spot inside me, rubbing the heel of his hand against my clit, and squeezing my ass with his other hand. Then his fingers are creeping between my ass cheeks, stroking around my tight hole.

"How's that, sweetheart?" he asks.

Good, strangely good. But I can't get the words out, not with the way he is winding my body higher and higher. I manage an enthusiastic murmur and then as I come around his fingers, jolting about on the bed, he slides another finger inside me. But not my pussy this time. My backside. I cry out, stars crashing against my closed eyelids.

He growls right by my ear, "I can't wait for us to have you together."

Together?

I remember how intense it was when we were together, the three of us in Stone's cabin. How they explored, kissed and touched every part of me, overwhelming my senses completely.

But the man in black means something more.

I try to imagine what that would be like as he flips me over onto my stomach angling up my hips, and thrusting inside me, his hand tight around my braid. His hips slap against my backside. Could I take two mates at once?

Do I want to?

As he fucks me hard, down deep into the mattress, tugging at my hair so my scalp stings in sharp contrast to the pleasurable sensations in my pussy, I know I do.

I want it really badly.

LATER, he insists on ordering takeout, laying out menus across the bed from every restaurant in the city.

"Choose whatever you want, order as much as you like," he growls. "We're going to have a banquet. I didn't treat you well enough last time you were here. And I'm making up for it now."

"I like you cooking for me," I admit, picking up the first menu and scanning the list.

He drags me onto his lap and nuzzles my throat. "You do?"

"Uh huh."

"Hmmm," he murmurs against my skin. "Not tonight

though, little mate. Tonight you're being spoiled with the finest food Los Magicos has to offer."

I smile. Being spoiled is a strange sensation but I think I could come to enjoy it.

"But I don't know what to choose. I've never tried half of these foods."

"Then I'll choose for you." He picks up a handful of the pamphlets and disappears out of the bedroom. When he doesn't return straight away, I pull one of his t-shirts over my head and go to investigate. I find him in the dining room – a room that looks as if it's been rarely used. He's busy setting out the table, lining up cutlery and crockery, several candles already flickering across the tabletop and an uncorked bottle of wine waiting in a cooler.

"This looks rather posh," I tell him, watching him work from the doorway.

"I'm spoiling you," he says simply, placing a white napkin next to a plate and then striding towards me and wrapping me in his arms.

"I think I'm underdressed. Should I go change?" I tease, not that I have anything to change into. I came in my jeans and hoodie.

"No, I like you in my shirt," he says, his hands disappearing under the hem. I sigh, quite happy to forget about dinner altogether, but then we're interrupted by the doorbell.

"That'll be the food," he tells me. "Don't go anywhere."

I take a seat, lying the crisp napkin over my knees and wait for him to return. When he does, he's carrying a tray laden with dishes – no plastic takeout tubs in sight. He places each dish onto the table telling me as he does what it contains and encouraging me to ladle a bit of everything onto my plate. There's food from across the republic – stews from the north, fried chicken from the south, as well as spiced buns from across the ocean and tight little meat bundles wrapped in pastry from the islands.

He takes the seat next to mine, pouring golden wine into both our glasses. He takes a sip of his as I sink my teeth into one of the parcels and moan, my eyes rolling in their sockets.

"You like it?" he asks, watching me, his own plate empty.

"I don't think I've ever tasted anything so good. You have to try it."

"I will. In a minute." I eye him.

"What?" he says.

"You're just going to sit and watch me eat?"

"I like watching you eat – especially when you make those delicious little moans of pleasure," he growls by my ear.

"Hmmm," I say, finishing my mouthful and swallowing. "Are you a feeder?"

"A feeder?"

"Someone who gains, you know, sexual pleasure from feeding another person. Only, you fed me all that food on our way to Los Magicos and now this." I sweep my hand over the table.

"You're turning me into a pervert, little mate, because I gain sexual pleasure from watching you do just about anything."

My bond spins with pleasure. I like that I turn him on. It feels powerful. I take another of the parcels from the plate and offer it up to his mouth. He meets my eyes, then takes a bite, capturing my fingers between his lips and sucking at them.

"Definitely a pervert." I giggle.

"You have no idea," he mumbles.

I'm half tempted to push the food aside, lie out on the table and encourage the man in black to feast on me, but this food is delicious and I haven't eaten all day.

I try some of the stew next, encouraging him to do the same.

"My aunt used to make something like this in the winter," I tell him. "But it wasn't as good."

"It's my favorite thing to eat," he says, lifting a forkful to his mouth, then pausing, "well, until I met you."

"Yep, you're a pervert." I grin at him. "But really, it's your favorite? Not the parcels? Or, you know, something chocolate and creamy?"

"No, my mother used to make us this. It reminds me of her." He stares down at his plate, before taking another mouthful.

"She's ..." I hesitate. He's never really mentioned her before.

"Dead, yes," he says, lifting his glass and taking a swig of wine.

I rest my hand on his thigh and he covers it with his own much bigger palm.

"How long ago?"

"I was 15. My sister was 8. She was killed in a car accident."

"I'm sorry," I say and he squeezes my hand. "You miss her?"

"Of course," he says, twisting his head to meet my gaze. "She was a good woman. A kind and funny one. Our home was never the same after she died. It felt colder, darker. There wasn't as much laughter or sunshine."

I think of what it was like after my aunt passed. How the nights felt longer, the days duller, the clouds heavier, the wind colder.

"She would have liked you," he continues.

"Unlike the rest of your family," I mutter.

"My mother was a good influence on my father. She hated my uncle and while she was alive, we didn't have so much to do with him. Then she died and ... everything changed. If she was still here, things would be different. She'd have cooked you this stew, and we'd be eating it at my family home."

I kiss his cheek, running my fingers through his dark hair. He's silent, thinking, his heavy chest rising and falling.

I lean closer to him, wanting to lift him out of his sadness. "Of course, dessert wouldn't have been as good."

"Dessert?" he says, jerking out of his reverie.

"Uh huh, dessert."

I climb onto his lap, straddling him.

"You are going to have *me* for dessert, right?"

"Shit," he mumbles, hands on my ass as I grind against him. "You think we could pause the main course and have our dessert now?"

I smile at him, then lean in to drag my teeth up his throat. He takes that as a yes, freeing his already-stiff cock from his pants and lining me up. I'm not wearing any panties and I glide straight down onto him, gripping his broad shoulders as I do. The food was good, but there's nothing quite like this, the feel of him full and deep inside me, my bond humming with pleasure. I wonder why we bothered with the food at all, why we didn't just stay in bed.

I grind myself on his lap and he tugs his t-shirt over my head so I'm completely bare on his lap, my tits bouncing as I rise up and down on his cock. Then his fingers are at my clit, getting me off as I find a rhythm that has us both panting.

"You're so fucking beautiful, Rhianna," he says, as my legs begin to shake and I lose control. "So fucking beautiful." I come, squeezing and convulsing around his cock and he lifts me up, slamming me down on the table, sending dishes and glasses tumbling. He sucks at my tits and then he thrusts back inside me, fucking me straight through my orgasm, his eyes locked on mine. "And I can't get enough of you."

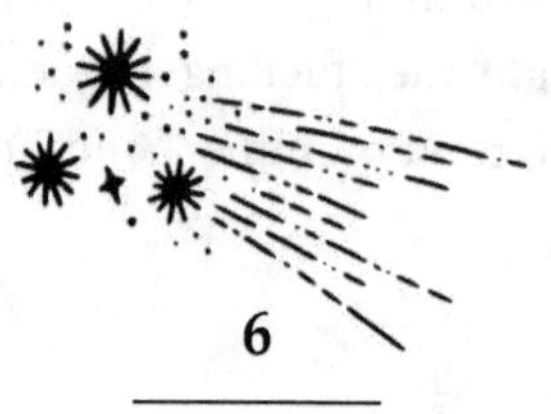

6

S pencer

THERE's an envelope waiting for me on my desktop when I arrive back from my run on Sunday evening.

I don't need to switch on the lamp, examine the handwriting, tear it open, to know who the letter is from.

My mother.

She is the only person who writes to me. The only way she actually communicates.

I haven't had such a letter for months and months. I'd almost begun to wonder if she'd forgotten about the existence of her youngest son.

I pick up a discarded towel from the floor and wipe it around my wet brow, neck and shoulders, eyeing the envelope the entire time as if I expect it to jump up and bite me any moment.

Then I discard the towel back to the floor, toss my phone and earbuds onto my bed, and stalk over to the desk.

Now I examine the handwriting, my name penned in her elegant hand across the crisp white paper.

I squint at that hand, trying to determine if it was written in pleasure or anger. A neutrality most likely. My mother is not an emotional woman.

Maybe that comes from raising boys like us.

I lift the envelope and turn it over, finding it fastened shut with the usual family seal. I run my finger over it – the outline of a powerful wolf – then I tear the thing open, shaking loose the single sheet of paper inside.

I run my eyes over the words. A short note, congratulating me on the dueling team's win, on my successful captaincy, on my powerful display.

She ends with words describing my father's pride. I laugh out loud, a sarcastic, hollow sound in the quiet of my room.

My father spends more time as beast than he does as a human these days, hidden away in the grounds of our family's compound. I doubt he knows anything about my match. I wonder why she wrote it at all. In case I shared it?

I scrub my hand over my chin, eyes hovering over the words.

It is my mother who has held the family together by the skin of her teeth over the years. Hiding our true natures, managing our affliction, negotiating and bribing those she needed to.

Could she fix this for me now? Stop this restless energy, the constant scrape of the beast inside me, his incessant stirring?

Once upon a time there was another person I would have asked for advice. Someone who would have helped me despite our differences. Maybe the only other person in the world who could understand this. But he's gone and there's no point in dwelling on it.

I rest the letter back on my desk and, grabbing a fresh towel from the pile of laundered washing the maid has left by my door, head to the shower. Under the water, I try to stay focused on everything but the pig girl, reliving both matches from yesterday in my mind – both the official and unofficial one – then raking over my performance, debating in my mind what I'd do differently next time.

But these distractions are useless. Temporary. My body and the creature within aren't the only things fixated on the girl. My mind is too. It keeps straying back to her over and over again. The picture of her in my mind's eye refusing to budge. Watching me from the stands in the stadium. Peering up at me from the ground outside the Venus common room.

I scrub at my body. It's far sorer than it would normally be.

My limbs are heavy, my muscles ache. I feel like I'm coming down with a cold. I'm never ill. What the hell is wrong with me?

I slam the shower screen back and stomp from the cubicle, forgetting all about the towel and trailing a puddle of water after me. I stare down at that letter again, water dripping from my chin onto the paper, a gray dot staining its surface. Then another and another, smudging the black ink.

I shake the water away from my face, bend over my desk and pull out my own piece of paper. I don't give my response too much thought, scribbling lines quickly across the surface before I can change my mind. When I'm finished, I shove the sheet into an envelope, affixing it with a matching family seal of my own and scribbling my mother's name across the front.

Then I straighten up and hover my hand above the envelope. It flickers for a full minute before vanishing completely from sight.

I gaze down at the empty desk.

There's no going back now.

I'M STANDING on the steps of the mansion at 9.55am sharp the next morning, just as directed. At 10am exactly, I hear the crunch of gravel under heavy tires and watch as her sleek silver car glides to a halt. A minute later, the chauffeur emerges from the driver's seat, adjusting the cap on his head and then turning to the rear passenger door.

I watch as his hand grips the handle and he tugs on it, the door swinging open and my mother's form emerging from the darkness.

I knew she would come. She shuns the crowds, avoids the matches. But today the campus is quiet, the visiting team long gone and the spectators departed, and my letter enough to tempt her out of the shadows.

The chauffeur offers her a hand and she takes it, climbing out from the dark leather seat and adjusting the satin-black jacket she's dressed in. She wears a matching satin skirt, black stockings and black-heeled boots. The same outfit I've known her to wear for as long as I can remember.

She peers upwards, her alert amber eyes observing me first and then the principal beside me.

Professor York takes this as her cue, descending the steps and holding her hands out towards my mother.

"Mrs. Moreau, so wonderful to see you. I was not expecting you." She smiles coolly at my mother. "To what do we owe this pleasure?"

"I've come to speak with my son," my mother says in her usually clipped tone, ignoring York's outstretched hands and walking towards me.

She looks older than she did the last time we met. More white streaked through her jet hair, more lines hovering above her brow. Although she's still strangely beautiful in that angular, frightening way.

The principal follows behind us. "Would you like to come to my office? I can have some refreshments sent for us and–"

"No, we'll go to the alumni common room. I have my key."

"And Spencer has classes," the principal says, a tad less friendly.

My mother snaps her head around to peer at the principal over her shoulder. "He played on Saturday. I expected him to be resting, recovering and recuperating today. Or do you wish him to gain an injury?"

The principal considers my mother, obviously weighing up whether or not to argue with her. My mother stares at her unblinking until the principal bows her head, conceding. "A mother knows best, Mrs. Moreau. If you feel Spencer would benefit from a day's extra rest, then I will sanction it."

My mother doesn't thank her, instead she spins her vivid gaze to me, climbing the steps to stop by my side and weaving her hand around my arm.

She's smaller than I remember too, frailer despite her domineering persona.

"Let's go for a stroll, Spencer," she says, "I need to stretch my legs after the journey."

"Thank you for coming," I say, when we've walked away from the front of the mansion, around its width and towards the paths that lead through the campus grounds.

"You should have sent for me sooner," she says.

I'm quiet. I don't want to talk about this out on the path. A few students hurry along, late for their lessons. I don't want them overhearing. I already see the way they glance at us from the corner of their eyes. They'll be spreading this piece of gossip as soon as their backsides land on their classroom seats. Mrs. Moreau seen out in the open. It hasn't been known for years. I don't care.

My mother senses my reluctance to speak out in the open and she's silent too, following my lead as I weave us along the paths. The day is overcast, the air thick with humidity and the coming fall. The light gray.

Her nails pinch the skin of my arm and her heels crunch the gravel underfoot. Under the perfume she wears, I smell her scent – sharp against the floral tones.

We walk around the gymnasium and the dueling pitch, deadly quiet today, and past the practical magical labs, its tall chimneys lost in the low-hanging cloud.

We're passing the door, when I hear a pupil hurrying on the path behind us, their breath panting loudly in the quietness.

I keep walking, eyes trained right ahead, refusing to look that way, even though the hook in my belly strains towards her, even though I'm damn curious to look.

But my mother stiffens.

She halts suddenly beside me, her head snaps over her shoulder and her amber eyes flash.

I can't help glancing too, watching as the Pig Girl swings the building door open and disappears inside.

My mother stares at the closing door.

"Who is that girl, Spencer?" she says, her eyes returning to their normal color.

"No one," I mutter, tugging gently on her arm.

"No one?" she says. "I do not recognize her."

"She's new. Joined the school several months back."

"From where?"

I pause. "The wastelands."

My mother snaps her head back around to me. "An unregistered?"

I nod.

"She's powerful." I glance towards the door. "Come on," she says, "I've walked far enough. Let's talk."

The alumni common room is a long ancient room that rests alongside the Great Hall, its floor formed of old wooden boards that creak as we walk inside, battered leather armchairs spread around its walls, more paintings of previous pupils adorning the wall. It's a room present students are not permitted to enter. Only those who are honored alumni of the school are allowed to use the room, each given their own key and permission to enter whenever they like.

My mother walks straight to the nearest window, opening the heavy shutters that block out the dull light. Then she turns to face me, resting her hand against the back of the nearest chair.

I stand facing her on the other side of the room. The distance between us feels vast as always.

"The pills are no longer working," she says.

"No, they aren't," I say, "I'm sure Principal York must have told you–"

My mother waves her hand through the air in irritation. "Yes, yes, but I assumed that was some boyish prank. If there's been a problem – if there is still a problem – you should have contacted me sooner, Spencer."

A problem? She has no fucking idea.

Suddenly, the weight of it. This burden – this cruel stupid burden – is too much. Too fucking much.

I sink into the nearest chair and bury my face into my hands.

"I thought I could sort it out myself," I say, my voice catching in my throat. "I thought I'd be able to control it, to get a grip on it."

She huffs with more irritation.

"Is there anything that's caused this change? The pills have always worked for you in the past."

I keep my face hidden in my hands. I don't want her to read the lie on my face when I murmur, "No, nothing that I can think of. Can't you make me stronger pills?"

"They're as strong as I am prepared to make them, Spencer. Any stronger would be dangerous." I peer up at her. I've been taking two to three times the number of pills I should but I'm not going to confess that either. "We need to find another way. A girl perhaps." I snort. "Or a boy. Some-where for all that pent-up energy to go."

"Are you telling me to fuck my way out of this situation, Maman?" I say with irritation.

I've been fucking plenty. Okay, maybe not so much recently – not at all recently – but before then I was, and it did nothing to help contain the creature.

My mother bristles at my bad language. Her eyes deepen. "You can scoff all you like but what do you think has settled your father? Me. A mate. A wife. A partner."

I lean back on my chair and cross my arms over my chest.

Bullshit! My father rarely leaves the compound these

days. He spends most of his time as beast. He's even less settled than I am.

Is that the only future she has to offer me? Living like a wild animal in a glorified zoo.

I'm cautious in my cynicism towards my mother though. She has a cold temper, one I have no intention of provoking.

"Papa isn't forced to live his days as–"

"How about that girl?"

I choke on my words and look at her in disbelief. She can't know. Even my mother, shrewd, clever, with an ability to see far more than most magicals, couldn't see that. It isn't possible.

I force my body to relax. Her hot gaze examines me.

"What girl?"

"The one on the path. The powerful one."

"She's not powerful," I scoff.

My mother walks towards me, stopping in front of me to hook a manicured finger under my chin and force my gaze up to hers.

"She is and I'm sure you feel her power just as clearly as I do, Spencer. A mate like her would provide you with the stability you crave. That the family craves."

Yes, can't have a little Moreau werebeast on the loose, causing havoc, destroying the good family name, exposing all our carefully guarded secrets.

"She's an unregistered. Unskilled. Untrained. With no family, no connections."

"All the easier to bend her will to yours. To manipulate her. I'm not saying you need to marry the girl, Spencer." She cups my cheek, patting it gently, the closest expression to warmth hovering in her eyes. "Simply use her for your own means."

"And is this the advice you gave my brother too? Go fuck some girl?"

"Your brother never had problems with control, Spencer."

Shame and sorrow swim through my body.

"She has to want me back," I say petulantly.

"Such modern ideas!" My mother laughs. "What does your beast want?"

I peer out towards the window.

She can't possibly know. She can't.

7

R^{hi}

After dinner, I make like I'm taking Pip out for a walk and head out into the dark evening. I feel guilty for using him like this, but no matter what people may sneer and snap, he is important to me – very important – and it's about time these mates of mine became better acquainted with him.

I take a deviating route, pausing twice to allow Pip to snuffle around in a bush, and then I double back, cutting across the meadow towards Stone's cabin, my tracking sense switched on and scanning for anyone nearby.

I know Stone's home tonight, our newly sealed bond humming with his presence, and I nearly trip over my feet in my bid to reach him.

The door swings open before I've even reached the bottom step of his cabin and he comes jogging down, his gaze swinging around the meadow.

I expect him to tell me off for coming to see him unannounced. It wasn't exactly our plan, but to my surprise he sweeps me up into his arms, lifting me so our faces are level and then kissing me, warm and passionately, as if he hasn't seen me for months, not hours.

"Fuck, it feels like years," he says. "This bond thing ... I didn't think it was possible to want you more than I did."

I grin at him and kiss him back, but then Pip's grunting unhappily by our feet and I slide out of the professor's arms, and crouch down to pat Pip's head.

"You brought the pig?" Stone says with obvious disgust.

"Yes, you haven't been formally introduced and I thought it was about time."

Pip snorts loudly at the man in front of him.

"I assume he's finally thanking me for that time I rescued him from the cellar."

"Nope, that's the noise he makes when he loathes someone."

"Seems a little unfair."

"You need to win him round if we're all going to get along."

"You're my fated mate," he says a little sulkily, "not the pig's." He attempts to take my hand and tug me back up, but Pip gets there first, barreling his way into my arms.

"Jeez," Stone mumbles. "Does he like Azlan?"

"They're growing on each other."

Stone shakes his head, plunging his hands inside his pant pockets and climbing back up the cabin steps.

"Come on. Let's get inside before anyone sees us."

I lift Pip into my arms and follow Stone inside.

Is it my imagination or has he spring-cleaned the place? It looks neater than it did the day before. Possibly even cleaner, the fragrance of citrus clear in the air and the piles of books and essays stacked away in a corner. Even the floor looks swept and the shelves dusted.

I drop Pip to the floor, and he immediately starts scurrying about.

"What's it doing now?" Stone asks suspiciously.

"*He* is exploring."

"Does *he* want some food?"

"He's a pig. He always wants food."

Stone marches over to the kitchen cupboard and draws open the doors. "Does he like cereal?"

"What kind?"

Stone peers over his shoulder and grins at me. "Rainbow candy pops."

"You're kidding me? Do you eat that stuff?" Stone nods. "It'll rot your teeth."

"I've been eating it for about thirty years, Miss Blackwaters, and my teeth are just fine."

"Damn, I thought I knew you, Stone."

"There's a lot you don't know."

I hop up onto the kitchen counter, swinging my legs as he shakes fluorescent-looking corn puffs into a bowl and drops it to the floor.

Pip eyes it suspiciously, giving a cautious sniff before licking one with his tongue.

"Like what?" I ask him. "What don't I know?"

His heated gaze flicks down my body, making me squirm on the counter.

"Oh no, don't distract me," I say, wagging my finger at him. "I didn't come here for that." The other reason I brought Pip along.

"Are you sure about that?" he says, stalking towards me and coming to stop in between my thighs.

"Well, no, but I need to talk to you first, before you distract me, okay?"

"You spoke to Azlan yesterday?" he asks, his tone turning serious.

"Yes, and he's fine. Happy, weirdly happy."

"Weirdly happy, weirdly sad, the dude's just plain weird."

"He's meant to be your best friend."

"Which is why I get to call him weird."

"I don't think he's weird," I say with a little huff.

The professor grins at me. "You're cute."

I straighten up on the counter. "I am not cute."

"You are incredibly cute, especially when you're pouting at me." He nuzzles at my neck.

"I'm not pouting," I totally pout.

"Sure you're not, sweetheart."

I push at his shoulder. "You're doing it again," I say as he ignores my attempt to push at him and nuzzles further down my neck.

"Doing what?" he mumbles at the neck of my top.

"The distracting thing. I'm serious about talking."

He pauses mid-kiss and drags his head up, taking a decided step away from me and holding up his hands. He dips his head to meet my eyeline and gives me his sincerest look. "I apologize. You have my full and undivided attention."

"Good," I say, "but you don't need to stand quite so far away." I grab a fistful of his shirt and tug him closer.

"Better?" he says, standing right in front of me.

"Hmm," I say, considering him, then taking both his hands in mine and resting them on the tops of my thighs. "Better."

"You know this is a huge distraction for me too."

I nod in a brattish way. I'm beginning to learn that being a brat totally winds the professor up in just the right way.

"Talk, Blackwaters, before I toss you over my shoulder and march you through to the bedroom."

"Promises, promises," I mumble.

He growls in return and I figure I'm playing with fire if I tease him any further.

"The memories. My mom."

"Did you talk to Azlan about it? Did you share what you learned from the old man?"

"No ... we were busy with other things."

Stone gives me a hard look. "Are you playing favorites already, Miss Blackwaters? He gets to be busy with you and I'm resigned to the talking."

"His sister came to visit."

"Ahhh," Stone says, looking the closest to sheepish I've ever seen him.

"Was that a flash of jealousy though, Professor, because you guys said–"

"I'm not jealous of the time the two of you spend together."

I can't help but reach up and stroke my hand over his cheek. "I don't understand how you can't be jealous. The thought of the two of you with another woman has my insides churning. I'm pretty sure I would kill any woman who tried to touch you."

"And I'm certain I would kill any man who touched you, sweetheart. Apart from Azlan. It's different. He's your mate like I am. It's hard to explain but it doesn't feel the same. It feels natural."

As natural as developing feelings for both of these men at once? No matter what they tell me, I know it's unusual.

Most people have one partner. One love. And yet, it feels so right, there's no way it could be wrong.

"What are you wondering about your mom, Rhi?" he asks me.

"I'm not done yet, Phoenix. I need to know what happened to her. What happened to my dad."

"Of course you do."

"So I want to explore those memories in my head again – only this time delve deeper, see if my aunt left me any clues."

"No, Rhianna, absolutely not. No way."

"What?" I stutter with incredulity. "Why not?"

"Why not?! The pain it caused you. The suffering. I'm not letting you go through that again."

"It wasn't that bad."

"It was, Blackwaters. It was worse. I had to drag you out of it. I was right there with you. I saw just what it cost you and we're going nowhere near those memories again."

"It's my choice!"

"We'll find another way."

"There is no better way."

"Blackwaters, I said no."

"These are my memories. It's my head!"

"Then find someone else to help you. Because I won't."

"And that's it? You say no and that's final."

"Yes."

"This isn't fair. It's my decision."

"I'm not arguing with you about this."

"So we can't even talk about it now?"

"There isn't any point. You're not changing my mind."

I glare at him. But to my utter astonishment no more feisty words come flying from my tongue. Instead, I burst out into goddamn tears. Big fat ones that streak down my cheeks.

"Rhi," Stone says, reaching with his thumb to wipe them away.

I duck my head from his reach. "I'm so damn angry with you. I'm so angry ... and frustrated. You know who you are, Stone? So does Azlan and Winnie. Shit, even Pip knew his parents." Pip looks up from where he's planted his face in the bowl of cereal and squeaks. "And you're denying me this."

"Rhi," he says softly. "Please don't ask me to do it. It was bad enough before, now you're my mate, I can't. I can't in good faith allow you to do something that will hurt you so badly. I can't watch you suffer like that."

"How can this work, Phoenix?!" I say, shaking my head wildly, the tears still coming strong. "All we do is fight."

He smiles. "The bond is pretty damn strong magic, but it isn't the thing fairytales make it out to be. We're still going to fight and disagree and really fucking hate each other sometimes."

"Do you hate me, Phoenix?" I ask him through my wet eyelashes.

"Hate you? Rhi, no, I–"

"Because some of the stuff you did to me, the way you treated me."

He scrubs his hand through his hair.

"You know I'm sorry about that Rhi, really fucking sorry. You know if I could turn back time and undo all those things, I would."

"But you can't. And now when I ask you to do this one thing–"

"Rhi, I'm trying to do right by you, make up for the

wrong I've done. I can't do that one thing. I just can't. I can't hurt you."

"Then what can you do, Phoenix?" I snap.

He huffs our air and takes my hand in his, fiddling with the rings on my fingers. "I've been thinking about that. I … I don't have a lot to offer you, Rhi. I'm not exactly swimming in money or connections. But, you know what, I am a damn good teacher when I want to be."

"Really?" I say, lifting an eyebrow.

He smiles sheepishly again. "Yeah, and I know how desperate you are to learn, to catch up with the others, so I was thinking I could help you, give you some one-on-one tutoring."

"Wouldn't that look seriously suspicious, Professor? Us spending even more time together?"

"It would give us the perfect reason to spend time together. And," he adds before I can interrupt, "I've already okayed it with York. First tutoring session can take place tomorrow straight after dinner if you want it to."

I sniff, considering his offer. I'm still angry with him, plus disappointed with his refusal to explore those memories, but I have to admit this offer is a good one. There is still so much I want to learn. I want to test my magic, push it, stretch it, but I've almost been too scared to try. With Stone I wouldn't feel afraid; with his help and guidance I'd be prepared to try anything.

"Okay," I say finally.

"I thought you'd be a tad more enthusiastic, Miss Blackwaters," he says a little sulkily.

"Hmmm," I say.

He examines my face, then tugs on my hand, pulling me off the counter and onto my feet.

"You're not satisfied enough? You don't think I've done enough to redeem myself?"

"I don't know," I say, shrugging and feeling confused. I want to climb back into bed with him. I want to be in his arms. I want him kissing me again. But in my heart I'm not sure I've completely forgiven him. "You did some pretty awful stuff to me, Stone."

He tugs me closer. "I know I did, and I'd do anything to make it up to you, Rhi. So, if you want to punish me, you go right ahead."

"Punish you?" I hiss. "What? Throw ham sandwiches at your head? Tip shit all over your face? Chain you to the bed?"

"If it makes you feel better. If it means you'll forgive me." He curls his arms around my waist and whispers in my ear, "Miss Blackwaters, if you'd like to chain me to the bed then you can."

"It's tempting," I say as he sucks on my throat.

He chuckles. "I bet it is."

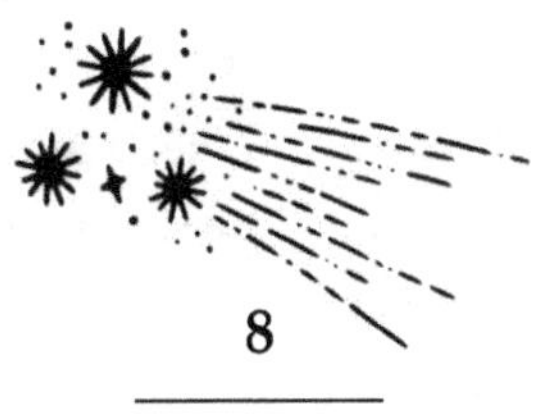

8

S tone

WHEN I MADE THE SUGGESTION, I'd made it in jest. I didn't expect her to take up the offer, but then I should know by now that this girl doesn't do anything by halves. Plus she's damn determined when she wants to be. Right now, she's angry with me, angry I won't unlock more of those memories, angry at how I treated her. She wants to make me pay and if paying involves her taking my hand and leading me to my bedroom, I'm not going to complain. In fact, I'm positively excited about the idea, my cock already hard in my pants as I imagine lying out on my back, chained to the bed as the little thing bounces on my cock, or sucks me off. Yeah, that's one punishment I can get on board with.

When we enter the bedroom, she strides over to the window and yanks the curtains closed, then she spins to face me, one of those fiery looks on her brow.

"Where do you want me, Miss Blackwaters?" I smirk. "I'm all yours to command."

"Do you promise that, Professor? Promise you're going to do as I say?"

"Scout's honor," I say, giving her a little salute.

"You were never a scout," she says with disdain.

"No, but I wanted to be."

"Just promise me," she says.

I meet her eye. "Rhi, I'm trying to make things up to you and I'd do anything you ask to make that happen. So I give you my word. You're in charge here. You're in command." Am I an asshole? Because this seems too easy, too enjoyable. I like the idea of the little bratty thing taking the reins, showing me just what she wants.

"Okay, then, Professor, take off your clothes."

"Not even a please, jeez," I say with a wink, unbuttoning my shirt, enjoying the way her eyes darken as I strip off the thing. "All my clothes?" I ask, as I toss the shirt towards her feet.

"All," she confirms.

I unbuckle my belt and slide my pants and boxers off together, throwing those onto the pile too and standing in front of her, my cock pointing right her way. I reach down to fist it in my hand but she shakes her head.

"Want to come touch me instead?" I ask her.

"Not yet," she says, "we haven't got to the chaining bit."

I chuckle. I'd almost forgotten that bit.

"Where do you want me, then, Miss Blackwaters?" I take a step towards her, hoping she wants me between her thighs.

"Lying on your back on the bed." A smile plays across my lips as that image of what's to come plays out in my mind. My cock grows impossibly harder, precome dribbling from the tip.

I slump down onto the bed, shifting along until I'm laid out in the middle. Then I lift my fists and offer up my wrists. "All ready for you, Miss Blackwaters."

"Hands by your sides, Professor." I do as she says, and she waves her hand through the air, cool metal chains weaving across the bed and coiling themselves around my ankles and my wrists. Just like mine had done that night in the motel. I tug against them, testing the constraint. They're tight, powerful. Nothing I couldn't blast through if I needed to though.

"Satisfied?" I ask.

She rests a knee on the mattress and leans over me, her hair tickling against my skin, her scent doing the same in my nostrils. She yanks on the chains, checking the strength and my cock twitches with her proximity. But she doesn't stay, she leans away and resumes her place by the side of the bed.

"Not planning to join me here, Miss Blackwaters?"

She smiles all coyly and my blood heats several tens of degrees. Then her hands are at the neck of her blouse, slowly threading the first button through the fastening. The stupid uniform has always looked sinful on her. I've dreamed so many times of ripping open her blouse, of burying my face between her tits, of lifting that tiny skirt of hers and discovering everything wet and hot beneath.

I growl, watching as she undoes more and more buttons, the blouse falling open and her bra coming into view next, her tits almost spilling out of the tight thing.

"You want me to take that off for you, Miss Blackwaters?" I ask, loving the way those tits jiggle as she shimmies the blouse down her arms.

"Your hands are bound, Professor."

"I could use my teeth."

She flashes me another coy little smile and then she toes off her shoes and turns her back to me. She bends in half, her skirt riding up the back of her thighs and flashing me her panties. Then she tucks her thumbs into the tops of her socks, caressing the soft milky skin there, and rolls them down her legs. Fuck, I want to do that. I want to roll them down and follow after with my tongue, lick her right the way down to the tip of her toe and back up again to her pussy.

She kicks the socks away and now she's standing in just her bra and her skirt. She looks incredible with her hair braided loosely, her eyes dark, her lips pink and parted.

"Take your panties off and come sit on my cock, Miss Blackwaters. Like a good girl."

"No," she says, shaking her head. "I'm in charge, not you, remember, Professor?"

I groan, taking back my earlier thoughts. This *is* a suitable punishment. In fact, it's torture. My bond strains for her, my cock aches for her pussy and I feel like my balls might explode. But despite how much she must feel me longing for her through our bond, she's determined to continue with this torturous strip show, this time undoing the button at the waist of her skirt and stepping out of it. Now she's in just her underwear.

I wait hungrily as she twists away from me a second time and reaches around to snap open her bra. She lets the straps fall down her arms and the garment tumble to the floor. My gaze trails down her beautiful back and my heart thumps in my chest. I've seen her breasts before. I know how stunning they are. Full and round with pink pert little nipples I want to suck into my mouth. And yet, my pulse is still racing, waiting for another glance.

"Miss Blackwaters," I groan. But she doesn't turn around yet, instead she squeezes her breasts in both her hands before hooking her thumbs into the waistband of her panties and gliding them achingly slowly down her legs. This time I'm rewarded with the glorious view of her ass – something I'd give anything to slap right now. When she straightens up, she gives a little wiggle, making her ass cheeks jiggle.

I hold my breath waiting for her to turn around and walk my way.

Once again, she surprises me. She remains exactly where she is, a foot away. Instead, I'm forced to lie here and watch as she slides her right hand down her body and then around to the front of her body. She moans and I can guess exactly where her hand has ended up – right where I want to fucking be.

"Are you touching yourself, sweetheart?" I ask, the desperation clear in my voice.

She doesn't answer but I can tell by the movement of her hand and the little noises that start to bubble from her throat that she is.

"Fuck," I mutter. "Fuck, Miss Blackwaters, turn around and let me see."

She continues to ignore me, those noises becoming louder, the movement of her hand more frantic. I swear I can even hear the squelch of her wet pussy. Fuck, I can imagine just how wet she is, can almost taste that on the end of my tongue.

I groan and tip back my head in frustration.

"Miss Blackwaters, get your peachy ass over here right now!"

"No!" she moans, her legs beginning to shake, color racing all over her body, her magic sparking in the air, pleasure swooping through her bond.

I yank against the chains, desperate to see what she's doing to herself, how exactly she's touching herself, wanting her to do that right over my face, wanting to add my tongue and my mouth to her pleasure.

"Oh Stars," she cries out and I grunt again, trying to blast my magic through the chains this time. But I'm too frustrated, too aroused, and I make a mess of it, her tight chains keeping me locked in place.

A long drawn-out sigh rushes from her lips, her hand stills and then her body jolts with waves of bliss.

"Blackwaters," I plead, "please, please come here. Please let me see you, touch you, fuck you."

I try again with my magic but it collides with hers.

"You promised," she moans as she continues to massage between her legs. "You promised."

"Fuck, Fuck! But you're so ... I'm so ... so fucking hard. Come here and let me show you just how hard."

"Hmmm," she says, running her hands over her body, her skin flushed with pleasure. "I don't think so."

"What?!" I say incredulous. "You don't think so?"

"No, Professor," she says, reaching down to pick up her clothes, her back still turned towards me. "I think I'm going to leave you right where you are and head back to my dorm room."

She peeks at me over her shoulder, giving me a bratty smile – one she's worked out drives me wild.

"You can't leave me like this!" I whine. I want her so badly, I think I might combust, set this bed and this shack alight and blazing.

"I think I can." She blows me a kiss. "I'll see you in our tutoring session tomorrow, Professor."

She sashays out of the room, hips swaying in a damn provocative manner. How the hell did she learn to do that? She shuts the door behind her. Through the thin walls, I hear the rustle of clothes, then she calls to the pig and both their feet pad towards the door.

"It's not too late to change your mind," I call out.

"Goodbye Professor," she says, the door slamming.

I let out a string of curse words, then fling my head back onto the pillows. A smile spreads across my face and I can't help chuckling.

What a brat!

But I think I may have deserved that.

9

R hi

"YOU CREPT IN LATE LAST NIGHT?" Winnie says as we climb into our uniforms the next morning.

"Did I?" I say as innocently as I can.

Winnie comes to stand next to me at the mirror, bumping her arm against mine.

"You did. And is that another love bite on your neck?"

"Shit," I mumble, moving closer to the mirror for a better look.

Winnie bumps my shoulder again. "Jeez, Rhi. I was joking. There's no love bite. But I'm assuming ..."

"Assume all you like, Winnifred Wence. I'm under strict instructions not to tell you every little detail of our love life."

"Hmmm," Winnie says, sounding unimpressed. "Men do not get to interfere in the ways of women and one of the fundamentals of such ways is: you must tell your best friend all about your love life in excessive, lascivious detail. Even if those men are the authorities' enforcer and one of the academy's hottest teachers."

"Hottest teacher," I correct with a grin.

"Want to tell me how hot?" she says with a third bump.

But before I can, there's a rap at our door.

We both look at each other. We know by now whenever someone comes knocking on our door, it isn't a good thing.

"I'll get it," I say, plopping my beret on the top of my head.

When I swing back the door, I'm greeted by the groundsman clutching a gigantic package in his arms.

"It's for you," he says, gruffly, obviously unhappy he's been forced to deliver the thing to my door. "Where do you want it?"

"Inside, I guess," I say, standing to one side to let him in.

"It isn't cursed, is it?" Winnie asks, eyeing the parcel with suspicion. "Someone did check?"

"'Course they did," the groundsman grumbles, dropping his load and swiftly marching away.

"That doesn't mean there isn't something sinister inside," Winnie says as I close the door. "Remember that ham?"

"I'd rather not," I say, trying not to vomit.

We both edge towards the parcel and peer down at it. Then Winnie squeals, her hands flying to her mouth.

"What?" I say.

"It's from *Colette's*."

I place my hand on my hip and give my friend a hard stare. She knows that means nothing to me.

"It's this super glamorous department store that all the rich magicals shop at. Practically everything Summer, Aysha and the others wear is from there – right down to their panties."

"I told him no designer," I say.

"Who? The man in black?"

I nod.

"Nonsense, it's about time he bought you something. He's a Kennedy–"

"–an estranged Kennedy."

"I bet he still has more money than the two of us put together."

"That isn't hard."

"Just open it."

I sink to my knees. I may be putting on an indifferent show for Winnie, but inside I'm super excited. We never had much money for presents at home. Birthday gifts consisted of whatever my aunt had managed to trade, scavenge or craft. I don't think I've ever had new shop-bought in my entire life.

I tear open the brown paper, revealing a lavish-looking velvet bag below with an embroidered *Colette* logo.

"God, even their packaging is beautiful," Winnie swoons.

Carefully, I drag open the golden zipper, finding layers of tissue paper beneath. I peel these back too, and what emerges from the soft dusty pink sheets of paper are dark-jewel colors of silk.

"Oooo," Winnie says, dropping to her knees and watching as I lift several pairs of panties from the parcel – each one beautifully crafted with lacy thrills or pretty ribbons. "Those look like they belong in an art gallery."

"Exactly, I won't ever be able to wear them. They're too beautiful."

"Oh, you are wearing them, Rhianna Blackwaters, and binning every other pair of grotty panties you own."

"My panties are not grotty," I say, offended.

"Are they this beautiful, though?" she asks, lifting another three pairs from the package.

"Has he only sent me panties?" I mutter.

"No, look," she says, "matching bras."

The bras are somehow even more beautiful than the panties. I take one from Winnie's hand and stroke my fingers over the soft silky material.

I'm almost mesmerized by the design of it, but then Winnie laughs and I drag my gaze away.

"What?"

"He's sent you a couple of sports bras and panties too – look." She throws several pairs at my head. "Now you'll have no excuses not to join the bouncing bunnies."

"No, thank you," I say, feeling more grateful for the hearty-looking thing with plenty of support than the pretty underwear.

"And there are socks."

My attention is drawn back to the parcel. The last remaining items aren't as beautiful or as expensive looking – a few plain tees, a new pair of jeans and some yoga pants. They don't look a whole lot different from my existing wardrobe of clothes – except they're brand new, not falling apart.

"Now, this is useful," I say, holding up one of the t-shirts to my chest. Could I get away with wearing one of those pretty bras under this, though? Would anyone notice?

"There's one last item in here, Rhi," Winnie says. She points to a small pink box buried at the bottom of the parcel.

I lift it out and examine it with suspicion, twisting it this way and that in my fingers.

"Hells Bells, Rhi, open it!" Winnie cries. "I'm dying of suspense here."

I lift the lid carefully off its base, my heart suddenly loud in my ears. The clothes were one thing, practical, necessary really and maybe not as romantic as Winnie would believe. I'm sure neither Azlan nor Stone appreciate a mate who looks like she dressed in the dark most days. They've probably been dying to get me into something more respectable.

But this ...

Inside is more pink tissue paper and Winnie groans in frustration.

I fold it back, and there nestling in a pink velvet cushion is a silver bracelet formed of interlocking tiny stars.

"Wow, Rhi that's so pretty," Winnie says. "And so you."

Carefully, I take the delicate chain out of the box and let it hang down in my fingers. It is very pretty and I stare at it stunned, unable to believe anyone would buy me something like this, let alone a man like Azlan. I have to pinch myself. Because this has to be a dream, right?

"There's a note too," Winnie says, fishing it out of the package.

"What does it say?"

"You're okay with me reading it?"

I hook the bracelet around my right wrist, my hand lingering on the chain.

"Winnie, you just said no secrets among girls."

"True." She unfolds the paper and clears her throat.

"'To my little mate' ..." Winnie peers up at me. "Oh gosh, that is so adorable."

"Keep reading."

"'Thank you again for taking me into your life and into your heart. Please accept this small gift as a token of my love for you. You are the guiding light – the one Northern star –

in my life now. Maybe you will wear this bracelet and think of me as I am thinking of you.

"'All my love, my heart and my world,

"'Azlan.

"'Kiss kiss kiss kiss.'"

Winnie waves her hand in front of her face. Then looks at me.

"He did not write this?"

I shrug.

"But it's so ..."

"Corny," I venture, even though my insides are glowing, my heart brimming and my bond humming.

"Romantic." She shakes her head. "The country is doomed," she adds dramatically.

"Why?" I laugh, taking the note from her hand and folding it carefully. I need to find a safe place to keep it.

"Because you've turned the authorities' enforcer – our key weapon against all the bad guys out there – soft. Next time they send him to make a capture, he'll probably recite them poetry."

"He's sweeter than you'd think."

Winnie watches me as I take the letter to my desk and find a special spot for it inside my top drawer.

"Good," she says finally. "You deserve sweet as well as hot, Rhi." Then she lunges across the room and wraps me in a large, unexpected hug. "I'm so happy for you, so happy everything's working out."

"Touch wood," I say, reaching up to tap her on the head. "Let's not jinx things, okay?"

I'm still uneasy by the way those other men have been making me feel and though I want to believe Winnie's explanation, I'm finding it hard. Winnie, however, seems utterly convinced I have my two fated mates and now I'm going to get to live happily ever after.

Stars, I want to believe that too. But Stone's stuck working here, forcing our illicit relationship underground, Azlan has been sent on yet another mission, and sooner or later I'll be graduating from this academy and heading with the others to protect the borderlands in the West.

I don't see us living happily together any time soon.

10

R^{hi}

"MY LOVE LIFE has really put you in a good mood," I say to Winnie as she hums cheerfully to herself as we walk the path to Dr. Johnson's class.

"I don't know. I just have a good feeling today."

"A good feeling that has nothing to do with what *you* were up to last night, I suppose." Winnie may be fascinated by my complicated love life but hers is proving just as successful and a lot more straightforward. In fact, Winnie and Trent are becoming inseparable. I'm happy for her. Trent is a total sweetheart.

"That definitely helped," she confesses.

However, Winnie's good mood takes a serious battering when we arrive at Dr. Johnson's classroom and find her waiting outside again with instructions to follow her down to the meadow for another lesson on combining magic.

Winnie grips my arm as we follow the others.

"Do you think we'll be paired with the same people again?" she asks anxiously.

"I don't know. Why? Do you have a problem with Dane?"

"Apart from the fact he was friends with that scumbag traitor, Andrew, no. But last time you got stuck with–"

"Tristan," I say, my gaze straying towards the back of his golden head.

"Will you be okay?"

"I'm not scared of Tristan Kennedy," I say a little too loudly, the girls in front of us peering over their shoulders to scowl at me.

"I'm not concerned about you being scared of him," Winnie hisses.

"Unlike everyone else, I am not infatuated with his hot ass."

The girls glance at me again, then pick up their pace.

"Good," Winnie says, squeezing my arm in encouragement. "Hopefully he won't be your partner this time. Hopefully we'll be allowed to pick our partners."

Any hope of that is dispelled pretty quick when Dr. Johnson calls out.

"Find your partners from last time and pick up where you left off."

I glance at Tristan, whispering to Spencer at the edge of the group and ignoring our teacher. I have no desire to pick up where we left off, particularly when he left me on my knees. I don't wait for Summer to protest my partner this time, I do it myself.

"Dr. Johnson," I say, walking through the group of dispersing students towards her.

Today her hair is bright pink, clashing slightly with the

large orange glasses hanging around her neck on a silver chain.

"Miss Blackwaters," she says, frowning slightly when she realizes it's me who's addressed her. "Is there a problem?"

"Yes, I'd like to swap partners."

"No," a firm voice says from right behind me, and I don't need to spin around to see who it is. I can tell by the sensation in my stomach. Shit!

I ignore him.

"I was unable to work with Tristan Kennedy last time. We were incompatible."

Summer's hanging to one side listening in to this conversation; Aysha a pace away looking pissed off with her arms crossed over her chest.

"Of course, they are incompatible," Summer chimes in. "They're totally unsuited. Tristan is one of the most powerful students in the academy, whereas Pig Girl ..." She snorts. "I'd be happy to partner with Tristan. We're much better suited. I'm much closer to his abilities and powers." I'm surprised she restrains herself and doesn't wink at him and blow him a kiss.

Our teacher looks exhausted and defeated this morning and, unlike our last lesson, doesn't seem to be prepared to put up a fight against Summer.

"Well, I suppose the two of them were partnered for the last lesson. I'm sure it won't hurt if they swapped this time."

Summer positively beams, while Aysha looks like she'd happily murder me, Summer or possibly both of us.

Tristan, however, draws himself up to his full height, towering above all four of us.

"No," he says again, this time with more venom. "The principal chose Rhianna and me to be partners. She must have had her reasons."

Summer glances up at his face and then scowls back at me.

"But Dr. Johnson is right," I say. "We already tried partnering as the principal requested, and it was unsuccessful."

"Then we try again. We're Arrow Hart academy elite pupils. We don't simply give up. We keep trying and trying and trying. We don't accept defeat. It's written on your goddamn crest, Pig Girl."

He points right at my tit and I can't help looking down at the embroidered crest on my blazer with its heart and arrow. I glance back up at Dr. Johnson, waiting for her to reprimand Tristan for calling me names. Of course, she doesn't. Instead, she swings her gaze between Summer and Tristan. Clearly, deciding who to side with. Determining Tristan to be the immediate threat, she says, "Mr. Kennedy and Miss Blackwaters will remain partners. No swapping."

Summer harrumphs, folding her arms over her chest, and the professor cowers and hurries away. Tristan, on the other hand, trudges off towards our previous spot in the meadow, a self-satisfied smirk hovering on his face.

I take an inhale and follow after him. But I haven't moved two steps, before Summer's blocked my path, grabbing my arm and digging her fingernails deep into my flesh.

"I'm not done with you, Pig Girl. Don't think I've forgotten the other night. I'm going to make your life hell from now on and completely destroy that face of yours."

"You mean, like I did yours?" I say coolly. "You know you didn't fix your nose straight, right? It's wonky."

"What?" Summer cries, snatching her hands to cover her face.

I don't wait for her to grab me again, I pick up my feet and jog after Tristan.

This time I find him standing, his blazer flung to the ground, his sleeves rolled up.

"Don't do that again," he says, pushing his sleeves further up his muscular arms.

"Do what?" I say, with the same bored tone I just used with Summer.

"You don't get to decide when this partnership ends. The only way it's terminated is if I say so."

"Why? You don't want to be partnered with me and I sure as hell don't want to be partnered with you."

"That's not what your magic's saying, piggie," he says, snatching my hands in his.

I gasp, the bond in my body sparking immediately and my magic firing into life. I should snatch my hands right away from his grasp but the feeling is incredible, like a shot of ecstasy right to the veins.

"Don't let go," he murmurs, his gaze locked with mine, his face the most attentive I've ever seen it – intelligent, cunning – not that bored rich boy he always tries so hard to project.

But I couldn't let go even if I wanted to. Our magic is already teasing one another; mine swerving and dodging around his and his leaping and chasing after mine. It's as if my magic has a mind of its own – a mind determined to frolic with Tristan's. Like two puppy dogs wanting to play.

His magic tries to catch mine, but it darts away and then our magic is dancing together, pulling out of my control as it twirls and twists like a dizzying spinning top above me.

I can't help but laugh, the colors so bright, so perfect, streaking against the clear fall sky.

He grips my hands tighter. But it's not like before, not violent or controlling. This time it's as if he just doesn't want me to break away, as if he never wants to let go.

"It's stronger," he whispers. "Stronger than before."

And I think it is. This is the first time I've unleashed my magic in days, since I sealed the bond with Stone, and although I suspected as much, I didn't know for sure. Now I feel just how vibrant and powerful it truly is. I wonder what I could do with it, how far I could push it, how much I could do.

Our magic breaks away, dancing over the tall pine trees that line this side of the meadow. For a minute we watch it shooting above the treetops like fireworks streaking through the air. Then, with my hands in his, I pick up my feet, taking chase after our magic.

"Come on," I tell him breathlessly, catching a glimpse of his emerald eyes, as deep and lush as the grass all around us.

He smiles at me and we follow our magic through the trees, out of the meadow, away from the others, and to the brow of the hill beyond.

We're panting now, my heart hammering in my chest and he swings me around to face him again as my magic streaks up into the air like an arrow from a bow and his shoots straight after mine. With my hair dancing in the breeze, I fling my head back to watch our magic, soaring higher and higher until my head tips so far back, I lose my balance, Tristan tumbling with me to the soft ground below.

Then we're rolling, down the slope, over and over each other, our magic spinning so fast the colors blur into one, merging with the picture of his face, the green of his eyes, the gold of his hair. And I'm laughing, the feeling so freeing, so pure, so beautiful. So magical.

We roll for what feels like forever, until there's no more slope, nowhere else to go and we land at the bottom of the hill, his heavy weight pressed on top of mine.

The magic stops spinning. It hangs sizzling in the air all around us. Like it's waiting. Like it's holding its breath.

My heart thumps. My bond shimmers. My body thrums.

Time stops.

Tristan Kennedy stares down at me, straight into my eyes, and then he kisses me.

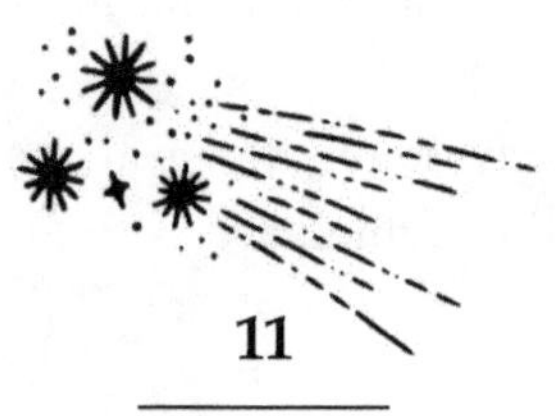

11

S pencer

I'm watching them from the corner of my eye the entire time. I can't help myself.

They were paired together. By the principal. Why?

And why wasn't it me?

And why the hell does Tristan seem so damn pleased about it?

He hates the girl. Or so he says. I've also never seen him as obsessed with anything or anyone like he is with her. Not that the majority of students or teachers in this school would notice. He does a very good job at acting nonchalant. But I see it, recognize my own fucking behavior in it too.

"Spencer," Dan says, snapping his fingers in my direction. Does he want a fucking beating? "Are we doing this or not?"

I roll my shoulders and nod but when he takes my hand in his, I jerk it away.

It's that laugh. The one that sounds like sunshine. The one that has me wanting to kiss her.

He hears it too, restless inside me.

I have the urge to drop to my knees and cover my ears with my arms. Is she a fucking siren? Is that what this is?

A powerful siren. One my mother wants me to …

My gaze snatches their way again and I catch a glimpse of them disappearing through the gap in the trees, hand in hand, running like they're a couple of kids in love.

The beast snarls inside me.

Except it isn't him snarling. It's me.

"What the fuck, man?" Dan says, taking several steps away from me.

And yeah, I'm done with this bullshit. Done!

I start to march away. Away from them. Away from him. Away from everything, the beast going fucking crazy inside me, the pressure in my skull so extreme I think my head might explode.

"Hey, where are you going?" Dan calls after me.

"Away," I growl.

"You're leaving? Johnson will have a fit."

If Johnson has a problem with me leaving, she can come talk to me about it. Or she can tell the principal and she can come talk to me about it. Then they can both talk to my mother together. I don't give a shit.

I'm done with this place. Done!

I did the match. I won it for them. Gave them the Cup. What more is there to stay for?

Nothing.

When I come to think about it, I know all there is to know. I'm ten times more powerful than 99% of the students in this academy. And the teachers too. Shit, even York would struggle up against me.

So what is the fucking point in staying here, in dicking around for six more months. It's just a vanity when I could be out there, like my brother, making a difference.

What is the point in staying when it's only torturous? When the beast becomes more restless inside me each day that passes? When I have to see her every day? Temp-fuck-ing-tation dangling right in front of my nose. It's too much.

I'm going to write to her again, tell her my decision. That's what I need to settle the beast, not some girl. Not *that* girl.

I falter, somewhere in the academy garden, leaning against the trunk of a tall oak tree, its bark rough beneath my palm, its scent strong in my nose.

I can't do what my mother asks. I couldn't do that to any girl, least of all her.

I've seen what it's done to my mother, under that high-buttoned shirt. All those scars. I know the sacrifices she's made.

I won't do that. The girl deserves better than me. What-ever the beast may think, whatever my mother might say, whatever fate has deigned, I won't do it. I won't ever tie another life to mine. I wouldn't make her suffer that way. I can't see her hurt.

Besides, the girl has her fated mate. The enforcer. And fuck maybe she'll have the golden boy of the academy, Tristan Kennedy, too.

I can't hang around to watch that shit, knowing I want her, knowing I can't have her.

No. I'll show the world what I can really do when you strip away the helmets and the safety vests, the rules and referee. I'll show them all.

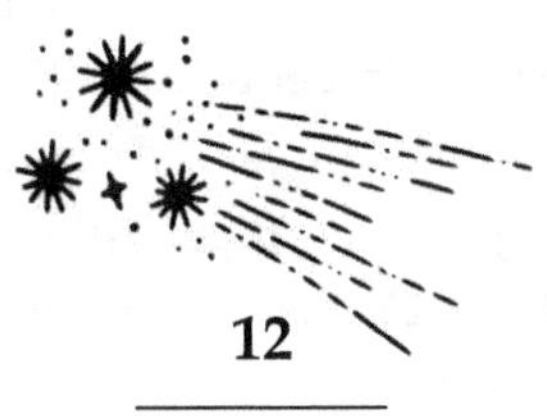

12

T ristan

RHIANNA BLACKWATERS KISSES me for one whole minute, her lips moving against mine, her tongue in my mouth, her fingers twisting with mine, her body warm beneath me, her heart loud in my ears.

Our magic spirals so electric, so fierce, it's dazzling, dizzying.

She tastes of mint and the flowers. Her skin is soft, her lips even softer and sweet moans bubble in her throat.

The sensation in my stomach – the one driving me to distraction – soars so fucking high it's like a goddamn orgasm.

Kissing her is like a goddamn orgasm.

It makes me hungrier and I kiss her harder, pressing her into the ground, grinding against her, wanting every part of her, wanting her to be mine. All of her. All my restraint vanishes, everything holding me back from this girl gone. In this moment, I surrender to it all.

As she kisses me, as our magic shimmers all around us wild and untethered, I forget about all my reservations, all my doubts. They're meaningless. Pointless. Insignificant. I don't care about any of it any more. All I want is her.

But just like that she's pushing me away.

I blink awake as if I've been pulled from a dream, some enchanting spell, and stare down into her face; her lips all kiss-swollen, her cheeks flushed, her pupils blown wide. One fuck-off deep frown wedged between her brows.

"You want to go back to the common room?" I murmur. I don't want to move. I want to take her right here on the ground with our magic dancing in the air, the grass rustling around us, the endless sky above us.

"Fuck you!" she says, giving my body one violent shove. Not that it does anything. I remain exactly where I am. "Get off me!" she shrieks, pushing even harder and attempting to wriggle free.

"I'm pretty happy where I am," I confess.

She stops shoving me and looks at me, her mouth hanging open in confusion. "Are you actually serious?"

"I am. I want to kiss you again. So we can play the little game where you pretend you're mad with me, and I apologize and look contrite, or we can skip that part and get back to the kissing." Kissing and fucking. Because I'm going to fuck her.

I don't care if she belongs to my cousin. Because she belongs to me, too. And I'm going to have her.

Screw everything else. Every concern, every worry, everything that's been holding me back. I don't give a fuck about any of it at all. None of it. I want her.

"Are you out of your mind?!" she says.

"Really? We're doing this," I say, all the glorious sensations I was feeling five seconds ago replaced with my usual frustration with this girl.

Why does she never – never – do what I expect her to?

"Get the fuck off me, Tristan. Get the fuck off me now!"

I don't move. Like I said, I'm perfectly happy where I am, with her body trapped under mine, her hands pinned to the ground. It's fucking turning me on.

She glares at me, then grips my hands so tightly in hers she must be cracking her own knuckles, and zaps me.

"Fuck," I say, snatching my hands away from hers and rolling off her reluctantly. She's not going to play. The moment has passed. And I may be an asshole, but not that kind of asshole. If she's coming, I want her coming willingly, enthusiastically, screaming my name.

She scurries backwards, rolling up onto her backside and scowling at me.

"You can't fight this," I say, meeting her angry gaze.

"Fight what? Your beautiful face, your irresistible magnetism, your legendary charisma? Yeah, I don't think so."

"The fated bond."

She jolts, color creeping up her neck and into her cheeks.

"I don't know what you're talking about."

"You have one fated mate already, Piggie, I think you do."

She hesitates as if she is going to tell me something, then changes her mind. I wish I was Stone, with his ability to read thoughts. I want to know what she's thinking. I *always* want to know what she's thinking. Even when she's sleeping. I want to see right inside her mind and understand every damn thing about her.

But right now, I want to see with so much desperation I can hardly contain myself.

Because she must feel it. There is no way it's so powerful in my gut and she doesn't feel it in return.

I don't need a stupid blood test to know what it is, to know that it's real. There's no doubt in my mind.

The pig girl is my fated mate.

"I don't know what you think is going on here – I don't know what delusions you're under–"

"I'm not deluded. You know that I'm not. And you also know that you can't resist this pull between us any more than I can. You saw with your own eyes how much our magic wants to combine together, wants *us* combined."

"Resist?" she says, spitting the word through her teeth and rocking up onto her knees so she's kneeling right in front of me. "Let's say I humor you here for a moment, Tristan. Let's say fate is pulling us together." Her hands drop automatically to hover over her soft belly, to the point mirrored in my own where I can feel that drag towards her. Always there. Always. So violent it's inescapable. "Then resisting it's exactly what you've been doing. Resisting every possible attempt to embrace it. You've thwarted fate at every opportunity. And ..." her voice falters for a moment before she regains her composure, "you've treated me like shit. Worse than shit. Like something not worthy to stick to the bottom of your shoe. And now, just like that," she clicks her fingers, magic exploding above our heads, "you've changed your mind and just expect me to welcome you with open fucking arms."

"You were welcoming me pretty damn enthusiastically right there on the ground less than five minutes ago," I say pointing to the ground.

"I hate you, Tristan Kennedy. I hate you more than the

men who beat my aunt unconscious, more than the men who tortured us, more than the man who tried to kill me, more than the soldiers who nearly killed Winnie. I hate you, I hate you, I hate you," she screams, frustrated tears in her eyes. "I hate you so fucking much!"

She jumps to her feet and I lunge for her but before I can stop her, she's running away, back up the hill and between the trees, her magic streaking through the air behind her. Chaotic, wild, untrained. Just like her.

My hands start to tremble and soon my whole body is shaking, my bones knocking together like wind chimes.

I stare down at the space she just vacated. At the flattened grass our bodies made together.

I think I could have handled that better.

A lot, lot better.

I DON'T BOTHER RETURNING to Dr. Johnson's class. What's the point? I'll only be hassled by Summer and her posse and their never-ending questions.

I can't stand that noise, their continual jabbering voices. I need peace and quiet. Away from everyone.

I lock myself in my room, pulling down the blind and lying out flat on the floor.

This is new, different.

I've never been rejected before. Never been told no. Not by my peers anyway, not by anyone in the academy.

I could have taken what I wanted anyway. She's strong but not as strong as me – both magically and physically – and besides the magic she does possess is untrained. Although she's been studying, practicing, she has a long way to go before she can wield it like me.

But I'm not my father. No matter how much he's tried to craft me in his image. No matter how many times I've tried to harden my heart like his, I can't.

"You want to be loved, boy." That's what he'd hissed at me. "It will be your downfall."

Is he right?

I rest one hand over my heart, one over my belly. My muscles ache, my body's still shaking, like the flu, my forehead damp with cool sweat.

God damn, it hurts. Stings deep, deep inside me as if she took the sharpest knife and plunged it right between my ribs.

Is this what it's like to be rejected? Tossed aside? Cast away? Is this what it feels like to be her?

I don't know how to fix this. I don't know how to do this. But I have to find a way.

I let my mind wander, let my body dissolve away and disappear into the carpet where no one can find me, where no one can hurt me.

It isn't until an hour later that my phone beeps. First one beep, then two, then a string of notifications making my phone light up and skid across the floor.

My first thought is Rhianna. Did she change her mind? Is she begging for my forgiveness?

But that hope fades as quickly as it appears. She isn't going to forgive me.

I bring myself back, rolling up to sit, every part of my body hurting, and pick up my phone. I glance at the first message, then the next and the next, leaping to my feet. Then I'm sprinting out of my room, down the stairs and banging my fist on the door.

He doesn't answer right away, but I keep on hammering and yelling his name, until finally it clicks open and I'm treated to the view of his retreating back. I follow him inside, noting the boxes already stacked up inside his room.

"You're leaving?" I say. It's a rumor, right? It can't actually be true.

"Yes, I'm leaving," he says, stopping by his desk and tossing things inside the box resting there.

"You can't leave. We haven't graduated."

"I've earned enough credits. My mother put in the request to the principal an hour ago and she agreed. I have permission to leave the academy and join the forces at the West immediately."

"What?" I say, his words spinning around my head, none of them making sense.

"I think you heard me the first time."

"I did, but it made no fucking sense. Why the hell would you leave? We have another half of a year to go."

"Staying is just a vanity. We already know everything we need to know. Hell, Tristan, you and I are a hundred times better than all the other losers in this place. I'd rather be out there fighting, making a difference, rather than sitting around with these deadbeats."

"You're wrong," I tell him. "There's more to learn. More that would be useful." I'm not even halfway done with all the knowledge I want to suck from this place. Every little piece of information, each nugget, is a step closer to being the best, to being better than him.

Spencer shakes his head. "I've had enough of this place."

I take a step towards him. I want to rest my hands on his shoulders and shake some sense into him, but I know he can't stand to be touched, not with the beast prowling inside him.

"Out there isn't like the dueling pitch, Spencer. Fuck, it's not even like the Warehouse."

"Do you think I'm fucking stupid?" he snaps. "That's half the reason I'm going. I'm tired of play acting, of pretending. I want to do something real. To push myself to the limits. Isn't that what you want too, Tris?" he asks, finally turning to face me, his eyes curious for my reaction.

Fuck, but it is tempting. To throw it all away. To give the finger to my father and head to the front. To show everyone just how powerful I've become, to show them just what I can do.

But there's more than just knowledge and information and the opportunity to grow and learn that's holding me back, keeping me tethered to the place.

Rhianna.

"We'll be giving them five years of our lives as it is. Why give more?" I say.

Spencer laughs bitterly. "Let's not pretend I have any kind of life beyond my time in the service. What I am, Tristan, the monster inside ... There's no life for me. No fucking position on the council, no pretty little wife, no family."

So this is the reason, the *real* reason. I've never thought any less of my friend for his affliction. Fuck, when I was young and he made me swear not to tell a living soul, I thought it was the coolest thing ever. Now we're older, now I understand more, I see it for the burden it is. For the prison. There's nothing cool about it.

"Your father has those things," I tell him softly.

"My father is one of the lucky ones." He looks away from me. "Look what happened to Tobias."

My heart aches for my friend and I glance down at my chest. I thought I'd ripped this organ from my body long ago. Seems I was wrong.

Seems I've been wrong about a lot of things.

But so is he.

"You can have whatever life you want." He shakes his head. "You can. Because, I promise, I'll be right by your side."

His chestnut eyes flick back to mine and for the first time I see he doesn't believe me. He doesn't trust me anymore and I have no idea why.

13

R^{hi}

I'm still shaking as I run away from the meadow and out into the countryside. Through the bond I can feel both Azlan and Stone hovering there concerned, anxious, wanting to know why the hell I'm so upset.

But what can I tell them? What can I say?

I've accused them of keeping secrets, of concealing the truth from me, but I'm as guilty as they are. I should have told them as soon as I understood what this feeling meant, as soon as I first suspected it.

I can imagine it now, the hurt in their eyes. The same hurt I've felt every time they've lied to me.

This is such a mess. So stupidly fucked up. Because that's the other problem, isn't it? What if they're in agreement with Tristan? What if they tell me I can't run from fate? What if they tell me I have no choice?

Because I don't want Tristan. I don't want Spencer. I don't want them anywhere near me.

And as for …

No, they're no better than those men who would terrorize us in the night, that haunted my dreams. They'll hurt me, crush me, destroy me. And I didn't fight to survive all this time just to end up an accessory to some man. His own personal punch bag. Loathed and despised.

I swipe the water from my eyes, my feet slowing. I'm out of breath, my lungs burning. I stop, resting my hands on my knees and attempting to catch my breath.

I peer out over the landscape, turning golden now, harvest time fast approaching, the trees in the distant orchard heavy with fruit.

It's so beautiful. The sky never ending above me, the sun's rays warm on my skin.

Maybe that's all this was. Maybe we were simply caught in the moment, the practice of combining our magic overwhelming us, sweeping us away in a wave of false emotion. Tristan will probably forget all about it before the day is out. He'll probably feign ignorance or a concussion or claim I seduced him.

I snort. I'm not even wearing the silky underwear Azlan gifted me. My powers of seduction are lousy.

I take another steadying breath and it seems to calm the two anxious men hovering through the bond as well as myself.

Then I pick up my feet and jog back in the direction of the campus. It's gym class next and I cross every finger and toe that, despite my already-tired legs, we're running sprints today and I won't be treated to a lesson from Spencer – even if the last one was actually useful.

However, when I arrive at the gym, I find a crowd of

students hovering outside the locker rooms whispering together. A couple of the bouncing bunnies are crying onto each other's shoulders and Summer is actually pacing. I push my way through the crowd finding Winnie talking to Trent and Dane.

"What's happened?" I ask, looking up into Trent and Dane's devastated faces.

"It's Spencer," Winnie says, pulling me to one side.

The world spins on its axis, the sounds of the chattering around me growing deadly quiet, my vision swooping in and out of focus. I sway on my feet.

Spencer?

Winnie grabs my arm. "Rhi? Rhi? Are you okay?"

I force myself to concentrate on her face, on her mouth. "Spencer?" I say my voice sounding distant. "Is he ..."

"He's leaving. Rhi? Did you hear me? He's leaving."

The noise around me returns with a deadly roar.

"Leaving? To go where?"

"The front. Apparently he has enough credits to graduate early, so he's leaving."

Trent rests his arm around Winnie's waist and leans his forehead on her shoulder. "I can't believe we're losing our best player."

"We already won the Cross-lantic Cup. I guess he's been waiting for that before he left."

"I didn't even know we could graduate early," I mumble, my insides a mixture of emotions I can't understand.

"You can if you've gained enough credits," Trent says. "Didn't your old roommate graduate early?" he asks Winnie.

"Yes," Winnie says. "But it's extremely rare. Most of us mere mortals struggle in at least one or two subjects and need the full three years to gain enough points."

I roll my eyes at my friend. As if Winnie struggles in any of her subjects?

I grab her sleeve and tug her out of Trent's grasp.

"Winnifred Wence, how many points are you away from graduating? You're not about to break out of here and leave me on my own, are you?"

"Are you?" Trent says, sounding alarmed.

"No!" Winnie says. "Even if I did have enough credits – which I'm not saying I do – I'm in no hurry to go back home." Both Trent and I smile at her. "My sisters drive me mad."

"Hey," I say, wagging my finger at her. "And you'd miss me, right? And maybe him too?" I jab my finger towards Trent.

"Pip's the one keeping me here," she says and Trent hooks his arm around her neck and lands a fat kiss on her cheek.

She giggles, but it quickly dies on her lips as the gymnasium doors crash open and Coach comes storming through looking like a rhinoceros in a bad mood.

"What are you ladies doing out here gossiping? Go get changed. We're doing killer circuits today."

Everybody groans until Coach glowers at us and then we're all battling to get through to the changing room.

Inside, several of the bouncing bunnies are clearly too devastated to find the energy or will power to change into their kits. Instead, they perch on the bench wailing about how much they're going to miss Spencer and how the academy won't be the same without him.

Summer is pacing up and down so quickly I'm surprised she's not wearing a groove in the floor and everyone else is avoiding her eyeline.

Winnie and I retreat to the corner, opening our locker

doors and continuing our conversation behind them as we strip out of our uniform, Winnie giving my new sports bra an approving nod.

"It all seems pretty sudden, don't you think?" I whisper to her. "All his friends seem genuinely shocked. Dan looked like he'd seen an actual ghost."

"I guess it's never really happened before. Saskia left last term because of her family situation and one other boy the year before that for similar reasons. But I've never known someone graduate early and volunteer straight into the forces."

"He likes to be different," I huff.

Winnie shrugs. "He always seemed to be living his best life here. Star of the dueling team – it's every boy's wet dream." She pauses to pull her top over her head, dragging it down her body as she says next, "They're saying he's leaving tomorrow?"

"So soon!" A sick feeling swims through my stomach and Winnie eyes me carefully.

"You'd think someone like Spencer would milk it for all it's worth. A leaving party – heck a leaving parade." Winnie shrieks and her hand flies to her mouth. "He's going to miss the ball!"

"I doubt he cares."

"Did you notice Tristan wasn't there either?"

"Wasn't he?" I say innocently, willing my face not to blush.

"You don't suppose he's leaving too?"

That sick feeling in my stomach becomes much worse and I force bile down my throat. Winnie continues with the inspection of my face and I force a cool smile. "We can only hope!"

Spencer and Tristan are both missing from gym class

and Coach's bad mood only seems to worsen. He has us all doing a circuit course so vicious, one girl actually faints and another boy collapses with severe cramp and has to be hauled off to the infirmary.

By the time we're back in the locker room, I'm incapable of uttering a single word, let alone an entire sentence, but it doesn't stop the bouncing bunnies from gossiping among themselves. It's clear there's another rumor flying round. One Trent fills us in on when we meet up with him on the path outside the gymnasium.

"Spencer's going to fight one last fight down at the Warehouse tonight – before he leaves."

I roll my eyes. Seems Winnie was right. Spencer couldn't just slink off without some big farewell. Although fighting at the Warehouse isn't exactly the killer party I'd expect from him.

"Are you sure it's not a rumor?" I say.

"No, Dan had a message from him and Tristan when we were changing in the locker room." Trent scratches the back of his neck. "I think I'm going to go. I've never seen him duel like that and it may be my final chance."

"Isn't it dangerous?" Winnie says, taking his hand.

"Only if you're fighting, not if you're watching. Will you come?"

"I don't know." He nods, kissing her on the cheek and heading off to some computer club.

"Don't you want to go?" I ask Winnie when he's gone.

Winnie chuckles. "I've wanted someone to invite me down to the Warehouse since the moment I stepped into this school, but it's too dangerous."

"Trent doesn't seem to think so."

"Rhi," Winnie says, stopping on the path. "It's too dangerous for *you* to go and I am not going without you."

"Why is it too dangerous for me?" Winnie gives me a hard look.

"Renzo Barone," she says.

"He wouldn't try something in a warehouse full of people."

"The Warehouse is full of *his* people," Winnie points out. "Plus he's a madman. Who knows what he'd do."

"Then go without me," I say. I've never understood the appeal of watching men play at fighting. Hell, I've no desire to see them fight for real either. I've seen enough violence, enough pain and hurt in my life. I don't understand the desire to watch it as a sport. "I don't need to go."

"Uh uh, I'm not leaving you alone."

"I'm choosing to stay, Winnie. You're not leaving me. You go with Trent – make it a date."

But Winnie's having none of it and we're still arguing about it when we arrive at the Great Hall for lunch.

There's hardly anyone inside and for once we're at the front of the line with a choice of all the best lunch options. I pick a salad which actually looks fresh and contains more than two vegetables and eye the empty central tables with suspicion.

"I guess they're all too sad to eat," I mutter, enjoying a large mouthful of actual avocado.

"I don't know." Winnie shakes her head, pointing to the group of students sitting nearest us. They're all hunched together, talking excitedly. "Seems the prospect of Spencer's fight has made them all forget he's leaving. This is going to be all anyone talks about for weeks."

I sigh and drop my fork.

"Then we have to go, Winnie." We're already enough of outcasts as it is. If Winnie and I are the only ones not to show up at the Warehouse tonight, we'll be bigger social pariahs than we are already, and while that doesn't bother me, I'm not inflicting that on my best friend.

"I told you already, it's not safe."

"Well," I say, "maybe there's a way it could be."

I HAVE no idea if Azlan's sister will approve of me going to watch Spencer Moreau fight an illegal duel in a warehouse in the city. I have no idea if she'll report the fact I've asked her straight to Azlan.

But Winnie's not going without me and, to be honest, the more I hear the buzz about the fight around me, the more my curiosity is getting the better of me. It wouldn't hurt just to see what all the fuss is about, right? It sounds like the entire school will be going, something that is confirmed when we receive messages on our phones informing us that our heads of house have given automatic permission to anyone who wants to leave the school tonight.

Winnie pretends not to care, reading the message before returning her attention back to the essay she's writing at her desk.

I decide I've got nothing to lose.

I step outside our room, Pip following me to snuffle around in our patch of grass, and dial Ellie's number.

The call connects straight to answer phone after two rings and I receive a message telling me she'll call me in five minutes. I drop down onto the ground and let Pip climb into my lap, stroking his ears while I wait for Ellie to call. After nearly fifteen she does.

"I'm so sorry, Rhi," she says, sounding breathless down the phone. "I had to find somewhere private to talk. Is everything all right? Is Azlan okay?"

"Oh no, I'm fine and so is Azlan," I say, feeling suddenly guilty that I'd alarmed her and doubting whether this idea was a good one. "I actually called to ask ... my cloaker – did you get anywhere working out how it works?"

"You need it for something?"

I debate whether to go with honesty or not here, but somehow I don't like the idea of lying to Ellie.

"Everyone in the school is heading down to the Warehouse tonight to watch–"

"Spencer Moreau duel. Yes, I heard. Tristan told me. Actually, he invited me down."

My mouth drops open on a shocked, "Oh. Your dad will let you go?"

Ellie laughs. "Not a chance in hell. But if it's Tristan taking me out, I'm never asked any questions and neither is he."

"Is it safe?" I ask, feeling way more concerned about her than me.

"Well," she hesitates, "if he finds out, I'll be in trouble, but I've risked it before. Are you going? Tristan says most of the school will be there."

"I'm thinking about it, only ..."

"Only what?"

"It may not be safe for me either." I don't know if the man in black has told his sister about the price on my head. But I decide I'm going to tell her.

"Hmmm," she ponders. "I can imagine Az wouldn't be very happy about you going."

"Yeah," I say, "but I have the cloaker. If I can get it to work, then no one will know I'm there. So I was wondering–"

"If I'd figured out how to use it?"

"Yes."

"Well you're in luck, because I have."

I smile into my cell phone. "Really?"

"Yep. I'm going to forward you what I found out, okay? And then I'll see you there. Or I won't, depending on whether you want me to see you or not." She laughs.

"And you're okay doing this knowing Azlan probably won't be happy?"

"You're not going to tell him?"

"I think it might be better to beg for forgiveness, rather than seek permission."

"I get it. He worries and that can be a little suffocating."

"He's not but–"

"Rhi," Ellie says, "you should totally come. Going to the Warehouse is a rite of passage at the academy. Everybody goes at some point. And this way, we get to go together."

"We can't be seen together, Ellie," I remind her.

"But you'll be wearing the cloaker. No one will see you. Not unless you want them to."

14

R^{hi}

It takes some convincing before Winnie agrees to the plan. Despite being desperate to go, she's wary about the cloaker and whether it will work, especially as it's the first time we've used it. I realize that if Winnie is nervous about me going to the Warehouse, the man in black and Stone will be positively neurotic. There's no way they'd agree to letting me go. But like Ellie said, this is a rite of passage. I'm not going to let assholes like the chancellor and Renzo Barone stop me from living my life.

I study the instructions Ellie's sent me on my cell and with Winnie, practice using the cloaker. It takes us a few attempts to nail the spell that ignites the charm, but once we do we see just how powerful it is, Winnie disappearing in front of my eyes, even though I can still hear her breathing – and I definitely feel her when she pinches my arm.

"Hey," I say.

She giggles, coming back into view as she takes the necklace off and hangs it around my neck.

"I wonder if the person who attacked me in the woods, who fought the werebeast off, was wearing one of these," I say, fiddling with the locket.

"Perhaps," Winnie says.

I look up at her. "So you're happy for us to go?"

She chews on her lip. "I still have a bad feeling about this ..."

"What's the worst that can happen?" I say, grinning.

She gives me a hard stare. "Don't even ... but yeah, let's go. My curiosity is totally trumping my caution."

"Mine too," I say.

We spend the next few minutes getting ready, although, as no one is actually going to see me apart from Winnie, Trent and possibly Ellie, I don't put in an amazing amount of effort with my hair and makeup. I braid my hair over my shoulder, add a little mascara and pull on some of the new clothes from the man in black.

Trent knocks soon after and we explain to him about the cloaker and how it works.

"So to everyone else," he says, scratching his head through his beanie, "it's going to look like just me and Winnie out on a date. They won't be able to see Rhi."

"That's right."

"You realize it's going to be packed?" he says. "You might end up trodden on, or squashed or something."

"I'll be fine."

Trent shrugs and we walk across campus, waiting at the bus stop for a ride. There's already a long line and we don't make it onto the first rammed bus, having to wait for the next one.

"What time is the fight?" I whisper into Winnie's ear as we squeeze onto the next bus and Winnie and Trent grab seats. This bus is as rammed as the last, and standing around invisible has everyone barging into me. To save myself from being squashed to death, I sit on Winnie's lap.

"It's not like that," she says, as if talking to Trent. "There is no fixed time."

The bus ride into town is incredibly uncomfortable, although more so for poor Winnie than me, and I wonder if Trent was right about the practicalities of this. I consider catching the bus back to the academy but the buzz of conversation around me is infectious. I start to feel excited and even more curious. I've seen just how good a fighter Spencer is out there on the dueling pitch. There he was restricted by rules and regulations. What will he be like when he's completely unbound? Free to fight as he wants?

However, when the bus pulls up in the docklands and everyone piles off, I'm hit by my first serious case of nerves. This was the place Andrew led me to. Where Barone nearly killed me. Where I nearly died. Even surrounded by people, all jabbering away, laughing and shouting, there's an eerie feel to the place – sea mist hovering above the sidewalk and the distant ships groaning on the water.

I take Winnie's hand in mine. I don't want to be separated from her, not here.

"Are you all right, Rhi?" she whispers, probably feeling the way my arm is shaking.

"Yeah, this place just gives me the creeps."

"Really? I love it."

That's because as well as all those sappy romcoms Winnie enjoys watching, she also has a weird penchant for horrors.

We follow the crowd, arriving outside a large warehouse,

black against the city's glow. There's a line to get in and I scan the people, looking for Ellie. She isn't there and neither is Spencer, Tristan or any of the bouncing bunnies. They either got here early or their VIP status allows them to bypass the line. Probably the latter. I huff and pull my jacket more tightly around me. The weather has turned nippy, especially out here near the water, the salty air cold against my face. Winnie leans into Trent's embrace and we wait as the line shuffles forward.

The entrance is flanked by five large, armed men who glare at Winnie and Trent and insist on patting them down and asking for their names. I hold my breath, especially when one of the men looks right at me, his brow crinkling. He takes a step forward, eyes scanning in my direction, and I begin to feel light-headed.

Then he shakes his head and steps back and we pass through into the dim corridor beyond. I gasp for air.

"We made it inside," Winnie says and I take a hold of her hand again and let her pull me into the main cavity of the Warehouse, the noise overwhelming.

I think there are more people here tonight than there was at the Cross-lantic match. Nearly everyone from school, plus many older people I don't recognize: some dressed in well-to-do suits; others wearing worn boots and ripped jeans. There's no stage, no raised platform, just people forming a ring under the rigged-up spot lights.

The crowd is at least ten people deep and I don't know how we'll actually see any of the fight. My stomach drops with disappointment.

Did I want to see him fight that badly? And why? Why do I care?

Because it might be my last glimpse of him, the last chance I ever have to see him, and despite the way he's treated me, despite all the bruises I have from all the times he's slammed me onto the ground, I can't help this strange sadness I feel about it.

"There's a bar," Trent says, pointing to a man behind a makeshift table, boxes stacked up behind him, and bottles of beers resting on the table in front of him.

Trent orders three, then corrects himself, grabbing two and I follow them back to the ring of people.

"I can't see anything, can you?" I ask Winnie. She shakes her head and I scan the crowd for a second time. I see Tristan's golden head bobbing above the crowd somewhere near the front. No Spencer.

Then there's an almighty cheer, so loud, the ground quakes beneath my feet. Winnie beckons to me and we push our way into the crowd as finally I catch sight of Spencer, caught in one of those bright lights. He strides through the crowd that parts to let him through. Then he's standing in the center, wearing only a pair of shorts, his chest bare and for the first time I appreciate just how strong and powerful he truly is. Everyone is calling his name, shouting it, chanting it. But he doesn't seem to notice. He stares blankly ahead, his face emotionless.

"He looks like he might kill someone," Winnie says a little unsurely and I know what she means. Even when he was hating on me, Spencer was full of energy, power and life, all of it reverberating round him. You could almost hear it humming in the air, you could almost see the air shimmering. But now he's still. That energy silent. It's unnerving. Not like him at all.

I can't drag my eyes from him and my bond tugs so hard I find I'm weaving my way unseen through the crowd, stopping at the front, right beside Ellie.

"Hey Ellie," I whisper. "It's me, Rhi."

She smiles, then flicks her eyes to me and back to Spencer.

"I can see you," she whispers. "Is the cloaker working?"

"Yes, only you and my friends can see me."

"What's that?" Tristan asks his cousin, his eyes fixed on his friend.

"Nothing," Ellie says, finding my arm and giving it a squeeze.

I go to whisper to her again, but another, older man steps into the circle, dressed in a black shirt, a heavy chain around his neck. He lifts his hands to the air and the crowd falls silent.

"Dearly Beloved," he cackles, "we are gathered here this evening in this great hall to witness the final fight of our dear friend, the Wolf. Named for his strength, his agility and his cunning use of magic. Undefeated in twenty-two fights. Can he make it twenty-three, can he leave us and head to defend our lands," he pauses for dramatic effect, some of the bouncing bunnies near the front of the crowd sniffling, "on a winning streak?" He grins, peering round at the crowd. "Maybe not, ladies and gentlemen, because I have a formidable opponent for our wolf tonight."

He spins around and holds out his arm. The crowd parts once again and this time a man strides forward: olive skin, dark hair, tattoos crisscrossing his body, rings in the lobes of his ears.

I gasp.

"It's the Killer, everyone."

I turn to Ellie, grabbing onto her arm.

But no one reacts with horror or dismay. In fact, they're cheering, some of the older people in the crowd calling his name.

No one steps forward to take him out, to strike him

down. Not even Tristan or Spencer, and in that moment I realize why.

They've all heard of the Wolves of Night's notorious assassin. They've all heard the stories of what he's done. They all know his name.

But no one knows his face. Very few have seen him and lived to tell the tale. It's possible in this warehouse full of hundreds of people, only Winnie and I know just who the Killer is: Renzo Barone.

I twist around, searching for Winnie but I can't see her anymore. I don't even know if she's seen him too.

The announcer is talking again, the crowd laughing and cheering but I don't hear the words. I'm too lost in my own thoughts, trying to work out what the hell I should do.

"What's wrong?" Ellie whispers, her face full of concern as she reads my emotions. I shake my head unable to speak, not sure what the hell to do.

If Spencer knew who the man facing him tonight really was, I have no doubt he'd try to kill him. But no matter how powerful Spencer is, Renzo is just as strong and clearly insane. If Spencer tries to kill him, he'll return the favor tenfold.

My stomach churns. I don't want Spencer hurt. I don't want him to *die*. But do I want Renzo to get away? To escape? Isn't this the perfect chance to capture him? Then I'd no longer have to live in fear that he's following me, watching me. I'd be free – or at least freer.

I screw up my eyes. Because there's another thought lingering at the back of my mind. One I don't want to acknowledge. That I don't want to consider. It's crazy, stupidly crazy for me to feel that way. But no matter how hard I try to stop that thought from leaping forward into my consciousness, it does anyway.

I don't want Renzo dead. I don't even want him hurt.

What the hell is wrong with me?

A crack of magic has me jolting, my eyes flying open; they're already fighting. It's already begun. I don't think I can stay and watch, and yet my feet are rooted to the ground. I can't move. I can't stop looking as they fling their magic at one another, twisting and lunging and spinning. Some magic slams into their bodies and despite the smell of burned flesh, they hardly flinch, continuing to fight. Other magic spirals overhead, or skids across the floor, the crowd scurrying backwards to avoid it.

It's mesmerizing, almost beautiful, the way they move like some violent ballet, choreographed to perfection.

"Come on, Spencer!" Tristan calls out from the other side of Ellie.

She squeezes on to me, speaking to him or maybe me or maybe no one in particular when she says, "That other guy is really strong. This is so evenly matched. Have you ever seen this man fight before, Tris?"

"No, never," Tristan hisses, wincing as a bolt of magic hits Spencer's leg. "I've never seen him before."

"When does it end?" I murmur to Ellie, as magic slices at Renzo's face, and blood slides down his cheek.

"When one of them concedes," she says.

I grimace. When one of them concedes?! I know both these men and I know conceding is not something either of them will do. No way. They'd rather fight to the end than give in. And I can't stand and watch that. I can't watch them tear each other apart, my bond smarting with pain every impact they make, until I'm hunched over, clutching my stomach.

I need to get away.

I turn, take a stumbling step forward and then all hell breaks loose.

The lights cut out. Someone bellows "cops!", and in the distance sirens blare.

People flee, pushing and crashing past one another, all trying desperately to reach the exit at the far side of the Warehouse. Some people are pushed to the floor. Some trampled in the stampede. People are shouting and screaming. Magic streaks above our heads and the floor is shaking again with the thud of a thousand boots.

I try to run too, but I'm buffeted and bashed, carried forward by the press of people, then knocked to the ground. People trip over me, their feet catching on my body. Somehow I pull myself back to my feet, dizzy and confused, my ribs aching where a foot kicked them. More people collide into me and the breath is struck out of me.

The sirens are blasting now and spinning blue light penetrates through the overhead windows. There's more shouting. People screaming for their friends. I don't know which way to go. I start to panic as I'm flung to the floor a second time.

And then a strong hand lands on my shoulder and drags me to my feet.

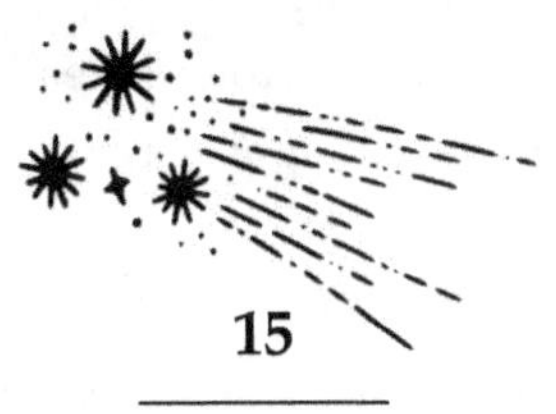

15

S pencer

"PIG GIRL," I shout right into her face. "What the hell are you doing?"

She looks right back at me as people crash around her, horror and incomprehension clear on her face.

Her hands fly to the locket hanging around her neck.

"You can see me?" she asks.

"What?" I say, frowning. "Of course I can fucking see you." I shake my head like she's insane. "What the hell are you doing standing around? Didn't you hear? The cops are coming – we need to get out of here."

I take a grip of her upper arm, ignoring the way she attempts to shake me off, and pull her along after me as I crash through the crowds of people, heading for the far exit.

"I don't need your help," she growls, tugging on my arm. "And I sure as hell don't want it."

"You want to be crushed then? Or maybe arrested?"

"What happens if we're arrested?" she yells at me, finally relenting and letting me drag her along. I push people out of our way. One or two spin around, ready to give me shit. When they see it's me, though, they have a swift change of mind.

"If *I'm* arrested, fuck all. They see it's me, they speak to my family. They let me go. If *you're* arrested ..."

I reach the door and yank her through it, out into the dank night. I'm only wearing shorts and the fall evening is cool. I don't feel it though. The adrenaline's still pumping through my veins and now, with her so close, with my hand gripping her body, it's even wilder. The beast practically purrs inside me, desperate to touch her himself.

I could leave her here, leave her to find her any way out of this mess. But I don't want to.

"If they arrest me, what, asshole?" she hisses, shaking her arm again as we run.

The beast inside me balks at the insult, but I let it fly.

"It's your first offense?" We skid down the slope behind the Warehouse, the water right there in front of us, black and ominous. I think about where to go next. I came with Tristan and his cousin in his ride, but that's parked in the lot round the front. Exactly where the cops will be.

"How was being at the Warehouse an offense?" she asks.

I scoff. Is she serious?

"That fight was illegal. Anyone watching it was breaking the law. They'd probably let you off with a warning and a fine. But it would go on your record, and considering all the trouble you've caused at the academy, York would probably kick you out."

"How about the people *actually* fighting?"

"No idea about that other dude," I say, peering back at

her. Her gaze falls to the ground. She can't even bear to look at me. "But like I told you, my family name gives me protection."

"That's so fucking unfair." I shrug. We're still running, both of us breathless, the people around us thinning as we weave through the streets of the dockland. "And," she continues, "I haven't caused any trouble at the academy."

I chuckle, coming to a stop. "You broke Summer's nose."

"I don't consider that trouble. I consider that justice."

"I think we're okay," I say, peering over my shoulder at the now distant Warehouse visible above the tightly packed gray buildings.

She hunches over her knees and catches her breath while I spit on the ground and examine the gash on my thigh and the graze on my side. They aren't too deep. Something I can heal easily with my own magic. I hover my hand over my leg and, closing my eyes, let my magic do its work. Is it my imagination or does it feel more vivid, more alive? Is that the effect of being so near her?

The beast strains inside me, wanting to break free, wanting his chance to be near her too and I let my hand fall to my side and concentrate everything I have on keeping him contained.

"What's wrong?" she says. My eyes open in alarm and I find her looking at me with curiosity. "You're not hurt from the fight?"

"Do I look hurt?"

She tugs her jacket around her body and I see only now that it's been ripped. "You know who that was, right? The other fighter?"

I frown. "Who?"

She opens her mouth to tell me but we're interrupted by someone calling her name.

"Rhi! Rhi!"

She steps out to the end of the road and I go to stop her.

"It's Winnie," she hisses. "Winnie!" she screams, cupping her mouth and using her magic to make her voice bellow. "Over here!"

A minute later, two of her friends come skidding around the corner. Spotting the pig girl, they race up to her and the tall girl with dark hair flings her arms around her friend and hugs her tight.

"Oh my God, Rhi! I was so worried about you! Did you see who that was? Did you see who the other fighter was?"

The pig girl's words are muffled in her friend's shoulder.

"Let's go! Let's get out of here before …" her friend says, releasing the pig girl but hanging on to her hand. "Trent found us a taxi." The friend peers over at me and frowns. "Was he …"

"I saved her ass," I mumble.

"Don't flatter yourself," Pig Girl mumbles.

"Hmmm," the friend says, eyes flicking between the two of us before she seems to settle on something. "Do you want to grab a lift with us?" she asks me.

My gaze falls to the floor. That wouldn't be a good idea. Dragging the pig girl to safety when she was in danger was one thing. Confined with her inside a vehicle, another – especially with the beast struggling to break free.

"No, I'm going to walk back."

"Walk?!" Pig Girl cries. "It'll take you all night."

"Spencer," the friend says seriously, "we'd be grateful if you came with us." My mouth opens. "The man you were fighting was Renzo Barone."

✳

WE'RE silent on the drive back to the academy, the three of them huddled together in the back, me in the front with the driver, staring out at the country lanes.

Renzo Barone.

Renzo fucking Barone.

I had him there in front of me, right in my grasp. I could have ended him, killed him. He was only a pace or two away. I could have destroyed him and ensured he never ever came for her again. I could have ensured her safety, kept her safe. Obliterated that danger. Instead, I fought him like it was a game, like it didn't really count.

Shit, it counted. Shit, it counted a hell of a lot.

If I'd known …

"You should have told me," I say.

"Pardon?" the driver says, eyes diverting from the road towards me.

I ignore him, catching the Pig Girl's caramel eyes in the rearview mirror. "You should have told me he was Renzo Barone."

"Renzo Barone!" the driver screeches, almost swerving off the road before he regains control and quickly crosses himself. "You're in trouble with Renzo Barone?" He peers at me anxiously and if I give him the wrong answer here, I think he might turf us out of the car.

"No," I say, crunching my knuckles. "I was fighting him at the Warehouse tonight."

The driver stares at me open-mouthed, before crossing himself a second time and putting his foot on the gas. He's obviously decided he wants to deliver us to the academy as quickly as possible.

"I didn't want him to know I was there," Pig Girl explains. "If I'd called out to you, if I'd tried to let you know …"

"You shouldn't have come in the first place," I say gruffly, snapping my eyes away from her gaze. "You had no business being there."

"Everyone was there, man," the guy sitting next to her says. "Everybody wanted to see you fight."

I snort. Yeah, that's all I am to these people. A source of fucking entertainment. Doesn't matter how beat up I get, how hurt or damaged, just as long as I'm putting on a show.

I crunch my knuckles again. I haven't healed that graze on my side and it throbs.

"You'd have to be an idiot to step foot outside the academy with Barone searching for you," I mutter.

"Barone is searching for this girl?" the driver asks, his hands gripping the steering wheel so tightly I can see his knuckles through the skin.

"Keep driving," I growl. Anyone knows if Barone is searching for someone, that someone has a price on their head and I don't want this dude getting any ideas. "I could have taken him out," I mutter, more to myself than the three people in the back of the car.

"It was pretty evenly matched," the pig girl says and I can't help turning in my seat to scowl at her. Unlike so many others, she doesn't flinch away from my scowl, simply stares right back at me, sending the thing in my stomach into a turmoil.

I snap back round and huff out a sigh of relief as the academy comes into sight. There are other vehicles on the road now too, Tristan's car somewhere up ahead as well as the campus bus, everybody returning home with their tails between their legs.

It wasn't the night everybody was expecting but I bet it will go down in folk legend anyway, everybody talking about it for weeks to come. Only I won't be here for those conversations. My gaze falls to my lap. I close my eyes,

I can hear the whistle of her breath behind me, loud above everyone else's. I can smell her sweet scent. Shit, I can feel the heat and the magic radiating from her little body.

The beast scrabbles inside me, scraping and snapping, desperate to break free. Desperate to claim her.

I focus all my attention on resisting him again, grinding my teeth, screwing up my eyes tight.

"Sir?" I open my eyes, the world swoops in and out of focus. "We're here."

"Th-thanks," I stutter, aware the others are already climbing out of the car.

I do the same, finding my legs unstable, feeling my bones start to crunch.

"Not now," I growl to myself, picking up my feet and sprinting as hard as I can through the academy, ignoring all the cheers and shouts as I pass the other students. In my room, I slam the door behind me and fall to my knees. My body jerks and jolts as I fight it, as I fight him with everything I have. I reach my bedside and grasp for the bottle of my mother's pills. I snap off the lid, half the pills tumbling to the floor as my arm shakes. Somehow I manage to tip the remaining ones down my throat. I don't know how many. I don't care.

He keeps fighting me and I slide to the ground, my body twitching and flinching until finally, finally it all dies away and I'm left there panting, staring down at the floor.

I am just as much of a danger to her as that psychopath, Renzo Barone. Fuck, maybe even more so.

I've made the right decision. I'm sure of that now. I have to go.

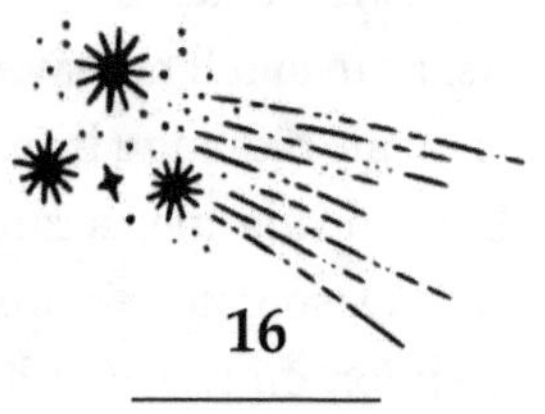

16

R enzo

I STAND in the crowd of deranged people, bumbling about like lemmings. Tripping and bumping into one another. Pushing and pulling at each other.

I yawn and scratch my head, scanning the crowd for my little rabbit. Where did the little thing scurry away to now?

I felt her the moment I walked into the ring – nearly fucking stopped me in my tracks. What is my little rabbit doing in a place like this? Didn't she learn her lesson last time? This place isn't safe for the likes of her. I may be the one tasked with hunting her down, but there's a price on her head and there are plenty of other fuckers who'd swoop in and do the job for me if it meant landing all that damn money.

But then I'd been sucked into the ring to face the wolf. His name is fucking laughable. It's even more fucking laughable how blind people can be. Wolf by name, wolf by nature. Can't they see it?

They didn't tell me it would be him I was fighting. I just got the call and a chance to visit the city – an excuse to be here, nearer to her – was fucking irresistible. Plus who doesn't love a fight? Not me. It's always been my most fun thing to do. Always has been. Ever since I could stand on my own two feet and swing my fists. It's how the Wolves of Night found me – fighting in the back alleys, making money to survive. And I still love it, even now – even if the fuckers here stop me from killing my opponent half the time. I mean, what's the fucking point in that?

Where is she? I caught a flickering sight of her standing there in the crowd, a haze of magic spinning around her. Her eyes had been all wide and scared. But what the hell was frightening her? Me? The thing in my gut spins. I like that I terrify her. It makes me hard. I also don't like it. I want to talk to her again. I want to touch her. And the little rabbit will bolt away if she's scared.

Then again maybe it wasn't me she was scared of. Maybe she realized just how fucking stupid it was to come here tonight.

I huff out air. Blue lights spin through the Warehouse and cops yell instructions out in the distance. They'll be here any minute. Bet they'd love to get their hands on me. I crack my knuckles. The fight ended too soon tonight, before it even started. But maybe there's still time to have some fun.

I shake my head. No! No time for fun, Renzo. The girl. There was at least one man here tonight, watching the fight, who would kill her if he caught her. One of Lowsky's footmen.

I spin the rings on my fingers. Perhaps there's fun to be had after all. Of course, Lowsky will be pissed – he doesn't like it when I kill one of his toys – but I could make it look like an accident. He'd never have to know it was me.

I crash through the remaining stragglers, out into the cold night, the mist curling off the water like a suffocating blanket. I squint through the dark, the lamp light low.

Has he already snatched her? Does he already have my little rabbit by the throat? I don't think so. I think I'd know. I think I'd feel it in my gut.

People are running in all directions. Engines roar, and behind me the sirens keep on wailing. I walk swiftly, hands in my pockets, fingering that knife, whistling to myself. People step away, give me a wide berth and all the time I'm looking, searching.

I spot him. He's big, jacked up. He thinks it makes him invincible. He thinks no one will ever touch him – especially the fucking cops. But his size makes him slow. I catch him with ease. It's almost disappointing. Two seconds and I'm on him. I tap him on the shoulder, he turns, recognition flicks across his face, then horror. He knows. He knows what I'm going to do. They always do. How is that? Is it something in my eyes? He starts to lift his hand, but then – snap – he's dead.

Fuck, I love that sound. Love how easily a spinal cord fractures like that. Like snapping a fucking bread stick in two.

I'd've liked to slice her knife through his neck. But that'd hardly look accidental. The man was dumb but not dumb enough to slam a knife into his neck. A neck that's now broken.

"He can't hurt you now," I say into the mist. I wish she was here. I wish she could have seen. I wish she knew how hard I'm working to keep her safe.

But she's not here. Her voice doesn't answer me on the

wind. There's only the sound of the black ocean, slapping against the concrete.

I kick the man's body, rolling him over from his back to his front and his back again.

"Roly poly, over you go," I say, kicking him again and watching as his body falls off the edge of the world and into the waiting embrace of the ocean.

There's a splash as his body hits the surface, water splattering up into the air and landing on my boots. The body lingers for a moment, drifting away, then slowly sinks into the gloom. He's fish food now.

I rub the toe of my left boot on the back of my leg and then the right.

I can't feel my little rabbit now. She's gone. She's safe. But it's only temporary and I don't fucking like that. I don't like it at all.

17

R^{hi}

I TOSS AND TURN, unable to sleep. Adrenaline still skates through my veins from the events of the evening but also unease about Spencer.

I don't like the dude. I never have. He's rude to me, obnoxious, cruel – he shoved me in that freaking locker. He's slammed me into the mat over and over again. He didn't step in and stop Summer when she attacked me. In fact, he just stood and watched. Yet all the time, all the time he must have felt it too, known what it meant, and he chose to ignore it just like the others. Ignore it and treat me like shit.

I should be rejoicing that he's leaving. I should be celebrating. But I don't feel happy about it. I feel this unshakeable unease. I can't help thinking about the time he kissed me. I can't help thinking about how he never told on me when I blasted him with my magic. I can't stop thinking about how he pulled me from the ground there in the Warehouse and out to safety.

It's confusing. And maybe him leaving is for the best. Except I still don't understand why he's going.

When Winnie's alarm sounds in the morning, I'm showered, dressed and out the door before Winnie's barely emerged from under the duvet.

"Where are you going?" she asks.

"The gym," I tell her. Winnie opens her mouth to ask me another question, my explanation obviously insufficient, but I'm already nudging Pip away from the door as I close it and hurry out of the building.

The excitement from yesterday has evaporated and that same sadness from before seems to hang about the few early risers meandering along the pathways. I ignore them, reaching the gymnasium and wondering what on Earth I'm doing here.

We had an arrangement, one that had hardly begun. But he's leaving today, the chances he'll be here are slim, very slim, and yet ...

I glance down at my gut and push open the doors. Maybe I want answers, maybe I want to see him one last time, maybe I am seriously fucked up.

He's sitting in the middle of the mats, forearms resting on his bent knees.

He looks up at the sound of the door and meets my eyes, the bond in my stomach spinning.

"I didn't know if you would come," he says, as I cross towards the mats, dropping down to sit in front of him.

"8am every Tuesday, right? That was the arrangement."

"I'm leaving," he tells me. "This morning."

I nod, rolling my eyes. "Yeah, I did hear that. Good news travels fast, you know."

He snorts. "Good news? You're not sad about it then?"

"Sad the boy who's been bullying me for the last few months is leaving? No, I don't think so."

"I haven't been–" he says gruffly, scowling at me.

"It doesn't matter now," I mutter. I don't know why I'm here but I do know I'm too tired to argue with him.

"You'll have to find someone else to teach you self-defense." He holds my gaze. "Tristan Kennedy, maybe?"

I frown. "You don't think I'm good enough yet, then? Despite your improved teaching techniques."

His whole demeanor is defeated and somehow he looks smaller and less intimidating than he usually does. Like someone in desperate need of a hug.

Well, he has an entire troop of cheerleaders for that!

"You've improved slightly, Blackwaters, but you've still got a long way to go. And you do have a propensity to land yourself in trouble."

He drops his gaze down to his hands. He scratches at his knuckles.

"Why are you leaving, Spencer?" I ask him, unable to help myself. Is it because of me? He hates me. He's made that clear from the start – even if some of his actions have been confusing. The majority have been hateful and cruel. Has he had enough? Can he no longer stand to be anywhere near me?

I look at him. Will he even tell me the truth?

He takes a deep inhale, his shoulders shuddering. "It's time."

"Time for what?"

"I've achieved everything I wanted to achieve here. I want to go somewhere I can be of use."

I tilt my head to the side and examine him. When I first met him, he seemed like such a brainless, arrogant jock to me. Not someone with a desire to truly serve his country, to help his people. Have I had him all wrong? Or is he lying to me? Why leave? Everyone worships the ground he steps on here at the academy – didn't the entire academy risk their necks to see him fight last night? I doubt he'll receive the same adulation in the protection forces no matter how good a fighter he is. I doubt that's how things work out there at the front.

"The whole school is going to miss you," I say.

He manages a limp smile. "Will you?"

I scoff. "About as much as you'll miss me," I tell him and his eyes lift to mine. The intensity of them has my bond spinning even faster and an awareness of something nudging at my consciousness. "Well," I say, rising back onto my feet, "I'm sure you have more important things to do this morning than teach me." I hesitate. "I just wanted ... I just wanted to say goodbye."

Why? Why did I want to see him one more time? To convince myself I don't feel what I feel? To convince myself I've filled my head with fairytales and foolish ideas? To convince myself I can watch him go and not feel a thing at all?

Because if that was my plan, I've failed completely. I feel it more than ever. Is that the reason he's going? The real reason. To be as far away from me as he can?

Good.

He's not my friend. Despite saving my ass last night, he's shown me over and over again just how much he despises me, and despite the stupid feeling in my stomach, the feeling is mutual.

Spencer lumbers up to his feet as well, towering above me like he always does.

"Be careful," he tells me.

"If you're going to warn me about Summer–"

"I'm serious. Don't take chances. Renzo Barone–"

"You're the one who needs to be careful," I cry out, my bond churning inside me like crazy. "You're the one going to the front." I can't think about it. I can't think about him there, risking his life. It's too … it's too …

He opens his mouth and closes it again. Clearly as taken aback by my outburst as I am.

"How about we make a promise to each other?" he whispers and I frown. "To both look after ourselves." He holds out his hand to me.

I frown harder. "If I shake this, will you throw me over your shoulder?"

He chuckles. It's genuine. I've never made him chuckle like that and my bond spins even more. "It would be tempting."

I hesitate, then look back up into his face, reaching out to take his hand. Electricity crackles against our palms, racing around our fingers and our wrists as our palms connect. But he ignores it and so do I. He's always been as stubborn as I am.

We stand, our hands linked, gazing into one another's eyes, knowing this is the end. The last time.

Maybe fate wants us together. But Spencer has chosen a different path and that is absolutely fine by me.

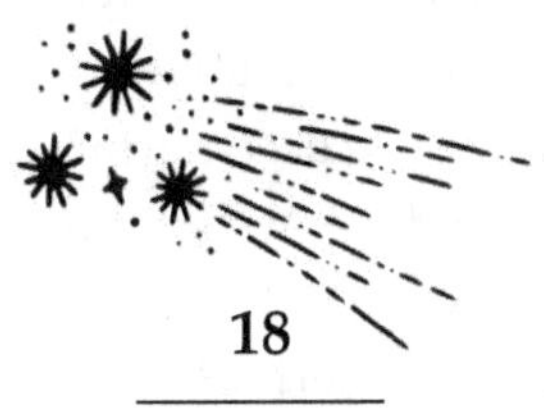

18

zlan

I've just finished packing up my bike when I receive the message.

The chancellor wants to see me. In the past, I've received a thousand of these summons and they've barely registered, certainly not sent my blood pressure soaring and my heart pounding.

Because now every summons feels like a gamble, a risk. Is this the time he challenges me? Reveals he knows everything? Delivers the ax down on my head? On Rhianna's and Stone's too?

I can't see him accepting this. Fated-mate pairs are rare these days. Some say just one forming every year. Others say it's not nearly that many. One every decade. The authorities have been quiet on the matter. There have been no official reports. Some say the waning of the fated mates is a sign of the times, a sign our powers are weakening.

But a fated-mate triad? I've never heard of one in my lifetime. The chancellor would view us as a threat, a challenge to his position. He'd come for us. Our names, the memory of us, would be wiped from the Earth before anyone knew.

Like Rhianna's mother? Her father? Is that what happened to them?

But what can I do? Refuse to see him? Abandon my post?

We need time, more time for Rhianna to develop her powers and skills, for Stone and me to destroy the threat from the Wolves of Night and to fix on a plan. Could we sail to Aropia? Away from here. Away from everything. Live like Rhianna was living, on the run, hidden, away from our people. And our family.

I try not to think of Ellie. Could I leave her?

For Rhianna, yes. Maybe I could persuade her to come with us.

For now though, these are idle thoughts. We're trapped, forced to play along.

And so I ride to the Council building, my face fixed in a passive mask, ready to receive my orders, determined not to give anything away, praying the ax won't fall this time.

If it does, I'll fight. I'll fight with everything I have, give the two of them the time to flee.

He's waiting for me outside the chamber, dressed in his heavy ceremonial robes today, the ceremonial chain hanging heavy around his neck, the glass dragon with its ruby eyes soaring on the ceiling above his head.

The sight makes my blood run cold. The man looks like the sinister politician he is today.

However, there are no guards. No guards flanking his sides, ready to arrest me.

"Azlan," he says, when he hears me approach, lifting his gray eyes to mine. "The council is waiting to speak with you."

"The council?" I say, my blood running so cold I suppress a shiver.

The chancellor motions for me to follow him and we make our way through into the great chamber, the glass dome alive with vibrant sunlight today, forcing me to squint against the assault. I blink, watching as the chancellor takes his place among the great magicals of the republic; my father and uncle included.

I lift my chin and hold my hands behind my back like a soldier, like the soldier I was trained to be.

I don't know what this is about – if my father and uncle have told the council about my fated mate – but I'm ready to face anything they throw at me.

"Enforcer," the chancellor says, "the council has requested a report from you about the ..." he hesitates, "disturbances in the West."

"Disturbances?" my uncle scoffs. "You can hardly call them mere disturbances, Chancellor."

The chancellor ignores my uncle's outburst – something I'm sure has my uncle seething – even as other council members mutter their agreement.

"What have you learned?" the chancellor asks me.

"That the forces in the West are becoming more organized."

There are several audible gasps around the council members.

My uncle, dressed in a black ceremonial gown of his own, thumps the arm of his high-backed chair. "How has this been allowed to happen? You've assured us – you've assured the people of this republic, Chancellor – that we are safe from the lawless and dark forces of the West."

An older woman with graying hair – one I recognize from the Darlian family – nods her agreement. "The dark magicals were driven from the new republic to the West in the last war. Their remaining forces were devastated and destroyed twenty years ago. We were led to believe they were incapable of posing any real threat or any real attack to our country."

"There has always been a threat," I can't help but growl. "There have always been attacks."

It's been many years since these older, high-born magicals ventured anywhere near the front. They've forgotten the horrors there. Not me though. I remember.

"Yes, at the border," the woman persists. "Never to our country. We drove them out. We drove them away. We destroyed them."

"That was long ago," I say quietly. The West is a barren wasteland with few resources and little wealth. Those banished there long ago were never going to be content with remaining there forever. The threat they would return has always been real.

"We will double our forces at the border – call up our reserves," the chancellor says. "I reassure you all, we are safe."

"Safe?" my uncle says with undisguisable amusement. The chancellor scowls at him but my uncle simply smiles. "My sources tell me that the West is not as ill-equipped or as poorly organized as it once was. That their forces have regrouped and rearmed."

There are more gasps and whispers around the chamber.

"Then we ought to strike them," the woman says, "strike them before they strike us. Before they are allowed to grow any stronger."

The chancellor goes to speak but my uncle cuts him off. "Now, now, Dorothea, there's no need to be alarmed. No need for an offensive. I'm sure the chancellor has things under control – or he will have given time." He nods at the chancellor as if he's being gracious.

The chancellor growls.

"But how has this happened?" the woman says again. "Who is leading them? Do we know?"

I shake my head. What information I have gleaned from sources closest to the border, from the western soldiers we have captured, has been sparse. If there is an individual leading and organizing the forces in the West, they are keeping themselves well hidden.

"I intend to find out." He holds the gaze of each council man and woman in the chamber. "And again, I assure you all, there is no need for worry or concern. We have our force of highly trained magicals stationed at the border, protecting this republic. The western forces cannot and will not pass them," the chancellor bellows, ending the council session with a flick of his wrist and marching to the door, motioning for me to follow him. "Let's go somewhere more private to speak," he says to me lowly as we pass beneath the menacing dragon.

I nod and follow him up the sweeping staircase and through into his office, my grandfather's face staring at me from the desk.

He doesn't offer me a seat. We remain standing, him with his hands clutched behind his back, mine by my sides.

"You think the threat grave?" he asks me.

"I ... I don't know. Gaining information about the West

has always been difficult. Illegal dealings happen between the gangs and traders in the West. Sometimes I can obtain information that way. But this time ..."

"You need to do better," the chancellor says with menace. He doesn't like the way my uncle humiliated him in the chamber. He doesn't like that I saw it.

"There are two other things I wish to speak with you about."

I nod again. My heart begins to race again. I'm sure he must hear it but somehow I keep my face blank.

"You are headed to the western border again tonight as instructed?"

"Yes, Sir."

"Then I would like you to take the youngest son of the Moreau family with you."

I frown. "Because?"

"He will be joining our forces there."

"Is he not enrolled in Arrow Hart Academy?"

"He was, but he's earned enough credits to graduate from the academy early and I received a request from his family yesterday that he be given special dispensation to join the forces immediately. Given his ... abilities," I frown, "I think he will be of use there."

"I see," I say. The Moreau family, though mysterious, is also powerful and the different generations have always made names for themselves in the force. The opportunity to take another of their powerful sons must have seemed opportune for the chancellor. Especially given the current circumstances. "Would it not be more usual for him to travel with the fresh reinforcements?"

"There are none due to leave until the end of the week and I see no reason to keep the boy waiting, particularly as you are heading that way anyway."

I nod a third time. The arrangement sounds less than ideal to me. The boy thinks he's a prince and probably expects to be treated like one too. He's going to receive a rude awakening when he joins the forces at the front.

"There was something else?" I ask, unable to bear the tension.

"Ahhh, yes, the Blackwaters girl."

I force my eyes to remain locked on his and my features to remain neutral, even though my heart now pounds so violently in my chest it's as loud as a drum.

"The Blackwaters girl?" I ask.

"Mmmm," he says, strolling around his desk and dropping into his chair. "There is something I haven't told you about her."

This time I falter. My body flinches in surprise, but the chancellor doesn't notice, too busy rifling through papers on his desk.

"Her mother," he continues, "was known to me."

I take an involuntary step forward, even though this could be a trap, even though it most likely is.

"I thought the girl was just another unregistered. No one of importance. I had no idea you knew who she was."

"And I understand the girl herself knows little of her family."

I nod.

"I had my reasons for keeping this piece of information to myself. In fact, only the principal knows, and she does not know everything. She has been watching the girl for me, reporting any signs of any unusual abilities or attributes."

I frown. How closely has the principal been watching Rhianna and has she really been reporting back to the chancellor?

"I don't understand," I say.

"Her mother was a magical with ... an interesting talent." I wait for him to divulge more but he doesn't. "Talent that the authorities found particularly useful."

"What talents?"

He smiles. "Talents that, unfortunately, our enemies found just as alluring, just as tempting. After she died, there were rumors of a child but any searches came up empty." He smiles and that cold smile reminds me vividly of my uncle. "And then you found her – or rather that gang out there in the wastelands did."

I suppress a growl, trying not to imagine what they would have done with my mate.

"Of course," he continues, "I couldn't let on that I knew who the girl was. I don't wish our enemies to know we have found the child."

"You think she has the same talent as her mother?" I ask him carefully.

"I'm rather hoping she does. It was a particularly useful talent – in fact it secured our dominance over the forces in the West, kept them at bay. However, so far York tells me the girl shows no signs of any unusual talents. Disappointingly, it seems she is nothing but a troublemaker."

I look at the chancellor. He's not as shrewd as my uncle but he's survived as chancellor for a long time. He's a skilled politician indeed.

"Why are you telling me this now?" I ask him.

"Ahh," the chancellor says, removing his glasses. "York doesn't understand how powerful the girl could be if she does possess her mother's gift. I wonder just how closely she's really been watching her."

"I imagine she watches all her students closely."

"But I imagine the students watch each other more closely still. I would like you to talk with the Moreau boy on your way to the West, determine if he knows anything about the girl, if he's noticed anything unusual."

"And if he has?" I can't help but ask.

The chancellor peers at me as he places his glasses back on the bridge of his nose. "Then you will report the information back to me and I will consider my next steps."

I want to ask him what he plans to do with Rhianna if she does have unusual abilities but there's no point. He won't tell me and it might only arouse his suspicions. Besides, there is no way in hell I'm letting him get his grubby little hands on my mate.

As soon as I'm out of the council building, I drive my bike around the nearest corner and park up. There's a chance the chancellor is monitoring my calls, but there are ways to ensure the calls I want to keep private are kept so.

"Phoenix," I say when he answers the call. Lessons will be over now and I imagine him holed up in his office, bent over his books. Or maybe he's in his cabin with Rhianna.

Do I want her to know of this?

I scratch at the stubble on my cheek. I promised no more secrets, to be honest and open with her.

"I thought you'd be halfway to the border by now," my friend says.

"The chancellor sent for me."

My friend is quiet for a long minute, then he asks, his voice strained, "Is everything okay, Azlan?"

I recount the conversation between the chancellor and myself, everything he told me. Phoenix is quiet again.

"This is dangerous."

"Why do you think I'm calling you?"

"What will you do? About Moreau?"

"I'll question him as asked and hope to God he's noticed nothing unusual about Rhianna."

"Azlan, he's best friends with your cousin. He may know about your bonding."

I screw up my eyes. Damn. Damn. If the boy was unobservant like every other dumb rich kid in the academy, this would be easy. Then I could carry out my order and forget all about it. If the chancellor decided to check up on my work, the Moreau boy would say I'd asked him some questions about the girl, and there would be nothing to cause the chancellor any alarm.

If he has something to tell me, this all becomes more complicated.

"I'll find a way to handle this," I tell Stone, "just … make sure Rhi is aware."

"You think that's wise?"

"No more secrets, Phoenix. And tell her what the chancellor said about her mom. She's keen for every scrap of information."

"I know. She wants to explore the memories in her head again."

I take a sharp intake of breath. "You can't let her–"

"That's what I told her."

We're both quiet again, his breath whistling into my ear down the receiver.

"I'll call you again when I arrive at the camp."

"Enjoy your time with Moreau," Phoenix says, then hangs up.

I tuck my phone away, and start the bike. I've been told to meet the boy outside the academy, the college having lent him a bike of his own for the journey.

I consider whether I could sneak to see Rhi before I meet the boy but the risk is too great and I have to content myself with gazing wistfully in the direction of the campus, knowing she's somewhere within.

There's quite a crowd waiting for me when I pull up. The principal, a handful of the teachers, most of what looks like the dueling team and several cheerleaders.

The Moreau boy, to my surprise, stands away from the rest of them, the principal next to him, talking to him softly.

He's dark like his elder brother was, only somehow bigger – and his brother was a giant. He's wearing a pair of dark jeans and a hoodie, a hiking backpack resting by his legs.

His bike is already parked up and I pull up alongside it and slide down to my feet, the crowd all watching me, one or two of the girls sobbing.

"Spencer Moreau?" I ask, stopping in front of the boy and the principal.

"Yes," he says, picking up his bag and slinging it over his shoulder.

"You're ready to go?"

"Yeah." He steps towards me, taking no notice of the sobbing that grows suddenly louder.

"Would you like to say some words before you go?" Principal York asks him.

He glances over his shoulder at her and shakes his head.

"Well, let me at least say some on your behalf. You have been a great asset to this academy, one of the best dueling players I'm sure this college will ever see. I know you will make an excellent soldier ...."

The principal's words fade in my ears. I'm too busy examining the boy; the slight sag to his shoulders. No grin hovering on his face. How did I expect to find him? Jubilant? Excited? Showing off to all his little friends?

But he's not. He's quiet, resigned. He doesn't look like the player who just won the academy the Cross-lantic cup.

The principal finishes her little speech and those around

her clap, then his team mates are stepping forward to slap his shoulder and wish him luck, the girls next, flinging their arms around his neck and begging him not to go.

It's my cousin who steps forward last, after the others have all shuffled away, one girl crying so hard she has to be supported upright by two of her friends.

He rests his hand on his friend's shoulder and meets his eye. "Take care of yourself, okay?"

The Moreau boy manages a half smile. "I always do, man."

"I'll see you, then."

"Yeah."

Tristan turns away, catching my eye for a moment, and then I motion with my head for the Moreau boy to follow me.

He settles himself on his bike and I rev the engine, waiting for him to do the same. He lifts his hand in salute to the crowd of farewell wishers and several wave back. Then we're winding down the drive, the boy riding by my side, several of his team mates and those girls chasing us until we're well away, lost in the lonely country lanes.

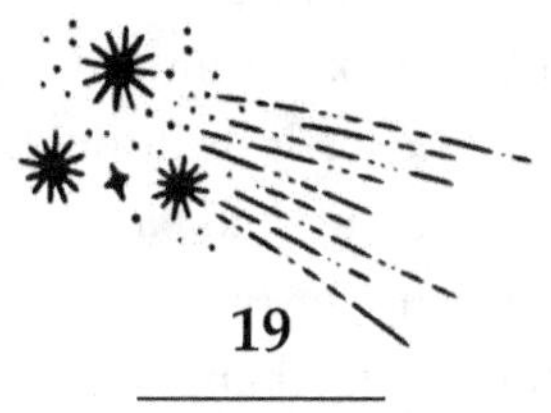

19

S pencer

WE RIDE THROUGH MOST of the day, the towns we pass through becoming dirtier and more decrepit the further we drive from Los Magicos; the shops on the high streets all boarded up; half-built tower blocks crumbling by the roadside; rusting machinery abandoned in fields. As the sun sets in the distance, the enforcer pulls us up outside a boarding house, no curtains hanging in the windows, the light bulbs bare. It's more run-down looking than the dorm building the pig girl was staying in.

I look down at my hand as the thought of her enters my mind for at least the one millionth time this afternoon. I can still feel the traces of electricity tingling across my skin where she touched me.

I didn't expect her to come. I didn't think she would. But

she had. And she'd let me go. Said goodbye and let me walk away.

All my suspicions confirmed.

The man in black talks to an old woman at the door, then hisses to me as she leads us through to a kitchen, spotless despite its meager stores and basic equipment.

"This may not live up to your usual standards but you're polite, all right, and fucking thankful."

I give him a stare, not saying a word as I drop into the seat the old woman motions towards, and thanking her for the glass of cloudy water she places in front of me.

She serves us some stew that looks worse than dog food but tastes pretty decent and then she leaves us alone. The enforcer doesn't speak to me, eating in silence as he scrolls through his phone.

I try not to, but I can't drag my gaze from his face.

She belongs to him. That's what she told me. She's his fated mate and whatever the hell Tristan Kennedy is up to, nothing can change that fact.

I try to imagine them together – the enforcer and the pig girl. His large hands around her tiny waist, her milky thighs open for him, his rough mouth on her tender ...

"Is there something you want to ask me?" the enforcer says, not looking up from his phone.

I nearly drop my fork in alarm.

"No," I say stiffly, forcing my attention back onto the chunks of unidentifiable food.

We share a room. Two single-wire cots laid out side by side. The enforcer doesn't undress, simply lies out in his boots, arms crossed over his chest, and closes his eyes.

I do the same, peering at him through the darkness, the electricity still dancing on my skin, imagining if that electricity dances across his lips every time he kisses her, dances though his soul when he fucks her.

I screw up my eyes. The monster is strangely quiet. No longer prowling, no longer busting to break loose. I hardly understand it. My mother said being with her was the way to solve this problem. But maybe, for once, I am right. Maybe getting the hell away from her was always the answer.

We drive nonstop again the next day. Although now the towns vanish, replaced by dirty villages, even those becoming fewer and further between the nearer we travel towards the border. By the time the sun is setting again, there's no sign of civilization, and the enforcer turns us off the main road, and under the cover of trees.

"We'll bed down here tonight," he tells me, already sweeping away the debris of the forest floor with his booted foot. "You go fetch kindling for a fire."

When I return half an hour later, my arms full of sticks, he's swept a considerable space, two sleeping bags laid out on the ground and some tins of food pulled out from his rucksack.

He motions to the floor and I drop the sticks, watching as he takes some in his hands, breaking them in half and building a fire between the sleeping bags.

"Couldn't we make a fire with our magic?" I ask.

"And signal to anyone nearby that we're here?"

"Are we in danger?" I ask, frowning. We're still half a day's drive from the camp at the border where our forces are stationed.

"There are the Wolves of Night and the Princes of Death. Both of them would like to see me dead." He pauses. "And you too, considering who your family is."

He's obviously not that bothered though, because he

clicks his fingers, lighting the kindling with a spark and then feeding the fire sticks until it's roaring.

He hands me a tin. "Here," he says. "I hope you like beans."

I shrug, rolling back the lid, and resting the tin next to the fire until the scarlet sauce inside is bubbling.

It burns my tongue when I lift the first bean to my mouth, but I don't complain, wolfing the thing down in three mouthfuls and then scrabbling though my own bag and pulling out the energy bars I'd had the good sense to pack.

"Want one?" I ask the enforcer. He looks up from his own tin of beans, clearly lost in his thoughts. "You want an energy bar?" I ask again.

"No," he says.

I shrug, ripping open the wrapper and taking a large bite, the thing sticking in my teeth.

The enforcer puts down his beans and holds his hands to the fire. Fall has arrived now and the nights are becoming cooler, especially out here in the West where the wind is renowned to have a freezing bite.

"Tomorrow we'll arrive at the camp and I'll take you straight to the commanding officer."

I nod, waiting for him to ask me why I'm doing this. Everyone else has. Instead he asks me something completely different.

"Your brother was stationed there."

I swallow my mouthful, the bar scratching all the way down my throat. "Yes," I say.

"Then you know what to expect."

"Not really. I haven't seen him in a long time." I take another bite, not wanting to think about it. "What should I expect?"

The enforcer looks up from the fire. "It changes you," he says cryptically.

I frown. What the hell is that meant to mean? "How?"

"People come back changed, different. What you experience, what you see – it changes you. The conditions out there at the front are harsh."

"I'm not worried."

"Dueling isn't the same as real fighting. Killing someone, taking a life, alters your soul. Watching someone die, withering away in front of your eyes, changes you forever." He pauses. "Seeing your friends die ..."

"But it happens rarely. Skirmishes with the western forces are few and far between."

The enforcer snorts, picking up his tin again and poking the remaining beans with his fork. "That's what the authorities will have you believe. There's constant fighting, constant battles, constant bloodshed."

I ball the wrapper in my hand and look at the enforcer, trying to determine if he's bullshitting me, trying to scare me, the new recruit. "If that were the case, why hide it?"

"The authorities like to keep the illusion that they have matters under control. But do you think they'd go to all the trouble of training us, of sending us to serve, if the threat was so minimal?"

"I thought we were more of a deterrent than anything else."

He shakes his head. "No, the force is there protecting our people, our lands."

"Good," I say. I want to be useful. I want to serve, to make a difference.

The enforcer shakes his head as if I'm stupid.

"How long ago did you serve?" I ask him.

The enforcer scrapes his fork around his tin, removing

the last traces of beans. Then he tosses the tin to the ground and drags his hand over his face. "It was a long time ago. More than ten years." He stares into the fire. "Turns out I was very good at killing people. At tracking them down and killing them." He glances down at his hands as if he can see all the lives he's taken with them. "I was in the forces less than six months before they recruited me to become an enforcer."

"You wanted to be one?"

"It seemed as good an option as any. Preferable to doing whatever my goddamn family would have wanted."

I remember Tristan telling me about it when we were kids, whispering with a kind of reverence about how his cousin had gone against his family's wishes.

"You still think it was the right decision?" Being an enforcer may be thrilling, adventurous, but I imagine it's also dangerous and lonely. An enforcer is not a great marriage prospect. Always away, always in danger. He has a fated mate now, he has the pig girl. Does he wish he'd taken some political position after all? Made her his society wife so they could live together in some grand mansion in the city?

"I think fate chose this path for me. I think it was inevitable," he says again in that irritatingly cryptic manner.

I go to ask him another question, but a distant noise catches both our attention. It's faint. A rumbling? No, it's boots hitting hard earth.

"Someone's coming," I say, the beast inside me suddenly alert, listening.

The man in black jumps to his feet and kicks dirt over the fire. I do the same. The flames smothered, plunging us into darkness.

"You think they're coming for us?" I ask.

"I don't know," he says, cocking his head.

"They're coming this way," I say, the beast's hearing far better than mine.

In the next moment, we see them breaking through the trees. Two ... three ... five ... eight ... so many I lose count. Magic thunders through the air towards us.

"Run," the man in black tells me, swinging around to face the men sprinting towards us.

"No," I say, as a bolt of magic explodes on the ground by my feet.

I'm not running. This is what I came for. This is why I'm here.

I pick up my feet and charge through the trees, pounding magic in the direction of the fuckers.

"Moreau!" the man in black calls after me.

But it's too late. There are no longer any boundaries, no rules, no limitations. I roar with anger as magic singes my shoulder and my hip, and then the beast is taking over. My body morphs as I run, bones snapping, muscles stretching, until it's paws that hit the ground not feet, and together we charge at the men, ripping them to shreds with our teeth and our claws.

I taste blood, metallic, and then everything fades away into darkness.

20

R^{hi}

"It's like someone actually died," I mutter to Winnie as we sit side by side in the Great Hall attempting to twist soggy spaghetti around our forks.

The hall is filled with the sound of sniffling and crying and the tear-stained faces of devastated-looking students.

"It kind of feels like someone did," Trent says from the other side of the table and I notice, like quite a lot of the other students gathered around the table, he's hardly touched his food.

"He was such a big presence," Winnie adds.

"Yeah, well, I don't remember anyone actually being this sad when they made that announcement about Andrew."

"Andrew deserved everything he had coming to him," Winnie says, waving her fork at me.

"Remind me to ensure it's you who breaks up with me and not the other way round," Trent mutters.

"Are you planning on breaking up with me?"

"No," Trent says. "I'm pretty fond of both my testicles."

Winnie sticks her tongue out at him as I laugh. "I hear she's pretty fond of your testicles too!" I say.

Trent grins, but the expression dies when Winnie stabs one of her meatballs with her fork.

I laugh again and several people throw us evil looks, one actually holding a finger to their lips and telling me to shush.

"Jeez, we're not at a funeral," I mutter.

The campus is just as somber as we make our way to our dorm room after dinner. The usual sounds of dueling practice or the cheerleaders rehearsing doesn't soar through the air and no one's playing any music.

It's actually a relief to arrive back at our dorm building. It's far too intense out there, the entire school wrapped up in some strange mourning spell.

Against our door we find another parcel waiting for us. This one is much smaller.

"Wow, he really is spoiling you," Winnie says.

I peer at my watch – I have half an hour before my tutoring with Stone. Then I scoop the parcel from the floor and peer at the label.

"It's for you, Winnie. Not me."

"Maybe, he realized he ought to spoil his mate's roomie as well as the mate herself," she says, but she examines the label and smiles. "It's from Nonny."

"It is?" I say, following Winnie inside our room and finding Pip with his head on his trotters when we enter the room. I go to pat his head, surprised by the lackluster response to our entrance. "Don't tell me you're sad Spencer's leaving too. We hate the dude, remember?"

Pip lifts his head ever so slightly then drops it back down to his trotters with a dramatic sigh.

"It's nothing to do with Spencer," Winnie says, dropping down onto her chair and unwrapping her parcel. "He's been like that ever since our trip to Nonny's."

"He's probably scared from your driving," I mutter, kissing Pip's head.

"There is nothing wrong with my driving, Rhianna. I think it's something else," she says cryptically.

I look at my pet with concern. "Do you think he's unwell?" I lay the back of my hand against his forehead and he grunts.

"Unwell, no. Sick, yes."

"Huh?" I say. I don't think he has a temperature, but now that I think about it, he ate his breakfast with a lot less enthusiasm this morning.

"He's lovesick, Rhi. He's pining for Cliff."

Pip's head pops up at the mention of that name and he grunts again.

"Who's Cliff?"

"Nonny's pup."

I stare at my oldest friend. "Seriously?" Pip sighs again and his body droops. "Jeez," I mutter.

"Ah ha!" Winnie calls out. "She found it!"

"Found what?"

"The old book of fairytales." She holds the book up to show me the cover – leather and battered with a faded gilded title. "This historian, Grace Emilie, collected them all together in the last century. They say she traveled up and down the country listening to the stories mothers told their daughters, fathers their sons, grandparents their grandchildren, and wrote them all down in this book." Winnie glides her hand across the cover. "This copy's been in our family for years. Nonny says, when her own mom was a child, her mom used to read it to her."

She flicks through the pages and colorful illustrations streak before my eyes.

"Why did she send it to you?" I ask, coming to lean against Winnie's desk so I can get a better look.

"Because I asked her to. There's this story in here ..." She continues to flick through the pages. "I couldn't quite remember what it was called ... Ahh, here!" The book falls open in her lap and she runs her fingers over the swirly calligraphy of the title. "Queen Æðelflæd and her five knights."

"Right," I say, my eyes trailing over the rest of the page. "And why–"

"When you were asking me the other day, remember, about fated mates, you asked me if there were ever cases of magicals with more than one fated mate and this is one. Queen Æðelflæd had five fated mates."

"I don't know the story."

"You don't?" Winnie says with a grin. She points to my desk chair and I wheel it over and sit beside her. She flicks over the page to a double-spread illustration. "This was one of my favorite pictures in the book when I was little. I used to stare at it for hours." Winnie points to the elegant-looking woman in the center of the page. "This is Queen Æðelflæd. See how she's dressed in armor and not some fancy ball gown. That's because she was a warrior queen. With the help of her five knights, she banished all the monsters from the land, and saved the people from the darkness."

I stare at the face of the woman. The artist had given her a beautiful face, her features soft and delicate, but there's a steely look in her golden eyes, and she grips a sword in both her hands.

"Who were her mates?" I ask, examining the faces of five men circling the figure of the woman.

"Now, let me see," Winnie says, tapping her finger on the page. "There was the prince – see this one?" She points to a young-looking man, his hair as golden as the crown he wears on his head. "The Scholar." She points to a man with a book in his hands. "He was my favorite. Then ... the huntsman and the shifter."

"The shifter? Well, there you go. It is all make-believe. There are no such things as shifters."

"There are werebeasts though, aren't there?" Winnie says, not looking up from the page.

I gaze back at the illustration. "And who is he? The last one." He's dressed in a dark brown robe, a hood pulled over his head.

"The monk. He's the one who saved Æðelflæd."

"Saved her?"

"The story goes that magicals were few and far between back then and when the village discovered that Æðelflæd had unusual powers and abilities, they called her a witch and sentenced her to burn on the stake." I gasp, my eyes returning to the woman. "It was the monk who rescued her and took her away."

"You said she was a queen."

"She rose to be one."

I stare at the woman and the five men, the blood in my ears ringing. "A wheel," I say. "She's their core. That's how Stone and Azlan explained it?"

Winnie tsks. "This is why boys need to read fairytales too, Rhi. It's not a wheel. It's a star. See?" She hovers her finger above the illustration, drawing colorful lines in the air, connecting the queen to her five knights and they to each of them. "A star."

I gaze down at the shape until the lines fade away.

"You're thinking this is like me?"

Winnie rests her hand on the page again. "Oh no, I'm not ... Maybe this is just a story. Then again maybe it really happened. Maybe it is possible for someone special to have more than one, more than two fated mates."

I harrumph at that idea. "I am not anyone special. And this is just a fairytale, Winnie. It's not true."

"Says who? Grace Emilie collected these stories – often she said the same story was told throughout the land. Sometimes varying a little in each town she visited. Sometimes almost the same. Who says they weren't histories passed down from one generation to the next? But who says they were made up stories?"

21

R^{hi}

I'M a little apprehensive about seeing Stone this evening. After all, the last time I did see him he was chained to his bed. Chained there by me. There's a very good chance the professor will be severely pissed off with me.

However, when I knock on his classroom door, he opens it with a look of excitement and hauls me into the room.

"Ahh, good you're here. We can get started." He's lost his tie and jacket and rolled up his sleeves and there are several artifacts laid out over the classroom desks. It looks like we are really going to do this. I half expected the whole tutoring thing to be a ploy to–

"I'm trying to be good to you, Rhi," he explains.

I'm not sure fucking me is exactly bad but–

"Rhi," he says, cringing. "It's going to be hard to keep my hands to myself but I promised you this."

I tilt my head to one side. "You did."

"And also there's every chance the principal may come to check up on us."

I roll my eyes. So that's the real reason he's going to keep his hands to himself.

"It's one of the reasons. It isn't the main," he explains. "Right." He bounces on his toes with obvious enthusiasm. "I thought we could start with more of the magical fingerprints–"

"Actually," I say, chewing on my lip.

"Yes?"

"What I'd really like you to teach me is how to keep you out of my head."

He looks a little taken aback, plunging his hands into his pockets. Then he regains his composure and smirks. "If you're that obsessed with me, that you can't stop thinking about me, then–"

"You know that's not what I mean."

"Right, you don't want me in your head?" He nods, hurt spreading across his features. "I have to confess, I like being in your head, Miss Blackwaters. You look at everything so differently to anyone else I know. It's kind of fascinating. No, it's more than that, it's beautiful."

"You said my mind was no better than a sewer."

He shrugs. "I was an asshole."

"I want it to be a choice," I explain. "I want to have control about when you enter my mind and when you don't. I mean, I know I'll probably never be skilled enough to keep you out–"

"Rhi, I think you could be. I think you could be strong enough to keep me out of your head if you wanted to. And if that's what you want, of course, I'll teach you."

I smile at him. "It is."

He steps towards me and takes my hand. "Close your eyes." I do as he says, and he laces his fingers with mine.

"I'm so sorry, Rhi," he whispers, "so sorry about Founders' Night. You know I'd never do that to you again."

I bite my lip. I think I do. I think I'm beginning to trust him, forgive him even. I want us to be happy. I don't want to carry around this heavy grudge on my shoulders for the rest of my life. I want to be free to enjoy our time together. Maybe even to love him.

I wonder if he's reading my thoughts right now. If he can't help himself. If he is, he doesn't say a thing.

"Clear your mind, Miss Blackwaters."

I peek open one eye. "I hate it when people say that. It's impossible. As soon as I try, I'm thinking about how to do it."

He chuckles. "Yeah, you have a very busy, chaotic mind."

"Beautiful or sewer, professor, make up your mind."

"It's messy and chaotic – that's what makes it so beautiful."

I close my eyes again. "Just tell me what to do."

"You need to use your magic to block me. Your magic is powerful. Even more powerful than it was."

"It's grown again. Since we bonded."

"Yes," he whispers. "I can see that. I can feel it. You need to ensure your magic is there in your mind, hovering in the recesses, there to strike whenever someone enters uninvited."

"How?" I say with frustration.

"Focus it there, let it seep into your mind."

I try, clinging onto his fingers as I strain to force my magic away from my fingertips, along my nerves and into my mind. But it's stubborn and it's not innate, not natural like so much magic is.

"I can't do it," I growl in frustration.

"You can," he whispers and I give him a very clear image of my middle finger in my mind.

"Miss Blackwaters," he warns. "A little less smart, a little more patience."

"My magic doesn't want to do it."

"Rhi," he whispers gently, stroking the pads of his thumbs over my fingers, soothing me. "It isn't something you need to force."

"But–"

"Rhi," he continues, "magic was something you kept hidden from others for so long, you've built a barrier in your mind. All you need to do is find that barrier and release it and then it will be as easy and as natural as breathing."

I screw up my eyes and search for the thing holding my magic back, for that barrier, for that lock. I begin to growl again, ready to give up, sure this is all nonsense, when something snaps, something strong and solid, and magic floods into my mind so powerful, it ejects Stone right out of my head, flinging him across the classroom, where he lands with a thud on his backside.

"Stone!" I cry, snapping open my eyes and racing towards him.

He groans, stumbling to his feet and brushing dust off his pants. "First the chains, then this."

"I didn't mean to."

He chuckles. "I know you didn't, sweetheart. I don't think you know just how strong you are half the time."

"Did it work though? Can you enter my mind?" I let my magic tingle behind my temples, ready to strike.

"Are you going to shoot me across the classroom again?" Stone asks warily.

I shrug with a smile and he swears, holding my gaze. I

feel him pushing, testing my defenses but he doesn't break through. His brow furrows and he grits his teeth. The pressure builds but I hold him back with ease.

"Well?" I ask.

"Nothing," he concedes, letting out a breath.

"Promise?"

"Promise."

"And now?" I let the magic seep from my mind, inviting him in, showing him just how much I want him, how and where.

"Yeah," he says with a grin. "Yeah, now I can see."

However, as much as I tempt him with ever more erotic scenes in my head, the professor is resolute. He's not touching me tonight, not when the principal could walk in unannounced any second.

I'm left to slink back to my room, thankful I've learned something new, but frustrated too.

Winnie's engrossed in writing an essay when I return, so I grab the discarded book from the floor and lift it into my lap.

I read the story of Queen Æðelflæd while Winnie finishes her essay, occasionally peering up to look at me. When I've finished that story, I climb into bed with the book and read all the others. Some are ludicrous – clearly complete fantasy. Others feel like they could have happened to someone I knew even yesterday. I'm still reading when Winnie climbs into her pajamas and brushes her teeth, continuing to flip pages as she turns off the overhead light.

It's the early hours of the morning when I finish, dropping the book carefully to the floor and curling up under the covers, not bothering to undress.

I lie awake, drifting to sleep slowly, the stories tangling

in my head as I do, the faces of those five knights swimming around and around in my mind.

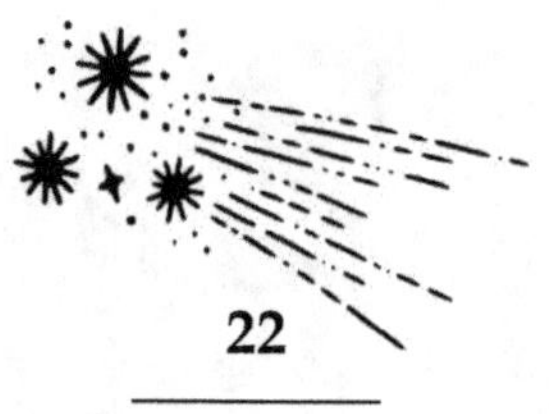

22

A zlan

FOR A MOMENT, everyone freezes to watch the massive beast crashing through the trees. Half wolf, half human, its eyes flashing with a wildness in the dark.

It's massive, a foot taller than me, and twice my bulk, its strength obvious in its every movement.

It's on top of the first man before he even has a chance to react, ripping out his throat in a torrent of blood. Then it's pouncing on the next and the others are fleeing through the trees, the werebeast swerving after them with the dexterity and speed of a creature half its size.

The men around me watch the beast go, caught in indecision for a second or two.

I take my opportunity, firing my magic at them. It knocks them back into action and they come streaming towards me. I duck and dive as they shoot their magic back at me. There are many of them, but they're poorly trained, their magic weak and ineffective, and half of them are dead before they make it through the trees.

Closer, I can see they're young – the same age as the Moreau boy, as Rhi. I hesitate and a bolt scorches across my shoulder, the smell of burned flesh singeing my nose. I grimace.

"We don't have to do this," I say, deflecting their magic with my own, dodging more blows.

"You're surrendering?" one asks me with a sneer, "because we were told to take no prisoners."

"I don't want to hurt you," I growl.

The man laughs. "You're outnumbered."

"Yeah," I mutter. I send a bolt of magic at his gut, and he flies through the trees, crashing into a trunk and collapsing unconscious. I should finish him off, but I can't bring myself to do it. Besides which, I'm dealing with the other five men hurtling their kindergarten magic my way. I slam magic into two, watching them collapse to the ground and then the remaining three are on me, punching, kicking and hitting. Luckily their combat skills are about as hopeless as their magical ones and I have two out cold in a matter of minutes.

The final one swings back his fist to punch my face, but I uppercut him right on the jaw. I flinch as I hear his neck snap and watch as the lights go out. Dead. Another one dead.

I didn't have a choice. It was them or me. And I have a mate. A fated mate, one I'm not prepared to leave heart broken.

Do these men have loved ones too? Mothers, fathers, girlfriends, boyfriends? People who will be left devastated when they don't return. I shake my head. Such a waste. Then I crouch down and inspect them. Are they the Wolves of Night? Or from some other gang? Or perhaps infiltrators from the West? It's hard to tell. They could be smugglers. Ones who didn't take kindly to us disturbing their racket. I look more closely at them. One has a vivid burn running up the length of his arm. Another the welt of a burn covering his left cheek. A third has his hands wrapped in bandages. What the hell caused those? Magic? Something they were smuggling?

I step away from the bodies and squint through the darkness. I can see the distant flash of magic, the roar of the werebeast and then silence.

I wait, catching my breath, clouds of it puffing through the air in front of my face.

I've never faced a werebeast before, but if it comes for me next, I'll be ready. I'll give everything I have. Unlike those men, I am going to return to my loved one. To my Rhianna.

Then I hear the soft pad of feet. I step forward, peering into the trees. Ready.

But it's the Moreau boy who comes stumbling forward, naked, his body battered, his hands bloody.

"You!" I roar, charging at him.

He looks up in alarm, raising his hands to defend himself, but then he sees it's me and his hands fall to their sides. His face floods with shame.

I'm on him in the next minute, smashing my fist against his cheek bone. He stumbles backward, and I hit him again.

"You're the fucking werebeast. You!" I hit him again and again. He makes no move to defend himself, to protect his face, his hands limp by his side. "You fucking attacked her!" I hit him again and this time he sways on his feet, stumbling down to his knees. "Rhianna! My mate! My! Mate!"

My heart pounds in my ears. I want to kill him. I don't

care about the blood on my hands. I don't care if it means another mark on my soul. Yet another bereaved family. He tried to kill my mate and now I will kill him.

He looks up at me, blood in his mouth, a cut slicing the skin beneath his eyebrow in half.

"He wasn't going to harm her." I growl, my hands forming even tighter fists. "He wasn't." A fat tear slides down his cheek, clearing a path in the blood. "He wasn't going to harm her. He ... he wants her. He wants to make her his." His bottom lip trembles. "That's why I had to leave."

He falls forward onto his hands, his head hung low, blood and tears dripping off his chin and onto the dried leaves below him.

The anger seeps away, my fingers uncoiling, my shoulders slackening.

How have I been so stupid? How had I not seen this?

"You love her ..." I say.

He doesn't answer but I don't need him to. Haven't I seen it before? With Stone? With myself?

The Moreau boy is in love with my mate.

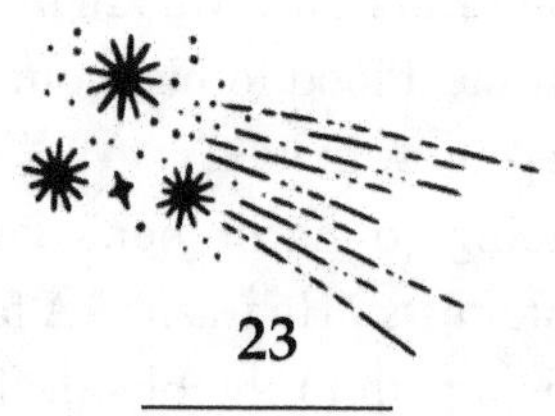

23

R enzo

I'M NOT good with a plan.

I get bored. I forget. The instructions jump around in my mind, tangling and muddling up.

Plans fucking suck. It's always been better to go with my gut, my instinct.

Apparently it makes me fucking unpredictable. Apparently that's a good thing.

But I need a plan now. A fucking good one.

I sit out in the forest. Only me and my bike. Away from people and their noise.

My legs jiggle and I chew on gum. Thinking. Trying to unscramble all the chaos in my mind and think.

What do I need to do?

Protect my little rabbit and make her mine.

But Lowsky wants her dead. He says he'll find someone else to do the job if I don't complete it.

I can't let that happen. So what do I do about it? Kill Lowsky?

My leg jiggles harder. He's the closest thing I have to family. The one who pulled me off the streets. But I'd do it. I'd do it for her. I don't give a shit about Lowsky. I don't give a shit about anyone apart from my little rabbit.

Killing him is risky, though. He may kill me first and then there'll be nobody to protect her. Only those pussies.

I shake my head. No, that isn't the solution here.

I need to keep thinking.

I knock my fist against my forehead, trying to force my thoughts into order.

I can't kill her and I can't kill him.

I smack my fist harder and shit, it works. The idea knocking loose and presenting itself.

I need to make him think she's dead. I need to make him believe it. Lowsky has bigger issues going on. If he thinks she's dead, he'll forget about her. It's not a permanent solution, he'll work it out in the end. But he has bigger ventures going on right now, stuff to distract him. It'll give me the time to work out what to do next.

I spit my gum to the ground.

"Ahh shit," I say out loud. I'm going to have to kill him eventually. I'm going to have to find a way to do it to keep her safe.

For now, though – for now – I'm going to make him believe I killed her.

Which means I'm going to have to go see her again.

My leg stops jiggling and I feel my cheeks tug upwards.

Fuck yeah, I want to see her again. And this time I really really want to touch her too.

TURNS OUT, seeing my little rabbit isn't going to be as hard as I thought it would be. Turns out the enforcer and the werebeast are both out of town. Of course, there are still two others watching my little rabbit, but the odds are looking more in my favor this way.

The academy is protected by all sorts of fucking impressive spells; spells designed to keep people like me out.

Although I have to say – many of them are looking old, creaking around the edges, fissures running through their surface. They need replacing, repairing. I should tell her that. I want her safe.

It doesn't matter either way, though. I'm not going in that way. I'm going in through the forest. The forest is impossible to enter through normal means, which means it's not protected by spells like the rest of the place.

I can enter if I want. With a bit of effort.

I return to Lowsky's compound to take a shower, brush my teeth, drag a comb through my hair and put on a clean t-shirt.

Want to look good for my girl.

I take a glance in the mirror. This older kid once said I had a pretty face. Tried to fucking stuff his hands down my pants. I broke his jaw, his hand and made sure he'd never father any perverted offspring like himself.

Since then, I've gained a fuck load of scars. I doubt my face is pretty any more. I run my fingers along the scar lines. Will she care? Does it matter?

I slam off the light, patting my pocket to make sure I have her knife as I stride back through the trees, ignoring all the busy little bees around me.

When I'm lost in the trees, I take a deep inhale and close

my eyes. The noise is there, chattering in my head, but if I listen real hard – real real hard – I can make out that humming. Time. Space. It has a sound all of its own, like a note on a piano.

All I have to do is reach out and bend that string, twist the note higher or lower and slip through.

When I open my eyes again, I'm in a different forest. A darker, denser one.

Bingo.

I take a minute, rubbing at my temples. It hurts, always does. That's why I don't do it very often. The pain intensifies if I do it too much.

This was worth it though. For a glimpse, for a touch, to ensure she's safe.

The forest is silent. Not a leaf stirring in the breeze. Not a branch creaking overhead. I snake through the trees, my heart doing this funky dance in my chest the closer I get to the boundary. Her place is right by the edge of the forest. I can see her window from the safety of the trees.

Her room is dark. The pig napping on the grass outside.

I click my tongue and snap my fingers and the pig lifts his head, his ears twitching. I do it again.

"Come on, boy," I whisper. "Come to, Daddy."

The pig does as he's told, jumping up onto its little piggy legs and trotting all the way towards me.

I huff in amusement when he stops in front of me.

"Good to see you again, little pig," I say, reaching into my pocket and hooking out a candy bar.

The pig grunts at me in annoyance.

"Yeah," I say. "I fucked up. But I'm here to help her now. You know that, right?"

The pig examines me with his beady little eyes.

"Come on. I brought you a treat and everything."

I hold it out to him and he takes a suspicious sniff.

Then he looks at me again, tilting his head first to one side then the other, squeaking at me the whole time.

I lay my hand over the place my heart is supposed to be. "I swear on my life."

The pig snorts, snatching the treat from my hand and dropping down on the ground. I watch as he snuffles his snack, telling him my plan in the quiet of the forest. When he's done, he settles down beside me and we wait together.

"You think she's going to be long?"

The little pig grunts. He's about as much of a fan of hanging around waiting for her as I am, but he doesn't know where she is.

"With the professor, you think, huh?" I say, peering out towards the mansion in the distance, its windows all lit up like a lantern.

In a different lifetime maybe I could have gone here. Studied magic, read a few books. Maybe I could have been one of the rich kids. Lived in one of those big houses with a mom and a dad. But life took a different path. A less fucking prissy one.

The pig grunts again.

"Yeah, you're right," I say. "It still brought me here, anyway, didn't it?"

An hour passes, and then I feel it. That sensation in my stomach. I sit up straighter and the pig lifts his head from his paws. A moment later, she comes into view, dressed in that hoity-toity uniform, her dark hair flitting in the breeze, chewing on her thumbnail, lost in thought.

I nudge the pig.

"Will you go fetch her for me, little fellow?"

His little curly tail flicks up and down as he considers

my request, then he lumbers to his trotters with a snuffle and trots off towards her.

I stand up too, brushing dirt from my pants and sinking further into the trees.

The little pig meets his owner outside the dorm room. He squeals at her, bumping his snout against her ankles. She bends down to scoop him up, but he jumps back. She quirks an eyebrow at him, her mouth moving but I can't make out the words over the distance. He bumps at her ankles again, running a little away from her and then back towards her. She laughs, the way her face lights up all happy-like, making my insides fucking somersault.

The little pig repeats his dance three more times before she gets the hint and follows him, hesitating slightly when they reach the edge of the forest, but having no choice but to chase after him.

I stay hidden in the trees until the pig reaches me, slowing his pace, waiting for my little rabbit to catch up with him.

He lifts his snout into the air and snorts, and I step out from my hiding place.

Her eyes – all golden like caramel sauce – alight on me and widen.

"You?" she says, lifting her hands ready to strike me.

"Me," I say. "Did you miss me?"

"No," she says, in such a forceful way I'm sure my feelings would be hurt if I had any.

"How the hell did you get in here?"

"Erm," I say those muscles pulling at the corners of my mouth again, "magic."

My little rabbit really is funny.

I take a step towards her. I can smell that sunshine scent

of hers from here, even above the dank organic stench of the forest. Fuck, I want to lick her. Like a lollipop.

"Come one step closer and I'll blow you apart."

"Fuck, yes," I say. "Blow me fucking apart!" I bet it would feel amazing.

She frowns. I'm doing this all wrong again. Frowning is bad. If she's frowning the likelihood is she won't let me touch her.

Or lick her.

I peer at the pig, appealing to him for help. He crinkles his snout and trots off to root about under a bush.

"What did you do to my pig? Did you bewitch him?"

"We have an understanding." She stares at me like I'm mad. But hey, she's the one with the pig. I've seen how she talks to him, how she babies him. "He knows I want to keep you safe."

"Safe?!" she spits. "You've been trying to kill me!" She takes an aggressive step forward, that hook tugging her closer.

I want to reach out and coil my magic around her, drag her right into my arms. But she'll probably scream and make a fuss about it.

"Yeah. Not anymore."

"You expect me to believe Marcus Lowsky has ... what ... forgiven me? Forgotten about me?"

"No, he still wants you dead."

Magic hisses on the end of her fingertips like snakes about to strike. Crimson magic. I want to see it again, want to see her wield it.

I also want to stay alive. For now anyway. Long enough to lick her.

"But I don't," I add.

"Why?" There's curiosity in her tone. I may be shit at reading other people, but with her it's different. It's clear.

I meet her gaze. She doesn't flinch away, not like all the others. She holds my gaze and her magic crackles in the air.

I can see her pulse dancing in her throat, can see her breath brushing against her pretty lips, can hear her heart pumping. Her skin is pale, translucent. I can see all the rivers of blood flowing beneath it. She's so fragile. So fucking beautiful.

I bet she's just as beautiful between her legs. Just as fragile.

I bet I could ruin her completely.

"I like you, little rabbit. I don't like people. People are like fucking riddles. They make my brain ache. But you ..."

"I don't like you," she says simply.

It's the way people talk to me sometimes. They think because I don't think like them. I'm dumb. So they treat me like a child.

I don't think I'm dumb. I think smart doesn't always look the same.

It's not always professors in their posh suits, sitting in their goddamn offices, surrounded by dusty books.

"That's okay, little rabbit. I can like you enough for the both of us." Her brow wrinkles. The pig scampers back over to us, grunting. I need to get to the point. "Lowsky wants you dead. He wants me to do it," her brow furrows further, "if I don't, he'll find someone else who will. I don't want to kill you and I don't want anyone else killing you either."

"Erm, thanks," she says.

"You're welcome." Her scowl is so heavy now, she looks like *she* wants to kill *me*. My kind of foreplay. "I figured out a solution, though," I say with pride in my chest. "I need to make him *believe* I killed you."

"What?"

"I need to make him believe I killed you."

"So go tell him you killed me. There's no reason in hell for you to be here, talking to me." She glares at her pig.

I shake my head. "No, Lowsky, he's all fucking dramatic and damn suspicious. He'll want proof."

"Proof," she says, her eyes returning to me and making the thing in my gut buzz. "What do you want? My little finger?"

I consider this. "Yeah, that would work."

But I'm guessing that's the wrong response, because her face goes all horrified and she takes a step away from me.

"You were joking," I mutter.

"Yeah," she says, examining my face. "How do I know you're for real? How do I know you're telling the truth? That this isn't some ... some ... trap."

Why's she asking me that? If she thought this was a trap – if she really believed that – she'd have blasted me into lots of teeny tiny pieces by now.

"You want my little finger?" I ask, holding it up.

"No!" she says. "You're fucking insane."

I shrug. Like I haven't heard that a million times before.

I take a step forward, and another and another. She watches me come, but she doesn't shy away, she stands her ground like the stubborn little rabbit she is.

"Little rabbit, you know why I won't hurt you – not unless you want me to – not unless you're into that kind of thing – in which case–"

"How will you convince him you killed me?"

"I'm going to give him a heart. I'm going to tell him it's yours."

Disappointment floods her face. Like I failed her and I don't like that at all.

"He'll know it's not mine."

I shake my head, lifting my hand.

Her cheek looks so soft, like snowflakes. I bring my fingertips nearer, closer to her face. She's very still. But it isn't my magic keeping her rooted to the spot this time, it's something else. She watches my face as my fingertips stray closer, closer. And then the pad of my fingers are touching her cheek. So much softer than I remembered. So much softer than my own. And flawless. No scars, no marks. Clear like marble.

"I can make him believe it's yours. I know a way. But I need something from you, precious little rabbit. It's why I had to come and see you, even though I know you don't like it."

"What?" she whispers, letting me trail my fingers down her cheek to the curve of her jaw. "What do you need?"

Her magic spins in the air around us and mine feels so dark in my veins it's like a drug.

I lean in closer, inhaling that scent of hers and my fingers stray down to her throat. Her pulse leaps against my fingertips and I bring my mouth right up against the shell of her ear, her hair tickling my face.

"Your blood."

24

R^{hi}

I SHOULDN'T BE SURPRISED. The man is a psychopath. But then I'm the one standing here, alone with him, in a forest, letting him touch my throat.

Am I the one who's lost her mind?

Possibly. This is the craziest, stupidest thing I've ever done. And I've done quite a few crazy and stupid things. However, something in my gut tells me he isn't a threat, no longer a danger. He isn't going to hurt me.

Who am I kidding? I know exactly what that 'something' in my gut is.

Then there's Pip. He never changes his mind about someone. Make an enemy of my pig and you've made an enemy for life. There was one particular chicken back home that he hated for no particular reason. They spent entire days locked in battle.

And yet Pip led me right here.

Maybe this man has bewitched us both.

"My blood?" I say. "I don't think so."

"Little rabbit, you still don't trust me?" I shake my head. "And yet we both know you're far stronger than me. You could blast me apart if you wanted to."

"Me?"

"You."

"I'm not–"

"I've seen it, little rabbit. You can wield crimson magic."

The magic crackles on the ends of my fingertips when he says those words, as if he's calling to it.

He grins and fleetingly he looks less man, more boy.

He drops his fingers away from my throat and the thing in my gut isn't happy about it. It wants his hands on my skin. But then he's tugging up his t-shirt and, taking my hand in his, he presses my palm flat against the rigid muscle of his chest. His heart beats right into my palm and I see the flash of his toned stomach, inks scribbled over every inch of his skin.

"You can kill me if you want," he says. "If you don't trust me. If you think my intentions are bad. Then end me now."

I look up into his face. His eyes may be mismatched but they're also beautiful, framed by long lashes any girl would kill for. They don't belong in the face of a killer.

I let him press my hand against his heart, the sensation in my stomach going crazy with it.

I swallow.

"How is my blood going to help?" I ask him.

"Magic," he says with another grin. I raise an unimpressed eyebrow at him. "I know a way." He looks out towards the academy. "A hoity-toity school isn't the only way to learn."

As if I need to be told that.

"Why didn't you go to the academy? Every magical is required–"

"The Wolves of Night found me first, little one, and my ... *education* took a deviating route. Anyway, my mom, she was a potion maker. Sold all sorts of crap to gullible non-magicals – some of which worked. I guess I learned some things before she kicked me out."

"She kicked you out? How old were you?"

He turns his gaze back to me. There's no emotion in his face now. He doesn't answer.

"I never knew my mom," I say, not sure why I'm telling him. "The only thing I knew about her was her name."

"You want to know more about her, don't you?"

I nod. I don't need to know how he knows that. He said before he's been watching me and now he seems to be best buddies with my pig too.

"What was her name?" he asks.

"Bronwyn."

He thinks for a moment, his heart still pounding, the rhythm of it crazy like the man himself.

"I only need a couple of drops. Nothing more. You can keep your hand right here," his gaze races up the length of my arm, "and if I try to kill you, you can kill me first. Fair?"

"Fair," I tell him. He reaches into his pocket with his free hand. "But Renzo?" His gaze flicks back to mine. "I warn you, I will do it."

"I know you will, little rabbit," he says brightly like I'm not threatening to end his life.

He pulls out my knife from his pocket and flicks up the blade as I offer him my free hand. He cradles it in his right, examining the lines that cross my palm and tracing them softly with his left forefinger.

"A drop," I remind him.

"Three," he counters, spinning the knife so the blade hovers above my palm.

"It was my dad's," I tell him.

"It's no ordinary knife," he whispers as he sinks the tip of the blade into my flesh. I wince, the skin splitting and bright red blood rushing to meet the blade.

"So pretty," he says, tossing the knife to the ground and reaching into his pocket a second time, this time pulling out a small bottle. He yanks off the cork stopper with his teeth. "May hurt," he whispers, squeezing my hand and encouraging more blood to rush to the surface. He tips my hand and lets the blood run over my palm and into the neck of the waiting bottle. I watch as the scarlet races down the glass, pooling at the bottom, his heart pounding even more chaotically. Then he stoppers the bottle and slides it carefully back into his pocket.

We're done. He has what he needs.

But he doesn't release my hand, instead he lifts it to his mouth, and, before I can stop him, he licks his tongue across my palm.

"Shit, you taste so good, little rabbit."

He sucks, drawing more of my blood into his mouth, groaning as he does, and I should be horrified, sickened, and yet I'm not. The bond in my stomach hums with contentment and my magic glides through my body.

"I can taste it, that magic of yours," he whispers against my palm, kissing it softly and then removing his mouth.

The cut is gone, healed – the only sign of it is the scarlet stain on his lips. He licks them, grinning at me again.

I give him a little zap of my magic as a warning. "I didn't say you could do that."

"Yeah, but I did it anyway."

He looks at me hungrily, like he'd like to taste me in other places too, and a shiver of desire skirts through my body unbidden.

This has gone too far. It's dangerous, really dangerous, and incredibly stupid too.

"You have your blood," I say. "You have what you need."

"I have the blood," he agrees, "but I don't have what I need."

I take a decided step away from him. "You should go, before someone comes looking for me, before they find you here."

His shoulders sag. He looks like a kid who just had his favorite toy snatched away. The sensation in my stomach strains towards him.

"Can I come see you again, little rabbit?"

My hand's still stretched towards him, ready to shoot magic at him if I need to. The hand by my side, balls into a fist, my nails pinching deep into my skin.

"No. No, I don't think that would be a good idea."

He nods, bending down to pick up my knife. "It's mine now," he tells me.

"Yes, I know." I say, but before I've finished the words, he's gone, vanished right in front of my eyes.

25

R^{hi}

PIP SQUEAKS at me all the way back through the forest and to our dorm.

"I don't know what you're trying to tell me but what just happened was entirely your fault," I tell him as I unlock our bedroom door. "You led me straight to him. You do remember who he is, right?"

I swear Pip actually rolls his eyes at me before trotting inside.

"Are you two arguing again?" Winnie asks, looking up from where she's scrolling on her phone on the bed.

"Do pigs go through a teenage period because I swear ..."

"Was he humping stuff again?" Winnie asks, shaking her head at Pip.

"Humping stuff? No! Ewww!" I drop down on the bed next to Winnie. "Has he really been doing that?"

"No, but it's what teenagers do."

Pip snorts at us both in a dignified manner and flops onto his bed.

"God," Winnie says, shaking her head. "Have you seen all the things people have been posting about Spencer? Like he really did die."

"Nope," I say.

Winnie shakes her head and continues to read. I chew on my lip.

I said no more secrets, but somehow I can't bring myself to tell her about the encounter I just had with the assassin who is meant to be trying to kill me. I'm not sure I'll be able to tell Stone or Azlan either. They are all going to kill me – which is pretty ironic considering Barone didn't.

I leave Winnie to her scrolling and go check my own phone. There's one message from Azlan earlier today in reply to mine thanking him for the gifts. He reminds me I can send him those images through the bond and tells me he loves me.

I read the words and read them again. They seem so innocent on the screen of my phone but also so important and so fundamental. Azlan loves me and somehow it makes all the other worries I'm harboring – about Spencer, about Tristan, and Renzo Barone and the Wolves of Night – dissolve away.

Dissolve away until the very next morning when I open our bedroom door, ready to head to class and find one large man towering the other side of the door.

For one fleeting moment, I think it must be Renzo again, back for another visit, but then my eyes focus properly and I almost do a double take.

Tristan Kennedy. Here. In our dorm building. Outside our room. In broad daylight.

"What the hell?" Winnie says, obviously as surprised as I am.

We both stare up at him. Whatever this is, it can't be good.

Tristan, however, simply stares back at us, combing his hand through his golden hair in a way I'm sure has half the school swooning.

"What do you ... why are you here, Tristan?"

"To walk you to class," he tells me, holding out his hands and motioning to the books I'm carrying.

"What?" Has the principal insisted I require an escort? Has news of Barone's visit got out? Or with his buddy gone, is Tristan hoping to find new ways of entertaining himself? Most likely torturing me.

"I've come to walk you to class and carry your books."

"Why?" Winnie says, narrowing her eyes.

"I'm trying to be nice," he says and if I didn't know Tristan Kennedy, I'd almost believe he looks a tad – a tiny bit – sheepish.

Winnie and I look at each other. "Nice?" we say together.

"Can we talk alone?" Tristan says in irritation, attempting to take my arm.

"No," I say, yanking my arm from his grasp. "I don't need you to be nice to me. I need you to leave me alone."

"Not going to happen," he says.

"You're failing at the nice thing," Winnie informs him. "You're being a jerk."

"Just give me your books," he says to me.

"No," I say to him, then linking my arm through Winnie's, I pull her out of the dorm.

"Well, that was weird," Winnie says, as we hurry down

the path towards the Great Hall, and I avoid the temptation to peer over my shoulder and see if Tristan's following us. "You think Spencer going has sparked a sudden surge of conscience in him?"

I shake my head. "He ... we ..."

Winnie stops in her tracks and spins me around to face her. Peering around us first, she then leans in. "You what?"

I swallow, my cheeks heating. "Kissed?"

Winnie takes a large inhale and I know she's going to screech something so loud half the school will hear. I slap my hand over her mouth. Her eyes bulge. "Mhen?" she mumbles.

"What?"

She harrumphs and pushes my hand away from her mouth. "When?"

"Out in the meadow. In Johnson's lesson."

"And you're only telling me now?"

"There's been a lot going on," I say, my even bigger secret suddenly feeling very heavy in my chest. "I'm sorry."

"It's okay ... I'm just struggling to keep up with your love life here, Rhi."

"Erm, tell me about it."

Winnie pinches me. "Don't do that. You are living practically every person in this academy's fantasy right now – probably including the principal. The man in black. Stone. TRISTAN!"

"Tristan is an asshole. A jerk. A terrible, terrible person who has done terrible, terrible things to me."

"Like kiss you? Was he a bad kisser? I can't imagine Tristan Kennedy being a bad kisser, but maybe he's all show and no–"

"Not like kissing. Like throwing a bucket of cold water over my head so that the entire academy saw my tits!"

"Aaahhh," Winnie says. "But does this mean that he really is–"

I squeeze Winnie's arm and lower my voice even further. "He seems to think so and I'm guessing he's had some kind of change of heart – for the minute anyway – I doubt it will last."

"Jeez, for a magical who is meant to be so darn smart, he really is an idiot."

"He is. And I'm not interested."

"Really?" Winnie says, looking unsure. "Because I'm pretty certain that's what you said about Stone and–"

"Winnie," I cry, picking up my feet and storming in the direction of the mansion.

We join the back of the line as usual, expecting our dose of gloopy porridge. However, when we reach the front of the line today, the woman serving peers at my face, then a piece of paper pinned to the wall and says, "Are you Rhianna Blackwaters?"

"Yes," I reply, glancing at Winnie again. Don't tell me I've been assigned more kitchen duties.

"We were asked to save you this." She reaches down and pulls out a plate piled high with omelet, croissants, bagels and fruit. "He didn't know what you liked, so he told us to save a bit of everything."

"Who did?" I ask, my stomach rumbling loudly as I stare at all that good-looking food.

The woman leans forward. "Mr. Kennedy," she whispers.

I can't help it. My gaze automatically snaps towards his favored seat in the middle of the hall. He's leaning back in it, scrolling through his phone like he always does.

What the hell is going on with him today?

"It's okay," I say. "I'll stick with porridge."

"She will not," Winnie says, snatching the plate off the

counter and marching with it towards our seats before I can stop her.

"Winnie," I say when I finally catch up with her. "I don't want to accept anything from him."

"You're not turning down the first decent breakfast you've been served since you got here." She picks up the croissant, oozing with butter, and tears it in half. "And also, you're sharing it with me."

I slump into my seat. "I don't want to encourage him."

"I don't think someone like Tristan Kennedy needs encouragement."

"Winnie, you're meant to be on my side."

My friend lowers the croissant from her mouth. There's a big flake of pastry stuck to her lip but I decide not to tell her just yet.

"Rhi, I'm always on your side. I've always got your back. You don't want anything to do with Tristan Kennedy, that is fine by me. I agree with you, he's a jerk." She lowers her voice to a whisper. "But if he is another of your fated mates then–"

"I don't want to hear it."

"Okay, but we can at least enjoy the benefits while they last." She hands me the other half of the croissant and I sink my teeth into it. It tastes heavenly. I could get used to food like this.

WHAT I DON'T THINK I can get used to is Tristan Kennedy popping up left, right and center. He's there waiting for me outside the Great Hall after breakfast and outside each of my lessons too. At lunchtime, I'm once again treated to the best the canteen has to offer and then it's back to him offering to carry my books every five seconds. I spend most of the day ignoring him. Hoping he'll get the message.

He doesn't. He's back again the next day and the day after, despite the fact I'm giving him the cold shoulder and refusing to even acknowledge his existence, let alone talk to him.

Unfortunately, as much as I'm trying to ignore this situation, it's pretty damn obvious to everyone else. At first, Tristan just receives the odd, peculiar glance but soon the corridors are alive with whispering every time I come strolling along with Tristan in my wake. And if the entire school has noticed that also means that one person won't fail to have.

However, rather than confront me about it like she usually would, she steps up her campaign of intimidation. The bouncing bunnies are extra loud jogging past our room in the morning, talking in especially loud voices about how ugly, stupid and annoying I am. Whenever Tristan isn't there, I'm bashed into as I walk down corridors or along hallways, and twice I trip when someone sticks a leg out in front of my path. My gym kit goes missing, earning a lecture and reprimand from Coach, and Pip's food fails to be delivered like it usually is.

Tristan may think he's doing me a favor by accompanying me everywhere but the number of bruises on my body would definitely suggest otherwise.

My time in the locker room is definitely the worst. Summer doesn't seem to want Tristan knowing what she's up to but he can't follow me inside – although I get the impression he's severely tempted – so Summer and her buddies can strike without consequence. There's no more waterboarding or attempts to physically hurt me. It seems since I broke her nose, Summer is being a little more cautious with me. Or maybe she's simply scared I'll go crying to Tristan if she hurts me and Summer is definitely afraid of him.

By the end of the week, I'm seriously considering bunking off gym but Coach is one of the few teachers I really like at the academy and I'm not sure I could cope with another disappointed lecture from him. Ignoring Tristan, I steel myself for whatever Summer has waiting for me this morning.

I'm guessing it's bad because when I enter the locker room it's deadly quiet and one girl actually seems to be trembling.

Terrific. I consider turning right around but Summer's already in my face.

She's quite a bit taller than me and I don't like the way I have to tilt my head back to look up at her. It gives her a sense of superiority. Like she needed any more.

"If it isn't the school slut," she hisses at me.

I roll my eyes. Honestly? I may have gained some sexual experience since arriving at the academy – okay, quite a few sexual experiences (I haven't been able to help but sneak round to Stone's cabin nearly every night and despite his protests about being careful, he hasn't exactly been turning me away) – but Summer doesn't know that and it's not like she is the Virgin Mary herself.

"I wonder," she says, with a smile hovering on her lips that makes me nervous, "whether your new admirer is aware of just how big a slut you are." She peers over her shoulder at her posse of bouncing bunnies, all of whom nod in agreement. "I think we ought to tell him that you're cheating on him."

I decide to go with ignorance. It's worked well for me most times. Kind of.

"I don't know who you're talking about."

"Oh, I think you do. You've spun him around your little finger with some crafty sorcery but I don't think he knows the real you, Pig Girl. I don't think he knows what you're really like."

"Like I said. I don't know who you mean."

Aysha tuts from behind Summer like I'm stupid.

"I think we should tell him just what Cindy saw you doing last night." My blood runs cold. Last night? She can't have seen us, can she? I've been so careful. But if she did ...

"I ... I ..." I can't think of a damn excuse. Shit, why didn't we prepare for this. Have our cover stories ready. Stone is going to lose his job. Worse, we'll be hauled in front of the authorities and then ... I sway on my feet.

Summer's smile morphs into a predatory smirk.

"Sucking off that jock in the library."

"Wh-what?" I mutter, blinking at her. The library? A jock?

"And Chloe saw you earlier that same night disappearing into some computer-nerd's bedroom."

"I'm pretty sure it was her best-friend's boyfriend, Sum," Chloe calls out.

Summer shakes her head in feigned disgust. "You really are disgusting, Pig Girl. Because I definitely heard you bragging to your little friend about some threesome in the toilets."

"And there was that Andrew dude she let fuck her over his desk," Aysha pipes up.

"And I saw her with one of the drama dudes out in the meadow – fucking right there in the open for everyone to see."

I stand there and wait for them to finish. I couldn't care less what they say or think about me. As long as they don't start spreading rumors about me and a particular teacher, they can go right ahead and make up anything they want to.

However, Winnie obviously doesn't agree and is suitably outraged on my behalf.

"This is such a load of horse shit, Summer, and everyone will know it."

"Winnie Wence," Summer says all innocently, pressing her hands to her chest. "I'm so sorry to break the bad news to you about your friend and her back-stabbing, slutty ways."

"Are you slut-shaming her, Summer?"

Summer flicks her ponytail and lifts her chin. "Pig Girl can sleep with whoever she likes – if they're stupid enough to want to catch some disgusting swine disease that's their problem. But cheating? Two-timing? I think it's only fair people know. I don't want people getting hurt."

Is she for real? Didn't she tell me herself she was sleeping with Tristan *and* Spencer?

"You can tell whoever you like," I say. "I don't give a shit. It might actually do me a favor."

Summer clearly thinks I'm bluffing because the smirk cements more firmly on her face. But I'm not. Maybe if she tells Tristan all that stuff, it will put him off me. He's an arrogant hypocrite after all. When it comes to relationships, I can well believe he's happy to apply double standards – insisting his girlfriend is faithful while he fucks whoever he likes.

I push past Summer and head for my locker, finding once again my kit is missing, replaced by something that looks like a pig onesie.

"Are you sure you don't want to give her a giant A to hang around her neck instead?" Winne snaps at Summer, throwing the onesie towards the head cheerleader.

"What?" Summer says, brow crinkling.

Winnie shakes her head. "I had a feeling this might happen again," she whispers to me. "So this time I packed you spares. It's my old kit, so a little worn, but–"

"Better than another lecture. Thanks, Winnie. I don't know why I didn't think of this myself."

"Because your mind's been on other things," Winnie says, patting my shoulder.

I have to hand it to Summer and her bouncing bunnies, their gossip-spreading skills are pretty darn effective. In fact, I wonder if they use magic, because by the time I step into the gymnasium, everyone seems to be talking about my sexual exploits and Tristan is standing to one side looking glassy-eyed.

Okay, maybe this is damn annoying, but maybe it's going to be the answer to all my problems with Tristan Kennedy.

26

R^{hi}

THE NEXT MORNING, we're woken not by the obnoxious abuse of the bouncing bunnies but by excited chattering out in the corridors. I roll over, plucking my phone out from under my pillow and glance at the time.

"Shit, it's 7.30 already, Winnie!"

"What?" she says, yawning from the bed beneath me. "Did we actually sleep through the bouncing bunnies this morning?"

"Maybe," I say, sliding off my bunk. But when we head into the corridor, we understand exactly why there were no cheerleaders this morning. Pinned to our door are two official-looking envelopes, gilded text printed on the thick luxurious-looking paper.

"It's our invitations to the ball!" Winnie yelps, plucking them off the door and handing me mine.

"And this is exciting because ..." I ask, tearing open the envelope and sliding out the piece of card within. "We already know the date."

"This will have all the details," Winnie says, taking much more care to open her own envelope. "Oh, it's going to be in the Great Hall. Drinks and dancing, followed by a banquet, speeches, presentations, and then more dancing."

Winnie presses the invitation to her chest and closes her eyes. "This is going to be amazing."

"If you say so," I mutter.

"Do you remember how amazing all the decorations and magical displays were for Founders' Night, Rhi? That was nothing compared to what this is going to be like. It will be off the scale. We will most probably never get to go to a party like this one again in our whole entire lives."

I don't exactly remember Founders' Night being all that wonderful and as for the decorations and magical displays, apart from my own, I caught a glimpse of the ones in the Venus Common room and that was it. No one else in the communal bathroom seems as skeptical or underwhelmed as I do, though. Our dorm building buzzes with conversations about the ball. It's actually pretty infectious and means everyone has stopped talking about me and is now talking about the ball.

In fact, they talk about it all through breakfast and practical magic, and still have things to discuss as we stand in the gymnasium at the start of our lesson. Coach doesn't have time for gossiping, though. He tells everyone quite firmly to shut up and then takes us outside for combat training.

I peer at Winnie in excitement. With Spencer no longer here, there's no one to give me one-on-one sessions and I'm actually permitted to join the group.

We gather around Coach who explains the moves he wants us to practice in this session and then tells us to hurry up and pair up.

"Be careful pairing up with Pig Girl, boys. Rumor has it she's riddled with all sorts of sexually transmitted diseases."

"Clutton-Brock," Coach says fiercely, "zip it unless you want to miss this session and spend the lesson doing burpees instead."

Summer shakes her head and grabs Aysha's arm.

I look up at Winnie. "Can I be your partner?" I ask.

"God, yes," Winnie says, grabbing my arm. "I usually end up left with one of the huge dudes no one else wants to partner with."

"So I'm not the only one who's used to being thrown around mats."

"No, that's just you," Winnie says with a grin. "Because, I'm not half bad at this, Blackwaters."

She swings round to face me and squats down, clearly ready to charge.

"Winnie?" I say, a little nervously, before she comes bowling at me.

We tussle, both trying to take the other's legs out from underneath them, and soon I'm collapsing to the ground in a fit of giggles, Winnie leaping on top of me.

"You're not taking this seriously," she says.

"I can't help it," I tell her, going for the dirty move and tickling her under the armpits until she's giggling too.

Soon we're both rolling around in fits of laughter, that is until we look up to find Coach glaring down at us.

"You think this is funny?"

"No, Coach," we say in unison, both trying our best not to laugh.

"This is serious, girls. It's not a laughing matter," he says and Winnie lets out a snort.

"Right," he says, resting his hands on his hips, "if you can't act sensibly, I'm splitting you up." We both go to argue but he holds up his hand to silence us. "Wence, you go with Malik. And Blackwaters you can go with Clutton-Brock." I open my mouth to protest but he starts clapping his hands together. "Come on, hurry it up."

I slump off towards Summer, who's waiting for me on her mat with her arms folded across her chest and a look of delight plastered on her face. She obviously thinks this is her opportunity to beat the crap out of me, which is funny seeing as I was the one to break her nose last time we stood off against each other.

"Hey Pig Girl," she says, grinning evilly at me. "Want to show me what you've got?" She beckons at me with her fingers.

And oh my stars, I want to go right at her, knock her to the ground and batter her with my fists. But I know that's exactly what she wants me to do. If I go charging at her, she'll find a way to use my own momentum against me and I'll be the one on the floor being battered.

I adopt my best bored expression, taking a serious leaf out of Tristan Kennedy's book.

"Not really," I say.

"Oh," she says, pouting her lip. "Is the lickle piggie wiggie scared? I'm not surprised, you look like you'd fall over if the wind blew hard. There's nothing to you." She pushes out her impressive tits as if to emphasize her point.

I can't help peeking down at my body. Maybe that assessment of hers would have been accurate a few months back, but I'm not as skinny as I used to be. There's more to me now and quite a bit of it is muscle on account of all these gym classes.

"How's the nose, Summer? Have you finally gotten it straight?"

"My nose is just fine. But yours could use a serious rearrangement, it would improve your face. In fact, I'm not sure why you bothered changing the snout I gave you. It looked much better than that honker of yours." She sniggers at her own joke and I really hate this girl.

"Girls!" Coach yells at us from the other side of the hall. "Stop yacking and start practicing." We glare at each other, neither one willing to back down and Coach comes marching our way. "Blackwaters, you're seriously trying my patience today." Summer smirks. "And you too, Clutton-Brock," he whips. "Stop talking and start fighting. Clutton-Brock show me a shoulder throw."

Summer positively beams and stalks towards me. I take a pace away from her. There's no way I'm letting her do that to me. This girl has pushed me around one too many times.

Coach throws his hands up in frustration with me. "How are either of you meant to learn, if you won't let each other practice?"

"I'll let Winnie practice on me," I say, turning towards him. Summer takes her chance, lunging towards me, attempting to sweep my feet from under me. But I see her coming and twist my body, we collide together, both grappling at each other's shirts, trying to pull the other to the ground.

"Enough!" Coach yells. "Out, both of you out." He grabs both of us by the upper arm and marches us out of the gym doors and onto the dueling pitch. "Right, I want three laps of the academy grounds."

"Three!" Summer whines.

"Three. And don't think I can't tell if you don't run the course properly." He releases us both and taps the side of his head. "I have ways of knowing. Now off! I don't want to see either of you again until you're out of breath, drenched in sweat, and begging my forgiveness. Go!"

To my surprise, Summer doesn't argue like she usually would. Perhaps she understands Coach well enough to know there's no point. She's kicking up her heels and sprinting off before I know it.

"Blackwaters!" Coach growls, and reluctantly I race after Summer. I hate to admit that Summer is better than me at anything, but when it comes to running she is. She's much taller than me, her legs stretching on for miles, and she can run a hell of a lot faster. I try to keep up with her just on account of my own pride, but soon she disappears into the distant trees and I'm left with only the pounding of my feet and the thudding of my heart for company.

The day is overcast, the weather changing now, the odd crimson leaf twirling down from the branches and overhead geese flying in formation across the gray sky. It reminds me of home. Of the changing season. Right now, we'd be pickling and canning the vegetables and fruit we picked a month ago.

A homesickness tugs at my heart and I realize it's been days, maybe weeks now since I experienced a pang like that. The academy seems more and more like home. Or maybe not the academy but the people – Winnie, Trent, Stone, Azlan.

Maybe it's not home then that I miss, maybe it's my aunt. My emotions about her have become confused. The more I learn about my past, about my mom, the more I feel resentment towards my aunt. Why did she never tell me these things? Why did she leave me so ignorant and exposed? But those feelings are always followed by guilt. She did her best. She worked hard every day to keep me safe.

I do miss her. I love Winnie to bits. I even appreciated the advice her grandma gave me on our brief visit. But it isn't the same as my aunt. I wonder what she'd make of my situation. I wonder what she'd think of the two men that are my mates. I wonder what she'd think of those other men too. I don't remember her ever having a special person in her life – a man or a woman. Another sacrifice she made for me.

The crisp, fallen leaves crunch under my soles as I run beneath the changing trees and into shadow, lost in my thoughts.

So lost I don't see her coming for me.

27

———

R^{hi}

THIS TIME she succeeds in knocking me off my feet, swinging a branch at me and smacking my legs from under me. I lift my hands ready to defend myself, ready for her to jump on me. But she's not stupid enough to make that mistake again. I guess she treasures her nose too much.

Instead, I feel the chain of my necklace catch at my neck. I try to grab at it, but it snaps and my locket flies from my neck and into Summer's waiting hands.

I roll up onto my backside and scowl at her. She's so fucking petty. I can't believe we're actually going to do this. And yet I can. I have something Summer desperately, desperately wants. Tristan Kennedy's attention.

"If this is about Tristan ..." I say.

"It's not," she says, her voice a little shrill. The girl may be an amazing cheerleader but she's a really shitty actress.

"I don't want to fight over some boy. He's all yours and you are welcome to him."

"It's not about Tristan Kennedy," she snaps.

"Then seriously, Summer, what is your problem?" I watch as she twirls my necklace around her fingers. I'm going to try and reason with her and if that doesn't work I'm going to give her what's coming to her. I am so sick of this girl.

"What is my problem?" she mocks, holding up my necklace and letting the locket twist one way and then the other. "You. You're my problem, Pig Girl."

"But why?" I ask, feeling anger and exasperation boil in my gut. "What have I ever actually done to you?"

Her eyes flash. "Except break my nose."

"Summer, you turned my nose into a snout!" A nose for a nose. It seems pretty fair.

"But it's not just that. It's your existence. Your presence. I don't like the way you look, or the way you act and I definitely don't like the way you smell."

To be honest, she has me there. I've just sprinted around half the campus. The sweat is running down my face and soaking into my top. I'm sure I do smell pretty awful.

I climb up onto my feet, brushing dead leaves off my body.

"Okay, so you don't like me. So can we please just call this quits? I'm more than happy to ignore you, go out of my way not to look at you, or talk to you ever again, if you agree to do the same." I hold out my hand. "Just give me back my necklace." I bet Coach is timing our laps. If he doesn't see us sprinting past the gym soon, he's going to come looking for us and he's already lost his patience twice with me today. I'm trying to stay out of trouble, not wander straight into it.

She twirls my necklace around her fingers and grips the locket tightly.

"Most of all I don't like the way you capture so much of everyone's freaking attention. I don't like the way people look at you, talk about you–"

"They're only talking about me because you spread all those stupid stories."

She smiles sweetly, the smile I often see her use on Dr. Johnson. "I don't know what you're talking about."

"Before those rumors, most people didn't even know I existed!"

"But *he* did!" she yells. Her cheeks swamping with color as soon as the words have left her mouth.

"It's not my fault if he's looking at me and not you Summer. Take it up with him."

"It is your fault. I know you've done something, something to bewitch him." She shakes the locket at me. "Something like a love charm. Something like this." She laughs. "You're so pathetic, Pig Girl. Did you actually think he wouldn't work that out?"

"Give it back, Summer."

"No fucking way."

"It isn't a love charm. If I actually wanted to seduce him, wouldn't I be with him? Instead of rebuffing him every chance I've had? Think logically, why would I use a love charm on him then ignore all his advances. I am not interested in being with Tristan Kennedy. Not one little bit."

She jerks, thinking about this. Realizing most probably that I'm right. Then she shakes her head. "You're playing hard to get. You want everyone to believe you're too good for Tristan Kennedy." She scoffs. "You're deluded."

"It's not a love charm, Summer."

"I can feel it's magic, Pig Girl. I know it is. I'm going to show it to him. Tell him what you've been doing." She stares at the locket and I see the very moment a thought occurs to her, something glints in her eyes.

"It's a cloaker," I say. "And it belonged to my mom. Give it back."

"No, I'm keeping it." She grins at me and hooks the chain around her neck and I see instantly she's changed her mind. She has no intention of telling Tristan her theory about this love charm. No, she's going to try and use it for herself.

I'd be laughing. Or perhaps letting her trot off with her new toy while sniggering behind her back. But that locket is mine. Apart from Pip, it's the only connection I have to my aunt, to my home, to my family, to my mom. I want it back.

"Give it back," I growl, feeling that dark magic curling inside me.

"No," she says simply, staring at me with defiance.

"God help me, Summer, if you don't–" I lift my hand, the sinister magic sizzles at my fingertips, making me dark, dark promises.

"You'll what? Blast me? Come on then, Pig Girl. You're always threatening to do it and I've been waiting all this time for you to try."

And I can't take any more of this, any more of her. The sight of my aunt's necklace around her neck is too much. She can call me names, spread rumors about me, even push me around, but I have so little and she has everything she's ever wanted. And yet, she has to take the one thing that's precious to me. And then something occurs to me. This isn't the first time she's taken something precious of mine. I growl right in the back of my throat, convinced more than ever it was her.

"Did you take my pig?"

"Your pig?" Her eyes dance with amusement and she

laughs. "Take it? I was trying to get rid of it. This school is no place for a smelly pig. I told you that the very day we met. I told you then to get rid of it."

"You bitch!" I cry and I'm flinging that dark magic at her before I even realize what I'm doing.

Summer ducks, the magic shooting over her head and crashing into the trunk of a tree behind her. Immediately the tree is enveloped in a darkness that crawls across its bark, hissing like it's burning it alive, and the tree shrivels before our eyes.

I stand staring at it in shock, too stunned to attempt blasting Summer a second time.

"What the fuck?" Summer says, her head snapping back to me. "Oh, you are so dead, Pig Girl, so dead."

She sprints away, my necklace still around her neck, but my eyes are locked to the tree and I'm too shocked to care.

I watch as my magic envelops more and more of the tree, streaking up the trunk and branches, turning everything rotten like some all-consuming disease. The tree groans, sways and I step back as it crashes in on itself, dissolving and shriveling until all that remains is a pile of ash.

I peer down at my fingertips. No longer sizzling, stone cold now. A frigid fear spreads up my hand and through my body.

Did I do that?

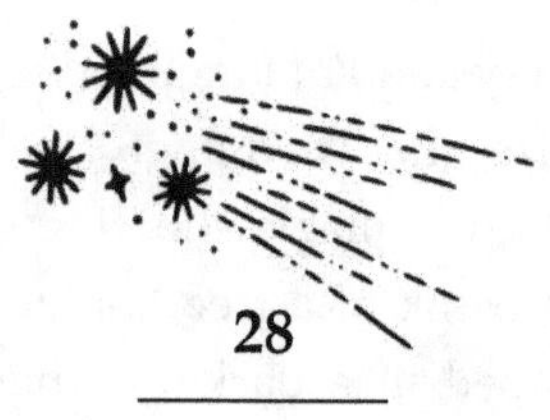

28

S tone

"BLACKWATERS!" I snap as she comes strolling into my classroom like nothing out of the ordinary is going on. "A word! The rest of you, open your books and start reading."

I march towards my office at the back of the classroom as all the other students watch us, open-mouthed. Yeah, this probably wasn't one of my best ideas. But shit …

Somehow I've managed to keep my hands off her for this past week (during the daytime anyway – the little minx has been sneaking to my cabin most evenings). But goddamn it, it hasn't been easy. I've been half hard most lessons, my bond shimmering so violently, there have been several occasions I've been this close to ordering all the other students out of the classroom just so I can bend her over my desk and fuck her.

And now this …

I wait for her to follow me into the office, her hips swaying and her ass jiggling in that way that has me almost falling to my knees. Then I slam shut the door, and wave my arms, sealing the office with an impregnable spell.

"Is this wise?" she asks, folding her arms over her chest and drawing my gaze straight to the neck of her blouse. Stars! "There are already several rumors circulating about my sexual reputation and inviting me into your office alone may trigger a whole load more. A whole load more that would be far nearer to the truth," she adds, her mouth twitching.

"What the hell is going on? Why are people saying this crap about you?"

"So you don't believe them, then?" Her arms loosen. "I was expecting an interrogation here about my sex life."

"Blackwaters, I've seen inside your head. I know all about your sex life."

"Maybe I'm smarter than you think. Maybe I've been feeding you exactly what I want you to see."

I smirk at her. "You're not and I have been dominating a considerable amount of your sex life. I'm quite confident that, apart from Azlan who is currently away in the West, there is no one else."

I close the gap between us and she takes a hold of the collar of my shirt. "You're very sure of yourself, Professor."

"I am, although ..."

"Although?"

"I was a little hurt when I heard you'd sucked off the entire dueling team and yet I haven't had that honor."

She trails her little hands down my chest, all the way down to the waistband of my pants, and now I'm completely hard.

"An honor, huh?"

I brush the hair away from her ear and lean in to whisper. "It would be an honor to come in that pretty mouth of yours, Blackwaters. To make you choke on it, to watch you gulp it all down. In fact, there's nothing I'd like more than for you to sink to your knees right here and now and let me fuck your mouth."

She shivers so hard, it takes every bit of willpower not to push her onto her knees.

This girl has warped my mind, scrambled all my common sense, bent my good nature. There's a classroom full of students out there already spreading salacious rumors about my little mate. Do I want to make things worse? Do I want our relationship to come to light and the chancellor's spotlight to swing our way? No, it's too dangerous. Far too dangerous.

I swallow.

"Tonight," I whisper, because I'm fucking weak for her and I can't resist her. "You'll come tonight?"

She whimpers a little and I can feel through the bond how difficult she's going to find the wait. Yeah, she's not the only one.

I unhook her hands from my shirt. "What prompted this wave of crap?" I ask.

"The rumors?" She rolls her eyes. "Who do you think? Summer."

I frown. I've been considering just how to deal with that little bitch. I'm going to have to be subtle about it because anything less than that will have the pain in our asses telling tales to her daddy and the last thing I need is Clutton-Brock breathing down my neck.

I kiss Rhi's mouth and then nudge her towards the door.

"Later," I tell her. She hesitates. "Miss Blackwaters ..." Then I sense the anxiety in her mind. "What's wrong?"

"Something happened."

She looks frightened and I take her hands in mine, my eyes crisscrossing her face.

"Are you okay? Hurt?"

"I'm fine."

I nod. "Then we'll talk about it tonight, okay?" I say, kissing her forehead.

Back in the classroom, I find a little satisfaction in directing all my most challenging questions on the topic of advanced alchemy directly at Summer herself. Usually, the girl adores the limelight, gloating because she thinks she knows more and is better than everyone else. It's pretty amusing to watch her squirm on her seat, unable to answer my questions.

I take even more satisfaction in rolling my eyes and tutting at her, communicating just how stupid I think she is.

"Really, Miss Clutton-Brock, this is pretty basic stuff." Winnie Wence frowns. She clearly knows it's not. "I thought you were smarter than this."

"I am. It's just–"

"Clearly, not." I nod with a feigned look of sympathy on my face. Rhi hides a smile behind her hand as Summer's face drops in dismay. "But not to worry, I will set you some additional homework which will help you to catch up."

I wave my hand and an assignment drops onto her desk. Summer picks it up, her eyes scanning over the three pages.

"But this will take me–"

"You can have it on my desk by tomorrow morning."

"I have cheerleading practice this evening!"

"Then I suspect you'll be having a late night," I say, glaring at her with such venom she sinks in her chair. That should keep the nasty piece of work busy and prevent her from spying on Rhi.

At the end of the lesson, Summer comes marching up to my desk, waving the assignment at me. I lumber up to my feet with a yawn, noticing as I do that Tristan Kennedy is loitering outside my classroom door, attempting to talk to my mate. That's the fifth time this week.

I snatch my gaze back to Summer.

"How can I help you, Miss Clutton-Brock?" I ask, folding my arms over my chest and perching on the edge of my desk.

"This isn't fair. Why am I the only one you've set homework for?"

"Because you are the only one who showed a distinct lack of apprehension and aptitude for the subject."

The girl flushes.

"That's not ..."

I look gravely at her. "I'm afraid it is. You're slipping behind. Perhaps your position as head cheerleader is interfering with your studies. Perhaps I ought to have a word with Principal York."

"No!" the girl cries, snatching the paper to her chest. "I can catch up. I can have this assignment done by tomorrow, I promise."

"I thought so." I smile and she starts to stuff the paper into her bag. "And Miss Clutton-Brock?"

She peers up at me. "Yes, Professor?"

"I've heard rumors that some members of the dueling and cheerleading squads think it appropriate to demand other students do their homework for them." Her cheeks burn and she's no longer able to meet my eye. "Of course, you wouldn't be one of those students, would you?" She shakes her head slowly. "Because I am one of those teachers who would know."

The girl is fairly efficient at shielding her thoughts, but

nothing I can't easily bypass. It's not usually something I have a desire to do. The girl is vain, cruel and really damn boring. Wading through her mind makes me feel dirty.

Today, I make an exception. What I find is a mind stewing in jealousy.

29

R^{hi}

I REGRET NOT TAKING the chance to tell Stone about the crimson magic when I had the chance. I'm a jumpy wreck, waiting for a heavy hand to land on my shoulder and lead me away. Summer isn't going to keep a secret like this. She'll use it to her advantage, and as her goal has always been to rid the academy of me, she'll be straight to York with tales of crimson magic. And how can I even deny it, the pile of ash where that tree once stood is solid proof?

No, I should have told Stone. If I'm arrested, or taken in, or whatever the hell they might do to me, then I'm putting Stone and the man in black at risk too.

I join the back of the line at lunchtime in a daze, my feet shuffling forward without my awareness, and the words Winnie's speaking floating right over my head.

If I'm honest, I know why I didn't tell Phoenix. Because I

am afraid. Afraid if he knows the truth about me, what I'm capable of, he'll look at me differently. He will regret bonding to me.

I gaze down at my hands again. What the hell *am* I capable of? I don't even know. But I don't think it's good. Certainly, Tristan, Spencer, and now Summer, too, seem to think it's bad.

At the front of the line, the lunch lady hands me my usual dish of impressive lunch choices, everyone around me glaring as they're served the crappy leftovers.

I stare down at my tray and inwardly groan.

It's clear Summer's master plan may be causing the entire school to gossip about me but it hasn't had the desired impact she wants when it comes to Tristan. For once, I'm probably as disappointed as she is.

I try to pass the tray back, but Winnie snatches it off me and carries it over to our usual seat.

"By taking that, I'm only making more enemies," I tell her. "Did you not see all those death stares?"

"It's not like we're popular, Rhi. We don't have tons of friends to lose. So what if a few idiots are jealous about our mealtime bonus? They should take that up with the school, not us."

She pinches a sausage from the plate and takes a big bite. A bite she's soon choking on as her eyes alight on something behind my head. I remember my first breakfast in the hall and for a moment, I think it's Stone towering behind me. Maybe he's heard what happened with Summer after all and is here to confront me.

My bond strains towards him. My cheeks heat of their own accord. Only the sensation in my gut is much stronger whenever Stone's near now we're bonded. And this is ... this is ...

I grimace.

This is Tristan.

"Rhianna."

I consider ignoring him, pretending I haven't heard his voice, but Winnie's eyes are practically bulging out of her head and I realize the Great Hall has fallen deathly silent. So silent, I can hear his breath behind me and there's no way I can pretend I haven't heard when he says, for a second time, this time louder, my name ringing around the huge, cavernous space, "Rhianna."

Steeling myself, I spin around on my seat and peer up at him. I almost double-take. He looks different. Somehow even more handsome than he usually does. His hair combed back from his face, his cheeks shaven smooth, his tie neatly knotted. Shit, I think his shoes may even have been polished.

What the hell is going on?

"Y-yes?" I whisper tersely, aware every person in this hall is staring at us. In fact, some have risen from their seats, necks craning just to get a better view. They're straining to hear every word between us too.

Before I have a chance to snatch them away, he takes my hands in his and tugs me to my feet.

A murmur ripples through the hall, people whispering to each other. The tension is palpable.

Tristan Kennedy never ventures anywhere near this section of the Great Hall. Why would he when his place is right in the center with the other popular kids? But here he is among us dweebs, dorks and losers and now he's actually holding hands with one. And not just anyone. Pig Girl herself. No wonder there isn't a person in the hall capable of dragging their eyes away from us.

"What are you doing?" I hiss, attempting to jerk my

hands away from his despite the electricity skating between us.

"Rhianna Blackwaters," he says, holding my gaze, projecting his voice so that every damn person in the hall can hear him. I wince, waiting for whatever verbal or physical blow is coming my way. Maybe Summer's plan worked after all. Maybe he's going to call me a slut in front of the whole school or start a new rumor of his own. Or maybe he's going to accuse me of bewitching him. "Would you do me the honor of accompanying me to the victory ball next Friday? Would you do me the honor of being my date for the evening?"

There are audible gasps all around the hall. One I'm pretty sure comes straight out of my own mouth, and one from Winnie's too.

I glance at my best friend. She's so shocked the sausage she was eating is still hanging from her mouth.

"Rhianna?" Tristan says and I look back his way. Is he for real? Or is this some kind of stupid joke?

Someone in the hall obviously seems to think so because a loud reel of laughter cuts through the whispering.

Summer.

She stumbles from her seat, clutching her stomach, laughing as loud as she can. Soon all the bouncing bunnies and half the dueling team are cackling too, obviously convinced this must be some kind of joke.

Tristan frowns, an expression that grows steelier as the laughter ripples across the hall.

I scowl at him, and keeping a tight hold of his hands, march out of the hall, dragging him behind me, everyone watching us go.

Summer yells out after us, "That was so freaking funny!" as we push through the doors.

"What the hell are you doing?" I hiss at him as soon as we make it out into the corridor away from all the prying eyes and ears.

"Asking you to the ball," he says simply, like that isn't the craziest thing he's probably ever done in his whole entire life. Ask *me* out? In front of the entire school?

I stare at him in exasperation. "Will you just cut this out – the following me around, the attempts to carry my books, the food and now this! Just cut all of it out, Tristan."

"I tell you what. I'll cut it out if you actually stop and talk to me."

"No," I say. "Nope. No way." I wrestle my hands free of his and start to walk away from him. I don't owe Tristan Kennedy anything, least of all my attention, even if my body has different ideas about that and wants to give him every ounce of my attention.

"You're being stubborn about this," he says in that infuriatingly bored voice.

I spin around, ready to give him both freaking barrels. But suddenly the hallway is bustling with students – most, I'm sure, have deliberately followed us out here – eyeing us eagerly like we're about to start sparring. I don't want to fuel the gossip train more than I already have this week.

I step towards the nearest empty classroom and motion for Tristan to follow me. Once inside, he shuts and locks the door, blocking the doorway with his huge frame, and I decide this is another one of my stupid ideas. I glare at him, thrusting my finger in his direction.

"I'm being stubborn!" I hiss at him. "Tristan Kennedy, just be thankful I'm not being something a whole lot worse because frankly you fucking well deserve it!"

That mask of nonchalance flickers and I see a brief

glimpse of anger in his eyes. It lasts just a fleeting moment and then he's smiling at me lazily.

"Why? Why do I deserve it?"

"For the way you've treated me."

"And how have I treated you? No differently to every other girl in this academy."

"Bullshit!"

"You're angry because I didn't welcome you with open arms. Because I didn't drop at your feet and kiss your toes. Because I didn't confess undying love for you from the moment I first laid eyes on you." He snorts. "Let me tell you something, Blackwaters, you've read too many girlie kissing books. It isn't how things work in real life."

"No, it's not because of that," I say. "It's because you treated me like crap."

"Did you treat me any better?"

"Did you give me a chance?"

He leans back against the door, folding his arms across his chest. "Just because my cousin–"

"This has nothing to do with him."

He shakes the hair that's fallen into his face and looks at me. "Did you think that there was any way that I'd be pleased about this, Piggie? Did you think I'd be happy that my fated mate is a nobody, a no one." He chuckles. "A fucking *unregistered*. You saw how my family reacted with Azlan. Well, he was already a lost cause. He's not the Kennedy heir. The one they're all pinning their fucking hopes on. You know how fucking angry they're going to be about this?"

Maybe those words hurt me weeks ago. Maybe they made my heart ache. But I've heard them so often from everyone around me, they hardly penetrate at all anymore. Hardly.

"If that is the case, then what the hell is this week all about, Tristan? Why the hell are you asking me to the ball? Nothing's changed. I'm still me. Still an unregistered girl from the wastelands. Still a nobody. Your family hasn't had some epiphany and forgiven all my sins. They're still going to disown you if you ... if you ..."

"Seal the bond," he says so lowly it makes my knees tremble.

His eyes brighten and the bond in my stomach shimmers at the idea of it.

I dig my nails deep into the palms of my hands until I'm wincing with the pain and force the idea away. Every word I just said is true.

He straightens up and takes a step towards me, ducking his head so our eyes are level.

"Piglet," he says, with something that almost sounds like affection, "I'm not saying it makes any sense. What I'm saying is that the way I feel about you has changed. I don't care about all those things now. My family, this school, the whole fucking country. I don't care what they think. I want you. I want to make you mine."

I shake my head. I'm so damned confused. His words are tying me up in knots. He must be lying to me. There's no way what he's saying can be true. Actions speak louder than words and his actions tell me everything I need to know.

Damn the bond. Damn the way he makes my legs tremble and my pulse flutter.

Spencer. Barone. Tristan. The things they've done. The way they've treated me. I shouldn't want them anywhere near me.

"It's too late, Tristan–"

"It isn't–"

I hold up my hand. "It is. I deserve better than you.

Better than someone who couldn't look past the end of his own privileged nose and see me for who I really am and not what he thought I was. So just leave me alone, okay?"

He straightens up, his jaw hardening.

"I can't do that."

"You're going to have to," I tell him, pushing past him to reach the door and ignoring the way his magic tingles against my skin as I do.

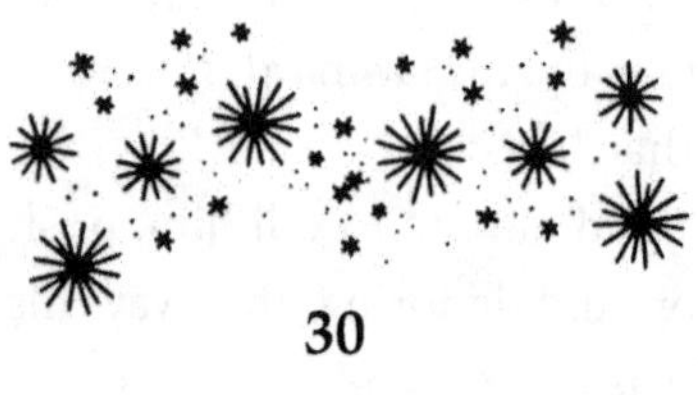

30

R^{hi}

WINNIE SPOTS me as I come marching out into the corridor and squeezes her way through the swarms of students to reach my side.

"Are you okay?" she asks, hooking her arm through mine.

"Oh, you know, just dandy," I tell her.

She looks at my face, and then at all the people hovering around us, clearly desperate to listen in to our conversation. "Wanna go somewhere quiet and talk?"

"And be late for battle strategy and theory?"

Winnie grimaces and I know exactly what she's thinking.

Summer's in that class with us.

Tristan's attention to me has sent her skating right to the very edge. But this? This will finally push her right over.

Everyone in the school knows Tristan should have asked her. With Spencer gone, he'll obviously be made captain of the dueling team. And when it comes to dances and balls and shit like that the captain of the sports team always takes the head cheerleader. It's written into some kind of hot-girl law.

But he didn't ask her, he asked me. The girl everyone hates. The girl everyone despises. Especially Summer Clutton-Brock.

It's a bitter, bitter pill for her to swallow. One she'll choke on, and spit up in my face. Yep, she's going to make my life a living hell. And she'll start by telling on me.

"We could skip it," Winnie suggests a little unsurely, "or claim we both have cramps."

"Both of us? At the same time?"

"It's known that roomies sync their cycles."

"Yeah, I'm sure old Professor Browne knows all about that," I say, rolling my eyes. "No, the gossip is going to happen whether I'm there or not. I'm not ashamed or embarrassed ... or scared," I add. Although, I'm not sure that's true. I may not be scared of Summer but I am scared of what's coming my way. For a moment, I consider if Winnie's plan is a better one. If I should claim a cramp and go find Stone.

Winnie peers at me from the corner of her eyes. "What happened?"

"What do you mean?" I say, my stomach twisting.

"After you left the hall," she whispers.

I shrug. "He wants to take me to the ball."

"Because ..." she prompts.

"I'm hot and gorgeous and irresistible, obviously," I say sarcastically.

"Obviously," Winnie says, grinning, "I've been telling

you that for weeks. So Tristan Kennedy has a crush on you, gee whiz, Rhi!"

"Gee whiz?" I laugh.

"So what did you say?"

"What did I say?! No, obviously!"

"No?!" Winnie cries, several heads snapping our way.

"Shush," I hiss. "Of course, no. He's treated me like shit and–"

"He's Tristan Kennedy and he asked you to the ball."

"I don't care who he is, Winnie. Would you really have said yes in my position?"

Winnie thinks about this. Then shakes her head. "I'd have been scared half to death though – I doubt someone like Tristan enjoys hearing the word no – but I would have turned him down."

"Exactly," I say.

I'm sure most of the school will consider me even more insane than they already did, but to me this is one of the most logical decisions I've made. However, Winnie is right. Tristan is unlikely to pay any notice to the word no. I'm not sure what that means. Some of his words come floating back into my mind and the bond in my belly aches uneasily. I don't like keeping secrets from my best friend, and while there are some I'm too petrified to admit to myself, let alone her, this one I need to tell her.

"Winnie," I say, leaning in close to her as we approach the classroom, aware of all the other students listening to us on the path, "me being gorgeous and amazing isn't really the reason he asked me out."

"Huh?"

"The reason he wants to take me to the ball." Winnie stops and turns to look me in the eye. "He feels it too." I lower my voice so low I hardly hear my own words. "The pull."

For once, she doesn't look shocked by my piece of news. No blinking, no paling, no wavering on her feet. In fact, she nods like she was half expecting me to say this. "I figured as much."

"How?" I say.

"The kissing. The way he's been acting. Tristan Kennedy has never shown any interest in anyone or anything before. It had to be more than just a crush."

"Yeah," I say, because didn't he say so himself? This is all fate's doing. I'm not the girl *he'd* choose.

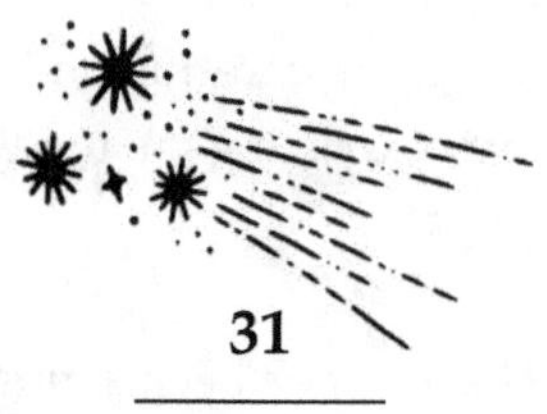

31

T ristan

I'M FUCKING THIS UP. I never fuck up. I've been a straight A-student, top of my year, award-winning athlete, all my life. I've never failed at anything. I've always succeeded in whatever I set out to achieve and I've always got exactly what I wanted.

And what I want right now more than anything is Rhianna fucking Blackwaters.

I sink onto the nearest desk, scrubbing my hand down my face. This shouldn't be this hard. She's my mate. Okay, so she's bonded to my cousin, but that isn't unheard of. It shouldn't stop her from falling at my feet. Falling into my arms. Falling into my bed. Right where I want her.

I scrub my hand more firmly over my face, the family ring on my finger catching against my skin. I flip my hand over and look at the family crest carved into the gold surface.

She's right. It shouldn't have mattered what they thought. I shouldn't have cared what anyone thought. Well, I don't any more. I know what's coming my way. It's only a matter of time before my father hears about my interest in the girl and I'm summoned to speak with him. And I don't give a fuck. I'm more afraid of never having her than I am of facing him.

I snatch the ring from my finger. He can summon me all he likes. He can rail and rave at me too. Fuck, he can beat me black and blue. It isn't changing the way I feel.

Not that it matters. Because my feelings don't matter to her and the efforts I've made this week have not made any difference. In fact, all they've done is provoke Summer into spreading ridiculous rumors about the girl. Fuck, anyone would believe she's sleeping with half the school.

I scoff, kicking my foot along the floor. As if she'd be sleeping with half the school and not sleeping with me.

No, I need to change tack.

I peer towards the corridor. I can't stand the losers in this school. I can't stand the way they talk about her. I want to beat every last one of them into a pulp.

I exhale. It won't help.

I step out, head held high, a look of boredom and disdain plastered on my face as if I don't give a shit about what's just happened, as if I'm oblivious to the way they're all talking about me.

I'm halfway down the hallway, when I spy Summer waiting for me. I groan, eyes flicking towards her and then flicking away. I could let myself fade away and slip through the throngs of gossiping idiots, but she's already seen me and there's no escaping her now.

She wears one of her phony smiles plastered to her perfectly made-up face and is surrounded by her usual groups of girlfriends.

I keep walking, dipping my head to them, hoping I might be able to walk right past. No fucking chance. Summer plants herself right in front of me and now she's laughing too, the other girls picking up on her cue and laughing with her. For a minute, I think they're laughing at me and I can't help frowning. Then Summer lands her palms on my chest and says, "Oh my God, Tristan, that was such a good joke. Utterly hilarious."

She's talking loud, too loud, making sure everyone in this hallway hears every word she says.

I wrangle my frown into a more neutral expression. I can't be dealing with Summer's bullshit right now, but I'm not interested in getting into an argument with her either. I just want to get away, to the sanctuary of my room.

"Making Pig Girl believe you actually want to take her to the ball," she continues. "She must have been peeing her pants with excitement. It's going to be so funny when she realizes you weren't serious."

"I was serious," I say quietly, but Summer just laughs again.

"We're actually thinking we won't do dates for the ball. It feels kind of wrong without Spencer here. We thought we'd go as a big group – all the dueling team and cheerleading squad together. We'll look so awesome that way – especially when we make our entrance."

"I'm going to be going with Rhianna Blackwaters," I say coolly, even though she hasn't agreed to go with me. She will though. I'll find a way to convince her. It's only a matter of time.

"But that's just a joke," Summer says, her voice ever so strained, her smile faltering ever so slightly.

"It's not."

Summer jabs a finger into my chest, and lowers her voice and all of a sudden all those friends are pretending to look elsewhere, starting up conversations among themselves.

"Are you fucking out of your mind, Tristan Kennedy? You're seriously asking that *girl* and not me," she hisses. "You're captain of the dueling team. I'm head cheerleader. We're meant to go together!"

"I don't care."

I look down at her with a blank expression and she scowls up at me. Then she looks around her. "Can we talk about this somewhere private? We could go to my room? Or the common room?"

"No."

"You don't know what she's like, what she's really like. You should have seen what she did to me today, Tristan Kennedy, firing cr–"

I grab her by the arm and yank her through the nearest door. It happens to be the girls' bathroom and the few stragglers in there stare at us in horror. One actually screams.

"Scram!" I bark and they scurry away like frightened little mice. I slam the bathroom door behind me and stalk towards Summer. "Out with it, Summer."

She tosses her hair. "Coach sent the two of us on a sprint in gym class today and Rhianna Blackwaters attacked me under the trees."

"Why?"

"Because she's a little bitch."

I lose all ability to keep cool. Thunder crashes across my face. I don't know if she's faking it or not, but Summer actually looks frightened. Good, maybe she'll leave Rhi the hell alone.

"Why did she attack you, Summer?"

"Because she hates me. She's jealous of me. She knows about us."

"Us?" I scoff. "There's no us."

"Tristan," she whines, crocodile tears pooling in her eyes. I can't be dealing with any of this.

"What happened?"

Summer sniffs, and looks up at me with big innocent eyes I'm sure she's been perfecting all her life. "She blasted crimson magic at me, Tristan. Right at me. *Crimson* magic! She's dangerous. Who knows what she might do next. If her magic actually hit me ..." She sniffs again. "She needs to be locked away."

There's a ringing in my ears and every hair on my body stands up on end.

"Who have you told about this, Summer?"

The innocence melts away, and she smiles at me now. The smile of someone who thinks they've won.

"No one ... yet. I suppose you're going to tell me I shouldn't tell anyone." I glare at her. Wary. "Well, I won't if you agree to stop all this stupid nonsense about taking her to the ball. It's not a good idea, Tristan. She might hurt you."

I think of the aching pain already resident in my body. Rhianna Blackwaters has already hurt me more than Summer could ever understand.

"That isn't a deal I'm prepared to make, Summer."

The smile falls from her lips. "But why?" she says petulantly. "She isn't even pretty. She has no family, no money, no friends." I stare at her. "And she smells like pig shit!" she snaps.

"She is pretty," I say.

"She's cast some kind of spell on you, Tristan. Some kind of love potion ... or charm. And you're too caught up in it to see." She steps towards me. "I can help you, help undo it."

"There's no spell. There's no such thing."

"She's dangerous. She's bewitched you ..."

I don't hear the rest of her words. The pig girl has bewitched me, just not in the way Summer thinks. It's no spell, no charm, no potion. And yet, I am completely and utterly bewitched by her.

"I'm going to tell York," she says, snapping me straight out of my reverie. "About the crimson magic."

"You're not," I tell her firmly.

"You can't stop me, Tristan Kennedy," she says, tossing her hair and moving towards the door.

"I can." I step forward, blocking her path, my voice deadly. "I'm not messing with you, Summer. This girl is important to me. If you tell anyone about what you know, if you hurt her one more time, I will kill you."

She laughs again, although it's a little nervous. She doesn't want to believe I'm serious, but I am. Rhianna is my fated mate and I won't let some silly spoiled bitch hurt her.

"Kill me? Right, sure you will." I grab her arm again, this time squeezing so tightly she yelps and struggles against my hold. "You're hurting me. Get off."

"I'll do a hell of a lot worse to you if you tell one other living soul, Summer, I promise you that." With my free hand, I weave magic through the air, whispering an old incantation. One Spencer and I made long ago. A binding promise. "Now, do you promise me?" The magic shimmers between us waiting for her response. I shake her violently so she's clear just how badly I could hurt her. "Do you promise to tell no one about this?"

Terror fills her eyes as the reality of her situation dawns

on her and she understands that I am not kidding. I will kill her.

"I-I-I-I promise," she says. The magic flashes, sealing the promise.

"Good." I let her go, and she scuttles towards the exit just like those girls did earlier. "And Summer," I say as she pushes against the door, "you understand what that was, don't you? So don't try anything clever. I will know if you break this binding promise." I growl. "And so will you."

When she's gone, I stride right past the classrooms and up to my room, my heart still pounding in my chest, the image of that promise still shining before my eyes. I burst through the door and beeline straight for my desk, pulling open the top drawer and finding my stash of pre-rolled joints organized all neatly alongside my pencils. I pick one up and examine it, bringing it to my nose and sniffing. Then I replace it and try another, and another, till I choose one I'm satisfied with.

I open the palm of my left hand and let a flame dance across it, snaring the tip of my joint and rolling it between my thumb and finger until the end is glowing. Then I bring it to my lips and puff it lightly, once, twice, until the thing is burning properly. The smell of weed floats through the air and I can already feel the buzz before I've even sucked on the thing. I've been smoking far too many of these joints but I can't help it. I feel like shit. The bond in my stomach a constant gnawing ache and my body painful like I'm ill with the flu. The weed helps.

I slink down into my chair, rocking it from side to side as I close my eyes and inhale the smoke, sucking it down into my lungs, the image of Pig Girl dancing in front of my closed eyes.

I huff and pull out one of those pencils from my drawer

next, testing the sharpness of the nib. It's not good enough and I spend the next minute grinding it in a pencil sharpener, the joint stuck between my lips. When I'm satisfied, I reach back inside the drawer for the final time, lifting the papers that lie inside until I find my pad buried beneath. I flick back the cover and stare down at the sketch. It's about two-thirds done. I have the structure of her face, the shape of her eyes, the form of her mouth. I take a long drag of my joint, before dropping it into the ashtray on my desk. I spin the pencil around my fingers, eyes flicking over that face, then I brush my fingertips over her cheekbone, smudging the pencil lines, adding shadow and depth.

It's like magic, like I'm touching her actual cheek. Soft, velvet. I touch the lips I've sketched next, remembering what those felt like pressed to mine.

Fuck, I want her so badly, it's unbearable.

I'm hard just thinking about her. Thinking about how her body quivered under mine. Thinking about how she rubbed herself against me.

Fuck!

I reach inside my sweat pants and curl my fist around my cock, hot and hard in my hand. I imagine how it could have gone in that meadow, how it should damn well have gone. Her thighs falling open, me reaching beneath her skirt and slipping her panties down her legs. I imagine how wet she'd be, how she'd mewl and rub herself against my fingers. How I'd nip at her throat, how I'd tell her to hold still and let me thrust inside her. Barebacked, raw, feeling all of her.

I groan, sliding my hand up and down my cock. Imagining it. Imagining the way she'd moan and whimper, the way she'd beg for more, how she'd come squeezing around my cock.

Fuck!

I open my eyes and stare down into her face. Her eyes would be all drowsy with lust, her skin all flushed from her orgasm, her lips all swollen from my kisses.

I'd fuck her even harder.

And then I'd come deep inside her tight, sweet, beautiful pussy.

I grunt. My cock twitching in my hand, ribbons of come spilling into my lap.

I toss the pad to the ground and flip back my head. For a moment, I feel calm, swimming in the drowsy buzz of my orgasm and my joint.

It lasts precisely one fucking lousy minute. And then the shame and the hatred, the frustration and the desperation come flooding back. Like a tidal wave, hitting me so hard, I nearly tumble from my seat.

I can't bear it.

I wave my hand through the air, cleaning up the mess I've made of myself, trying hard not to imagine her licking it up with her tongue.

Then I stub out the joint and scramble to my feet. I need to see her again.

SHE KNOWS to keep her dorm room locked with magic these days so there's no longer any chance of slipping inside, of watching her while she sleeps. Instead, I linger outside in the darkness. It's pathetic. If anyone knew, they'd laugh at me. If they believed it. Tristan Kennedy loitering outside some girl's room like a love sick puppy? Yeah, it's usually the girls loitering outside mine.

I'm not sure I care. The ache in my stomach is less

intense closer to her, even if there's a fucking wall separating the two of us. My body – fuck it, probably fate too – wants me close by her and it's too hard to resist that pull.

So I stand here and I wait, straining to hear a whisper of her voice, peering at the window for just a glimpse of her.

It's obsessive. Maybe it's more like me than anyone will ever know.

For once, my obsession and my patience is rewarded because her door opens and she comes scurrying out, her hand buried in the pockets of her jacket, her hood pulled up and her pig trotting by her side.

She turns and says something to the roommate and then she's pushing the doors of the building open and stepping outside, peering into the darkness as she does.

She hurries along the path, taking a meandering, unusual route that makes no sense. Is she out walking the pig? She's never done that before. Usually the little creature seems happy enough hanging out in her room or on the small patch of grass below her window.

I close the distance between us a little and she peers over her shoulder, squinting through the darkness, and frowning. But she doesn't stop, and she doesn't challenge me. She's too engrossed in her thoughts. Just when I think she's heading back, when I'm considering intercepting her, she takes a sudden left turn, hugging the back of the laboratory building and cutting across the back way to the meadow.

The meadow. Why the hell is she heading to the meadow at this time of night? To exercise the pig? Its tummy certainly has rounded over the last few weeks but it doesn't look like the kind of animal that endures exercise.

At the edge of the meadow, she hesitates, glancing over her shoulder again and then peering out over the long grass, swinging her gaze left and right. When she determines there's no one about, she hurries across the grass, straight through the trees at the far side and then down the slope where I'd kissed her and through another meadow to ...

I halt.

What the fuck?

Stone's cabin. He's there standing on the porch. Is he waiting for her? Did he know she was coming?

They must be meeting to discuss my cousin. He was ordered to accompany Spencer to the front. He'll be gone for days. Maybe weeks. Maybe the professor has a message from his friend for the girl.

When she reaches the bottom of the cabin steps, the professor smiles – not his usual sardonic grin, something genuine, happy even. An expression I don't think I've ever seen on his face before. Rhi races up the steps, the pig lingering behind her, and falls straight into the arms of the waiting professor.

This can't be right. Am I seeing things?

I stand there, peering through the starlit night, too shocked to move as the professor draws my fated mate right against his body and kisses her mouth. Then he's lifting her into his arms and carrying her inside his cabin.

And if I didn't think my world was fucked up enough it comes crashing down around me.

What the actual hell?

I'm racing up the steps to the cabin before I know what I'm doing and blasting through the doors. They stand there, horror all over their faces, his hand tight on her waist, hers fisted in his shirt.

"Tristan!" she cries.

I charge at him, pushing her out of the way and swinging for the professor. He ducks, my knuckles grazing his cheek bone.

"He's your best friend! You fucking dickhead! Your best friend!"

My hand fisted in his shirt, I draw back my fist to hit him again.

"No, stop it!" Rhianna yells, grabbing a hold of my elbow and attempting to pull me away. I shake her off.

"Everyone's been calling you a slut," I hiss at her, keeping my angry gaze fixed on the professor's face. "And I thought it was bullshit. All pathetic rumors spread by Summer. And yet, here you are sleeping with–"

"Let go of me right now, Kennedy," the professor growls, "or I will break your fucking neck."

Rage scorches through my body, the bond in my stomach thrums violently. I should kill him. I should blast him into a million pieces.

His best friend's girl – his best friend's fucking mate. A student. The man is sick, twisted.

I should kill him. Kill him for daring to lay one finger on her.

I drop a hold of his shirt and take a step away. I don't need to kill him. I can destroy him.

"I'm going to tell York," I say firmly. And then I'm going to tell Azlan.

"Tristan. No," Pig Girl pleads, attempting to hang on to my arm again. "You don't understand."

"Oh, I understand perfectly." I glare at the professor who stares back at me stony-faced.

"Kennedy, I'm warning you ..."

I scoff and then I unhook her fingers from my arm, spin on my heels and race away, into the darkness, into the shadows.

32

R^{hi}

"We have to stop him!" I cry, swinging through the door.

"Rhi!" Stone calls but I'm already chasing down the steps on Tristan Kennedy's tail.

I can't see him in the darkness of the night, no matter how hard I squint, no matter how many flashes of light I send spinning from my palm, but I can feel him, feel that tug towards him in the pit of my stomach. Why hadn't I felt it earlier? He was following me. Because I was lost in my own thoughts, too concerned with the upcoming conversation with Stone to pay proper attention to my surroundings. Stupid, stupid, stupid.

I let the sensation in my gut pull me up the hill, under the trees and into the brightly starlit meadow. So bright I can see every blade of glass. Every blade of grass but no Tristan Kennedy.

"I know you're here," I yell into the emptiness, sprinting after him. "I can feel you!"

I sense him halt and I draw to a stop, too. I can feel him only a few paces in front of me, but all I see is the meadow beyond, the grass and sleeping flowers rustled slightly by the evening's breeze. Then slowly, slowly, he appears right in front of me, see-through and transparent at first and then more and more solid until it's him. All of him.

I stare at him in disbelief.

"And what do you feel?" he spits, his eyes hissing with anger. "A bond? A bond you're determined to disregard."

"What?" I say, shaking my head. "How ... how did you do ..." Then an idea sails into my mind. My mouth falls open in disbelief. "It was you! In the forest. You attacked me." I frown. "And it was you ... you who saved me from the werebeast."

He glares at me, not saying a word.

I hesitate. He saved me. He also attacked me. My heart thumps in my chest and my lungs burn. I'm out of breath from chasing after him. I'm also confused. Damn confused. So confused I want to sink to the ground and sob into my palms.

But what good would that do? I can't let Tristan tell on Stone and me. I need to persuade him not to, which means revealing more to him than I want to. Because despite all his declarations this week, I don't trust him. And now I think I have even less reason to do so. It was he who attacked me in the forest! He who crept into our dorm room.

And yet ... and yet, it was also Tristan who saved me from the werebeast, who may have saved my life.

"You can't tell York about me and Stone," I say.

"Can't I?" he says.

I've never seen him look so angry, his whole body taut

with it, his magic crashing and swirling around him with violence.

"No, because I'm not cheating on Azlan. He knows about this."

"Sure he does," he growls, without any of his usual humor.

"Tristan, he does. Because ..." I swallow. Telling him this, confessing it, makes the situation between the two of us a lot more complicated. But I can't afford to let him tell York. Because if Summer's also been to the principal telling tales, York will be marching straight to the chancellor and then all three of us are in danger. "Because ..."

"Because!" he snaps. "Out with it, Piggie, I'm fascinated to hear your excuse, to learn how you've convinced yourself that what you're doing with that jerk is somehow–"

"He's my fated mate, Tristan!" He takes a stumbling step backwards as if I slapped him right across the face. "Stone is my fated mate."

"No," Tristan says, staring at me in horror, shaking his head slowly, "no, that isn't true. You're lying to me."

"I'm not lying!" I step forward, the bond in my stomach aching for him. "You know your cousin, you know Azlan. And you know Stone. They are the closest of friends. Do you seriously think Phoenix would go behind his back and–"

He shakes his head. "They can't both be."

"Tristan," I say gently, far more gently than he deserves, "they are. Which is why you can't go telling York. If she learns the truth ... if she tells the chancellor."

He stares at me and I can almost see the cogs turning in his brain as he deduces the consequences.

"Who the fuck are you, Rhianna Blackwaters?"

The question strikes me deep in my chest. Because who

am I? Tears pool in my eyes. "I don't know," I whisper. "I don't know."

He watches as a tear trails down my cheek. For a moment his face seems to soften, then he shakes his head, his shoulders stiffening.

"And this is why you don't want me? Why you're denying the bond between us?"

"There is no–"

"How else did you follow me here then, Rhianna?" He glares down at me and I say nothing. "You have your two mates and so you're going to deny your third. But do you know how rare this is? Do you know what the hell it could mean?"

"I don't care what it means."

"But two's enough."

"Fuck, Tristan. How the hell would I know?"

"It's the reason you're denying this bond between us."

"It isn't the reason and you know it. I told you already. You treated me like shit. Hell, you told me yourself how much you despised me, how strongly you tried to fight this."

"I also told you, that that was before."

"And I told you, you're too late."

His shoulders visibly slump and his gaze drops to the ground. For the first time ever, I look at Tristan and see defeat. Defeat and a deep, deep sadness.

My bond strains even harder towards him, wanting me to comfort him, to wrap my arms around him and forgive him. But I can't. I just can't do it.

"Are you going to tell York?" I ask softly.

He keeps his eyes fixed on his shoes. "You know I can't. And I've also made sure Summer doesn't tell her about your little incident in the woods." I stare at him in shock and he raises his eyes to meet mine. "Because, whether you like it or not, Rhianna Blackwaters, fate has determined that I'm mixed up in this. Just like Azlan and just like Stone.

✳.

STONE'S WAITING for me under the trees that line the meadow, a frown planted between his brows, Pip snuffling around his feet.

"He's not going to tell," I say. I want to wrap my arms around him and rest my cheek on his chest but we've already been caught once tonight, I don't fancy it happening again.

"He thinks you're fated mates."

I jolt a little. I've not shielded my thoughts. Stone can read my mind. No doubt he can read Tristan's too. It's not surprising he knows and yet these thoughts have been hovering around, half-formed in my mind for some time, and he's never picked them out before.

"Half-formed ideas are very hard to read," he explains. I nod, not quite able to meet his eye. "How long have you known?" he asks.

"I'm not sure that I know anything," I snap, kicking at loose earth with the toe of my boot.

"Rhi ..."

I glare up at him, those tears threatening to overspill again. "How can fate bind me to someone I hate? Someone who hates me? That can't be right. It just can't be!"

"He doesn't hate you," he says softly.

I scoff at that. "You don't know the half of what he's done to me, Phoenix."

"Rhianna Blackwaters, you don't owe him anything. You don't owe anyone anything."

"But?" I say, because there's always a damn but.

He shrugs. "Going against fate, refusing your fated mates–"

"Is what you were doing."

He sighs, then takes a hold of my arm and drags me towards him. "I'm a far bigger fool, far more stupid, far more of an idiot, than you are, Blackwaters."

"That must make you an exceedingly big one, Professor."

"Yep," he says, "because see what I was missing out on."

My bond thrums as he leans down to kiss me, sliding his warm hand into my hair and cradling the back of my head. And now, right now, is the moment I should tell him about the crimson magic. That I should confess all the dark things I suspect I might be capable of. But I can't. I can't do it. He's already learned one of my secrets tonight. To confess another, one far worse, feels too dangerous. I can't lose him. I can't. So instead, I whisper:

"Someone might see."

He waves his hand through the air, whispering the enchantment and the air seems to shimmer in a cocoon around us. "Now they can't," he says, kissing me harder this time, walking me backwards until I collide with the trunk of a tree.

"I almost feel sorry for him," he murmurs as he kisses his way down my throat, my eyes drifting shut.

"Who?" I say, my train of thought completely disrupted as he slides his hand under my shirt and squeezes my breast.

"Kennedy. You're so delicious, Blackwaters. So fucking delicious. It must be driving him mad to want you and not to have you. I know it drove me to the fucking brink."

His other hand finds the waist of my jeans and he twists

the buttons through their holes, opening the fly and tugging them down my legs.

I wrap my hands around his neck, and scrape my nails against his scalp – something I've learned that he likes.

"Hmmm," he moans as he slides his hand between my legs. "So delicious, so deliciously wet."

"I can't bear to be apart from you," I whisper, as he tugs down his fly and, taking a hold of my thighs, hoists me up against the tree. "You and Azlan. When we're apart, all I can think about is you and the things you do to me."

"I think you do a fair bit to me, too, Miss Blackwaters," he says, grinding his hard cock inside me. My bond sparks to life and I moan as he rubs against every sensitive spot. Despite how much I plead, he grinds and grinds until the tears in my eyes finally spill and my nails are deep in his shoulder, then he pounds me against the tree, his words turning wild as both of us wind higher.

"I can't wait till he's home either, sweetheart. I can't wait until we can pleasure you together, share you between us, fuck you at the same time."

"Oh," I call out, coming messy and loud as he does the same. We float together, high above the shadowy trees and the pale meadow, somewhere up in the stars where our magic swirls and curls around us.

And when we float back to earth, buffeted along the way by more feelings of bliss, he whispers in my ear, "You like the idea of that, Miss Blackwaters? You want us to fuck you together?"

"Yes," I whisper. Yes, I want that very much. So much so that I don't think I have the words to describe it.

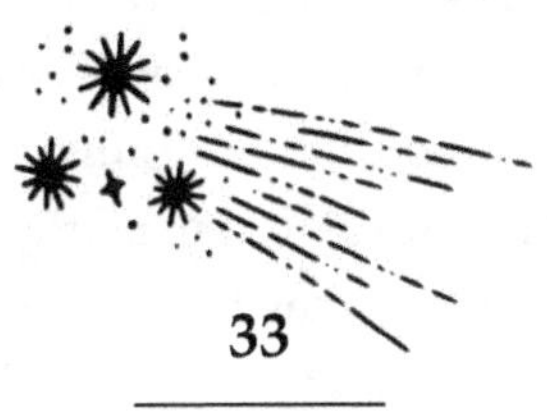

33

S pencer

WE TAKE it in turns to stay awake after that, one of us watching for another attack while the other sleeps. In daylight, we travel cautiously, the man in black avoiding the main route and weaving us along unpaved tracks and twisting lanes, all the time both of us watching, listening.

I think he watches me just as much as he does the trees and the roads. I can feel his eyes scrutinizing me, although whenever I look at him, his gaze is trained elsewhere. But despite his curiosity, we don't talk of it again – he doesn't ask me. Not until we spot the tall barracks clear above the tree line on the horizon, and beyond trails of smoke and flashes of magic.

"That's it," he calls to me over the roar of the bikes.

As if it were in any doubt. I can smell the magic in the

air, smell the death and destruction too. The beast stirs inside me. Curious as always.

The man in black motions with his head, and we pull onto the side of the road, both disappearing into the bushes to relieve ourselves and then returning to our vehicles. The man in black pulls out his water bottle from his rucksack and stares at me as he takes three long swigs, wiping his gloved hand across his mouth when he's done.

"How do you know?" he asks as I settle myself back on my bike.

"I don't–"

"How do you know the beast wasn't going to hurt her? How do you know he wants her?"

I close my eyes. How? Can I explain it? Would he even understand?

"He talks to you?" the man in black asks, his dark eyes alert with curiosity.

"Not exactly."

"Is it him who wants her or you?" My eyes leap to his. I don't answer. "You control him."

I scoff. "No, we are not one and the same. He does not control me and I do not control him."

"Then how do you know?"

I screw up my face. Finding the words to describe this is impossible but I realize no one has ever asked me before – not even Tristan, full of unending amounts of curiosity. And I find I want to tell him, I want to try.

"He's inside me all the time, hovering right beneath my skin. Sometimes straining to break free, sometimes strangely content. In those moments, I receive flashes of his emotions, of his thoughts."

"But when you're in beast form?"

"Nothing. I wake up unable to remember what I've done or where I've been."

The man in black considers this, sliding his bottle back into his bag and tying it closed. "And what does he ..." he hesitates, "'feel' for Rhianna?"

"He's obsessed with her."

"Yeah," the man in black says with some feeling as if he can relate to that. I'm not surprised. I bet being bonded to her is obsessive. I have to force my body not to shake with the mere thought of it. He slings his bag on his back, then peers at me once more. "Why? Why is he obsessed with her?"

The beast is all alert inside me. He has his answer. But it isn't one I'm prepared to share with the man in black. That's between me and her, and we've made our choices.

"I don't know," I say, revving the engine and pulling away, giving him no chance to read the pained expression I'm sure marks my face

WE HIT the main road bustling with traffic – trucks, tanks and magical-looking machinery trudging along the road, some in the direction of the barracks, some back towards the capital. We weave through the convoys and I see the rows of soldiers, men and women sitting on benches inside the vehicles, their hair shaved short, their caps balanced on the crown of their heads, guns resting against their thighs. I'll be joining them soon enough. Just another recruit. No longer Spencer Moreau, star of the dueling team, heir to his family. Just the same as anyone else.

I wrench the throttle, eager to arrive, hurtling at a speed

so fast, several trucks blare their horns at me and I lose the man in black in the throng of traffic.

I'm forced to stop though as the traffic comes to a standstill and a huge wire fence looms in front of us. Beyond is the barracks building, an ugly brown monstrosity, that looks more like a cardboard box than anything else. The man in black pulls up alongside me, then motions with his head and we bypass the line, coming to a stop at the line of guards inspecting the vehicles entering the barracks.

The enforcer stops in front of the most senior-looking guard, several red stripes running along the arm of his jacket, and, taking off his helmet, goes to speak to him, beckoning me to follow.

The soldier greets him with a curt nod of the head.

"Enforcer," he says.

"Sergeant," he answers. "I have Spencer Moreau here. He'll be joining the new recruits."

The sergeant takes the paperwork the man in black passes to him, and scans it, although his eyes keep skipping up to me.

"You're joining early?" he asks me.

"Yes, Sir."

The sergeant glances at me. "Was he kicked out of the academy? Is he a troublemaker?"

"I was told by the chancellor that the decision was the boy's. He had enough points to graduate early."

The sergeant scoffs. "His brother was a trouble maker."

I take a menacing step towards the weedy little man. "My brother was a hero."

The sergeant shakes his head, folding the paperwork in half. "That what they told you?"

I growl and the man in black lays his palm on my shoulder.

"It's been a long journey, Sergeant. There are gang members out on the roads. We were attacked two days ago."

"How many?"

"Ten, fifteen," the man in black says.

The sergeant whistles, looking up at me this time with a little more admiration.

"You need to report to the major's office." He whistles and a small, female soldier leaves her post and comes jogging over to us. "Private," he tells her, "show Mister Moreau where to leave his bike, then take him to the major's office."

"Yes, Sir," she says, clicking her heels together and saluting. Then she smiles at me and beckons for me to follow her.

I peer back at the man in black.

"Thank you," I say to him.

His gaze flickers over my face. Then he grunts and turns away and I'm left to follow the little figure of the private.

She chats nonstop as I push my bike through into the giant yard, as I park it up, and as she walks me to the door at the side of the towering building. I know she thinks it makes her seem cheerful, trying to convey that she's fine, but underneath it I can tell she's nervous, jittery; of me or of the continual booms that rattle the yard I can't be sure.

I wasn't sure whether to believe what the man in black told me days ago. Whether he was trying to shit me up, scare the recruit. Now I wonder if there was truth in his words.

"Is that–"

"Battle? Yes," she says, the smile on her face becoming even more stretched. "There have been ongoing skirmishes up at the border the last few days."

"Anyone hurt?"

Her smiles stretches wider.

I squint out in that direction, smoke billows in the air and there's the hint of burning on the wind.

"There's a fire."

"Yes, that's new." She glances that way, her shoulders hunching. "There's talk the enemy has some kind of new weapon," she whispers, then seeming to collect herself, straightens and she points to the door.

The beast bristles, aware of something I'm not.

"This is it. Good luck. I'm sure I'll see you around."

And then she's gone, scuttling across the yard, jumping at every new explosion.

I pause, looking at the sign nailed above the door.

This is it. If I enter through this door, there'll be no going back. I'll be committed. There'll be no way home, no way back to the academy, no way back to her.

The ground shakes under my feet, the door handle rattling in my palm with the force of another explosion. The ache in my gut is stronger than ever and I am surprised I have the strength to remain on my feet.

I grip the handle tighter, blowing through my teeth. Fate doesn't want this. The beast sure as hell doesn't want this. But I do. I can be useful here. Back there I'm only a danger to her.

I swing the door open and march through. At the desk that awaits me beyond, I click my heels together and salute just like that little soldier had done. Only I'm bigger, stronger, more of a soldier than any of them will ever be.

"Can I help you?" a man with spectacles asks me from the other side of the desk.

"Spencer Moreau reporting for duty," I say.

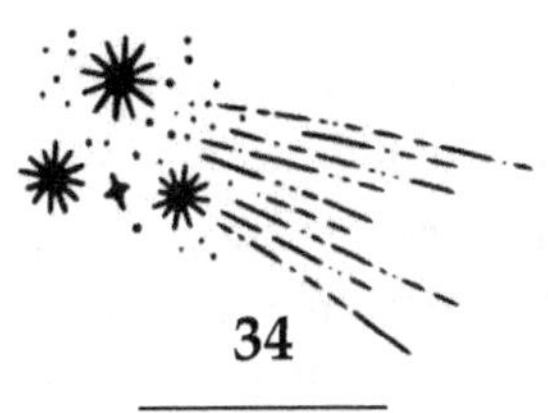

34

R enzo

I LIE ON THE BUNK, her knife in my pocket, the vial of her blood in my hand. I twirl the little thing in my fingers and lift it to the light of the setting sun streaming through the window. It hits the glass and plunges the room into a dark scarlet.

It's fucking beautiful.

Blood mesmerizes and captivates me like nothing else can. All those rivers of it flowing right beneath the surface of the skin. Just waiting to be released. Blue and green and purple little streams hidden under the veil of flesh, only revealing its true vivid nature when that veil, that flesh, is peeled back.

I like the way it moves. Sometimes trickling and oozing to the surface, sometimes squirting in great violent fountains, sometimes pouring out like a waterfall. So red. So very red, staining everything it touches. Impossible to remove, to wash away. Once you've soaked your hands in blood, you're forever marked.

I hum in satisfaction, peering at the blood in the vial. There's magic in her blood. I can hear it humming to me in return, can feel its energy, its intensity.

Just how it felt in my mouth, on my tongue, on my lips. I lick them now, sure I can still taste her there.

Fuck, that was so good. Best fucking thing I've done in my life. Better than the maiming and the torturing and the murdering. And those are a few of my favorite things.

I grip the vial more tightly in my hand and bring it to my mouth now, kissing the warm glass and inhaling, catching the scent of her, my blood humming too and that hook in my belly.

Should have lied to my little rabbit. Should have told her I needed six, seven, eight drops of blood. Some for the potion, some for me. Then I'd wear this fucking vial of her blood around my neck, resting against my fucking heart.

Instead, I have to waste the precious stuff.

I frown.

I don't want to. I want to keep it. She gave it to me. It's mine.

But if I don't go ahead with the plan, then all of her pretty blood could be spilled, lost forever.

It seems unfair. I've never had anything of my own. Even as a kid, even now. It's never bothered me before. I'm not like those other dudes who collect things and people. What I've done has always driven me, not what I fucking own.

But now look at me. I have a knife you'd have to pry from my stone-cold hands and a vial of a little rabbit's blood. I want to add more to my collection. The little rabbit herself. I want a little collar to place around her neck so I can tether

her to my side. Or maybe I want that collar around my own neck and the lead in her hand.

I chuckle and swing my feet to the ground with a thump. I'm even more fucked up than I realized. Ain't that a surprise.

The heart of the man I killed rests in a basin by the sink of this cabin. It smells rank – nothing like her blood – and it's too fucking big to be hers. But a little magic, a little potion brewing.

I stretch my arms above my head, tilting my head from side to side and listening to the vertebrae crack.

The light's fading quickly now, the sun no longer reaching the window, and the inside of this cabin falls darker and darker. I snap my fingers and a lantern hanging on the wall flames to life. Then I slip my feet into my boots and stalk towards the sink, sliding my hand into the bowl and squeezing my fingers around the heart.

It's cold and wet, all squidgy, yet strong; solid. The muscle that kept that dude alive. This is the organ they say I don't possess. Sometimes I think they might be right, even though I can hear the thing beating in my head day and night. Letting me know it's there.

But I guess what they mean is that I have no feelings, no remorse ... no empathy. People talk some serious crap. This ugly, smelly organ controls nothing but the blood pumping in your arteries. And the only thing it has to do with love is pumping the blood to your cock when you want to fuck a girl.

If any of those crackheads had held a heart in their hands, they'd know that.

I turn to the other ingredients I spread out on the counter, the herbs and the concentrates. It had been fucking hard to track some of these ingredients down, but a little arm twisting here, a little neck squeezing there, and I'd found everything I needed.

I think of my mom doing this, standing at the kitchen sink in her holey socks, the radio blasting, noise to cover up all the shouting and screaming out there on the streets. She used to balance on her tiptoes and hum along with the music. So I hum too, that tune that's humming in my belly. That's where those feelings really lie, deep in the pit of my stomach. That's how I know she's mine and I'm hers. Nothing to do with this lousy muscle.

I slop the heart back into the bowl and concentrate on concentrating. I can't fuck this up. It needs to be perfect. It needs to work.

I concentrate so hard I give myself a fucking migraine as I shake the herbs and mix the liquids and finally pour my little rabbit's blood into the bowl, swimming my hands in intricate patterns over the bowl, humming the old words, letting my magic creep into the core of the muscle and molding and shaping it, changing it into something different, smaller, prettier, feminine. When I'm done, my hands stained red, I fall back onto that bunk, the lantern still blazing, my feet still inside my boots, and close my eyes. My head hurts so badly I think my skull will crack in two.

I DON'T KNOW how long I sleep but when I wake, the lantern has burned itself out and a night owl hoots somewhere out there in the wood.

I find a torch under the bed, then search through the cupboard finding a small wooden box at the back full of notes and coins. I tip them into my pockets and then carefully, admiring my work as I do, I lift the heart from the bowl and place it in the box, snapping shut the lid with satisfaction, and hooking it under my arm.

At the door of the cabin, I roll the mutilated body of the man – some dude who liked to ship women over the border for fuck knows what – out of my path with the heel of my boot and open the door.

Am I going to go to Hell for all the bad stuff I've done? I think as I step over the corpse and out into the darkened forest. That's what my mom said. Hell, that's what half of my victims said too. One last-ditch attempt to stop me from the inevitable. But what do I care if I am? Where I am now, here on the Earth, with my boots sinking into the damp ground isn't that great. Or it wasn't until her.

I kick away the stand of my bike and sit on the machine, the box resting on the seat in front of me.

I'm going to tell Marcus I killed her. That I crept into the forest at the academy and lured her under the trees, pretended I was her friend, that I was going to help her, then wrapped my hands around her throat – her pretty, tender throat – and squeezed her life away.

Ahh shit, that is some fucking fantasy. One that makes me hard. I want to wrap my hands around her throat, feel that heart of hers pumping against my palms.

"Shit," I mutter, the word loud in my ears. I need to concentrate.

I go over my story again and again in my head, all the way to Marcus' compound. When I arrive they tell me he isn't in the boardroom. He's asked not to be disturbed. So I ignore the instruction and jog up the stairs, the box tight in my hands, finding him in bed with some girl, different to the one before. A girl who looks almost relieved when I barge into the room and interrupt them.

"Barone! What the fuck?" Marcus says, rolling off the girl

and taking the sheet with him, leaving her bare and exposed and scrabbling to cover her tits with her arm. "I said I was not to be–"

"It's done," I say, tossing the box towards the bed where it lands with a thud on the mattress.

"What is?" Marcus says.

"The girl. She's dead."

Marcus stares at me and I stare right back. He can't read me. No one can. One of the advantages of having no fucking heart.

He reaches for the box and lifts it onto his lap, peering up at me again before he opens the lid.

The girl can't help her own curiosity, she leans over to look inside too. Then she screams scrambling away so quickly, she tumbles off the bed.

Marcus studies the heart for several long minutes and I kick at the ground and study my fingernails, whistling a tune under my breath.

"This is hers?"

"Yep."

"I'm going to need to test it. Check that's true." He presses down hard on a button on the machine by his bed. "Send Carlton up here."

"You don't usually test the gifts I bring you."

"How did you do it?" Marcus asks, closing the lid.

I grin at him and lift my hands, miming wringing her neck. The girl on the floor whimpers, but Marcus simply stares at me some more.

He's a cunning fucker. I don't know whether he believes me. It's clear he senses something's not right about me, about this.

"The little bitch deserved to suffer," he says lowly.

I peer at my hands. "Did I say she didn't?"

Marcus nods. "Good ... good." He drops the box on the table beside the bed. "I was beginning to think you'd turned soft, Renzo. That maybe you'd grown a heart of your own."

"Me?" I chuckle. Then I thump my hand against my chest, right above where my heart pounds against my ribs. "Empty. Completely empty."

"I thought as much," Marcus says, rubbing his hand across the stubble on his chin.

"So what's the next job, boss?" I say.

"Renzo," he says, reaching over the edge of the bed and hauling the girl back onto the mattress. "Fuck off."

I do as he says. There's no point provoking him. Especially as my curiosity is gnawing at my insides. I want to know what's going on, what he's plotting. I've never cared before. I've never been interested. The killing part has been the interesting bit. The motives, the reasons, I don't give a shit. But now I have something to care about. And so now, I need to know.

It was Marcus who spotted me that day on the street, fighting. Marcus who saw my potential and tempted me home. He wasn't in charge back then, it was his father but even then it was clear Marcus was going to inherit the throne. He was smart, clever, fucking beguiling.

I've never cared what he's done, why he's done it, but the things he's done have always made sense to me. He wants power and money – nearly as much as I want to make people hurt. Every move he's ever made has been motivated by those two things.

But this?

I step out into the compound yard to watch all the busy bees. But am I seeing it wrong? Did I confuse it in my head? I blink my eyelids, strain my vision.

Soldiers from the West. I can tell by the way they speak,

by their hollowed-out cheeks. They look half starved. Is that why he's loading up the sheep and sending them over the border?

Along with weapons?

It makes no sense.

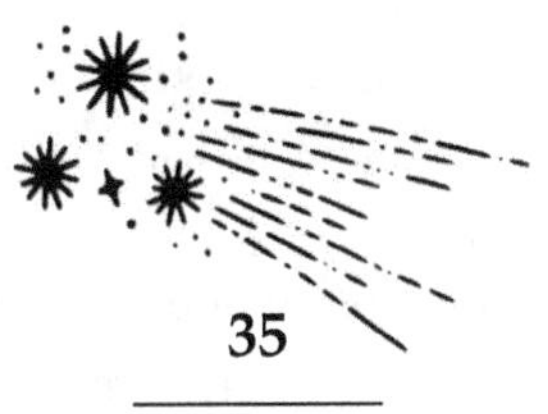

35

zlan

I'VE BEEN AWAY TOO LONG. FAR longer than I intended. The attack meant the need to take deviating, less obvious routes to the border but I'm not prepared to piss about getting back, no matter the danger. I don't like being away from her and that's not just because I'm concerned for her safety, concerned to have her lying back in my bed. No, I miss the little thing. She's burrowed under my skin. Fuck, she's burrowed into my heart and I miss her voice, her face, her scent. I miss everything about her.

Despite the crazy speed I drive, pushing my bike and my body to the fucking limit, the journey passes achingly slowly, every yard, every mile creeping past so that I want to scream with frustration.

I think of the assassin and his ability to slip through space and time. Shit, I don't think I've ever envied anyone an ability as much as I do him. If I could do that, I could be with her now. I could be with her whenever I liked. Creeping into her room, creeping into her bed.

I drive right through the night and right through the next. It's stupid, of course it is, especially when my eyelids droop and the road swims and swerves in front of me. But I grit my teeth and plow on, messaging both Rhi and Stone when I stop at a cafe to pump my veins full of coffee.

I am going straight there, to the academy. It's a risk, but one my bond tells me I have no choice but to make. I can't stand to be away from her a minute longer.

A sort of elation blossoms in my chest as Los Magicos comes into view. I'm nearly there. Nearly with her. I can almost smell her scent in the air, almost hear her voice on the wind. The busy traffic forces me to slow down but I don't care now. Home is in touching distance.

Of course, all my plans go to shit as I glide down the main street of the city, my phone beeping in my jacket. I'm tempted to ignore it. It will be Rhi, or Stone, and I'll be seeing both in a matter of minutes. But then it dawns on me the message may be important, a warning, a hint to proceed with caution.

I pull up, and not leaving the saddle of my bike, pull out my phone.

The chancellor.

I groan like a man gutted with a blunt carving knife. My presence in the city has been noted and he has a request. I snort. Request? Like everything he asks of me isn't a mandatory order.

I scroll down, my thumb halting as I read the words.

He's become impatient. He's no longer intent on waiting for my report, no longer bothered by what the Moreau boy may have to say about the girl. He wants to talk to her himself. And he wants me to collect her.

My hand drops to my thigh and I stare out at the passing traffic, blurring and merging into one as I think.

Is this dangerous? Is she in danger?

I don't know.

I glance down at my phone. Should I call them now? Tell them to run? To get the hell out of Los Magicos? Would that work? How far would they even get?

I rub my knuckles over my forehead. The caffeine has long ago waned and now I'm hit by the full force of my tiredness, making every thought a struggle.

He knows nothing. The chancellor knows nothing. If he did, she'd already be in some cell somewhere, and, hell, so would I.

For the time being, there's nothing for him to discover. Not if we're careful. The Moreau boy and his secrets are far away at the border. And as for my cousin, if he were going to blab to anyone it would be his father, and as I've had no word from my family, I can assume, for whatever reason he's chosen not to.

I'll take her. I'll take her to the chancellor. But I'll stand right outside the door. Right there in case ... I stare right ahead. If he touches one hair on her precious head, I will end him, damn all the consequences.

I answer his message and then tuck my cell back inside my jacket and start the bike.

The last part of my journey, through the country lanes towards the academy perched up there on its hill, seems to pass much more quickly, as if fate is choosing to torture me with the passing of time.

I'm going to have to report to the principal, do this by the official route. No time even for a stolen kiss, to hold her against me and tell her how much I've missed her.

The gates at the outskirts of the grounds open for me automatically and I climb the drive up to the front of the mansion, parking up and finding the principal waiting for me on the steps.

"You were expecting me?" I ask, walking towards her as I tug off my gloves.

"Yes, the chancellor said you were on your way to collect Miss Blackwaters."

"Correct."

"Do you know why he wishes to talk with her?" she says, an anxiety I'm not used to observing in the woman hovering in her eyes.

"No."

"He's shown an unusual curiosity in the girl," she mutters, peering over her shoulder. "I don't understand why. I haven't observed anything unusual about her." She peers back at me. "Have you?"

I keep my face blank. "No," I hesitate, then add, "apart from her age. Most unregistered magicals I pick up are much older."

"Yes, I suppose they would be." The sound of gravel crunching catches her attention and she peers around again to catch sight of Rhianna walking towards us. The summer's passed now and she wears a worn jacket. I need to buy her a new one. "Miss Blackwaters," the principal beckons her forward. "The enforcer will escort you to see the chancellor."

She catches my eye for a flicker of a second and nods. The principal hesitates as if she's considering saying more, but then she turns and leaves the two of us.

"Rhianna," I whisper, my bond straining towards hers.

She peers over her shoulder, checking the principal has gone, then smiles up into my face.

"Azlan," she says and why does my name sound so good in her mouth?

"I missed you," I say, daring to take her hand in mine and stroke my thumb over her knuckles. Her entire body trembles with my touch and this is going to be agony I can tell.

"Why does he want to see me, Azlan?" she asks.

"I don't know, sweetheart, but I'll be right by your side. I'm not going to let anything happen to you."

A crinkle forms between her brows and she squeezes my hand. "But what if he tricks me, tricks me into telling him something I shouldn't? What if he already knows?"

"Rhi," I say smiling back at her, unable to help myself, "you're very good at keeping a secret."

She frowns harder still and before she can take umbrage with what I've said, I tug her towards the bike and we're both climbing onto the saddle, back here again, her arms wrapped around my waist, her thighs pressed to mine.

As we fly through the lanes back towards Los Magicos, I'm no longer tired, I'm wide awake, her presence electrifying and stimulating, my body and bond pulsing with her proximity. How did I have the strength to leave her in the first place? How did I tear myself away? Because being with her is like heaven, addictive, something I can't live without.

As we enter the city, I feel her body stiffen and her arms tightening around me. I reach down and squeeze her thigh, projecting through our bond all my intentions to keep her safe.

It does little to reassure her, and though it wounds my pride, I understand. I'm one man. One man against the chancellor and all his guards. But what she doesn't understand is, they have nothing to fight for, while I have every-thing. If it came to it, I'd fight to the bitter end to protect her.

The council gates part just like the academy's and we glide through, around to the side entrance I brought her to all those months ago. That seems like a lifetime ago. I had no idea back then how much my life would alter, how much I would. Or maybe I did. Maybe I always knew.

"Okay?" I ask her, as she yanks off my helmet and shakes out her dark hair.

"I'm fine."

I want to pull her towards me and hold her. At the very least I want to squeeze her hand again but there's too many pairs of eyes now so I have to make do with signaling for her to walk through the entrance way, and as she does, lightly pressing my hand to the small of her back.

The chancellor's secretary meets us under the glass dragon in the hall. It seems extra sinister today, its ruby eyes glinting as if its gaze is real, piercing through us all, its wings taut as if it's about to soar right out of the building. The first dragon to fly through the Los Magicos skies in centuries.

"Rhianna Blackwaters," the secretary asks me and not her.

"Yes," she answers anyway, frowning at the man, tall and skinny and not much older than Rhi herself.

He gives her a sickly smile that has me bristling. "The chancellor is waiting for you in his office. If you'd follow me." He motions to the staircase and I go to follow them both. The secretary halts. "Enforcer, there is no need to come with us. You may wait in the–"

"I'll be required to escort Miss Blackwaters back to the academy. She is a known flight risk. I will wait outside the chancellor's door."

"There's really no need ..."

I glare at him and he visibly slinks backwards, obviously deciding an argument with me is one he won't be winning.

At the top of the staircase, we find two guards flanking the chancellor's doors and they inspect Rhianna carefully, running their hands over her body in a way that has me grinding my molars and fisting my hands. Then the secretary knocks on the door; it opens, and she's walking through into the chancellor's office.

It's too risky for her to look back at me, too dangerous for me to whisper her any words.

The door closes, and it takes every ounce of my self-control not to break it down.

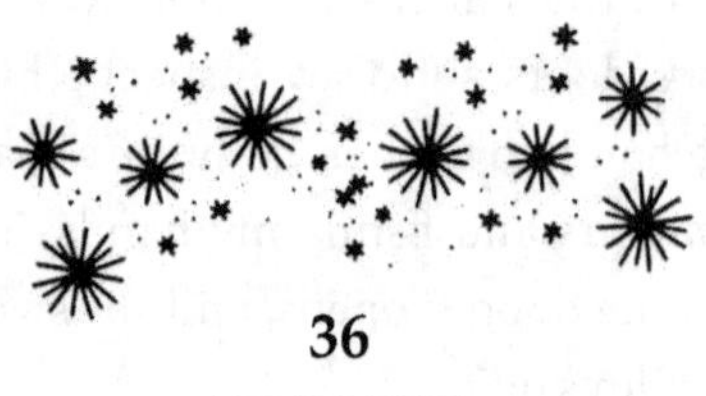

36

R^{hi}

HIS OFFICE IS DESIGNED to intimidate. I can tell that straight away and so is the way he sits behind his grand desk and takes no notice of me, scribbling away on a piece of paper with a golden pen.

I stand and wait, determined I'm not going to play any of his games. I was naïve and uninformed the first time we met. I didn't know how the world worked – how people ticked. But the academy hasn't only taught me how to handle magic – it's also taught me how to handle people. And if I can handle a vicious bitch like Summer Clutton-Brock, if I can escape the clutches of the Wolves of Nights' assassin more than once – then I can handle this man. This man who thinks he's far more clever than I suspect he actually is.

"Ahhh Miss Blackwaters," he says at last as if he's only

just noticed my presence. "Thank you so much for coming to see me." Like I had any say in the matter. He replaces the lid on his pen, leans back in his chair, and points to a wooden one in front of me. "Take a seat."

I desperately want to peer behind me at the door, where Azlan is waiting for me. I know he's there – my bond yanking me in his direction as if it wants me as far away from this man as possible and in the arms of my mate instead.

I draw out the chair, its legs scraping against the highly polished floor and slide into the seat.

The chancellor looks me straight in the eye. His are cold and calculating. He reminds me of the snakes that would slide into the chicken pen sometimes. How one moment they'd be still and watching and the next they'd strike, sinking their fangs deep into a chicken's neck. It's not only my bond ringing out a warning, my magic is suddenly alert too.

"I thought it was about time we spoke," he says.

I concentrate on breathing, on not letting my heart race away. It's not just my own neck on the line. It's Stone's and Azlan's too. Shit, and Pip's. I wait for him to say more, not trusting my own voice, knowing if I speak I'll likely trip myself up.

"You see, I haven't been completely honest with you." I frown unable to help myself. "I've suspected for a while now that I knew your mother."

"My mother?" I say, again unable to help myself. That the chancellor has been hiding secrets about my mom is no big surprise. Azlan told me as much. But to hear him admit it, to speak about her ... I lean forward on my seat. I'm so desperate to know more about her, even if it means trading secrets with a snake.

"I believe so." He smiles with what I suspect he thinks is sympathy. "She died when you were young."

"A baby, yes. I never knew her."

"And your father?"

"I ... I'm not sure what happened to him."

"But you know who he was?"

I have a name. I have a photo. Neither of those I am prepared to give him.

He examines my face, then reaches under the pile of papers and produces a file. He turns over the flap and twists it towards me.

"I believe this was your mother. Bronwyn Eden."

"That wasn't my mom's name," I lie. Although that last name is new. A name I've never heard before.

"And yet you look so very alike."

I lean even further forward and gaze down at a picture of a young woman. A beautiful woman. A woman who looks like my aunt. Who looks like me. The photo is far bigger than the one in the locket and I can see more clearly the colors in her eyes, the texture of her hair, the smoothness of her skin.

"She was a very talented magical ... uniquely talented. She possessed a powerful gift–"

"What gift?" I ask.

The chancellor smiles again. Does he suspect that I already know? "She was a great asset to the authorities."

I glance at him. There's an eagerness in his eyes now.

"What happened to this woman?" I ask, my fingers desperate to grasp the photo and slide it into my jacket.

The chancellor frowns and slides the folder away from me. It's painful, physically painful to watch it go, and I have to force myself not to snatch it back. He closes the file and drops it into a waiting drawer.

"I've been very careful, Rhianna, to keep your parentage secret. I believe that if I revealed it, you'd be in danger."

I bristle on my seat. "Why?"

"Like I said, her gift was unique and powerful. It gave our side an unprecedented advantage in our continuing struggle with the gangs and with the West." He leans forward in his seat. "I wasn't chancellor back then. But I was already on the council and chosen to work with your mother–"

"You don't know if she was my mom," I insist.

"–I saw the full extent of her ability."

"What ability?" I snap in frustration.

"The ability to read the future."

I swallow. Is that such a gift? Such a talent? Would knowing what the future was to bring, stop it from happening, make it any less painful? Because she died, didn't she? Did she see her own death too? Did she try to stop it?

I think of those memories in my head. Of the dreams I had as a girl. Knowing what was to come never prevented it from occurring. Those men still came in the night. They still beat and abused my aunt.

I screw up my eyes, those memories rising, swirling in my head.

The future came no matter what and all those dreams did was torture me, frighten me half to death.

"Miss Blackwaters?" the chancellor says, pulling me back to the present, to this room that's too hot and too stuffy.

"I don't see how that was a powerful ability," I say.

The chancellor scoffs. "We had less control over the forces in the West back then. Our country – our way of life – was threatened daily. There were frequent battles at the border that spilled into our lands. We lost lives. Many lives. Not to mention the infrastructure and resources that were destroyed too. We were at a very real risk of straying into another war."

I nod. My aunt had told me of those darker days.

"Your mother–"

"She's not my mom," I insist.

The chancellor smiles like he doesn't believe me. "Was able to predict when the enemy would strike, how they would strike. She could see their plans and their weapons. She gave us an advantage that turned our struggles around. We had the upper hand and we used it to our advantage."

I think of my aunt. Strong willed, determined, brave. Most of all principled. She had her beliefs – a sense of right and wrong – and she stuck to it. She hated the authorities and everything they stood for. She told me time and again they could not be trusted.

I always assumed my mom was just like my aunt. Same strength, same beliefs. But she aided the authorities, she worked for them, she helped to destroy their enemies. Could that really be true?

Unease whistles through my veins. The more I learn about my past – about who I am, where I came from – the more confused I feel.

"You can't change the future," I mumble.

"How would you know, Miss Blackwaters?" he asks. "Have you ever tried?"

That unease inside me seems to grow in the room too, curling around me, squeezing me tight. It presses against my lungs making it hard to breathe. It presses against my skull causing pain to spike through my brain.

The chancellor smiles and I see it's his doing.

"No," I say, sinking my nails into my palms. I won't give him anything. I won't betray myself or my aunt or Azlan or Stone. He squeezes a little tighter still and my skin prickles with discomfort. "But fate is a powerful force – that's what all the books at the academy say – you can't go against it."

"But fate gave us your mother as a weapon in our struggles. Fate wanted us to know what we were facing."

I blink. Is that true?

"She told me," the chancellor says quietly, "that one day a girl would come with abilities even greater than hers." All his focus is trained on my face.

I stare at him. "What girl?" I say.

"I don't know, Rhianna Blackwaters, but sometimes I wonder if she is you."

I manage a smile. "Me? I've been teased, laughed at … bullied at the academy for my ignorance and my hopelessness. I am no more some powerful magical, chancellor, than my pet pig is. I'm not the girl you are looking for." I laugh. "Or perhaps this woman lied to you. Perhaps there is no girl."

"Can you see the future?" he asks, no mirth on his own face. He has me in a vise now, like a giant hand has hold of me and is squeezing me more and more tightly. Or perhaps I'm caught in the invisible coils of a snake.

My ribs creak, dark spots swim on my vision, vicious pain smarts all through my body. I keep my eyes locked on him, not showing how much it hurts. What choice do I have? If I blow his magic apart, he'll see just how powerful I am. And if I scream out in pain – if I let any of the agony I'm feeling spill into the bond – Azlan will be bursting into this office all guns blazing and it will be game over for all of us.

"See the future? No," I say. "No more than you can."

I grit my teeth, concentrating with all my might on not letting my pain spike through the bond.

"Maybe I'm not giving you enough motivation to think,

Rhianna Blackwaters. Maybe you need that motivation to focus."

He holds out his hand and clicks his fingers. A flame jumps to life, hovering above his palm before swimming slowly towards me. The heat of it smarts against my face, the brightness of it making my eyes water.

"I know how vain young women can be," he says, "how highly they prize their faces. And you do have a pretty, if not very cultured, face. It would be such a shame to ruin it."

He edges the flame closer and the heat is unbearable, my skin scorching.

That memory in my head comes searing to the forefront. Of fire. Of everything burning.

"I'm telling you the truth," I say, glaring at him through the dancing flame.

"Are you?"

He holds my gaze, letting the flame burn against my skin. I don't move. I don't feel. He thinks he's the first man to try and hurt me. The first man to try and take something from me. He's not. And I'm not scared of him.

Eventually he falls back with a sigh of disappointment, the flame extinguishing in a puff of smoke, the tight hold on my body opening like spring.

I'm forced to smother my own sigh of relief as he picks up his pen. I know he's going to dismiss me. But I'm not ready to go yet. He knew my mom. Does he know what happened to her?

"What happened to that woman?" I ask again.

"I am most certain that woman was your mother."

I shrug like I don't care.

He smiles coldly. "Our enemies learned about her, learned of our weapon, and they snatched her from us. Used her against us. Of course," he shakes his head, "we rescued her eventually, brought her back home, where she belonged. But by that point she was already carrying a child. Some say the father was a dark magical from the West."

The words echo around my head. A dark magical? My father? I think of the picture in my locket – the one Summer now has. The man in that picture looked kind, gentle. Was he?

"Wh-what happened to her?" I repeat.

"Murdered," he says, and the flash of the snake returns, cruelty hovering in his eyes. I wait for the strike, for the fangs. "Brutally tortured and murdered."

"How?" I say, the room suddenly even hotter, spinning in front of my eyes. All the pain now concentrating right in the depths of my heart.

"Crimson magic."

I want to fold over my knees and vomit. I want to curl up into a ball and sob. I want to be far, far away from him and from everyone.

But I'm stuck on this seat, the chancellor's eyes perusing my face, squashing every emotion I'm feeling deep, deep down inside me.

"Who?" I say, my voice loud in my own ears.

"I don't know, I'm afraid. But, of course, it's of no real interest to you anyway, seeing as she wasn't your mother." The chancellor picks up his pen and snaps off the lid, ruffling the papers in front of him. "Thank you for coming to see me, Miss Blackwaters. This was a most interesting conversation." Heat creeps into my cheeks. Was it? Did I give too much away?

I take this as my cue to leave and stand, my legs weak beneath me, every step towards the door a struggle to appear normal, composed.

As I reach for the handle, Azlan so close I can feel him

on the other side of the door, the chancellor calls out, not raising his gaze from his paperwork.

"If you do remember anything more, Miss Blackwaters, about your childhood, about your aunt or your mother, you will be sure to tell me, won't you?"

"Y-y-yes."

"Same goes for any unusual abilities. We're always keen to pick out the best talent from the academy."

I push down the handle and stumble out of his office almost falling straight into Azlan's arms as the door slams behind me.

"Rhi!" he says, with concern.

I shake my head, pulling myself upright.

"I'm okay," I whisper, although every part of my body screams with pain.

He looks at me and then the guards still flanking the doorway and the secretary hovering off in the distance.

"Let's go," he says, stiffening his stance and taking a grip of my elbow. To all the pairs of eyes watching us, I'm sure it looks like he's marching an uncooperative brat out of the building, when really I'm relying on him to keep me upright and moving, my legs so weak they might give way any moment, air struggling to reach my lungs.

He picks up the pace, sensing my distress, and we crash through the exit and into the daylight. I fling back my head and gasp, sucking fresh air into my lungs, Azlan's grip still tight on my arm, his other hand stroking circles over my lower back.

"Breathe, Rhianna, just breathe."

I close my eyes, focusing on the low tenor of his voice, of his warm touch, of the comfort of his bond. My body relaxes. The feeling of panic subsides. I blow away the anxiety and open my eyes.

"Okay?" he says.

I manage a nod. I can tell he wants to ask me what happened, but it's too dangerous here. Too many prying ears and curious eyes.

He helps me up onto his bike, wrapping my arms tight around his body, squeezing my hands, and then getting us the hell out of here.

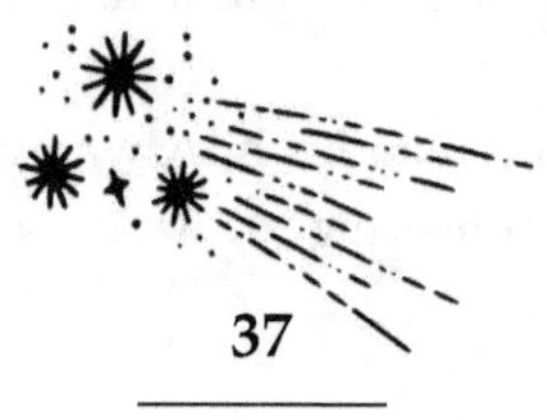

37

S tone

I PACE THE FRONT ROOM, peering at my watch, pacing and peering some more, the ticking hands on my watch barely registering. I know they are safe, I can feel it in the bond in the pit of my stomach, but until I see it with my own eyes, until she's safe and sound in my arms, I'm not going to truly believe it.

I hover by the window, watching the street, then pace some more, scrubbing my hands through my hair and feeling like I might go insane.

Finally – *finally* – I hear the rush of his bike and immediately I skid through the room and hallway, waiting by the door.

I hear their footsteps, the turn of the key, the creak of the door and then she's falling into my arms. I catch her, dragging her close into my body, and peer up at Azlan.

"You weren't followed?" I ask.

"No, we took a deviating route. York will be expecting us back soon though."

"What happened?"

"I don't know," Azlan says anxiously, closing the door behind him.

"Rhi?" I say.

She's shivering, her skin pale and cold.

"Let's get her a drink," Azlan says, "bring her through to the sitting room, Phoenix."

I lift her into my arms, cradling her against my chest, and carry her through, lowering her down onto his couch.

"What happened?" I ask again, brushing the hair away from her face. "Sweetheart, what happened?"

She looks up at me with sad eyes that nearly break my heart and invites me to see. I hesitate, then taking her hand in mine and kneeling by her side, I enter her thoughts.

"What the fuck?" I growl. "I'm going to kill that wrinkly bastard." She shakes her head limply, imploring me to look further. There's more? Apprehension shivers down my spine. He tortured her, threatened to burn her face, how can there be more?

It's not as bad as I feared, though. He doesn't know about our bonds, about her fated mates. He's ignorant – at least at the moment – about the powers Rhianna possesses. But she's hurting.

"Your parents?" I whisper, as Azlan joins us, offering her a steaming cup of cocoa.

"I added a shot of whisky," he says. "Drink some."

He holds it to her lips and, cradling her hands around his, she sips at the concoction, bringing color to her cheeks.

"He said my father was a dark magical from the West. He

said my mom was killed, tortured with ... with crimson –
scarlet – magic."

Azlan looks at me, then drops to his knees alongside us.

We've been waiting for this, for her to tell us, to broach
this subject. To know for sure.

"Crimson magic," Azlan repeats.

"That kind of magic is bad, isn't it? Evil, dark."

I tilt my head to one side. "That's what you've heard?
What you've read?"

"Yes," she says, then hesitates, "and what I've felt."

I glance at Azlan meeting his dark eyes. Then I turn
back to our girl. In this moment, she looks so young, so
small, so vulnerable. Not the powerful, fiery woman I know
her to be. All I want to do is hold her in my arms and
promise her that everything is going to be all right. But the
more we're pulled into this strange web, the more I'm beginning to doubt that it's that simple.

Rhianna had dreams. Okay, dreams long ago, but
dreams nonetheless that showed her the future. Just like her
mother. She has not one, but three fated mates. She is no
ordinary girl.

"Rhi," I say gently, "that image in your mind, of that
injury."

"To Spencer Moreau," Azlan adds, and my eyes flick to
him briefly.

"Did you do that?"

Her entire body shakes and she drops her gaze to her
lap, unable to look at either of us. For a long moment, she
doesn't answer me, and I can hear the hands of my watch
again, ticking away. But then she swallows.

"Yes," she said. "Yes, it was me. I did it. And ..." She peers
up at me, fear and defiance shining in her eyes. "It
happened again, when I was trapped by Barone. I felt it

again, sizzling on my fingertips, begging me, pleading to …
kill him. And out in the forest with Summer when she stole
my necklace."

"It might not have been–"

"Spencer said it was. And Tristan. And Barone. Even
Summer. They all recognized it for what it was."

So had I. I knew what it was. It was why I'd been so
desperate to pry that thought from her head.

"What does it mean?" she says, chewing on her lip.
"Tristan said it would get me locked up."

"It's old magic," I say carefully, "ancient and powerful
magic."

"Dark magic?" she asks.

"Sometimes, yes. Not always."

She shivers. "I don't like the way it makes me feel."

"How does it make you feel?" Azlan asks.

"Like a killer."

"Sometimes we have no choice but to kill," he says
sternly, staring down at his own hands. "Sometimes it's
justified."

"If Renzo was trying to kill you–"

"But Spencer wasn't. And neither was Summer," she
snaps, "they just really, really pissed me off and I … I … I
nearly …"

"But you didn't. You're a good person, Rhi," I say,
clasping her hands in mine. "You know that. This ability
doesn't make you–"

"Evil," she says.

"Twisted," I joke lamely. "Slightly disturbed, and maybe
deranged. Not evil."

She manages a lame smile back, although it fades
quickly. "The chancellor said my mom made a prediction.
That a girl would come. A powerful girl."

Azlan scoffs. "People have been making predictions for centuries. The return of the fire queen," he says dismissively.

"From the fairytale?" she asks.

"Exactly, from the fairytale."

"The chancellor seems to believe it."

"You think you're that girl," I ask with a nudge of my elbow.

Her cheeks pinken. "I don't know."

"The chancellor wants it to be true, Rhi. That's all."

Azlan glances at his watch. "We need to get going. Otherwise York will ask questions."

"No, not yet," Rhi says firmly.

"If we delay–"

"Not yet," she says, grabbing a fistful of my shirt and fistful of his jacket and dragging both of us onto the sofa. Azlan looks like he might argue about this, but I simply shrug. If she has the ability to wield crimson magic, I think we'd better start doing what this woman wants, and if she wants to rest her head against Azlan's chest and her feet in my lap, so be it.

"I've been parted from you both for too long," she says, snuggling up, "and my bond has been mighty unhappy about it."

For once my stubborn-assed friend seems happy to fold. He wraps his arm around her shoulder and kisses the crown of her head. "You're right, too long. I'll think of some excuse for York."

She smiles and murmurs like a contented little cat, and I guess I should be content to just snuggle like this, comfort her after the rough day she's had. But the way she's laid out between us is giving me ideas, hot, freaking explicit ideas.

Besides, there may be far better ways of offering her comfort.

"You know what else has been a long, long time since we did?" I growl.

"We did that only yesterday," she murmurs, eyes closed, although she rubs the sole of her foot against my groin making me instantly stiff.

"But it's been a long time since the three of us were together," I say and her eyes flicker open, registering the heat in mine.

"Oh," she says.

"Rhianna has had–" Azlan begins but his words are interrupted as she cups her hands around the back of his neck and drags his mouth down onto hers.

My bond sparks into life watching the two of them and I can't help thinking about Azlan's cousin. The golden boy of the academy. Was he really made for her too? Could that even work? The boy is arrogant, self-obsessed and fucking good looking.

"Professor?" she says, grinding her foot against me now.

"Yes, Miss Blackwaters?" I ask.

She crooks her finger and beckons me closer and I kiss her while Azlan busies himself removing her clothing. Soon she's perched between us in only a bra and her panties. I double-take.

"What the hell!" I say, taking in silk and lace and a serious lack of material overall.

"Azlan bought them for me," she says.

"Dirty bastard," I say, grinning at my friend.

"I couldn't fucking help myself," he mumbles.

I trail my hand up her ribcage, cupping her tit and squeezing it through the silky material. "Fuck," I say, "you look like Christmas all wrapped up in a pretty bow. One I want to tear apart with my teeth." I growl, diving towards her.

"Nope," she says, batting me away, "you are not ruining my nice new underwear, Professor."

"Are you sure you've not ruined it yourself, little mate?" Azlan asks, sliding his fingers inside the gusset of her teeny, tiny panties and making her whine. "Ahh, yes. Yes, you have. Already so wet for us."

She grinds against his fingers, squealing with frustration when he draws his hand away.

"It's been a long time and I want you coming round my cock, not my fingers."

She gives him one hell of a bratty scowl – the kind of look that does something unhinged to me and I'm pinning her down on the sofa in the next heartbeat and tearing away those panties.

"How about I come around both your cocks," she says breathlessly, as I line myself up with her glistening-wet pussy.

"You will. First mine, then his," I say, taking her hands in mine and pinning them above her head.

"No," she says wildly, shaking her head as I thrust into her. "Together. I want you together."

I halt, peering up at my friend, his eyes dark with lust, and then down at hers, all needy.

"Together?" I choke out, close to coming inside her at the very thought of it.

"Y-y-yes," she mewls, circling her hips and making me groan. Such a freaking brat!

"You're not ready for that yet, sweetheart," Azlan says, his voice straining with tension, the tendons on his neck looking like they might pop out.

"I am."

"No," he insists, "we'd hurt you."

"I want you both inside me," she says, circling her hips more desperately now, and squeezing my fingers tightly.

"You're so tight, Miss Blackwaters," I groan, "and you may have noticed we're both pretty big." I grin and she whimpers. "If it's something you want to do, we need to prepare you first."

"How about ..." she pants beneath me, using her strength to roll up so we're kneeling together on the sofa, her legs wrapped around me, "how about ... the other place?"

"The other place?" I ask with a quirked eyebrow.

"Uh huh."

Azlan edges closer so she's sandwiched between our bodies. "Do you," he says, his voice so strained now it sounds on the verge of snapping, "mean here, sweetheart?"

Over her shoulder, I watch as he slips his fingers between the plump globes of her ass and tickles her tight hole.

"Hmmmm," she says dreamily.

"Fuck," I say. "Have you ever ...?" I peer up at my friend eagerly but he shakes his head. "I'm sorry sweetheart, but we'd need to prepare you there too. Loosen you up, stretch you a little."

"Professor?" she says with more than a little hint of frustration. "Are you telling me there isn't a spell that can do that for us?"

My eyes leap back to my friend.

"Do you know it?" he asked me.

Do I know it? Like every magical teenage boy hasn't had the thing memorized forward and backward by the time he hits sixteen.

Have I ever used it? Not for a while.

"Are you sure about this?" I ask her, leaning back a little so I can see her properly. She has that drowsy, dreamy look about her – it's nearly as hot as the brattiness – but her eyes are bright and eager and through the bond I can feel how much she wants this.

Fuck, I want it too. I've been fantasizing about it over and over again in my mind, not really believing it was a fantasy that would ever come true.

"I can do the spell, sweetheart. But it doesn't mean it won't be uncomfortable, especially for your first time."

"I'm not afraid," she says, lifting her chin in that defiant way she does.

"Of course, you're not," I say, smiling at her and brushing the hair from her face. Then I close my eyes and whisper the words, letting my magic get down and personal with her backside, something that has my cock twitching in her pussy.

"Ohhhh," she moans, and maybe I'm wrong. Maybe this won't be uncomfortable, maybe she's going to enjoy it a lot.

I expect my friend to go straight for the jackpot. After all, he's been away from our mate for days. Instead, he's falling forward on his hands and knees and nuzzling his nose between her ass cheeks. She whimpers and then he's nuzzling her with his lips and his tongue, showing that tight hole of hers a whole lot of love.

"Do you like that?" I ask her, grinding into her pussy as Azlan licks out her backside.

"Yes," she whimpers and I think I fall that little bit more in love with her. The things she's willing to try, to do, to risk. Fuck I really do love her.

I lift her right leg, wrapping it higher around my waist, opening her up for me and Azlan and then I kiss her, raking her bottom lip through my teeth, making her moan some more.

"Ready?" Azlan asks, rolling up onto his knees and coming closer, his hands on her little waist.

She nods, but it's not good enough for him. He wants to hear her say it.

"Rhianna, words," he growls.

She rolls her eyes, but thankfully only I see. I jerk my eyebrow, and mouth. "Don't keep him waiting, sweetheart, you have no idea how fucking irresistible you are."

She rolls her eyes a second time, then says, "Fuck me."

And the lady doesn't need to ask twice. Azlan grips her tight, keeping her still, pushing his way inside her tight hole. And I can feel him, feel him through her delicate walls.

She gasps, her head falling backwards and knocking against my friend's broad chest.

"Okay?" I whisper.

"Hmmmm," she moans, and I lose my ability to hold back. I thrust into her, Azlan doing the same, her little body buffeted between our two larger, bigger, stronger ones.

For a moment, I worry it's too much for her, too forceful, but then her magic is spinning in the air, bright and beautiful, lighting up the darkening room, leaving me in no doubt how much she wants this, how good it's making her feel.

She cries out, the magic casting her skin in a multitude of colors, her eyes so bright and vibrant, they're almost otherworldly, and then she's coming, sweet sounds I've never heard her make rushing from her lips, her body jolting with pleasure. And I think she's never looked so beautiful.

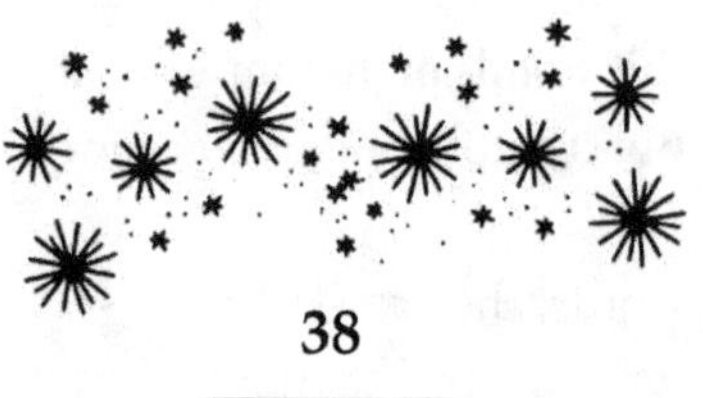

38

R^{hi}

I**T'S SO** hard to drag myself from these two men, especially when I know being left on my own will mean being left with my thoughts. Their words have gone some way to reassuring me, but not completely. Stone may be able to read my thoughts – the man in black may be able to sense my emotions – but neither of them can know what it feels like to have crimson magic sailing through their veins. The power, the danger, the buzz it elicits. Part of me is desperate to play with it, to try my best to unleash it again, to see what I could do with it. The other part of me is petrified.

Am I a monster? Like my father? The kind of monster who tortured and murdered my mother? Is that what my aunt was hiding me from, protecting me from, all that time: myself?

These thoughts circle around and around in my mind all through an interrogation with York – the principal wanting to know why the chancellor had summoned me – still there as I walk the path back to my dorm. I guess York's not the only one curious about that, because as I near my building, Tristan Kennedy emerges from the shadows to stand in front of me.

It's dark, the campus quiet, only the fall wind frisking the changing leaves from the forest branches. They spin in the air, falling like confetti around our feet.

"The chancellor sent for you," he says.

"Wow, news really does fly at a phenomenal speed around this school." I tilt my head. "Or have you been spying on me again?"

"What did he want?" He frowns. "I didn't tell. I haven't told anyone."

I chew on my lip. For all Tristan Kennedy's many, many faults that much is true. He hasn't spilled one single one of my secrets – not about being unregistered, chased by the Wolves of Night, bonded to two men, or wielding crimson magic. Anyone of those secrets would be hot collateral in a place like the academy. Anyone else would have spread them like wildfire.

Then again, I'm not stupid. The reason he's kept my secrets is to protect himself, not me. He wouldn't want his golden boy reputation tarnished by a wayward fated mate.

"I know," I say simply, unable to help scowling back at him. I'm still mad as hell at him but my bond and my body don't seem to care. Neither does my magic. It's a damn flirt, fluttering near his, provoking it to come play. I wish my bond, my body and my magic would stop being so damn horny for such an asshole of a man and get a damn grip.

"Does he know?" he says, taking a step forward.

It's dark, but the night is a cool, clear one, the frigid air nipping at my nose, and I can see his face. He's worried, anxious. There are deep, dark circles under his eyes I've never seen before and his cheeks look almost sunken. Is it just a trick of the moonlight? Or maybe I'm right. He's concerned about being dragged into my mess if all my secrets are revealed.

"About what, Tristan?" I snap.

He fidgets on the spot, shifting his weight from one foot to the other and scrubbing his hand through his hair. I've never seen him look so uncomfortable.

"About your mates, about the bonds."

I shake my head. "No, you're perfectly safe."

"Are you?" he asks anxiously, eyes flicking to mine.

"Me?"

He nods.

Am I? The chancellor is cunning. I don't know if he saw through my act, if he knows more than he showed.

"I don't know."

He scrubs his hand through his hair a second time. "Maybe I should speak with my father. He's the only one the chancellor is afraid of. If the chancellor is going to–"

"Isn't your father far worse?"

"Yeah," he says, nodding his head quickly, "yeah, you're right. That's a stupid idea."

"It's okay, Tristan. I won't tell anyone about–"

"What did he want?" he asks, frowning again.

I sigh. I want to crawl into my bed and snuggle up with Pip, dissecting everything that's happened today with Winnie. I don't want to be standing out here in the cold with a man who makes me feel things I shouldn't.

"He wanted to talk about my mom."

"Your mom?"

"He knew her. She was ..." I peer into the crystal blue of his eyes. Can I truly trust him? Why am I even having this conversation with him? "She was a seer. I guess he's keen to know if I'm one too."

He holds my gaze and peers into my eyes with the same intensity. "Are you?"

My brow crinkles. Maybe I could lie and bluff my way through a meeting with the chancellor but it's harder with him, it's always been harder with him. I'm already fighting, controlling so many other emotions.

"I think I had the gift when I was young, a little girl. I don't think I have it anymore."

"Did you see ... did you see anything about us?"

My hand flies to my head. Those memories. Azlan crashing through the door. That hand stretching out to touch me – Barone's hand. Burning – everything burning.

"Rhi?" I feel his warm hand on my shoulder, and my bond ignites. I jerk out of my reverie and take a stumbling pace away.

"Don't touch me!"

He frowns harder, thunder clouding his expression now, all that anxiety gone. He opens his mouth as if he's going to argue with me, then slams it shut.

"I'm glad you're okay," he mumbles and my jaw falls open in disbelief as I watch him storm away. He's glad I'm okay? That might be the nicest thing he's actually ever said to me.

I laugh, shaking my head and scurry out of the cold and into the dorm.

Winnie is at her desk, a duvet snuggled around her shoulders and Pip in her lap.

"Jeez," I mutter, as I shut the door behind me. "I think it's colder in here, than outside."

"Probably," Winnie says, "this dorm is a shithole."

I pull my own duvet off my bed, wheel my own chair closer to Winnie and Pip, flopping down onto it.

I've already given Winnie a summary of my meeting with the chancellor over text message but I guess my demeanor is a giveaway that more's happened since.

I tell her about what happened with Stone and Azlan first. Pip grunts grumpily all the way through my recounting as if he really, really doesn't want to hear this. Unfortunately for him, my best friend is pretty darn insistent, wanting to know all about the mechanics in a lot of detail.

When she's satisfied, she asks me, with a dead serious expression, "Did you enjoy it, though? I mean, I know lots of dudes want to do that stuff, but you're under no obligation if you don't want to so–"

"Winnie, it was freaking amazing!"

She sighs with relief. "Thank God, you'd have shattered a hell of a lot of my fantasies if you'd said it sucked."

I shiver remembering just how good it did feel and Winnie shakes her head.

"I should be really, really jealous of you, Rhianna Black-waters, but you're just too darn cute so I can't be."

"Me? Cute?"

Winnie rolls her eyes. "Here we go again. You've just had one super-hot threesome with two of the sexiest men on the planet and you've been asked to the ball by the hottest guy at the academy, but, noooo, there's no way you might consider you're actually cute."

I shrug and Pip snorts. I tug the duvet more firmly around my shoulders.

"Talking of Tristan Kennedy–"

"Oh, so you do concede he's hot then?"

"Winnie, I'm not blind. I know he's hot." I can feel just how hot he is every time I'm near him. "That isn't the point."

"What did he want this time?"

I consider this question. "I don't really know. To check I wasn't blabbing to the chancellor I guess."

"Probably just an excuse to talk to you." I snort. "Rhi, I'm serious about him. He's never acted this way before about a girl. He thinks you're his fated mate. He's not going to give up that easily."

My shoulders slump and Winnie changes the subject.

"Well, seeing as you aren't going to accept Tristan's invitation to the ball. Who are you going to go with?"

"You?" I say hopefully.

Winnie grins. "Yeah, you can come with me and Trent. Although, no telling him about your threesome antics. I don't want him getting any ideas. I am far too jealous to share that boy with another girl. In fact, I don't know how those two big, growly men of yours do it. They both seem really, really ... possessive."

"Yeah," I say. Another reason why accepting Tristan as my fated mate – accepting anyone else as my fated mate – would most definitely not work. Stone and the man in black are friends – the best of friends – linked by destiny herself. Their willingness to share I am pretty certain is reserved to themselves and themselves alone, no matter what they might say about the matter.

"Have you thought about your dress?" Winnie asks, pointing to her desktop which is covered in cut-out pictures from magazines. "Nonny is going to make me one. She sent me all these clippings so I could get some ideas." I wheel my chair closer and pick a few of the clippings up. One is a sleek sophisticated-looking dress; the other poofy and princess-like. "I'm sure she'd make you one too if you wanted."

"Is there enough time?" I ask. The ball is less than a week away. I'm surprised Winnie has left the dress-making so late.

"Rhi," Winnie laughs, knocking my shoulder, "magic, remember?"

"Oh, yeah," I say grinning at her. I guess despite all my time here and all the magic I've used, it still feels unnatural to use it so freely and so often. I wonder if I'll ever get used to it.

"Then again," Winnie says with a cunning smile, "you could ask the man in black to buy you a dress. I bet he'd buy you something truly amazing and eye-wateringly expensive – something to rival even Summer's dress."

"She would most definitely kill me if I turned up in a dress better than hers."

"Oh do it, Rhi," Winnie says, clapping her hands together. "It's so clear she thinks she is going to be the most beautiful girl at that ball. I'd love for you to turn up and knock her off her throne."

"Me?"

Pip squeaks at me and Winnie thumps me harder on the shoulder this time. "Why do you think that girl hates you so much, Rhi? I bet you turned up at the academy and her magic mirror told her she was no longer the fairest in the academy."

"I love you, Winnie, but I think your mind has warped."

Winnie scoffs. "So will you ask him?"

I shake my head. "If I turn up in a really expensive dress, everyone will want to know how I got my hands on it and then ..."

Winnie groans. "I guess you're going to have to make do with one of Nonny's designs then."

"I'm sure Rosa's creations are far better than anything we could buy in a shop."

"Hmmm," Winnie says, examining a halter neck dress with a lot of fake flowers pinned round the neckline.

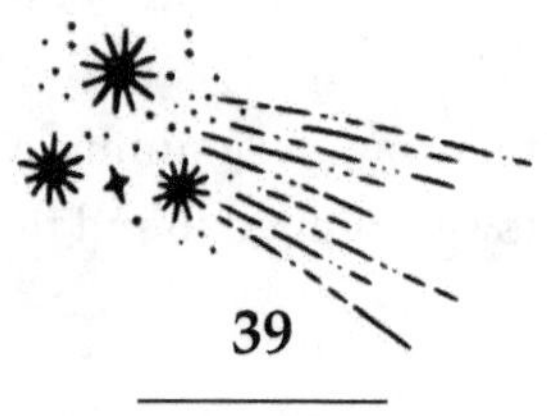

39

S pencer

A WEEK PASSES and I fall into the routine easily. Up at the crack of dawn for physical training in the yard, breakfast in the mess hall, then duties – mopping and cleaning the barracks, scrubbing the washing, inspecting the weapons – combat training in the afternoon, dinner, lights out and try to sleep with the boom and blasts of real battles somewhere out there in the dark.

They won't let me out there yet. I've asked – pleaded often enough – but out here it doesn't matter who my family is, doesn't matter I won Arrow Hart the Cross-lantic cup. I'm just a new recruit like all the other new recruits and despite our training and study at the academy, they aren't prepared to put us out there to fight yet. I'll have to wait.

Instead, I'm here outside, cleaning windows, slapping cloths against murky panes of glass, washing away grime and dirt. The frigid wind sweeps in from the West, bringing the stench of fire and burning. But it's eerily silent today. No booms, no blasts, no fighting. Although something in the distance, something faint, and barely discernible – the crack of wings? – has me twisting my head to squint against the low clouds out in that direction.

What's it like out there in the West? It's where they pushed the dark forces all those years ago, during the war that formed the republic. I've been told for as long as I can remember it's a barren place, a sinister place, a dangerous place. But all I see, squinting even harder, is trees and scrubland disappearing all the way to the horizon. It's not how I imagined it as a kid. No black clouds hovering over the land, no dead trees, no forest of thorns. I scoff. I read too many fucking stories as a kid.

"Are you scheduled a break, soldier?" a deep voice says, and I turn to find one of the commanding officers scowling at me.

I give him the obligatory salute. "No, Sir."

"Then why the pause? Keep it up. This isn't the academy. There'll be no maids to follow after and do this for you."

I nod and return to my work. It's not the first time one of the commanding officers has alluded to my privileged lifestyle back home. They seem to think I'm incapable of hard work, despite all the times I've shown them how hard I can work out there on the training ground.

I drop my cloth into the water. It's tepid now and I warm it with my magic, swishing the cloth around in the bubbles and slapping it against another window. Of course, this could all be done in mere minutes if they let me use my magic but I guess that's not the point.

The commanding officer stands watching me and then I

hear the pound of boots, another officer coming to stop by his side.

I drag the cloth over the glass, dragging the dirt and scum along with it. The commanding officers converse in tense, low voices and I strain my ears to listen, watching them in the reflection of the glass.

They don't tell us a thing out here. I feel like I knew more of what was happening when back in the capital.

"Any news on what the scouts found?" the first one asks the second.

The second shakes his head. "The major's keeping the information close to his chest."

"What do you think that means?"

The second one drops his gaze to his boots. "It can only be bad news, if it were good, why not share it?"

The first one chews on this, quiet for a moment. "There're rumors among our soldiers of a weapon."

"There've always been rumors like that."

"But have you ever known the major to send scouts into their lands?"

The second shakes his head again and together they walk away.

A weapon? I haven't heard rumors like that among the new recruits. But then hardly anyone talks to me and we're not at the front. Perhaps the rumors are yet to spread to us.

I smooth the wet cloth against the window, water racing down the pane.

What the hell could it be?

✳.

I LIE out flat on the lumpy bunk, staring up at the ceiling where the plaster's cracking and listen to those distant booms. I think of my brother. Think about how he died. About what happened to him. They say he died a hero's death – at least that's what they told my parents. But there's never been any more detail than that. And no one treats me like the brother of a hero. In fact, most people give me a wide berth, ignoring me as best they can.

It makes me think of the pig girl. Of how they treat her back at the academy. Maybe I'm beginning to know how that feels.

Except, maybe they have more reason to avoid me than they ever did the pig girl. She was different: skinny, scrawny in her old ill-fitting clothes, with not a clue about one damn thing. Okay, she may have been an unregistered too – certainly some people suspected it, whispered about it – but very few actually knew it to be true.

Me, on the other hand, there's every reason in the world to avoid me. The werebeast. The cursed boy. The dangerous monster. Do they know? Did my brother let our secret slip?

I think back to the moment the man in black and I were attacked out there in the forest. It had been instinctual. I'd changed before I even knew what I was doing. Had the same happened to Tobias? Did he give himself away in the heat of battle?

I roll onto my side, tucking my hands under my cheek. Fucking bastards. A werebeast in battle is powerful, strong, unstoppable. An ally any of them should have been thankful for.

There's some big lad snoring on the bunk next to me and somewhere at the other end of the dorm, another dude is muttering in his sleep.

They all look the same. Shorn hair, dazed eyes. I think I'm the only one who volunteered to be here and yet I'm stuck with these losers doing nothing useful but scrubbing floors.

I can't stand it. Not with the wolf prowling inside me eager to be released. Being here has done nothing to tamper down his restlessness. My mother was probably right all along. But I can't think about that. Can't think about what it would have been like to make Pig Girl mine. She's far away from me and him. Safe.

The monster growls. He disagrees and he's pissed about it. Really pissed.

I toss back onto my stomach and try to focus on falling asleep but those snores and those booms and the air thick with other people's breath drives me half mad.

I snap upright, swinging my gaze around. Everyone else in the room is asleep and through the window I can see the tiniest sliver of moon.

I slide off my bunk, my bare feet hitting the cold floor almost soundlessly, then I creep through the room, along the gangway between the rows of bunks and to the door. I peer over my shoulder. All still asleep. I push open the door and step out into the cold night wearing only my boxers and a vest.

The air stinks like it always does out here, of putrid magic, singed flesh, and gunpowder. I stare up at that moon, the beast inside me suddenly silent and alert, waiting to see what I'll do.

Did the smell bother him too? The confinement? The battle just out of reach?

I thought this place would be an escape. Now I wonder if it's a prison.

I want to know what happened to him. I want to know so badly. My brother. My big damn brother. He was never as strong as me, never as confident. Always nervous, chewing on his nails, eyes flicking around the room. He hated the affliction, I think, even more than me. It made him jumpy.

But that came later, there was a time before that. When we were younger. When she kept us hidden, away from others. So long ago I hardly remember it. Flipping between our two forms, chasing each other, rolling in the earth, nipping at each other's fur. I remember how strong the smells were then, how vivid, how close to him I felt. Before we knew. Before we understood. It wasn't a gift, a game, a prize. It was a god damn burden.

Did it break him?

I stare down at my hands. Find them trembling in the dark. I should have talked to him about it. I should have talked to him full stop. I can't stand not to know. Not to understand. I can't stand that he's no longer here. I want him back.

He'd be the only one to understand. The only one who would tell me the truth. Who'd look in my eyes with no judgment, no disgust.

I'm running, before I know it, running out here in the darkness, away from the barracks, away from the training ground, towards the magic flashing violent colors above the tree line.

And one minute I'm me, one minute I'm him, I hardly notice it happen, a scent on the wind pulling both of us in one direction.

It takes him through the trees. I catch glimpses of it from the abyss, of the crescent moon, the hard earth, the fallen leaves. The scent grows stronger in his nose. It's not right. Not how it should be. But it's a scent we both know.

The booms from the magic grow closer, louder, rattling his bones, shaking the ground beneath his paws. That scent grows stronger too and then he's halting, sniffing the earth, pawing at the ground.

And I come back to myself. On my hands and knees. Naked, covered in cold sweat, shivering against the cold. That scent – my brother's scent – so clear in my nostrils. I sink to my stomach.

This is where it happened.

In the distance I can hear the shouting of soldiers, the crashing and colliding of magic.

It happened here.

I rest my cheek against the cold mud. His scent has sunk into the earth, becoming one with it.

I close my eyes. It happened here. Was he alone like I am now? Was there someone with him? Holding his hand, promising it would be okay?

My face is wet. I burrow my nose right into the ground. His blood's in the earth. Our blood.

On the surface, I have so much. All the riches of my family. Their name. My strength and power. My reputation.

But hasn't my brief time here already shown how little those are worth?

The only thing I ever had – the only real thing – was him.

When it comes to it – when I get my chance – I'm going to kill every last one of them.

40

R^{hi}

Luckily, the upcoming ball proves a massive distraction to every student and teacher at the school, and Tristan's little stunt in the Great Hall seems well and truly forgotten. At least for the time-being. It helps that, despite Winnie's prediction, he appears to have given up on me. No more public declarations, no more ambushes in the hallway or attempts to carry my books. In fact, I hardly see him, although occasionally, I have that feeling he's nearby, invisible and watching me.

Perhaps Summer really has found a way to use my necklace as a love charm. She still has it, slung around her neck. I catch glimpses of it tucked into her school blouse and her gym kit. It's clear she's wearing it all the time. I want it back. I'm going to get it back. I just haven't thought of how I'm going to do it yet.

I glare at her now in Dr. Johnson's lesson as she sits at the front of the class talking obnoxiously loudly about the dress she's going to wear to the ball – the dress her father has had especially commissioned and shipped in from Aropia. She casually lets slip how much it cost – enough to have fed me and my aunt for a year easily. It makes me feel kind of sick, and I'm glad I didn't ask the man in black to buy me a dress after all.

We're meant to be practicing changing pencils into butterflies. Unfortunately, rather than telling Summer to be quiet and get on with her work, Dr. Johnson is happy to be an obliging audience and so we're all forced to listen to every single miniscule detail about Summer's dress – the number of crystals sewn onto the bodice, the exact shade of blue, the matching tiara she's borrowing from her grandmother's priceless collection.

"Do you have your dress?" Trent asks Winnie as he wrestles with his wriggling pencil.

"Nonny's making my dress and Rhi's dress too. It should be here in the next day or two."

From the corner of my eyes, I notice Tristan's eyes flick up from his own completed work, to peer over at the three of us. He's sitting in the back row, a colorful butterfly perching on his desktop.

"How about you, Trent?" I ask him. "What are you going to wear?"

He grimaces. "I hate wearing a tux," he says, ringing a finger around the inside of his collar and rolling his shoulders.

"So don't wear one," Winnie says, inspecting her own perfect butterfly.

"You wouldn't mind?" he says. "I thought you'd want nice photos and all that shit."

"Oh there will be photos," Winnie says smiling, "but just wear what you're most comfortable in. I can look glam enough for the both of us."

Trent smiles and I decide the two of them really are perfect for one another.

I concentrate on my pencil which seems very reluctant to change its shape. I close my eyes and say the words, caressing the stupid object with my magic. It's much harder than it looks, the pencil stubbornly refusing to shift its form. I frown. I don't see how this will be of any benefit in the real world, anyway.

"You're not doing that right," a voice whispers by my ear and I flick open my eyelids.

There's no one there, but of course I know just who it is by the sound of his voice and the familiar tug in my stomach.

I ignore him, even though he's very close, so close I can feel his warm breath against my cheek. I am not about to start talking to him when he's invisible. People think I'm strange enough owning a pig. I don't need them thinking I talk to myself, too.

I close my eyes and concentrate even harder now, which is very difficult when I feel his arm brush against mine and his magic tingling in the air, begging mine to come play.

I open my eyes again. The pencil is still a damn pencil. I huff.

"It's a very easy spell, Piglet."

"Go away," I hiss under my breath, smiling when Winnie turns around to look at me.

"I need to talk to you," he continues.

Now? He needs to talk to me now. Perhaps it's him who is insane.

I don't respond, instead keeping my gaze locked firmly

on that pencil. I'm not playing his games. I keep staring at the pencil, even when I feel his knuckles brush the bare part of my thigh between my socks and my skirt. Even when I'm sure his lips press against my throat.

"That isn't talking," I hiss.

I am going to kill him. As soon as we're out of this class-room, I will–

"Do you need a dress?" he whispers so quietly in my ear, only I hear. I shake my head. What I need is for him to go away. Having him so close – touching me – is confusing. My bond thrums with pleasure, a pleasure I feel reflected throughout my body. And I can't help thinking about that kiss. A kiss I've been resolutely blocking from my mind – a kiss that set my entire body on fire. "I'll buy a dress for you if you like."

His whole hand is resting on my thigh now and I could bat it away. I could zap him with my magic. I could jump to my feet and pretend I need to fetch a book from the other side of the classroom. Something stops me from moving though. The bond. Or maybe just him. His scent is deep and his touch more than magic. It's so hard to resist both when he's this close, when his magic brushes over my skin and makes me shiver.

"I'll buy you anything you want," he breathes, his voice deep and husky, his warm lips pressing my ear. "Give you anything you want." His wet tongue sweeps around the shell of my ear and then he plunges it into my ear hole, making me shiver even harder, my legs and my hands beginning to shake.

I don't move. My own breath is loud in my ears. I try to focus on that pencil but all I can concentrate on is his hand on my thigh, tingling with magic. A hand that's dipping under my skirt.

Shit! What is wrong with me?

Am I just like all the other girls? A hopeless sucker for Tristan Kennedy. Am I that pathetic that I'm going to let him touch me like this, trail his fingers up the sensitive flesh of my inner thigh and graze the gusset of my panties.

"Stop," I mutter really damn pathetically, stifling a little moan.

"I can't," he breathes back and I bite my lip, everything between my legs already pulsing with the electricity of his touch.

My heart thumps in my chest. My breath turns needy. He waits, the thin fabric of my panties the only thing separating my most intimate part from his fingertips. Despite telling him to stop, I'm not pushing him away, I'm not getting up to leave.

"You really want me to stop?" he asks, nibbling at my earlobe.

I screw up my eyes. What do I want? My body, my bond, are screaming at me. They want him to touch me. They want it so badly I can't fight against it.

I shake my head. A tiny, almost indiscernible movement.

But it's enough. It's enough for him.

He slides his fingers under the silky material of my panties and gasps as his fingertips connect with the sensitive flesh that lies below. Already sensitive and swollen.

"Fuck, you're so ..." He groans. I can feel his other arm hooked around the back of my chair, his strong body pressed up against me. "Gonna make you ..."

He barely has to brush his fingers against me, his magic does the rest, gliding around my most intimate parts, stroking against my clit in delicious circles that has me biting down even harder on my lip.

"Yes," he whispers and then his mouth is back on my

neck, nibbling and licking up and down my throat. I think I might actually pass out. I want him to stop. We're in a classroom, surrounded by students. And I hate him. Everything about him. Everything he's done to me. Except I don't hate this. I don't hate it at all. I want it so badly. I don't want him to stop.

My breath turns panty and ragged, my pussy throbs, clenching and releasing.

"Shhh, you need to be quiet, Piglet, really quiet," he whispers.

But I'm losing control. His magic thrums against my clit and I slide lower in my seat, lifting my hips, wanting more, wanting more of his touch and his magic and the way he makes me feel.

I guess for once I'm grateful for how loud Summer and her adoring fans are, because the tension he's building inside me is too much. I fumble for his arm, gripping his wrist tightly with both my hands, and when I come, I come with a sigh I can't disguise and can't muffle.

As I do, I feel two of his fingers slide deep inside me and I clench around them in rhythmic waves. His free hand comes to cover my mouth, smothering the groans I'm making as he massages my spot.

"Shit," he mutters and I'm even more grateful Trent and Winnie are distracted by each other and not looking my way.

I come again with his fingers inside me and his mouth on my throat, scraping his teeth against my skin. This time it seems to go on and on forever – wave after wave crashing through my body and he has to hold me down in my seat.

When the bliss finally subsides, and I'm limp and breathless, I feel him slide his fingers from me.

Suddenly, I'm hit by a wave of shame and embarrassment, my cheeks growing incredibly hot.

What the hell have I just done? What the hell was I thinking?

By my ear I hear him slurping and sucking and I know the fingers he just had inside me are now in his mouth.

"Your pussy tastes damn good, Rhianna," he growls, making my stomach turn somersaults. "Want to meet me in the empty classroom at the end of the hallway and I'll eat you out? Make you come all over again. Shit, I could make you come all day and all night. Shit, I will if you let me."

My cheeks glow so hot, I'm pretty sure my skin must be melting.

I shake my head and lean over my pencil, pretending to be fascinated by it and not him.

He's quiet, and if it weren't for the press of his leg against mine, I'd have thought he'd gone.

Finally, he whispers, "I'll find you a suitable dress." And then he's moving away, reappearing a moment later at his desk, everyone too engrossed by Summer or their pencil spells to have noticed.

I rub my thighs together. I'm wet and sticky. What the hell am I doing?

41

___

R^{hi}

AFTER THAT I avoid Tristan Kennedy like the plague, trying to convince myself what happened in that classroom was a figment of my imagination, a little daydream – an extremely hot, explicit daydream – gone very wrong.

I certainly don't tell Winnie or Stone. I don't know what either of them would think. Especially as I don't know what to think myself.

Instead, I concentrate on my studies. I don't even engage in all the gossip and chatter about the ball, much to Winnie's frustration.

However, come Friday evening, Winnie is growing increasingly agitated by the fact our parcel from Nonny hasn't arrived, jumping every time one of our phones beep or there's the sound of heels crunching gravel outside on the path. Which means when there actually is a knock on the door, she practically dives across the room to answer it, jumping up and down with joy at the sight of yet another parcel.

"Our dresses!" she squeals, snatching them from a disgruntled groundsman's arms – seems he's been delivering lots of parcels in the runup to the big event, the biggest event of our lives Winnie keeps reminding me – and heaves it into the room.

"Jeez," I say, "that looks heavy. What on Earth did she make our dresses from?"

Winnie pays me no attention, ripping open the parcel and then tugging down the zipper on the clothes bag inside.

"Oh," she says, pulling the first dress from the bag.

"Oh?" I repeat. "What's wrong? Is it not how you wanted?"

"No, this isn't one of Nonny's creations. This is," she holds the dress up, staring at it with obvious admiration, "designer."

"What?" I say, coming closer to look at it. It's a jet-black dress with a bodice formed of silk petals and a pretty tulle skirt.

"Did you ask Azlan to buy you something after all?" Winnie asks, sounding a little put out. "You could have told me because Nonny worked–"

"No, I didn't ask him," I say, reaching inside the bag to pull out another designer dress, this one a midnight blue, strapless and silky.

"Maybe he decided to buy you some anyway," Winnie suggests, finding yet another dress inside the bag. This one a forest green.

"I doubt it. We haven't really talked about the ball." We've had other more important things on our minds. "Maybe Ellie told him to get me one." Ellie and I have been texting on and off and she definitely knows about the ball. "Although I already told her I was having one made."

Winnie pulls out another dress, this one a pale cream that almost reminds me of the dress I wore on Founders' Night. Then she rummages around in the bag, finding a small business card and examining it as I hang the dresses over the side of my bed, letting them drape down and admiring how pretty and elegant they are.

"I don't think it was the man in black or his sister."

"Well it wouldn't be Stone," I say, "he tells me on a regular basis how pitiful his teaching salary is."

"No, not the professor." Winnie twists the card my way. Over its surface is scribbled the name Tristan.

"You're kidding me," I say, reaching for the dresses to stuff them all back in the bag.

"What are you doing?" Winnie says.

"Sending them back to him."

"You can't, Rhi. They're too beautiful."

"I already have a dress. One Rosa is making me."

"I hate to shit on my grandma, but her work cannot compete with this."

"I don't care. I bet it will look beautiful anyway."

"Not as beautiful as these. I bet they cost ten times as much as Summer's. I mean this one – look at the label, Rhi. It's vintage *Mona*."

"You know that means nothing to me."

"They're priceless. Actually priceless." Winnie picks up her phone and starts typing, then thrusts the screen my way. "See how much this one went for at auction. I knew Tristan was loaded, but this ... I wonder how he even got hold of one."

"Still don't care," I say.

"Well, we may not have a choice. We may have to wear them if that parcel doesn't arrive from Nonny."

"I'd rather wear your nightie again," I say, "or a bedsheet."

"Rihanna Blackwaters, sometimes you are too stubborn for your own good. You have two other mates who might actually like to see you looking all glammed up and stunningly beautiful. In fact, *you* may like them to see you that way. Imagine the sex–"

"Firstly," I say, wagging my finger at her, "the professor will be on strict teacherly duties and won't be able to come within twenty feet of me. And secondly, the man in black won't be coming."

"Poor you," Winnie says, with a not-very-sympathetic-looking grin. "I am intending on looking so good that I give Trent a mild aneurysm. That or a boner so intense he has no choice but to fling me over his shoulder and march me to the nearest horizontal surface."

"Cruel."

"The sex will be worth it." She gazes longingly at the green dress, stroking her hand over the bodice. "Are you sure we couldn't wear these?"

"I don't want to give Tristan Kennedy any kind of encouragement." Even though what happened in the classroom was one hundred percent, most definitely, encouragement. Inwardly, I cringe.

"Let's hope that parcel from Nonny arrives, then."

My phone beeps as she says the words and she glances eagerly at the phone, obviously hoping it's a message about another parcel.

"It's from Stone," I say, sitting down on my chair and reading the message.

"What does it say?" Winnie asks. My cheeks heat and

Winnie's eyes narrow. "I thought you were no good at the sexting thing."

"I'm not, but he is. Very good," I say, reading the message. "Very, very good."

"Why am I not surprised?" Winnie says, flopping down on her chair. "I bet that man is good at everything." I can't argue with that. "Are you going to give me the gist of it or leave me hanging?"

"It seems like you might be right about the looking-forward-to-seeing-me-all-dressed-up-tomorrow-night thing."

"Really?"

"Uh huh," I say, rubbing my thighs together and rereading the long description about how he's looking forward to taking any such dress off me, before it disappears. "Oh ..."

"Oh?"

"Erm, it also seems you were right about the man in black."

"Of course I was ... which bit?"

"He is coming to the ball. He managed to wangle an invitation on security grounds."

"Because he doesn't want to miss out on seeing you, too."

"No, probably because he is actually concerned about security here at the academy."

Winnie scoffs. "The academy is one of the safest places in Los Magicos, in the republic."

"And yet a werebeast got in and–" I halt my words and glance up at my friend. She peers up from her own phone.

"And?"

"What?"

"You said a werebeast had broken in *and* ..."

"Did I?" I say, feeling horrible for hiding this from

Winnie. So guilty, I think I might actually be sick. This girl has done so much for me – including risking her life. Shit, she nearly died following me on one of my stupid adventures. Don't I owe her more than secrets and lies? I clear my throat. "Renzo Barone."

"You think he was the one that nailed that ..." she swallows, morphing a sickly green, "to the bed? I always suspected that was Andrew. I don't see how someone like Barone would be able to infiltrate the academy's security."

"He did. He has."

Winnie brows crinkle together. "How do you know?"

"I ... I saw him. I spoke to him."

"Rhi, what the–"

"It was his fault," I say, pointing to Pip, snoozing in the corner.

"Pip's?" Winnie looks at me like I've lost my mind. "I'm so confused."

"He was waiting for me in the forest. Pip led me straight to him."

"Pip would never do anything to put you in danger."

Pip lifts his head and snorts in agreement. "Well, I'm telling you–"

"He probably didn't know he was there." Winnie's eyes widen in horror. "Or maybe he bewitched him."

"Maybe," I say, not believing either of those explanations to be true but not wanting to argue with Winnie about it.

"But did Barone attack you again? Did he hurt you? I can't believe you haven't told anyone!"

"Because he didn't want to hurt me, or kill me, or whatever, he wanted to talk. Which was ... pretty confusing."

"Talk!" Winnie snorts. "What the hell about? How he'd like to chop you into lots of tiny little pieces? How he plans to slit your throat?"

"I don't think he wants to hurt me." In fact, deep in my gut, I know he doesn't want to.

"He works for the Wolves of Night. He's Marcus Lowsky's assassin. There's a price on your head. A vendetta. Of course he wants to hurt you."

"This is why I didn't tell you, because I knew you wouldn't understand," I say in frustration.

Winnie's face falls, hurt shining in her eyes, and almost immediately I wish I could take back those words. Winnie has put up with so much of my shit. She's been understanding through all my craziness. She's been there by my side, encouraging me and helping me.

"I'm sorry, Winnie, I didn't–"

"No, you're right," Winnie says, shaking her head. "I don't understand this, Rhi. You need to be careful. He's a clever man, a cunning one. He's murdered a lot of people. You cannot trust him."

I nod, but only because once again I don't want to argue with her. But I think she's wrong. I trust him. And maybe that's really fucked up, but I do.

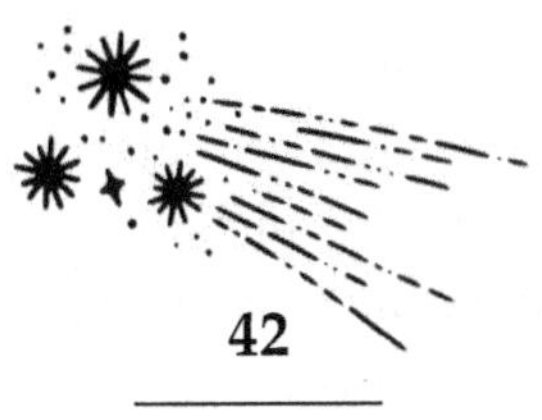

42

S tone

I PICK UP MY PHONE, staring at the screen. My fingers twitch. I consider sending her another message. I consider ordering her to get her ass over here early for her tutoring. I toss my phone back on my desk, it skids across the surface, catching in the light of my desk lamp and then disappearing into the shadows. I lean back in my chair, scratching my fingernails through my beard.

I can't stop thinking about her. I can't stop. It's like an itch I'm addicted to scratching. One I have no self-control over. I can't help myself. I think about how fucking beautiful she is. About how she looks when she comes. I think about the other day with her and Azlan, how that was most definitely the best moment of my life.

But I also think about the memories in her head. About her run-in with the chancellor. About Tristan Kennedy –

about how that spoiled brat fits into all this. Whether he really does.

I peer at the edge of my desk, bathed in shadow, knowing my phone is there.

I pick up a book. I've been attempting to study up, to read up on everything that might be of use. I've exhausted every source out there about fated mates. Now I'm trying to deduce if there's a way I could look at those memories for her without her having to relive them too. I don't want her going through that pain again but I know there might be answers in there, ones that might help us. The chancellor's interest in my mate worries me – it worries Azlan too – I'm sure there is more he's not telling us. More we ought to know.

However, no matter how hard I squint at the words – no matter how much I know this is of importance – for her, for us – I can't make the damn words focus. They swim across my vision, turning gray and blurring, rearranging to form her face.

Shit!

I'm obsessed. There's no point denying it. Probably no point resisting it.

At 7.57pm, I slam shut my book and go linger by the classroom door. At 8.03, she knocks.

"You're late," I tell her, opening the door and pulling her inside.

"By three minutes!" she says with a huff, flinging her satchel onto the nearest desk. "You need to learn some patience, Professor."

I quirk my eyebrows. Is she kidding? *I* need to learn some patience?

Although, if I'm honest ...

"I can't help it if I'm impatient to see you," I say.

"Because you're so keen to teach me?" she asks, resting her hand on her hip.

"There are so many things I want to teach you, Miss Blackwaters," I growl, then wipe my hand down my face, struggling to regain my composure. "But tonight we're going to focus on your own control."

"Control?" she says with a look of disappointment. I'm guessing she was hoping we'd be going over something big and fancy.

"Yes, control. You're very powerful, Rhi." She looks up at me with those big wide eyes. "And some of that magic is dangerous." She flinches. "We need to be realistic here, Rhi. There's no point pretending you don't possess it."

"Okay," she says, straightening her body. "How?"

"You're good at the big, over-the-top, dramatic stuff," she opens her mouth to argue with me, "can you do the small and delicate? Can you crystalize a snow flake from the water droplets in the air? Can you weave a cobweb? Can you electrify one single nerve?" I say, flicking my fingers and igniting one very seductive nerve right between her legs. She gasps, color rushing into her cheeks.

"I don't see how that will help me control the ..." she swallows, "crimson magic."

"You have to trust me, Rhi. It will."

I beckon her towards me and when she stops right in front of me, I turn her around, wrap my arms around her body and cover her hands with mine.

"Let's start with the snow flakes," I whisper into her ear. "You need to tune down – tamper down – all that energy inside you. Let it settle, let it still, let everything quieten inside you."

Her body softens, melts into mine.

"That's it, sweetheart. Now reach out for a water droplet,

tempt it to you – carefully!" I warn when she tugs too hard. "Don't force it."

Her breath softens too, her heart rate mellows. I see her beckon a water droplet into the palm of her hand and settle there.

I smile. She's a natural. So easy to teach. So keen, so eager to learn. In fact, teaching her, sharing all my knowledge with her, is becoming as enjoyable as taking her to bed. Perhaps, maybe, even better.

"Now gently, ever so gently, cool it."

The first few times, she's too quick, the water droplet cracking or splintering in her palm. But soon she masters it. The tiny speck of a perfect snowflake resting in the center of the palm.

She laughs. "I did it!" she says.

"Of course you did."

She twists her head to look at me right behind her.

"But how do I–"

"Remember what this felt like. This quietness, this stillness, this control. You had to subdue your magic, master it, to do this, Rhi."

She nods, understanding me.

"Full marks, Miss Blackwaters." I brush her hair away from her ear so I can lean down to whisper in it. "You are fast becoming my favorite student. How ever will I reward you?"

She shivers and I take her hand in mine, and lead her through the rows of desks and into my office, closing the door and casting an impregnable spell around us.

"Isn't this a bit risky?" she asks, jumping up onto my desk and swinging her legs. "Didn't we just get caught?"

"You want to go?" I ask her with a seriousness, a lump of apprehension in my throat. I don't want her to go; now she's here right in front of me, I'm even more damn desperate for her.

But she shakes her head and relief swims through my body.

I stalk closer to her, gripping her waist and leaning down to kiss her mouth. I'm millimeters away from her soft lips when something flickers through her mind. She knows how to keep me out now, and yet most of the time she keeps her thoughts open to me.

I stop. She's unhappy.

I lift my head and look down into her face. Her eyes are closed. She's waiting for me to kiss her. "What's wrong?"

"Huh?" she says, opening her eyes.

"Something's bothering you."

"Oh," she says, glancing away from me and worrying at her lip.

I pinch her chin and twist her face back to mine.

"What is it?"

"Nothing, it's silly." She finds the hem of my shirt and tugs it out of my pants, reaching under the material to stroke her warm hands over my chest. My blood warms several degrees and if I was a jerk, I'd fuck her over my desk and disregard the fact she's upset about something. But I'm trying not to be a jerk. I'm trying really hard for her sake.

"Tell me, Miss Blackwaters."

"I don't want to talk about it."

"Well, if you want me to fuck you," I say, moving further between her legs and grinding against her, "you're going to have to."

She huffs. "Me and Winnie had a fight."

I almost laugh. That's it? But her face has fallen and I know she's upset about it.

"What did you fight about?"

"A couple of things."

"Yes ...?"

"Erm ..."

"Rhi?"

"Dresses."

"Dresses," I say flatly.

She nods. Then inhales. "Tristan sent me a bunch of really expensive dresses."

I blink. "I'm struggling to follow here."

"Winnie thinks I should accept them. I want to send them back."

I shake my head. "He's trying to win you round. It's hardly surprising. He's your fated mate."

"He's not my ..." She trails off.

"Rhi," I say, "I think we're past that now, aren't we? He is and at some point we're going to have to deal with it."

"How? I hate him. *You* hate him," she says, pointing at me.

"I don't hate him," I say, a little taken back. Sure I think he's arrogant, spoiled and self-centered. But so are most people in the academy. So are most people in Los Magicos. I don't hate him.

"How could we ever make it work?"

"Fuck, Rhi," I say, stroking my knuckles over her cheek. "I think I could endure hell itself for you."

She rolls her eyes. "I don't want you to endure anything. And I don't want to have to deal with him," she says, wrapping her arms around herself. "I want him to leave me alone."

"I'll have a word with him," I say darkly, then I chuckle, shaking my head. "Trust Tristan Kennedy to throw his money at the problem."

"Yeah," she says. Her eyes drop, and something flickers

through her mind. Something to do with a classroom ... and ...

"What the fuck?!" I say.

"Huh?" she says, eyes leaping back to mine.

I take her chin in my grip again and twist her gaze back to mine. "Care to explain, Miss Blackwaters?"

Her eyes are all wide and innocent but the girl is a brat, a minx.

"Tristan Kennedy can make himself invisible? How the hell do I not know that?"

"I guess keeping it a secret works to his advantage."

"Yeah, it's one hell of an advantage," I say, trying to deduce what I just saw in her mind. "He ..." My eyes flicker over her face. I'm trying damn hard not to infiltrate her mind here. But I'm curious as hell and frankly whatever went down looked hot as hell too. "He made you ..." I growl, "come."

Her eyes widen with horror. "Are you strolling around inside my mind again, Professor?"

"Are you keeping secrets again, Miss Blackwaters?" She scowls at me and I scowl right back. In the end, it's me who relents first. Of course it fucking is. I'm weak for this girl. "Sometimes, I honestly can't help it, Rhi. When you're not blocking me, I end up strolling in without meaning to. I see things I genuinely don't mean to see."

She looks at me with suspicion, then tweaks my fucking nipple.

"Ow!" I say.

"Don't do it again."

"I'm not making any promises," I say, reaching inside her top and rubbing her nipple between my finger and thumb in retaliation, making her bite her lip.

"What happened?" I ask again. I rub the pad of my

thumb around the hardening nub of her nipple and graze my teeth up her throat towards her ear. I nip the lobe, then whisper into the shell. "Tell me all about it, Miss Blackwaters. And then we can see if you need punishing at all. Misbehaving in class ..."

"You really want to know all the gory details?" she asks.

She has no fucking idea. "I want to know what he did to you. I want to know if you liked it. I want to know how it felt."

"You're not ... you're not mad at me."

"Oh I'm going to punish you, Miss Blackwaters," any fucking excuse, "because I have a feeling you're going to enjoy me slapping that plump ass of yours, but I'm not mad."

"Really?" she says earnestly.

"We already had this conversation, Rhianna," I say, lifting my gaze back to her anxious eyes.

"Yes, but talking and doing are two different things."

"He's your fated mate. No matter how much you may protest this, no matter how much you may try and resist it, it's darn near impossible." Don't I know all about that!

She smiles like she's the one reading my thoughts. "And you really want to know?"

"Miss Blackwaters, it's hot. Don't dissect it. You already know I'm a deranged pervert." I squeeze her tit.

"I do," she says with a grin and I squeeze her ass even harder.

"So what happened?"

"He ... he made me come ... in class."

"No, Miss Blackwaters, I want the details. All the details. You invited him to come sit next to you in class?"

"No, he made himself invisible and came and sidled up to me. He was asking me stuff in my ear."

"And?" I say. Her heart is beating that little bit faster remembering this, and it makes my own do the same.

"He put his hand on my bare thigh."

"Where exactly?"

"Between my skirt and those stupid socks."

"Here? Like this?" I ask, laying my own palm on her supple thigh.

"Yes."

"Go on," I urge her, brushing the pad of my thumb over her nipple and making her shudder.

"Then he slid his hand up the inside of my thigh, all the way up to my panties."

"And you didn't stop him?"

She shakes her head.

I stroke my own hand up the inside of her thigh, but she's wearing pants and it isn't the same. With a grunt of frustration I reach the waistband and motion for her to lift her butt, sliding them over her ass and off her legs.

"Better," I murmur, gliding my hand back up her warm skin. "What happened next, sweetheart?"

"He wanted to know if I was wet so he slid his fingers inside my panties."

"You're always fucking wet." I chuckle, reconstructing what he'd done and making her moan as I brush against her pussy lips. "Wet and sensitive. And noisy." I kiss her throat. "How the hell did you stay quiet for him? Or is Tristan Kennedy all talk and no orgasm? Was he no good with his fingers?" I ask, nudging her legs open further for me and ringing her clit with my touch and my magic.

Her hands jerk from the inside of my shirt and she grasps the edge of my desk, her head falling backwards.

"No," she mutters, her legs already starting to shake, "he was good. Really good."

I almost roll my eyes. It isn't hard with this little one. She's so freaking sensitive. I'm sure I could make her come just by breathing on her clit.

"So what did he do to you with his fingers inside your panties, Miss Blackwaters? Where exactly did he touch you? Here?" I press my finger to her throbbing clit.

"Y-y-yes, there," she says, bucking her hips to try and gain some friction.

"He played with you here, until you came?" I ask, circling her now.

She moans out her yes and I can't help leaning back to look at her, perched on the edge of my desk in her panties, her shirt pulled up exposing her silky bra, her hair already a mess around her head. It looks like every perverted professor's fucking nightmare.

I flick at her, using my magic to vibrate at her sensitive nub.

"I'm not surprised he touched you, you're so fucking beautiful, Miss Blackwaters. How the hell was he meant to resist?"

"I should have resisted," she chokes out, as her legs shake so hard the desk rattles and her body tightens.

"That's not what fate wants, sweetheart. She was always going to tempt you, at every twist and every turn."

Her clit thrums against my fingertips. She's close, so close, her pussy getting wetter and wetter.

"You don't have to be quiet for me. You can be as loud as you fucking like." I give her one last flick and she falls apart, bucking against my fingers and screaming my name. I can't help myself, I thrust my fingers deep inside her warm, wet pussy just so I can feel her inner muscles clench around me.

"Did he do this too, Miss Blackwaters?"

"Yes," she cries out, as I massage her spot and have her dancing on my fingers a second time.

"Yeah, I bet he fucking did." Slowly, I slide my fingers from her and, taking her hand in mine, tug her off my desk and onto her feet. She peers up at me with intrigue. "But I bet he didn't do this," I say, twisting her body around and, with my palm firm between her shoulder blades, pressing her down onto my desk so she's folded in half, her ass on display. I yank away her panties and thrust into her, lifting her up onto her toes, her hands scrabbling for purchase across the desk.

"Phoenix," she gasps, throbbing around my cock.

"Yes, Miss Blackwaters?"

She moans as I slide from her and slam my way back inside, the desk wobbling beneath us.

"Am I right? He hasn't had you this way, has he?"

"Noooo," she cries out.

I shake my head, pressing her down more firmly as she begins to squirm beneath me, wriggling her ass and begging me for more. As if I could ever deny her this. I shake my head again, pounding into her.

Poor fucking bastard, I almost feel sorry for him.

Almost.

43

———

R^{hi}

WINNIE SPENDS the whole of Saturday morning with her hair in curlers either pacing up and down our room or barking down her cell phone at some poor postal worker. In-between, she glances longingly at the clothes bag with the four designer dresses inside which I've stuffed into the wardrobe.

Pip, sensing something isn't right, is cowering in the corner under a blanket, attempting to avoid us both.

"Are you sure we can't wear those dresses?" she asks me for the fifth time in the last hour.

"Nope," I say, not even looking up from the book on advanced magic I'm reading. I tried to return the dresses to Tristan's room yesterday, but they'd simply turned up outside our door again this morning and I don't have the energy or the inclination to play silly games with him. If he won't take them back, I'll donate them to charity or something. Because I'm not keeping them and I'm definitely not wearing one of them either.

"Well, we might not have a choice," Winnie says, stamping her foot and throwing her phone across the room. "There's no trace of Nonny's dresses anywhere and there's less than," she peers at her watch, "eight hours until the ball starts." Pip squeaks and burrows further into his cover.

"You're scaring Pip," I tell her, flipping a page.

"Rhianna!" she snaps, "you're not taking this seriously."

I sigh, closing my book and sitting back in my chair. "I'm sorry, Winnie, but I'm finding it really hard to get excited about some snotty event which is going to be full of lots of snooty people who hate my guts. Especially when there are bigger, more important things going on in my life."

"And there aren't in mine, I suppose. I suppose you think I'm shallow and stupid for being excited about this." I look up at my friend and see tears glistening in her eyes.

I jump onto my feet and take a hold of her hands in mine. "Winnie, no. No, I'd never think you were stupid or shallow." I pull her in for a hug, standing up on my tiptoes to wrap my arms around her shoulders. "You're one of the most amazing people I know. That I've ever met."

Winnie sniffs. "Then you'll put away your books and let me style your hair?"

"Yes, and you can do my make up too. You're a million times better at makeup than I am."

"And we can wear the dresses Tristan sent," she says in a very quiet but high-pitched voice.

"Winnie!" I say, releasing her from my embrace.

"I did nearly die helping you escape from those soldiers."

I glare at her and she smiles sweetly, fluttering her wet eyelashes.

"Urgh! Okay, but you get to blackmail me emotionally with that once and one time only, Winnifred Wence," I say, stabbing my forefinger at her.

"Promise," she says, bouncing on her toes and then diving in to give me another hug. She squeezes me tight, then lunges into the wardrobe and pulls out the clothes bag. The dresses inside are no longer looking as elegant as they did. They're crushed and creased but Winnie lays them out over our desks and waves her hands, muttering a spell, and I watch as all the crinkles melt away.

"There," she says, clapping her hands together. "Good as new. Now, which one are you going to choose?"

I bite at my thumbnail. I hate to admit it but I do have a favorite, one I fell in love with as soon as we pulled it from the bag. I know it will look good on me, hugging my body, emphasizing my figure. But I don't like to admit that Tristan Kennedy knows me that well, knows my size and my body, knows what will suit me and what I might like. It makes the bond in my gut spin and my stomach bubble with nausea.

"I don't know. You choose first."

"Rhi, these are your dresses. I know I'm pushing my luck borrowing these as it is."

"Winnie, you're welcome to take them all! I'm not even sure I should go."

"No, I need my best friend with me at this ball."

"You have Trent," I remind her. I love Winnie but I suspect I'm going to feel like a spare wheel tonight. Another reason I'm not as hyped as everyone else about this ball.

"Yes, but you're my best friend. And I've never had one like you before, Rhi. I never got to go to parties with my bestie. And now I have one. And it won't be the same if she isn't there."

"Okay, okay," I say, peering over at Pip who's watching us intently. He meets my eye, his brows wrinkling. I inhale. Should I pick the one I really like? Is it fucked up? Probably, but I can't help imagining both Stone and the man in black's reaction when they see me in it. Because, okay, they look at me with heat and lust and all that stuff, but they've never looked wowed, bowled over, or knocked off their feet. I'm usually in my hoodie and jeans, not exactly designed for seduction. It would be nice to feel beautiful for once. Like a Princess and not Cinderella in her rags. "The black one."

"Totally," Winnie says, clapping her hands again. "I agree. You will look so good in that one. Try it on, Rhi, and we can work out how to do your hair and makeup."

I nod, still unsure whether this is a really stupid, stupid idea. It's too late now, though. There is no way my best friend is going to let me backtrack.

"What one are you going to go for, Winnie?" I ask, dragging my hoodie and t-shirt over my head.

"Would you mind if I picked the green one?"

"No way, I think it would look amazing with your complexion."

"Thanks, Rhi," she says. "I know I'm being a pain in the butt here."

"You're not," I say, tugging down my jeans. As usual, it's cold in this room and I shiver in my panties and bra.

I look at the bodice and then at my underwear. The bodice has a deep V cut into it and clear mesh at the back giving it a backless effect. There's no way I can wear a bra under this dress.

"Do you think this dress is going to be, you know, secure

enough?" I ask Winnie as I carefully step into all the silk and tulle and shimmy it up my body.

"Secure for what?"

"My boobs," I say, removing my bra and wriggling the dress into place.

Winnie looks at me and her jaw falls open. She stares at me for one whole minute, then her hands fly up to her mouth.

"Rhi, it looks gorgeous and freaking, freaking, freaking seductive."

"Seriously?"

Winnie walks me round to stand in front of the mirror and my reflection whips my own breath away. She's right. I don't think I've ever been one to blow my own trumpet, but it does look stunning and the way the bodice is cut out at the front shows off the curve of my tits. In fact it shows off a hell of a lot of tit.

"See what I mean?" I say, waving my forefinger around in front of my chest. "The entire school has already seen my tits once. I don't want to fall out of this dress and flash everyone again."

"Rhi, that won't happen. This dress is magical."

"I know, it looks great but–"

"No, Rhi. It's really magical. Look." She taps my shoulder and the dress comes to life, I feel it suck me in in some places and release me in others and it takes a very firm grip of my breasts.

"Oh," I say, bouncing up and down and finding the dress is more secure than most of my sports bras. Then I catch a sight of the skirt. It's twinkling.

"Do you see that, Winnie?" I ask.

Winnie flicks her fingers and the curtains draw closed, plunging us into almost darkness. The effect becomes more clear. My skirt twinkles like the night's sky, as if hundreds of thousands of tiny stars have been caught in the fabric of my skirt.

"Wow," Winnie and I say together. And if I had any misgivings about wearing this dress, any ideas that maybe I wouldn't wear it after all, well they have been well and truly tossed out the window. I'm wearing this dress. Even Death himself couldn't wrench it from my body.

SEVEN HOURS later we're both standing in our dresses with our hair and makeup done too. Winnie has swept all her dark hair up, showing off her long, elegant neck and she's wearing long dangly emerald earrings that match the deep green of her dress.

We decided to leave my hair loose in waves, although Winnie pinned some bright silver stars into my locks as well as my ears, and has given my eyes a smoky effect that makes me look like someone else entirely.

I gaze at myself in the mirror.

"Winnie, you really are magical," I say. "I look like a real princess."

Pip snorts, scurrying around our feet.

"Uh uh, mister," Winnie says, nudging him gently with the toe of her foot. "No trampling your muddy trotters on our dresses. You'll have to admire us from a distance."

I pull up the skirt of my dress and examine my feet. They are the only thing that let me down. I had to borrow heels from Winnie that she adjusted to fit me. She's done a great job, but I've had very little practice walking in shoes like this, and I'm nervous I'm going to end up on my ass.

Especially with people like Summer and Tristan in the vicinity.

I'm about to kick off those heels and ditch them in favor of my sneakers, when there's a knock on the door.

"Trent," Winnie hisses. "How do I look? Do I have anything in my teeth?" She draws back her lips and bends forward so I can see.

"Winnie, you look gorgeous, you know you do. Go give him that aneurysm."

Winnie smiles wider than I think I've ever seen her. "Thank you, Rhi. I know you really, really didn't want us to wear these dresses."

"I may have warmed to the idea of wearing this one," I say, swishing my skirt, "just a little bit."

Winnie giggles and opens the door and the gurgling, incomprehensible sound that comes from the doorway leads me to believe her dress has had the desired effect on her boyfriend.

That noise is followed by some definite smooching noises, and I pretend not to hear, bending down to tickle Pip's ears instead.

Finally, the lovebirds break apart and Trent steps into the room. It seems he's gone for the tux after all, complete with an actual bowtie and a red rose in his buttonhole, that matches the corsage made up of roses Winnie's wearing around her wrist. He's also removed some of his piercings and slicked back his hair. I don't think I've ever seen so much of his face, which is a shame because he's actually pretty good looking.

"Look what Trent got me," Winnie says, holding up her wrist.

"Err, I got you one too, Rhi," Trent says. "I didn't make it matching ... well ... because ..."

"You didn't want to look like a stud with two girlfriends?" Winnie teases. The tips of his ears burn.

"You two look so amazing together," I say, taking the corsage from Trent's hands and tying it on my wrist. It's made up of black roses and I'm assuming Winnie was behind it after all.

"I know we do," Winnie says, with a grin. "Will you take our photo to send to my mom and Nonny?"

"Sure," I say, "but I think we can find a better background than our room."

Winnie peers around our dilapidated bedroom. "You're right, let's go outside."

"I'll be right out," I tell them as they walk out hand in hand.

I crouch back down, swaying slightly in my heels, and beckon Pip towards me. Frankly, I don't care if he muddies or slobbers on my dress. I need a Pip cuddle because all of a sudden I feel nervous.

"Do I look stupid?" I ask him. I'm not Summer. Can I really carry this off? Do I look like a little girl playing dress up?

Pip snorts at me.

"Thanks, Pipsqueak, I appreciate it," I say, scratching his ears; even if he doesn't ruin the dress, I'm going to smell of pig, but oh well, I'm not called Pig Girl for nothing. He squeaks some more. "Yeah, I know you smell nice. After all, you had a bath only last month." He grunts. "Teasing." I kiss his head. "I'm guessing it might get a little noisy and raucous tonight, but I'm going to put the locking spell on the room so you'll be safe. I'll tell you all about it when I get back." His brows lift. "With some required edits to make it PG-friendly if required."

I know Pip is not a big fan of my newly acquired sex life.

"See you later, love," I say, giving him a final kiss and wrapping him up in his blanket. Then I shut the door and cast the spell.

As I spin around into the hallway, I hear other people, several of them gasping and one actually muttering a wow. My cheeks heat. Have I misjudged this? Is the dress too much? Do I have piggy slobber on my face?

But then one of the girls steps forward with a genuine look of admiration on her face.

"You look amazing, Pi– Rhianna. Is that an actual *Mona* dress? It's gorgeous!"

There's a murmur of agreement and I thank them and hurry out, my cheeks feeling even warmer.

Who knew all it required to win these people round was a designer dress and a ton of makeup? I shake my head, finding Winnie and Trent waiting for me by the edge of the forest.

"Isn't it a little dark for a photo here?" I ask.

Winnie shakes her head at me and clicks her fingers, and the trees light up with lanterns illuminating the couple in a halo of soft light.

"Right," I mutter, "magic."

Winnie passes me her phone and I take some snaps of her and Trent, before Trent takes some of me and Winnie. Winnie spends the next few minutes forwarding the photos onto a long list of family members as well as me.

"Are you going to send one to ..." she peers at Trent who's texting on his phone and mouths, "Stone and the man in black?"

"No, I think I'm going to give them the full effect in person."

"Love it," Winnie says, hooking her left arm through

Trent's and her right through mine and pulling us both along the path. "Come on, let's go. We can't be late for the ball."

Just after the labs, we meet up with Trent's friends Harry and Fabio, both with their dates. After we've all told each other how great we look and taken some more photos, we carry on towards the hall and I lean in to whisper to Winnie.

"I'm going to be the only one there without a date, aren't I?"

"Well, you could have had a date," Winnie reminds me and I screw up my face. Winnie shakes her head. "Although, if I'm honest, I'm surprised no one else asked you, especially as there are more guys at this academy than girls."

"So someone should have been desperate enough to ask me!"

"That's not what I'm saying. I'm just surprised."

"Surprised!" Trent says, overhearing us. "After Tristan Kennedy asked her out, no one would be brave enough."

"That's true. Men have fragile egos," Winnie says, "they don't do well with rejection."

Trent laughs. "It's not that. It's because most men are pretty fond of their testicles."

"What?" I say.

"You think Tristan Kennedy wouldn't remove the balls of any dude who asked you out after you turned him down in front of the entire academy?!"

"Right," I say, staring out towards the path. Tristan. I am not looking forward to seeing him. In fact, he's not the only one. The rumors spread by Summer have only gotten more vile in the last few days and I can only pray this ball will be a big enough distraction to keep them both occupied and not interested in me.

I peer back at my friends. Everyone else around me is bubbling with excitement about tonight and yet I can't shake this feeling that it's going to end in horror.

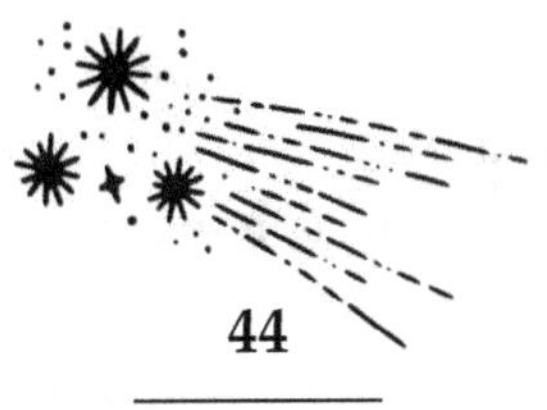

44

A zlan

FATE, Rhianna and my own weakness have dragged me back to the academy more times in the last few months than in the more-than-decade since I left, but most of those trips have been perfunctory, secretive or just a chance to catch up with my friend. None have required me to change out of my enforcer cloak and boots and into an actual suit. I don't like it. The collar is suffocating around my neck and the dress shoes pinch my feet. I'm sure I look like a gorilla in a suit and it reminds me too much of all the functions I was required to attend when I wasn't estranged from the family.

However, I'll take an ill-fitting suit and feeling foolish for a chance to be here tonight. I stand at the entrance to the Great Hall observing the people entering. I'm not actually checking tickets. There are some security underlings doing that – but I'm here to ensure everything goes smoothly – to ensure with several outsiders attending tonight – that Rhianna is safe. No Renzo Barone sneaking in with the crowd.

The pathways have been manicured since I last visited, the stones all raked, the bushes pruned, banners with the academy's and house crests hung at regular intervals and flaming torches lighting the way.

There's already a line, moving slowly into the hall – a mixture of students and guests. There's a tightness in my chest and it's not the suit. It's my fears for Rhianna. This mysterious girl I picked up from the wastelands with her fierce scowl and deadly smile has caught everyone's attention.

And she does it again now.

At first I don't understand, there's a slight commotion at the end of the line. I stroll that way, the tightness growing, my fingers ready to strike any threat.

The line of people have turned away from the front of the line and are peering behind them, nudging each other and whispering. My eyes scan the line, all the way to the end, to the place they're all staring at.

I halt. My feet frozen to the spot. That tightness in my chest floats away.

It's her. Rhianna.

She looks ethereal, otherworldly, so beautiful I can't breathe.

She senses me, feels that familiar tug of our bonds in the core of her soul, and raises her face, her eyes meeting mine over the distance, and I'm reminded all over again of the clearing, of that first time.

How is it possible? How can someone so beautiful, so precious, so strong and so fragile, belong to me? Why would fate give her to me?

But I know the answer. To protect. I will protect her from all those who would use her, who would harm her, who would threaten her. That mantra beats in my chest as if it's the rhythm of my heart.

Rhi smiles at me, a little shyly and mouths, "Do you like it?" She takes the skirt of her dress in her hands and shifts to one side and then the other, showing me how the dress falls away and leaves her back bare.

I nod, unable to find the words, hoping she feels my emotion through the bond. Feels how badly I want to whisk her into my arms and carry her into that hall, hold her close and dance with her until the sun rises.

There's no chance of that though. Too many eyes watching us tonight. All I can do is stare at her with an intensity I hope she feels in her bones, before I turn and return to my station at the entrance to the Great Hall.

"Everything okay, Sir?" one of the underlings asks me.

"Nothing of concern," I reply, my eyes flicking constantly to her position in the line, watching as she creeps closer and closer towards me. Then she's by my side, in touching distance.

"Good evening," I say gruffly to her and her friends.

"Good evening," she says, she's shivering in the cool air, her teeth chattering together.

"You're cold," I say.

"Yep, but Winnie says we have to suffer for fashion."

"It'll be warm inside," Winnie says.

There are goosebumps running down her arms. I flare out my fingers and encase her in a blanket of warm air.

She startles, then peers up at me. I nod stiffly.

"Have a good evening." And then they're shuffling forward to the front of the line.

Everyone is looking at her. She's like a goddess in a sea

of mortals. Everybody is captivated by her. They can't drag their eyes from her. It's like they finally see what I saw from the start – how damn special this woman is.

I watch from the corner of my eye as the security guard checks her ticket and she passes through the great doorway and into the mansion, the Great Hall lying just beyond; music and laughter drifting our way.

I want to follow her inside. I don't want her to leave my sight. But I can't neglect my post. I can't risk allowing someone dangerous to slip in.

The separation has never felt so intense and I loathe it, that tightness lodging itself back inside my chest almost immediately.

45

R ^{hi}

WE STEP through into the Great Hall and it's as if we've entered another land completely, somewhere even more magical and bewitching than the one we inhabit.

The sights and sounds of Los Magicos and the academy have often amazed me with their grandeur and beauty – something missing from the wastelands back home – but this … this is …

The usual tables, portraits and suits of armor have been removed, and the Hall transformed completely. The ceiling is a swirling mass of stars and planets, casting their light on the revelers below and six crystal chandeliers lit with more starlight float high in the air above their heads. The floor gleams like marble in shades of reds and blues and purples and heavy scarlet drapes hang across the walls. An orchestra fills the space with music and waiters dressed in white suits mingle in the crowd with trays full of canapes and glasses of champagne.

"This is crazy," I whisper to Winnie.

She nudges me. "I told you it would be."

"I know but I never expected anything so ..."

"Beautiful."

"Exuberant."

"Well, the Moreau and Kennedy family both had children on that winning team. I suspect they reached into their pockets for this celebration."

"And yet Spencer isn't even here."

"Really?" Trent says, scanning the crowd. "I thought he'd come back for this."

"I doubt it," Winnie says. "He's serving in the forces now."

"But he's a Moreau. Captain of the team," Trent insists.

Winnie shrugs her shoulders and I scan the crowd myself, not wanting to admit that the thought of seeing Spencer again has little sparks of apprehension bursting in my stomach. The same way I feel about bumping into Tristan. I'm hoping I might be able to somehow miraculously avoid him for the evening. I don't want to have to explain why I'm wearing one of the dresses he sent me.

The hall is bustling with students and their guests, several faces I recognize from the academy and the match and several more faces I don't recognize at all. Everybody is dressed in their finery, jewels, and diamonds twinkling under the lights. Spencer's nowhere in sight and both relief and disappointment battle inside me.

"Shall we get a drink?" Winnie says,

"I'll get them," Trent says, disappearing into the throng of people.

I stare up at Winnie. "So what does one do at a ball?" I ask her.

"One dances."

"Yep."

"Mingles."

I pull a face.

"And drinks and be merry."

"That I can do," I say, "only not too much." My first and only hangover is still acting as a very vivid and effective deterrent from drinking too much.

"You have to get wasted at a ball. It's like the law."

I pull a face at her but her attention is diverted by Trent who's tapping her on the shoulder.

He passes Winnie a glass of champagne and then one to me before whispering into his girlfriend's ear and making her giggle.

I take a gulp of my champagne and the bubbles fly up my nose, making it crinkle so much I sneeze.

"You're meant to sip champagne," Winnie says and I stick my tongue out at her. "You're ruining the sophisticated look, Rhianna."

"We both know I'm not sophisticated."

Winnie leans in to whisper in my ear. "Says the woman who's been having hot threesomes with two older guys."

I can't deny that, scanning the crowd again for those two older men. The man in black must still be outside which is probably just as well. The way he looked at me out there on the path had my blood heating. In fact, the way he looked, all dressed up in a suit that was straining at every seam – most definitely had my blood warming. We're meant to be subtle tonight. I'm hoping at some point we'll grab a moment together but if I'm seen hanging out with him the entire night people may get suspicious, and quite frankly hanging off the man, climbing him like a tree, is all I feel like doing right now.

It takes me a while to spot my other mate, too. He's standing with a group of the teachers and he has his back to me.

Maybe it wouldn't be so obvious if I went and spoke with him.

As if he knows I'm looking his way, I see his spine stiffen slightly and the man glances slightly over his shoulder.

It decides me. I'll pretend I have a question on ancient magic that needs answering urgently.

I tell Winnie I'll be back later and weave my way through the crowd. It's a strange experience. People don't dive out of the way to avoid me like they usually do, or turn away to ignore me. In fact, several of the girls from my gym class stop me to say how great I look and how amazing my dress is. And one guy – who I think is in my practical magic class and most probably laughed at me that day Summer turned my nose into a snout – grabs my arm and tries to persuade me to dance.

I wave him off and keep making my way towards Stone, stopping right behind him.

"Professor?" I say and his shoulders rise and fall as if he's steeling himself, before he turns slowly to face me. His features remain completely neutral although his eyes smolder as his gaze snakes all over me.

"Miss Blackwaters," he says, and I notice how tightly he's gripping the stem of his glass.

"I'm sorry to interrupt but I had an urgent question for you about the assignment you set yesterday."

Stone pats Professor Browne on the arm. "Excuse me, Jack," he says.

Then he motions with his head and we step to one side away from the other teachers.

"The assignment, huh?" he asks, eyes swimming all over me with a hunger that's making me dizzy. Maybe coming over to speak with him wasn't such a great idea after all. "I'm guessing that, seeing as I set you no assignments this week, this is just an excuse to show me in close quarters just how good you look?"

I smile and tilt my head to one side. "I look good?"

"You look fucking incredible, Miss Blackwaters, and you know you do."

I smile even more and lift my glass to my lips, remembering to sip this time.

Stone reaches out and takes the glass straight from my hands. "No drinking. We all remember what happened last time you drank."

"You flung a pile of shit at my head."

"I nearly passed out on the account of second-hand alcohol fumes."

"I wasn't that bad."

He chuckles, sipping at my champagne before handing it back. Then we both stand there staring at each other with such heat I'm surprised we don't set the hall on fire. I'm sure it would be obvious to anyone who looks how badly we want each other, how hard it is to keep our hands off each other.

"You know I'd ask you to dance if I could, sweetheart," he whispers.

"You would?"

"Of course, I wouldn't want any of these other losers getting their lecherous hands on you." He leans closer, lowering his voice further. "I'd hold you in my arms, right up against my body, let you know just how good you really do look, make you a little needy and desperate grinding against you in such a way only the two of us would know. Then, when I'd be satisfied you were well and truly swollen and wet for me, I'd take you outside and I'd have you."

"That's not very romantic, Professor."

"I'm afraid if you wear a dress like that my thoughts are going to be as dark as the depths of hell, little one, and not romantic at all."

I smile at him again.

We'll find a way later? I ask him in my mind and he nods. *With Azlan too?* He nods again, this time unable to help but smile darkly in a way that has me shivering with desire.

I turn away quickly, pretty sure if I stay any longer I'll give myself away.

I gaze across all the faces searching for Winnie. The hall is full to the brim now, some people dancing to the music – classical re-imaginings of some popular rock songs – others are talking and laughing, others sampling the food and the drinks. I keep searching, pretending I'm not looking for another face too. But no matter how hard I search, I can't find his face. He's probably choosing to be fashionably late, to make some statement of an entrance. Like he needs one. There will already be some kind of presentation to the dueling team half way through the ball and with Spencer absent, Tristan as vice-captain will be collecting all the adoration and all the praise.

I shake my head and go back to searching for Winnie, wondering if she's made good on that promise to drag Trent to the nearest available empty room.

I can't find her anywhere and instead my gaze lands straight on Summer, glaring straight back at me.

Her white-blonde hair is scraped back from her face and an impressive-looking tiara balances on the crown of her head. Her dress is an icy blue color that enhances her violet eyes and it clings to her body like water, showing off her curvy hips, and even curvier bust. The dress is strapless with a slit all the way up to the top of her thigh and she's wearing matching gloves that stop just past her elbows. She looks gorgeous – of course – or at least she would if she weren't scowling at me with a fucking murderous frown on her face.

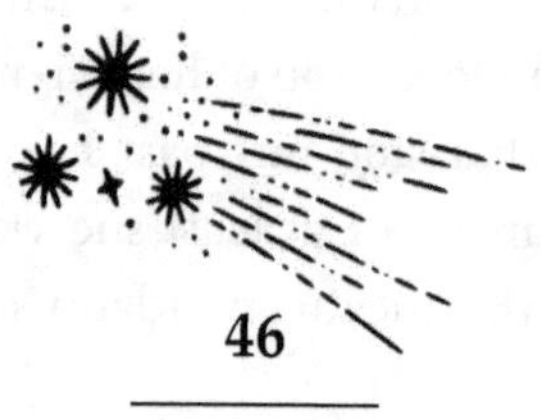

46

T ristan

I STAND in my old childhood bedroom and let my mom fuss around me in a cloud of some expensive floral perfume. She ruffles my hair, her long nails catching slightly against my scalp.

"Are you sure you won't let me trim a bit off, darling," she says. Her eyes are just that tad, tiny bit, unfocused. She's not high as a kite yet, hasn't taken enough of her pills. But that's probably down to my presence. I'm sure as soon as I'm gone she'll be popping them like candies.

"No," I say, jerking my head away from her hands and then almost immediately feeling like a jerk when hurt shimmers in her eyes. "I like it this long," I say, kissing her cheek and trying to make up for the damage.

"You know your father prefers it short. He can't stand it when it's too long."

I turn and look at myself in the mirror – some dark family heirloom hanging on the wall, the glass a little cloudy, totally unsuited to a kid's room. No wonder I had nightmares most nights sleeping here as a kid. Half the furniture in here looks like it was stolen from some haunted gothic house. It scared me half to death. That and the shouting. The screaming.

I smile flatly at her, a smile both of us can see doesn't reach my eyes. "It's fine." I mess it up and let it flop forward, knowing it will infuriate my father even more.

Right now, I don't give a shit. I didn't even want to come here tonight, seriously considered ignoring the summons.

It would enrage him, at best have him boot me from the family like Azlan, at worst have him scrabbling for ways to punish me. What does it matter? It's only a matter of time now until those consequences are realized. Because Rhianna Blackwaters is going to be mine. She may be fighting it, she may tell me that she doesn't want it, but I felt her come on the end of my fingers, I felt her squeeze around those fingers, I heard her soft sighs and her sweet moans and that tells me everything else is lies and bullshit. She wants me as much as I want her. She can't escape fate and her bond any more than I can, than Stone or Azlan could either. We're all destined for her, and maybe that is fucked up or troubling or worrying, but maybe I don't give a damn.

"Do you want me to do up your bowtie for you?" my mom asks, still hovering at my side.

"Sure," I tell her, cringing when I see how much that little concession pleases her. I do up the top button of my dress shirt and bend my knees a little so she can thread the tie around my neck and tie it at the bottom of my throat. She bites her tongue as she does it, concentrating, and when she's done, she rests her hands on my chest and beams.

"There! You look so handsome. I always knew you would be. You were such a beautiful baby."

I chuckle. "I was a fat baby. I've seen the pictures."

"Exactly like a baby should be. Chubby and gorgeous." She peers up at me with such obvious admiration it makes me feel guilty. When it happens, when they find out the truth, will she be disappointed or might she understand?

I think she loved my father once upon a time. I've seen the photos, her gazing up at him with the same admiration, hanging on to his arm like she never wanted to let go.

Could I tell her? Would she understand?

I shake the idea from my mind. It's too risky. For her. I already fear she'll be forced to face my father's wrath when he discovers my intentions. Better she can plead ignorance.

"I'd better get going," I tell her, "can't be late for the ball."

"Your father wants to see you before you leave," she says, still smiling, although now it's straining at the edges.

I nod, kiss her cheek and leave her, padding down the staircase towards my father's room. I knock but he's not in there and instead I find him at the dining table, today's newspapers spread out in front of him.

"You're in all of them," he says, not looking up as I enter the room.

"Am I?" I ask coolly.

"Well, of course, the victorious dueling team and their victory ball. Talk of the town." My father slams shut the paper he was reading and glares up at me. "Idiots. Don't they know there are more important concerns than little boys and their playing?"

I don't react. I've learned not to. Instead, I adopt that placid expression. Betraying no interest or emotion at all. I don't move either, no twitch of a muscle, no jerk of a limb. Completely still, nothing to provoke him.

It's how I first learned I could do it, disappear. I guess I wanted to be able to so badly I found a way. To melt away, to hide from his view, to disappear into the shadows. Somewhere he couldn't find me.

It saved me a beating numerous times, although there were plenty of times it didn't. Times I had to let him find me, see me, so he wouldn't learn my secret.

"I hope you're not letting this get to your head," he says, his hateful gaze scanning me, lingering on my hair. He frowns.

"No, Sir. It was just a match. One match."

"Exactly, although it obviously did something to that Moreau boy. Do you know why he left?"

"No," I answer, thankful for once I don't have to lie. I still don't understand it. Why would he choose to leave?

"He won't be back tonight?"

I shake my head. I've messaged him but I've only received a handful back. Short. Perfunctory. Telling me fuck all. I wonder what did happen to him. If I should have talked to him more. We were always rivals, sure, competing, challenging each other. But underneath it all, he was my friend. My best friend. The only one I could trust. I don't understand what happened.

Was it the werebeast attack? In all the years I've known him, in all the years I've known his secret, I'd never known him lose control like that. Did it shake him more than he let on? Because I handled it for him, didn't I? I stopped him doing any real damage. When it came down to it, I had his back, just as I expected he'd always have mine.

I blink, realizing my father is still watching me.

"What is it?"

I open my mouth, nearly confessing how much I miss

my damn friend. But what would he care? All it would do is hand him knowledge he'd use against me.

"Just thinking about my speech that's all."

"The one you'll be making at the ball?"

"Yes, Sir."

He examines me some more. "Have you heard from Moreau?"

I force myself not to frown. "A little."

"What does he tell you?"

"Not a lot," I say honestly.

My father stands and stalks towards me. "There are rumors of trouble at the border. Azlan has been sent there twice now. The chancellor doesn't usually send him there."

I nod. "Spencer hasn't said anything."

"The forces in the West are growing in strength and number." My father comes closer and this time I concentrate on not shrinking away from him. I've never liked his odor. Or the soulless quality of his eyes. It makes my skin creep. "But my sources tell me we need to be prepared."

I can't help it, my eyes flick to his. The amusement and cruelty I see hovering in them making me feel sick. "Prepared for what, Sir?"

"An opportunity," he says.

I know he wants me to ask more, but I'm not prepared to play his cryptic games, games designed for him to win and me to lose. The odds never ever in my favor. No, I won't play his games anymore.

"I have to go," I tell him. "I'm the star of the show and I can't be late."

I can't help the dig, one I know will grate him. He may want me to follow in his footsteps but he certainly doesn't want me to steal his limelight.

"Your mother should have cut your hair. You look like a hillbilly."

My voice tenses. "She wanted to. I declined the offer."

He grips my arm, his magic coiling tightly around my muscle, so tight it cuts into my flesh, makes my fingers tingle. I keep that blank expression.

"Take care tonight, son," he snarls. "The eyes of all of Los Magicos will be on you. They'll be depending on you."

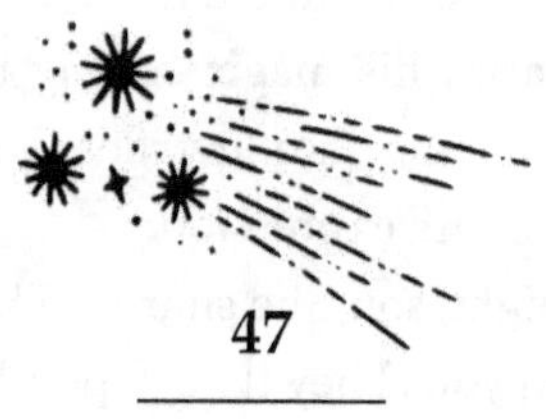

47

S pencer

IT's the night of the victory ball. As captain, as the player who won the match for our team, they would probably have given me special dispensation to attend. But I never asked. I made a promise to myself to stay away. To stay far away from her. To protect her. It's one I'm going to keep.

The beast doesn't like it. But it only confirms in my heart that I've made the right decision.

It doesn't mean I'm happy about it either though, so I'm grateful I'm on patrol tonight, marching the perimeter of the barracks with one other soldier I think is called Tim or Tom or Sam. We've already circled the eastern half of the barrack grounds, marched past the sleeping barracks and the other soldiers stationed at the gates, and we don't speak as we near the western edge. I've nothing to say and soon the thwack of our boots in the mud is muffled by the distant booms of magic. I've become used to those booms by now. I hardly notice them, a background track to our daily lives here.

We take the path through the trees, gaze swinging obligatory left and right for any signs of intruders, anything unusual. I've been here for two weeks. Not once has anyone on night patrol discovered or encountered anything. It seems pointless to have us marching up and down like this when there are trackers among us anyway, magicals who can sense the presence of others.

I huff, my breath coming out in a misty cloud in front of my face, and rub my hands together, the tips of my fingers cold. The soldier beside me peers up at me from the corners of his eyes. I suspect he's more scared of me than he is of any potential threat out here in the trees. He's seen me pound others in training. Seen me take down everyone they've put me up against. He's not the only one who looks shit scared of me.

"You hear there's talk they're going to send us to the front next week," he says.

No, I hadn't heard that, but it triggers a little excitement in my gut. I'm more than ready to stop messing around here at the barracks and face something real.

"About time." The other man grimaces. I guess he's not as keen as me. "You don't want to go?"

"I'm in no hurry," he says nervously. He eyes me. "They say you volunteered to come here."

"It's obligatory, mandatory. All registered have to do their service."

"But you came early? Left the academy early?"

I nod stiffly. I don't want to think about the academy. Not tonight.

"I remember you. You were a couple of years below me.

Already on the dueling team. Weren't you captain of the dueling team in the end?"

"Yes," I mumble.

"Man," he says wistfully, "I'd give anything to be back at the academy. The freedom, the parties. Fuck, the girls." He chuckles. "I bet you got laid all the time. The captain of the team back in my day had girls queuing up outside his door."

I glare straight ahead. I don't want to talk about this.

We reach the end of the path.

"There's nothing here," he says, smothering a yawn.

I nod and we turn.

The cold is bitter, biting. I miss the relative warmth of Los Magicos. I tug at the collar of my jacket, blow warm air over my fingers. I want to get back to the barracks. Away from this man. I don't want to reminisce about the freaking academy. Or girls. A girl.

We turn and as we do, the sky bursts with color. It entrances us both for just a fraction of a second. Then a boom thunders through the air and sweeps us off our feet.

My face hits the mud, the ground beneath me shaking. I spit out the earth from my mouth and scrabble to my feet, skidding in the mud.

"What the hell was that?" the other soldier says, climbing to his feet, but another crashing boom sends him flying back down into the mud. This time I keep my balance. The sky is alive with exploding magic, like a million fireworks let off all at once, colliding and slamming into one another.

"What the fuck," the other man shouts.

"We're under attack," I yell and then I'm picking up my feet and running back through the trees, down the path towards the barracks. It's chaos. An alarm blares. Lights flash and spin. Soldiers dash from the barracks, half dressed, rubbing sleep from their eyes. A couple of commanders stand in the middle of the mayhem bellowing orders but it's unclear if anyone is listening. I sprint to the nearest one.

"What do we do?" I yell above the commotion.

"What the hell do you think? Get to the front line!"

I swing my gaze around and see some soldiers already heading that way, I start after them. Then I freeze. We all do. A giant dark shape glides across the sky, blocking out all the light. We stare as it swoops above us and then the sky is alight again, this time with fire, soaring from whatever the hell that is, towards us on the ground. People scream, yell, run for cover.

But I'm still frozen, frozen to the spot, gaping up at this weapon, at this ... beast. Fire courses around me. A man catches alight, falling to the ground, rolling about in a desperate effort to smother the flames. A tree catches fire too, its burning branches flickering like some grotesque candle.

"Dragons!" someone yells, and I see another and another filling the sky.

It can't be? Dragons? There haven't been dragons for several hundred years.

I start to run for cover, expecting them all to swoop down together and burn – raze – everything to the ground. But they don't. They fly right over our heads.

"They're heading for the capital," that same commander yells as he runs past me, "we need to warn them." But he never makes it to the door, his body consumed in a ball of fire.

The capital? Los Magicos? Under attack?

Rhianna!

Every cell in my body screams.

I can't let anything happen to her. I need to protect her.

A strange compulsion overtakes me. I'm moving before I know I am, racing towards the barracks and up the fire escape, up and up and up until I'm four stories high, sprinting across the roof. The dragons soar closer, low enough I can see the ruby glint of their reptilian eyes, see the strange glistening of the scales that cover their tails, see the strong claws tucked into their bodies, and the strange swish of their tails in the air behind them.

The first two are too high, and the third swerves away, but the fourth is low, low enough, if I could …

The beast roars inside me and I know he is stronger, better, braver. I let him take control and together we leap into the air, grabbing a hold of the dragon's tail and clinging on with every piece of strength we possess.

48

R^{hi}

"Uh oh," Winnie says, spotting Summer too as she slides up beside me. "Someone doesn't look happy."

Summer's expression becomes fiercer and she begins to push her way towards us.

"Wanna run for it?" Trent asks on my other side.

"You guys can if you want," I say, facing Summer front on, "I'm staying right here."

Trent glances at Winnie who shakes her head. "I'm not going anywhere."

Trent shrugs nervously. "Okay."

Summer barges the remaining girl out of the way and halts right in front of me.

"Hi Summer," I say with what I hope sounds like sweetness. There really is no need for a scene and I would rather avoid one if I can. "You look nice."

Summer's eyes flick up and down my gown and her face turns bright red. She looks like she might blow a gasket. I half expect steam to start billowing from her ears.

"Where did you get that dress?" she hisses.

"Do you like it?" I say, ignoring her question.

"Where did you get it, Pig Girl?" she says and I realize there's no hope of avoiding a scene. There's already a crowd gathered around to watch this confrontation. Internally, I groan. This was half the reason I wanted to avoid coming tonight. It seems I can't go anywhere in this school without someone attempting to start a fight with me.

"None of your business."

"It is my business," Summer says, tossing her head and nearly losing her tiara in the process. "Where did you get it?" She snatches her arm forward and grabs a handful of my skirt, rubbing the material roughly between her fingers. "It's–"

"*Mona*," Winnie says with a grin.

"Vintage *Mona*," Summer growls. "This is the fucking dress Evette Saphire wore to the premier of *Moonbeams and Candlelight*." For a moment genuine admiration for the dress flickers over her face but as quickly as it comes it's gone, replaced by pure rage. "How the hell did you get this? There's no way you could afford it!"

She tugs on the skirt and I'm almost pulled off balance.

"Be careful, you'll rip her dress," Trent says. Summer turns her head slowly hand glares at him and he takes a decided step away.

"Did you steal it, Pig girl?" Summer hisses. "Or did you suck some withered old dick in exchange for–"

"What's going on?" Stone comes striding through the crowd of onlookers. His gaze swings from Summer and then to me. He stutters for a moment, his eyes smoldering with want. Then he regains his composure.

"Pig Girl is wearing a stolen gown."

"Miss Clutton-Brock, I think we've spoken before about calling people names," Stone says darkly and Summer's cheeks actually pinken.

"*Rhianna Blackwaters* is wearing a stolen gown. A highly priceless stolen gown."

Stone's lip twitches and his eyes dance with amusement. "Miss Blackwaters, Miss Clutton-Brock claims this very beautiful dress you're ..." he clears his throat, "barely wearing," I scowl at him, "is stolen. Is this accusation correct?"

I want to shrug. I actually have no clue where or how Tristan landed this dress. I'm guessing there is a possibility he stole it, although that doesn't seem very likely.

"I don't know," I say.

Summer huffs in triumph, folding her arms across her body. "She should be made to take it off."

"Miss Blackwaters, how has it come to be that you are wearing a dress that you are unsure whether is stolen or not?"

I scowl at him some more. I am going to torture him so badly when we are alone.

"It was given to her as a gift," Winnie says, bringing herself to Summer's attention for the first time. Summer makes some weird gurgling sound and points at Winnie in outrage.

Stone ignores her.

"Who gave you the dress, Miss Blackwaters? It may help us to determine if it is indeed stolen."

"It isn't," another voice says from somewhere in the crowd. A voice recognizable to everyone in the school.

The crowd parts and this time Tristan Kennedy comes

strolling through looking like he stepped straight out of a movie and into the Hall. He's wearing a tux, but the bowtie is loose around his neck and his shirt is undone, showing a flash of golden collarbone. He's slung his jacket over his shoulder and rolled his sleeves up showing his muscular forearms. He looks like he's been partying for hours, rather than just arrived.

"Mr. Kennedy," Stone says, his expression flickering somewhere between amusement and tension now.

Tristan comes to stop between me and Summer, facing the professor head on and my bond tugs at them both, pulling me in both directions ... and then a third. Azlan's nearby, probably watching this entire silly altercation. He's probably cursing the fact he's bonded to someone so young, still caught up in childish schoolyard crap like this.

"It is stolen," Summer insists, "that girl has no money. There is no way she got her hands on it through legitimate means. If someone gave it to her, they gave it to her because she ..." Summer's words trail away under the fierceness of Tristan's stare.

"I gave it to her," Tristan says. "It isn't stolen. I bought it for her. You can see the damn receipt if you want."

Summer's face falls, real hurt suddenly clear in her eyes, and for the first time since I arrived at this academy, I actually feel sorry for the girl. It lasts precisely thirty seconds.

"Why, Tristan? She's a slut and a nobody. She has no powers, no family, no influence. And most of the time she looks and smells like pig shit."

"I think we both know she doesn't, Summer. I think even you can see she's the most beautiful woman at this ball tonight."

Summer takes an angry step towards him, jabbing her

finger at him like a knife. "So what? She's still unregistered scum."

There's a communal intake of breath and many shocked faces turn to me in disbelief. Including Trent's.

"Oh yeah," Summer says, smirking at me. I guess she's been sitting on that piece of juicy gossip, waiting to expose it in a moment just like this. "Don't think I didn't know your dirty little secret, Pig Girl."

"Summer," Stone warns, stepping between her and me. But Tristan's the one she's really interested in, not me.

"An unregistered, Tristan. Your pretty little Pig Girl was an unregistered."

"I know," he says calmly, causing more shocked gasps from our crowd.

"Are you fucking kidding me?" Summer spits. "You can't seriously ..." She shakes her head, cackling. "You can't be serious about her."

Tristan lifts his chin, staring at Summer and then out towards all those people gaping at us, before finally landing on me. "I am serious. I am very serious. Because Rhianna Blackwaters is my–"

But he never gets to utter those last few words because there's an almighty roar and then the ceiling of the Great Hall cracks right in half.

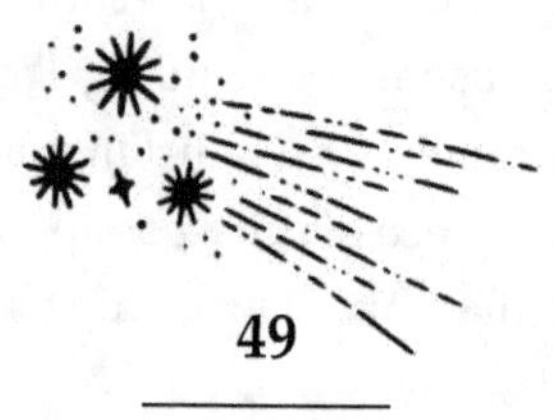

49

T he werebeast

I CLING to the reptile's tail, my claws digging into its scaly flesh, determined that I will not be dislodged. Twice the creature attempts to throw me off, thrashing its tail about wildly, shaking me so hard my bones rattle. But I only dig my claws in deeper, snapping my jaw into its muscle, making the creature moan.

In retaliation, it skims low across the trees, branches scraping at my body, at my own flesh.

I cling to the creature, despite the pain and the injury, my blood seeping from my skin as the branches cut me.

The girl – our mate – is in danger.

We are returning to the capital to protect her.

The boy was a fool to leave her side in the first place. She may be strong – stronger than even perhaps he deciphers – but she is just a girl after all. Mere flesh and blood. It would be so easy for us to lose her.

I growl at the thought, anger coursing through my veins, and clasp my claws tighter into the reptile.

The boy believes I intend to hurt her. It's why he took us far away from her. To keep her safe.

I snarl. I am not the one who intends to harm her. She's mine. My mate. My pet. I want to build a nest for her and rut her full of pups. I want to shield her away from harm and danger. I want to be with her, guarding her, keeping her safe. I am not the danger. I am the protection.

Two magicals ride the giant reptile's back. I can tell from their scent they are human. Which explains their lack of observation. They have not seen me. And they curse the reptile for its erratic behavior. It means the rest of the flight is smoother, the reptile flicking its tail occasionally, still determined to shake me loose.

Nonetheless, my shoulders scream with pain as the minutes flick to hours and my paws are stiff and aching.

I wonder if, caged inside the boy, I have weakened, if I can hold on long enough to reach her. But then the city lights appear on the horizon.

The human magicals chatter together in excitement and the dragon flaps its gigantic wings, cracking the night's air. We soar faster through the sky, the other dragons by our side, flying in a formation.

Do the humans know we are coming? Are they prepared?

As we fly closer, the formation breaks. Most of the reptiles soar away to the city. The one I am riding veers to the east with five others and we sail over countryside, the scent of it familiar, and then a hill appears, a great house perched on its peak.

I recognize it. The boy called this place home for many years. It is also where the girl should be.

I inhale, sure I can already smell her familiar scent even over this distance. We will find her. We will keep her safe. I will rip the throat out of this great creature with my teeth if I have to.

The night is eerily silent, cold air rushing through my fur, the pound of the reptiles' cold hearts and the crack of their wings the only noise. Then music, as we soar closer, music and then the lead dragon crashes down onto the roof of the school, smashing its snout and it claws through the turreted roof, until there's nothing of it left but a gaping great hole.

The beast I cling to swoops over the building and below I see the faces of a hundred young human magicals.

And her. Her eyes golden in the darkness, calling to me.

I pull back my claws, release my arms and fall. Through the sky, through the night, into the scattering students below me, my body twisting and contorting as I do, returning to his form, his body.

He needs to find the girl and together we will protect her.

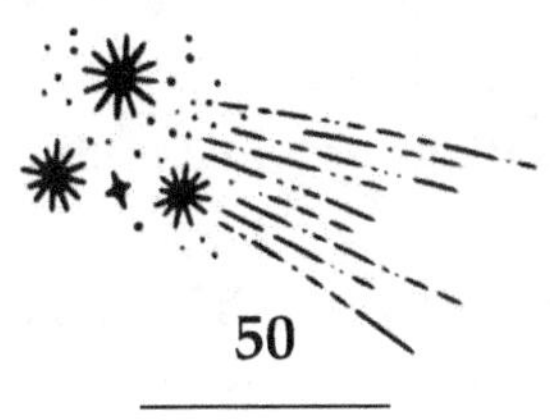

50

R enzo

THE TRUCK SPEEDS along the country roads, dim beams illuminating the ghostly trees and spindly bushes. I bounce on my seat, Marcus beside me, behind us ten other trucks. All full of soldiers like this one.

He won't tell me where we're going. But I ask again just for the hell of it.

"You don't need to know. Just be prepared for one hell of a fight when we get there," he says, grinning at me.

"Might help me with the fighting if I knew the details, if I knew *who* we were fighting," I say, fidgeting in my seat. We've been driving straight for two hours. My legs need to move. My muscles are twitching. I rub at my chin, at my chest, slide my hands down my thighs.

I've never been able to sit quietly. My mom tied me to

my chair once, screaming at me to keep the fuck still. Couldn't do it then. Can't do it now.

"You've never cared about the details before, Renzo," Marcus says, eyes narrowing.

"Maybe I'm getting more discerning in my old age." I flick lint off my leg.

I'm fucking 26 next year. It's hilarious. I never expected to make it past 20. I don't think anyone thought I would.

Just goes to show I'm good at my job. Nah, maybe it's not that. Maybe I'm good at surviving. Good at something anyway.

I peer back at the soldiers lined up on two benches either side of the truck. Some of the men are Marcus's, the inks on their arms and their necks making that damn obvious. The others are from the West. My eyes flicker back to Marcus. What the fuck is the crazy motherfucker up to? And is it going to get us killed?

I remember what it was like as a kid. My mom with her ear glued to the radio, puffing on cigarette after cigarette. Some dude with a plum in his mouth reporting of attacks and battles, people dying, of dark forces. Somewhere distant. Just words.

I close my eyes, my body jolting around by the stupid truck and its fucked-up suspension.

Do I care if I die? It never bothered me before. Live. Die. LiveDie. DieLive. Never gave a fuck. Probably why I'm still here, lungs expanding, heart pumping. If you hang on to something too desperately, like your life for example, it's usually the first thing you end up losing.

I think of my little rabbit. And something behind my ribs aches. I look down at my chest. I'm wearing an old leather jacket. It's my favorite. Took it from the body of the very first man I killed. Still makes me shiver every time I slide my arms inside the sleeves and shake the thing up onto my shoulders, even though it's been a long time since it smelled of him. It stinks of me now. Wonder if my little rabbit would wear it. I like the idea of her all wrapped up in my scent, unable to stop thinking about me, like I can't stop thinking about her.

I shake my head. Marcus eyes me through the darkness.

"Brother," he says, and it's been many years since he called me that. Are we? Not by blood, but they say there are other kinds of family. He was the one who saved me – a half starved kid, scrapping to survive. The one who took me in. "Don't do anything stupid tonight," he growls near my ear.

My eyes snap open. "Me?"

He didn't want to bring me. Which made me all the more determined to come. Okay, so I don't ask about all his plans, but he's never been so reluctant to tell me either. I don't like it. And so that's why I'm here.

"Yeah, you. You follow instructions, orders, don't go off doing your own fucking thing."

"*Moi?*" I repeat, this time pointing to my chest.

"Yes, you." I draw my finger down then across my chest. Marcus snorts. "I'm serious, Renzo. No bullshit."

"No bullshit," I say, scratching my cheek. "Whose orders?" I ask him. "Yours or ..."

Marcus doesn't answer. He's working with someone. Shit, maybe even *for* someone. Someone in the West. Why? I wish I'd paid better attention. I wish I had a brain that could pay attention, one that could slot all the pieces together.

My gaze pulls to the window, and now I see where we're going.

"Los Magicos," I whisper. Seems he is out to get us killed after all.

"No," Marcus says, attention diverted by his cell. "Not the city."

No, not the city. I see that as we skirt round it, the glow of the capital fading behind us.

I sit up in my seat and my gaze swings towards my boss, my brother.

The academy.

R hi

A DRAGON, the size of a small truck, crashes through the ceiling of the Great Hall, two men sliding from its back as it roars fire, and then there's another and another.

I stand captivated by the sight. The creatures are beautiful, their skin covered in emerald scales, their eyes glowing a violent red. They're huge and yet they move with elegance, swooping through the now exposed sky, landing deftly on clawed feet. I didn't know such creatures still existed. I thought they'd been lost long ago.

But I'm snapped back to reality by Winnie yanking on my arm and screaming in my ear.

I blink, focusing on the carnage around me. People are scattering, some screaming, some running. The heavy drapes that lined the walls are blazing with flame. Everything is blazing, roaring with fire. Just like ... just like that memory locked inside my head.

The magicals jumping from the backs of the dragons fire bolts of magic towards us. They streak and scream, skimming over our heads, one crashing into a crystal chandelier and shattering it into a million pieces of shards that shower on those below.

There's more screaming. Winnie tugs harder on my arm.

"Rhi, we need to get out of here!"

"What's happening?" I ask her, my brain struggling to compute what my eyes are showing it.

"We're under attack, Rhi, come on."

"Here at the academy?" I say, too stunned to move. "How can this be?" I thought we were safe here. I thought this was the safest place in the country.

"Dragons!" Winnie yells like that's some kind of explanation. "Come on Rhi!" Winnie screams and pulls me and Trent to the ground as several magical bolts stream over us. "We need to get out!" she repeats, screaming again and covering her head with her arms as another chandelier plummets to the ground.

But I'm already up on my feet.

Phoenix? Azlan? Where are they? I scan my eyes through the mayhem, my eyes moving more frantically than they did only ten minutes ago, the scene in front of me so different. Many of the students are sprinting for the exit, some cowering behind upturned furniture, but others are standing and fighting. Stone and the man in black among them, side by side facing off against two, five, seven – I lose count – magicals firing magic towards them.

I start to run, kicking off my stupid heels and gripping the skirt of my dress. I dodge another falling chandelier, leap over someone moaning on the ground and duck as the tail of a dragon whips through the air. I run as hard as I can but they're still so far away, outnumbered and in need of my help.

My foot catches on something sharp on the ground and I wince but keep moving. Magic grazes my arm but I hardly notice. The noise thrums in my skull. Magic thundering and booming all around me.

"Stone!" I yell, "Azlan!"

Azlan's head whips round and his eyes meet mine, alarm and determination clear in his expression, blaring through our bond.

His mouth moves and, though I can't hear what he's saying, I read the words on his lips: "Get away!"

Then I scream as he throws himself to the ground, a bolt exploding just where he'd stood one second ago.

I curse, ripping away the stupid netting of my dress. I can't run in this, I can't breathe. Then I'm moving again. I'm nearly there, nearly by their sides – where I'm meant to be, helping them, protecting them.

That dangerous magic, that dark magic, the magic that both scares and delights me coils through my veins, coming alive, my blood soon as hot as the fire, my fingertips sparking. I'm going to destroy anyone or anything that harms one single hair on my mates' heads. I lift my arms, ready to strike.

Then something catches my eye.

One of the dragons has a girl cornered, the blazing drapes at her back, the beast blocking her escape. It roars, smoke whooshing from its nostrils and the girl lifts her arm to protect her face, her pale blonde hair coated in ash.

Summer. Summer Clutton-Brock.

The dragon snaps its jaws at her and she shoots magic at

it, magic that bounces off its scales like raindrops bouncing off a tin roof.

The creature prowls closer. She can't step backwards; the flames are hot at her back.

I hesitate.

The crimson magic hisses with pleasure. She deserves this. Summer is a bully and a bitch. She's made my life hell. She's abused me, hurt me, humiliated me. Stolen something precious from me – the only link I have to my mom. And I'm not the only one. She makes everyone's life here at the academy a misery and she relishes in doing it.

I should let her die. Let the dragon snap its jaws right through her. Rid the world of her. I owe her nothing, nothing at all.

I screw my eyes closed, my hands balling so tightly my nails pinch into my palms. I struggle against it, against the dark thoughts, against the anger, and vitriol, the need for revenge. I beat it back as it hisses and protests, attempting to seduce me with all its promises. How good will revenge taste? How sweet?

My body shakes, the magic burns in my blood, roaring for release. I beat it back. My teeth grinding together with the effort.

Then I scream, thrusting the magic deep, deep inside me, and then I fling my arms to the right, sending powerful – light – magic lightning through the air and into the side of the dragon. It howls in pain, stumbling backwards, then sideways, attempting to twist its head to examine the gaping wound on its side.

Summer's head snaps in my direction and our eyes connect: hers in astonishment, mine in determination, and then she's running for cover, running from the danger.

"Rhi!" A hand lands on my shoulder and I jolt awake

from what felt like a dream, all that hot angry magic hissing away as a calmness overcomes me. "Rhi, are you okay?"

Tristan. He no longer looks like the suave, sophisticated heartthrob from fifteen minutes ago. His hair is tangled, his shirt ripped, blood oozes on his arm.

He shakes me a little.

"Is she okay?"

My gaze flicks from Tristan to the speaker. Spencer. Spencer Moreau, looking even more beat up than Tristan. His entire body is covered in soot and ash – his entire unclothed body – scrapes and cuts up and down his legs, his arm, his torso, his face.

"Sp-Spencer?" I say.

"We need to get her out of here," Spencer yells at Tristan, deflecting away a flurry of bolts that come cavorting towards us.

I pull against Tristan's grip and then all our heads are snapping to the Great Hall's entrance, people screaming and racing from that direction, as more of these fighters – soldiers – charge through the grand doorway.

"What the fuck?" Tristan gasps. "There's so many of them."

Spencer smacks him on the arm.

"Tristan!" he says, drawing his friend's attention to him. "You take her and you go! Take her somewhere safe!"

Tristan frowns, opening his mouth to argue, but then Spencer falls forwards onto all fours, his body jerking and jolting, just like I've seen before. Only this time it doesn't stop. His body morphs in size, grows even larger, even stronger, doubling in stature. His head twists and distorts, jet fur sprouting all over his skin. It happens so quickly I wonder if I'm seeing things. One moment Spencer Moreau, right there in front of us, and then ... and then ...

the werebeast. Black like the night. The werebeast that attacked me.

I spring back in shock as he leaps forward, but he's not coming for me. He charges straight into the wall of soldiers, bowling them over like tenpins.

I take my chance, shaking Tristan's hand loose from my arm, and running again.

"Rhianna!" he yells, chasing after me.

I keep running. Except I can't see Phoenix or Azlan any more, they're gone from the spot they just were and now the hall is filling with smoke. I cough as it catches in my chest. I can't see, can't see through the fog of smoke.

"Azlan! Stone!" I lay my palms on my stomach, coughing and spluttering as I do, searching for that pull, that tug, the bond. I feel them, both of them, they are alive, safe. And I almost sob in relief, but I've no time to savor the feeling as more magic thunders around me and the surviving beams of the ceiling groan, crashing down onto everyone below. I throw myself onto the ground, rolling through the smoke and the debris, hoping I'm moving away from the danger. Then I'm back on my hands and knees, firing magic at the men who've come to attack us.

A hand yanks me onto my feet. Tristan again.

"Get off me!" I yell at him. "I don't need your help."

"Tough shit, little Piglet. You're getting it anyway." He swings me to one side, and shoots his magic at a man racing straight towards us. The man crumples like a rag doll and then Tristan's firing again, his magic stronger, brighter, than all the rest, lighting up the smoke in a rainbow of colors.

I twist my arm in his grip, pulling and tugging. I don't want his help. Not his. I don't care how much my magic begs to join his, to combine with it. I don't care how the bond strains so much it hurts.

"Rhi!" he barks. "There's too many of them. I need your help. We need to combine our magic." I shake my head violently. "Rhianna!" he snaps. "You want your friends to die? You want your *mates* to die?"

Pain sears through my gut at the very thought of it and my magic races from me before I can stop it. It swims through the air, straight towards his and when they collide, it's like lightning, electricity streaking through every nerve, every bone, our magic so bright it blinds me.

My magic bleeds into his and his into mine and it's never been like this before; I feel everything, every part of him, all his power, all his anger, all his fears, all his love.

My bond sings in my stomach and I don't know what it means, what we've done.

But then he's calling my name again through all the noise. My eyes find his and I know what he needs me to do without saying a word. Together, we fling our arms forward, launching our combined magic across the hall towards the men streaming inside. It explodes into them and they fall like dominos.

Then we send a torrent of water at the blazing drapes, dousing them completely, steam hissing and curling into the air. We do it again before thundering magic at more soldiers, more and more of them falling. We're winning, taking control, driving them backwards.

"The dragons," Tristan yells and we fling our magic at a giant beast in the air, watching as it's blown high, high, high up into the air, till it's only a twinkle of a star like all the others.

I look at him, smiling, his magic curling and caressing around mine like it never wants to stop touching mine. His gaze drops down from the sky and he smiles at me in wonder, looking more beautiful in that moment than I think he ever has. Real and genuine. I smile right back at him, right up into his beautiful face, the warmth in our bond making me light-headed and giddy, and then it happens.

A bolt of magic streaks towards me. And I've no time to react. Nowhere to go. Tristan darts in front of me, shielding me with his much bigger frame. The magic slams into his body, his eyes widen in shock, he peers down at the massive wound in his stomach.

"I'm s-s-sorry," he stutters.

And then he falls to the ground.

52

———

R^{hi}

His MAGIC, so vivid, so alive, so raw, so powerful, lingers in the sky like smoke, then fades, slips away from mine. I cling to it, grasp at it, but it slides from my own and I'm alone, all alone.

I howl, the pain in my body so intense, I don't know what to do with myself.

I claw at my skin, pull at my hair, fling my pathetic magic all around me.

He can't be, he can't be! Please no! Please no!

I didn't mean it. I didn't. All those times I said I hated him. All those times I swore I wanted him gone. All those times I promised I didn't want him. It was lies. All lies.

I want him. I need him. He's mine and I am meant to be his. And he can't be gone, snatched from my grasp. He can't be.

I fling back my head and howl, pain and misery thunder through me and I start to lose my grip on my mind, on my thoughts, on my awareness. The pain is too great. The misery too deep. I'm drowning in it.

Around me the battle continues. Magic exploding, dragons roaring, men fighting. But now it's as if everything is slowed down, yanked under water. The sound is muffled, unclear, the colors dim, bleached, the movement dragging.

What do I do? What do I do now? Because he's gone and I don't know what I'm meant to do.

My head spins and spins. I barely know who I am. What I am. I grip my head in my hands.

Then I remember. Rhianna. Rhianna Blackwaters.

Is someone calling my name? Running my way?

I shake my head and they pull at me, yelling in my face, dragging me from the burning shell of a building out into the night. There're more people yelling at me, hands reaching for me.

I shake my head. I can't hear them. All I hear is my own heart, struggling to beat against all this pain. Broken, smashed, shattered into pieces. It hurts so much. And I don't even know why. What is happening? What has happened to me?

The world swoops and swirls. I'm being tugged further and further underwater, down into the murky depths.

Someone's missing. Someone important. Someone whose absence is making my body hurt this much, every step away from them agony.

"No," I call out, "wait."

I strain to remember, to make sense of it all as the pain ravages through me, licks me like hot hot flames.

There's someone missing. Someone I need. Someone

who means the world to me. Who I can't live without. Someone I can't leave behind. I can't.

Pip!

I throw magic at everyone in my path and then I'm running, so fast no one can catch me, away from the blazing mansion, along the pathways, into the darkness. I swerve the magicals coming for me, crash through fleeing students, blast away anyone who tries to stop me, sprinting towards the forest and my dorm room.

It's quiet this side of campus, the battle not penetrating this far, and our dorm building lies in darkness, all the lights gone out. I race through the entrance and to our door. I'm so agitated, so confused, it takes me four attempts to undo the locking spell, my hands shaking more and more with each failed attempt. I can't seem to concentrate, can't seem to make the words stop swirling in my head, the pain making everything spiral.

Finally, the spell releases and I crash through the door.

"Pip?!" I yell, "Pip?! Where are you?!"

The room is dark, the curtains drawn against all the light from outside, but as my eyes adjust I make out the silvery outline of our furniture.

I careen to Pip's bed.

Empty.

"Pip," I wail, falling to my knees. The pain inside me is so penetrating, I can no longer stand. The world spins even faster. My stomach lurches. Bile rushes up my throat and I sway on my knees.

But then there's a familiar squeak. A squeak I know so well. And he comes wriggling out from under the bed, squeezing out his behind and popping forward. I lunge for him, scooping him into my arms, burying my face against his.

"It's okay," I tell him as he quivers in my arms, jolting when a boom shakes the windows. "It's okay, little man, I got you."

I hug him to my chest. I found him. He's safe. Everything should be better now. We're okay, the two of us. We have each other, like we always have. The pain should stop, shouldn't it? And yet it is still there, lodged against the overwhelming sensation that something is wrong. It radiates through my entire body and I don't know what's happening to me.

I stumble to my feet and stagger towards the door, clutching Pip as tight as I can. I concentrate hard on placing one foot in front of the other, on keeping myself upright. It takes everything I have and that nausea swoops up my throat.

I don't understand what's wrong with me. I can't think straight, my head all a muddle. Something's not right and I don't understand what the hell it is.

I try to focus.

I need to get away. Yes, that's what I need to do. Get Pip and me to safety.

I reel out of the room and out of the building, but that's as far as I get. As I step onto the path, a bolt of magic slams right into my shoulder and I'm smacked to the ground, all the air crushed from my lungs. I lie on the hard, cold ground gasping, Pip nudging his snout anxiously against my face.

He's telling me to get up. To fight. But I can't. I can't breathe and my legs and my arms won't work.

I gasp again, my lungs refusing to work, burning in my chest. I stare up at the sky, burning with magic and fires and beasts that should no longer exist. Am I dreaming?

Then all that light is blocked out by the silhouette of a man. Tall and broad. He peers down at me with no compassion, no emotion, his eyes deadly cold. He's dressed head to toe in camouflage, only his face exposed. A cruel face. I can tell by the twist of the mouth, the deadness of his eyes. A tattoo runs the length of one side of his face and his dark hair is slicked back. He glares at me as the world explodes and burns around us.

"The unregistered girl from the wastelands," he says.

Do I know him? Pip squeals and burrows into my side. There's something about this man ... something familiar. But I can't make my brain work. Everything hurts and I can't breathe. I can't breathe.

"It is you, isn't it?" he growls, swinging back his leg and kicking me hard in the ribs. "I thought it was you, you little bitch."

I'm already in so much pain that the strike to my body hardly registers, but it seems to awaken my lungs, air rushing to fill them.

I stare up into his face as the oxygen floods my brain.

It's the eyes ... something about the eyes ... the shape, the color, the cocky self-confidence.

And then I see it. Then I remember.

My knife in that skull. Those same eyes, staring unblinking at the ground, never to close again.

"Marcus Lowsky," I gasp, my throat raw and raspy. And suddenly everything is clear, crystal clear. The sounds, the sights, everything coming into sharp focus, the dark lines of his tattoo, the chain around his neck, the leaves above his head, the aroma of burning in my nose.

"I had a feeling you weren't dead," he hisses, kicking me three more times, so hard my body skids across the path each time, before he crouches down beside me. "But not to worry. This is better. This is the way it should be."

I need to be fighting, saving myself, saving Pip, but

everything hurts, my magic refusing to come when I command it. My fingertips useless, like wet matches. I lie there helpless, staring up into his venomous eyes.

"This way," he continues, examining my face, "I get to make you suffer, hurt, pay for what you did."

He hovers a hand above me and sends electricity searing through my body. I scream as my body jolts and jerks and my muscles and nerves scorch.

"Yes, much better." There's no expression on his face. It's blank, completely blank, only those dark eyes glinting.

I glare right back at him. I could try to reason with him. Make him see I didn't know it was his brother, explain I was saving another. But who am I kidding? This man wants revenge. Blood. It's all he's ever wanted. He's been damn persistent about it. There's no way he's going to let me live.

Again, I try to move my arm, to call my magic to my fingertips, but everything is an effort, my arm so heavy I can't move it.

His eyes flick all over me and Pip takes his chance and attacks him, launching at the man and snapping at his nose. The man is too quick though, he swerves backwards, swings his arm through the air and sends Pip flying away. I hear my pet hit the ground behind me with a squeal.

"Pip!" I moan, my voice barely audible.

"I'm going to break every bone in your body. Then I'm going to slit your throat and watch you bleed to death," Marcus says. "So where shall we start? Your fingers?" He takes my left hand in both of his and I try with all my might to zap him. I reach deep inside myself, searching for that dark, crimson magic, knowing it would save me now. But there's nothing, only emptiness and pain.

"And while we're doing this," he says, uncoiling my fist and straightening my digits. He grips my little finger, "you can tell me why Renzo Barone didn't kill you. Why he brought me a heart that wasn't yours. Why he lied to me."

He snaps my finger backwards and white light sears across my vision. More pain. Hot and wretched.

I screw up my eyes and when the world stops spinning, he's still there, gripping my hand. His breath loud and menacing. He's gripping my next finger now, my pinkie dangling at a grotesque angle.

"Tell me why," he growls, his dark eyes spitting with anger and bloodlust.

"Because she's my fated mate, you fucking cunt!"

A black cloud of magic pounds into Marcus Lowsky, dragging him onto the ground and curling all over him, coiling around and around his neck like a noose. The man scrabbles to release his throat but his hands swim through the shadows and the ligature squeezes. He fires magic into the air but the coil grows tighter and tighter, his face growing red, then purple, the veins on his temple popping out against his skin, his eyes bulging. His legs scrape against the earth. He wheezes and gurgles. I turn my head away, unable to watch and my gaze falls right upon Renzo Barone, Pip tucked under his arm. He reaches for my shoulder, gripping it tightly.

"Let's get out of here, little rabbit."

There's a flash of light and then the world bends and stretches, the sounds of the man being strangled, the explosions and the fire, twist and stretch. There's a pressure in my head. I feel as if I am being squeezed to death and then it releases. I gasp for air and open my eyes.

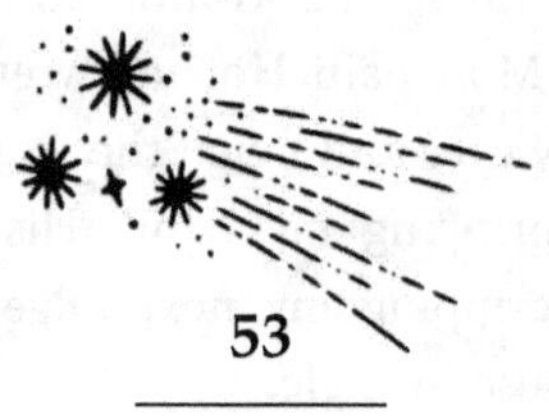

53

S pencer

I COME BACK to myself in a pile of bodies, the battle thundering around me, magic clashing in the air, the Great Hall a blazing wreck.

I scan the vicinity, searching a way out. I told Tristan to take Rhianna and leave, but as I climb through the wreckage, deflecting and firing magic at the remaining soldiers, I spy him. On the ground. His eyes closed. His body lifeless.

Blood rushes to my head. I sway on my feet. I think of my brother. My dead brother. His blood sunken deep into the earth.

Is he dead too? Tristan dead? So full of life. So strong. So powerful. And if he is dead then ...

No, it can't be! I rush towards him, barreling through men charging at me, throwing them over my shoulder, smashing my magic through their bodies, and then I'm sinking to my knees beside him.

At first I don't want to touch him, nausea and panic and fear swirling through me. If I touch him, then I'll know for sure. Then there's no more maybe, no doubt, no possibilities. If he's dead, he'll be dead, and there's nothing I can do about it.

I steel myself and reach out and take my friend's body in my arms.

He's warm, barely, but he is, and his brow furrows ever so slightly as I move him.

Relief rushes through me with such force, I let out a laugh, loud and crazy sounding among all the groans and moans of dying men.

"Tristan?" I say, "Tristan, can you hear me?"

I've always been able to feel his magic, feel how powerful and forceful it was, like an aura hovering around him. I close my eyes and feel for it now. It's there, feeble, faint, waning.

There's a gaping wound in the center of his chest, blood bubbling from it. I furrow my brows, grit my teeth and hover my hand above it, willing my magic to heal the wound, to seal the broken flesh. But I can't. It's a curse, deep and dark, seeping into his veins, and his magic fades that little bit more.

I need to get him to a healer, to a hospital.

I lift him and carry him out of the hall, away from the fierce battle, out into the night, deflecting all the magic fired in our direction.

As I emerge onto the path, gaze swinging desperately from side to side, seeking someone who can help us, the enforcer comes hurtling towards me.

"Rhianna?" he asks, his eyes wild, his breath coming in

ragged pants, his heavy shoulders rising and falling rapidly. His own arm is injured, hanging limp by his side, his jacket missing, his shirt torn, his face and hands bloody.

I shake my head. "She was with Tristan."

The enforcer's eyes fall to the body I'm carrying in my arms and he jolts with alarm. Then his face cracks, devastation racing like raindrops all over his face. He reaches out to touch him. His mouth quivers.

"He's dead–"

"No, alive, but barely," I tell him. "He needs help."

The enforcer's body sags in relief. He closes his eyes and exhales. "Take him to his father's house."

"His father's? I'll take him to the hospital–"

"The whole city is under attack. The council has fallen."

"Wh-wh-what?"

"Take him to my uncle's," the enforcer says, pushing at my shoulder. "To his mother."

I shake my head, not understanding. "It'll be safe there," he explains, pushing me forcefully now. "Go!"

I stand staring at him in bewilderment and Professor Stone and two of Rhianna's friends come racing towards us.

"We can't find her anywhere!" the professor says, his eyes as wild as the enforcer. "Nowhere! Where the hell is she? I can't feel her close by, Az! I can't feel her!"

I look at the enforcer. His shoulders have stiffened, his jaw hardened. "She's gone."

"What?!" I cry. "Gone? Have they taken her?"

The girl's friend whimpers, clinging to the boy beside her. They're all as disheveled and injured as the enforcer.

The beast roars inside me. He wants to tear the world down.

Gone? She can't be.

"We have to find her," we say together.

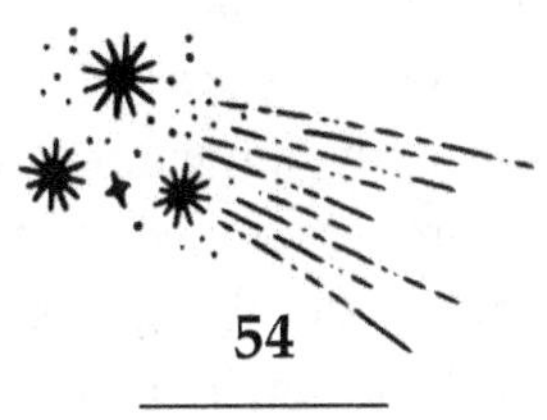

54

R enzo

I CLING to her and her little piggie with all my might and pull them with me, through time, through space, landing us with a thud on the kitchen floor. The same kitchen I sat in waiting for her only weeks ago. Except it's dark now, the first rays of dawn creeping in at the little window.

I peer down at my little rabbit's face as the pig stumbles away from me and vomits in the corner.

"Yeah, it's not everyone's preferred mode of travel, little fellow," I tell him, sweeping back damp hair from my little rabbit's face. Her eyes are screwed tightly shut, her brow all wrinkled.

"Shush," I whisper, holding her close, and rocking her, back and forth, back and forth, "hush now, you're okay. Safe."

She shakes her head, pain radiating in the creases and furrows scarring her pretty face.

I trace my finger over them, fascinated by them, fascinated by her. She's so soft. So warm.

She cries out, her body tightening, and I remember the finger. I take her hand carefully in mine. Anger flares through me like a bolt of deadly lightning when I see what he did to my rabbit. Took something so perfect and broke it. I think of him squirming on the floor, not even able to take one last breath and I wish I'd broken his fucking skull, his fucking spine, his fucking legs.

"Focus," I remind myself as my little rabbit shudders, murmuring nonsense. I lean down and shush her again, whisper against that creased forehead. "Gonna fix it for you."

I close my eyes and focus on the bones. Turns out it's a hell of a lot harder mending bones than it is breaking them, but somehow I manage, concentrating so hard to ensure it's as perfect as it was, sweat beads along my brow.

I slump back when it's done, peer down at my little rabbit.

The finger is fixed, but she isn't. Her body jerks, her head rocks from side to side.

Something's wrong.

"What is it, little rabbit?" I say, not sure she can even hear me. "Tell me what's wrong and I'll fix it for you."

She shivers and I squeeze her tightly against my body, radiating my warmth into her.

The shakes subside a little, the tight coil in her body loosens, she murmurs again and opens her eyes, her blurry gaze meeting mine.

"What's wrong?" I ask. I'd do anything for her, I think. Anything at all.

"Tristan," she whispers with pain and grief and longing and all those things I don't understand, "Tristan."

Read Book Four next, *Burdened Bonds*

Want to read a bonus scene from this story? You can find all my bonus material on my website here

For sneaky previews, spoilers and all the latest news, join Hannah's reader group

Thank you so much for reading. If you enjoyed this book, please consider leaving a review or rating — it's a great help to indie authors like me!

ALSO BY HANNAH HAZE

All available on Amazon and Kindle Unlimited.

Fantasy Romance RH
The Arrow Hart Academy
Fractured Fates
Twisted Ties
Shattered Stars
Burdened Bonds
Destined Dawn

The Firestone Academy
Storm of Shadows
Spark of Sorcery
Taste of Thorns
Lure of Lightning

Contemporary RH omegaverse
The Rockview Omegaverse
Pack Rivals Part I

Pack Rivals Part II
Pack Choice
Pack Gamble Part I
Pack Gamble Part II
Pack Education Part I
Pack Education Part II

In With The Pack
In Deep - Rosie's story
In Trouble - Connie's story
In Knots - Alexa's story
In Doubt - Giorgie's story
In Control - Sophia's story
In Stockings (Christmas Novella)

Contemporary MF omegaverse series
The Alpha Rock Stars
The Rockstar's Omega
Rocked by the Alpha
Fourth Base with the Alpha

Contemporary MF omegaverse standalones
Oxford Heat
The Alpha Escort Agency
Omega's Forbidden Heat

Contemporary MF omegaverse novellas
The Omega Chase
Online Heat
Christmas Heat

Alien omegaverse MF romance series

The Alpha Prince of Astia
<u>Alien Desire</u>
<u>Alien Passion</u>

ABOUT THE AUTHOR

A recovering cynic, Hannah grew up swearing she would never marry. Then in 2001, she met her husband and has been a card-carrying romantic ever since. Despite being an avid writer and reader, Hannah decided to do the sensible thing and study science at university, putting authoring ideas to one side.This all changed when she discovered the joys of a good romance book and came to the realisation that love stories are always the best ones.

She now uses her knowledge of chemical bonds and reactions to ensure her books are full of sparks. In fact the electricity between her characters is sure to set your pulse racing and your heart fluttering.

Hannah loves reading to her three children, including doing all the silly voices, and going for long walks in the country-side (the muddier the better). Her head is always full of new story ideas and you are most likely to find her avoiding the demands of her very naughty cat as she attempts to write them all down.

Sign up to my newsletter:
www.hannahhaze.com/about

Join my reader groups:

https://www.facebook.com/groups/hannahhazehotro
mancereads
https://www.facebook.com/groups/softandsteamyomega
verse

Visit my website:
www.hannahhaze.com

Catch me on TikTok:
www.tiktok.com/@hannahhaze_author

ACKNOWLEDGMENTS

Once again a massive thank you to all my readers for giving this story a chance and for all your amazing reviews, comments and messages. I really hop you enjoyed this book and can't wait to deliver the next part of the story to you!

I'm truly grateful for my team of wonderful beta readers who help me shape this story into the best it can be. Thank you Courtney, Sara, Jessie, Morgan, Leandri, Aimee, Alanys, Jenna, Melissa, Lili and Kiki.

Thank you to Christian for another beautiful cover and James for editing my smutty words.

And lastly thank you to my family for all their love, support and encouragement. Love you x

www.ingramcontent.com/pod-product-compliance
Lightning Source LLC
Chambersburg PA
CBHW070743120726
47910CB00001B/155